Hanging by a thong near the rock on which he was bound, the skull had many companions. Some were more yellowed with age, but all had the telling ridges of bone for ears and large oval eyes.

The beating of the drums increased and one of the dancers whirled away from the ring of men circling the fire. In his hand was a sharp stone dagger. As he danced round the rock, shrieking with delight, the dagger added one more slash to Redlance's back.

From their hiding place behind the bushes, Cutter and Skywise winced in horror. **Cutter, those skulls—** came Skywise's mental question.

"Don't worry," said Cutter aloud. "Redlance's won't hang among them. I swear it!"

Skywise gulped. To rescue Redlance meant fighting the humans. He could think of many other things he'd rather do. . . .

REDLANCE'S EYES OPENED
TO MEET THE UNNERVING STARE
OF A POLISHED SKULL...

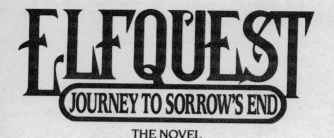

ELFQUEST
JOURNEY TO SORROW'S END
THE NOVEL

WENDY AND RICHARD PINI

ACE BOOKS, NEW YORK

This Ace Book contains the complete text of the original
edition. It has been completely reset in a typeface
designed for easy reading, and was printed from new film.

ELFQUEST: JOURNEY TO SORROW'S END

An Ace Book / published by arrangement with
the author

PRINTING HISTORY
Playboy edition / November 1982
Berkley edition / March 1984
Fourth Berkley printing / March 1986
Ace edition / January 1993

The Putnam Berkley World Wide Web site address is
http://www.berkley.com/berkley

ISBN: 0-441-18371-9

ACE®
Ace Books are published by The Berkley Publishing Group,
200 Madison Avenue, New York, New York 10016.
ACE and the "A" design
are trademarks belonging to Charter Communications, Inc.

PRINTED IN THE UNITED STATES OF AMERICA

10 9 8 7 6 5 4 3 2

To the friends who have supported us,
to the foes who have strengthened us,
and to us, 'cause we done it ourselves!

Foreword

Elfquest is a comic about elves. At least, that's how it started. With Wendy as artist/writer and Richard as editor/publisher, *Elfquest* has existed since 1977 as a successful alternative comic that can be found around the world in comics specialty shops.*

But the story itself, co-plotted by the two of us, seems to have a life—and a will—of its own. It struggles against the restrictions that independent publishers face. Our first wish for *Elfquest* was to see it grow from a black-and-white magazine into a series of full-color books. That wish has come true. Our grandest dream was and is to see *Elfquest* produced as a full-length feature animated film. Within a very few years, we know we will realize that dream too. But *Elfquest* the novel? That project, we must admit, came in through the side door!

There is a world of difference between scripting a graphic story and writing a novel. To tell a comic book tale effectively, words and pictures must meld smoothly and interdependently. But straight prose must create its pictures in the reader's mind, and this we have tried to do in "Journey to Sorrow's End." It was an instructive collaboration.

We didn't plan, in the beginning, to reincarnate *Elfquest* as a novel, but we discovered, as we wrote together, that the doing of it gave us a chance to expand greatly upon the original story. To the readers of *Elfquest* the comic, we hope the details and events we've brought to light here will help

---

*Those who are interested can obtain information about *Elfquest* the comic by writing to: Warp Graphics, 2 Reno Road, Poughkeepsie, NY 12603. Please enclose a stamped, self-addressed envelope for the reply.

you to appreciate the story and its many complex characters on a new, perhaps more intimate level.

Those who are discovering our story for the first time in these pages, we leave it to you to decide what *Elfquest* is and what it means to you. Is it an adult fairy tale? Socio-political allegory? Science fiction? Adventure? High fantasy? Romance? We don't know, and we are terrible at self-labeling. Ever since these insufferably beautiful, free-thinking little people came into our lives, we haven't been sure of much except that we must tell their story. They insist on it. We're happy to oblige.

Wendy and Richard Pini

One

Little Moon had already sunk beneath Land's Edge in the direction of Sun-Goes-Down. Lagging behind, Big Moon grinned a thin, crescent smile as it wheeled across the star-sprinkled sky to join its vanished smaller brother.

The Land was level and wide, stubbled with thick patches of rough grass that trembled in the rising breeze. Boulders like teeth fallen from some monstrous skull littered the ground. The lightning-blasted bole of a long-dead tree stood at a forlorn angle beside a large pool of water. Once the pool had served as a meeting place for an odd and incongruous variety of beasts, a place where, for the moment, predator and prey maintained an uneasy truce to lap the cool liquid.

The Humans owned the pool now. They had come from Sun-Goes-Up in leisurely pursuit of a migrating herd of tree-horns. The tall, magnificently antlered deer seemed no more annoyed by the two-legged hunters who followed and fed off them than by the gnats that occasionally swarmed about them.

Where the herd moved, there followed the Human tribe. This time the small group had been lucky. The deer had led them to water; with their clubs, sharpened throwing sticks, and bone knives, they had taken possession of the pool. For many warm days, life had been comparatively easy.

On a flat-topped rock that stood a little higher than the rest, Strongest Man kept a lazy watch. His long club rested across his insteps. His broad nose sniffed the air contentedly. The wind carried a damp smell, and clouds were beginning to move across the sky. The slender Big Moon, just setting, cast a silver-gray light, and Strongest Man knew that rain would come before morning. More water, more growth, more food. He swung his massive head to glance at his tribesmen and tribeswomen gathered around the pool. An infant had been born shortly after they had settled. Another was on its way, if a woman's hard bloated belly always meant the same thing. Never had the nomads known such a time of abundance. Surely the good spirits had made this place for them, thought Strongest Man.

A little way in the distance from the pool was the edge of a forest, and as the wind rose to press against the trees, birds began to wake and chirp their discomfort. Strongest Man grunted to himself. A storm then, he decided, as the first growls of thunder came from faraway Land's Edge. For Strongest Man, the Land was a great circle as far as he could see, and he was at the center. Wherever he settled with his people, that Land belonged to him. He liked a storm. He was brave. The others might cower in their rocky shelters as thunderbolts tore the sky, but not he. Strongest Man would stand up in the wind and rain and laugh at the noisy skyfire. It would not dare to strike him as it had once sundered the tree beside the drinking pool.

Strongest Man frowned, his heavy brow beetling. Something strange was happening to the clouds. Even his tribespeople were beginning to sense that the rapidly gathering turbulence was not a storm like other storms. The very air seemed to swirl as if some giant hand had reached down from the stars to stir it up. The clouds themselves, instead of scudding across the sky, were whirling faster and faster about a center, spun into feathery wisps by the force of their rotation. Odd, unnatural colors flashed in the boiling air, independent of the blue-white lightning that ripped the sky in spasmodic bursts. The thunder was a continuous terrible roar that grew steadily in volume. Now even the sky seemed to be spinning, falling into itself. Clouds and stars and double moons (hadn't they already set?) were visibly distorted and sucked into the eye of the incredible maelstrom.

Strongest Man stood on his perch of stone and gaped, too stupefied to know that he was afraid. His small piggish eyes bulged, showing the whites all around. A string of drool dribbled from his slack mouth; his dense stubble of body hair stood on end. Wind battered his thick, naked body and whipped his coarse hair about his face. Still he stared upward, craning his almost nonexistent neck back as far as it would go. Strongest Man stood unmoving against the storm, but he did not laugh. Nor did he know that most of his tribe had already fled in terror; only a youth and a woman, as paralyzed as he, remained by the pool. The woman's father lay nearby, dead of fright.

High above, the lightning seemed to converge into one massive ball of brilliance in the center of the roiling sky. The light spread outward, edged by rainbow colors that turned the land below incandescent.

Suddenly, within the sky-glow, something appeared: a structure, immense in size, with peaks and sharp edges like rocks piled in regular patterns to unthinkable heights. Blinding white, the Mountain Thing hovered for a moment like a newborn sun and then began slowly to descend. Around it, streamers of multicolored cloud continued to spiral, as if guiding it to the ground. The Land seemed to shrink back, loath to receive the alien object that laid everything bare with its unearthly brilliance.

At last the shining mass settled to the ground with a rumbling shock that could be heard and felt above the rolling thunder. Overhead, there seemed to be a great hole, ragged and gaping and infinitely black, torn out of the heavens by the object's passing. The damage was not permanent, though, for the wound in the sky at once began to close. Sparks of lightning and flashes of ethereal color spiraled upward and back into darkness as stars peeked out timidly from whatever black shelter they had taken. The last sliver of Big Moon could be seen wisely retreating behind the shield of a mountain range in the far distance.

But in the center of the wide, rich circle—Strongest Man's circle, his place, his center—there now towered an alien mountain of glowing stone still half concealed by tendrils of swirling mist.

Strongest Man clenched his right hand slightly. It was the only voluntary movement he could make. His cheeks twitched by themselves. His body shook with tension. He stared at the Mountain Thing.

What was it?

It stood many times taller at its highest point than the tallest tree in the woods. Its base covered a vast expanse of ground. Its majestic walls appeared to be made of some strange kind of rock that shimmered, opalescent in the predawn light. Delicate spires encrusted the entire upper parts, giving the structure the random and yet orderly appearance of a splendid crystal formation. It hummed softly, a single thrilling chord made of many notes, and though it stood firmly where it had settled, the Mountain Thing seemed to vibrate in sympathy with its own humming.

What kept him rooted in place, Strongest Man could not guess. The impulse to flee was strong in him, had been since the moment the sky opened up. Yet he stayed and stared and wondered. He felt the weight of his wooden weapon on his feet and absently picked the club up. That was part of his own magic—his skill with the club—and he was emboldened to find that he could still work it. The sudden appearance of the Mountain Thing apparently had not stripped him of all control over his body.

He stepped cautiously off the flat rock and turned to see what had become of his tribe. Several of his braver hunters peered from behind rocks and bushes, their blunt faces masks of terror and bewilderment. The woman and boy who had, like Strongest Man, been transfixed with fear still squatted by the water's edge, near her father's twisted corpse.

Whether it was curiosity or only bravado that caused Strongest Man to approach the alien construction, his watching tribemen took heart from his action. Several of them began to inch forward in imitation. He looked very small as he prowled around the looming object's base and avoided touching the strange stone. He sniffed at the subtle and odd odors coming from the Mountain Thing and the vapors that still clung to it, and suddenly he sneezed. Brought up short, he listened, tense and still, for any unwelcome reaction to his noise. There was none. He continued his exploration.

Turning a corner, Strongest Man discovered a feature he had not seen before. Recessed deeply into the vast iridescent wall of the Mountain Thing was an opening. Strongest Man knew about openings in walls, for he and his people had at times lived in caves, but this was not like any cave he had ever seen. Within the opening there rose a barrier of gleaming yellowish material that the Humans could not begin to identify. They stood in a group before the mysterious object and grunted their confusion.

Suddenly they became aware that theirs were not the only voices to be heard in the cool, gray dawn. From behind the tall yellow barrier came cries of distress, thin and faint in the still air. The Humans, chattering, shrank back in alarm. Slowly, noiselessly, the yellow wall began to open, splitting in two halves down the middle. Thick smoke billowed from the opening, obscuring sight, but even before the acrid fumes began to clear, the Humans knew that beings were coming out: beings from the Mountain Thing, evil spirits, perhaps, come to take the Land away from them. The Humans clutched their crude weapons in fear.

Coughing and crying out as they staggered through the smoke, the beings appeared. They were tall and graceful, slender and exquisitely fluid in their movements. They were garbed in strange, colorful fabrics that flowed lightly, shimmering despite the stillness of the air. They did not in any way resemble the squat and hairy members of Strongest Man's tribe. They were not human. Their skin was translucent and milky pale and seemed to glow from within with the rosy tints of a perfect sunrise. Males and females alike, for there were several of both, were possessed of an ethereal beauty. Yet their faces, surrounded by feather-soft clouds of shining hair, inspired fear as much as awe.

It was their eyes—eyes that were larger than the eyes of deer, eyes that were as deep and clear as cold spring water, eyes that were slanted like the eyes of animals. The Humans' skin went cold, for surely no eyes could be shaped so or gaze so piercingly unless they belonged to demons, evil spirits who could destroy with the power of a glance. The Humans saw further proof of the presence of evil, for beneath their soft hair the strangers' ears were pointed, delicately tapered like the crystalline spires of the Mountain Thing itself. The creatures must be kin to beasts, then, cousins, especially, to the great fanged wolves that tore their prey to shreds and sang the moons out of the sky at night to keep all in darkness. Like the eyes of evil wolves, the eyes of the slender strangers could look right into the soul of a hunter and draw out his life force. Like wolves' ears, the pointed ears of the tall beings could hear the lifeblood pounding through a frightened man's veins and find him wherever he tried to hide. Strongest Man believed this, and his tribe believed it with him.

So when the apparent leader of the strangers stretched out his slim, four-fingered hand in greeting to the Humans, with a small and almost apologetic smile curling his delicate mouth, Strongest Man swung his club and shattered the stranger's skull in one blow.

The dead one's companions gaped horrified as his thin blood spread in a widening pool on the ground. Strongest Man stood over the body and roared a challenge; he was terrified, but he knew in his marrow that the Evil Ones must be slain quickly before they could gather their wits to strike back. Already his hunters had begun to charge, scattering the aliens like so many brightly plumed birds.

A female was trying desperately to find some shelter within the walls of the Mountain Thing. Strongest Man seized the trailing end of her gown, holding her fast as she struggled to tear away. A tiny, winged creature flittered about her hair, squealing its distress, trying to encourage her to follow it in flight. Suddenly the female seemed to lift off the ground, to float weightless in midair. Strongest Man cried out but did not release his grip; he clubbed her to the ground and ended her life as easily as he might crush a wind-borne seedling. Her diminutive companion flew in a frenzy at Strongest Man, beating its multicolored wings against his face and spewing sticky threads, like spider's webbing, into his eyes. The beast-human swiped at the air with his club, but the butterfly creature, having done all it could, had already flown out of reach.

A killing lust came upon the Humans then as they realized that the tall strangers did not seem to know how to defend themselves. Within moments, graceful ruined bodies littered the ground; and the Humans, emboldened now, began to invade the Mountain Thing itself, seeking out other demons to kill.

When it was over, only a few of the elfin strangers had managed to escape into the dense woods, concealing themselves among the trees. Other creatures, small and apelike, also fled the Mountain Thing, scampering in another direction and burrowing underground to find shelter from the Humans' flailing weapons.

Strongest Man bellowed a roar of triumph as he emerged from the now-lifeless structure and surveyed the carnage he had wrought. For a while he and his hunters waited to see whether anything else would happen, but all remained silent. Even the Mountain Thing's humming had ceased. At last, hunger began to distract the Humans, and they turned away from the alien object to attend to the more pressing task of filling their grumbling bellies.

Time passed. The sun continued to rise and set as before, giving its rhythm to the world. The moons, with their ever-changing faces, slid through the night sky along their ages-old paths. Rain fell. Rocks and shrubs remained fixed. The life motion of the Land had been interrupted briefly but not permanently changed by the coming of the Mountain Thing.

Almost immediately, the animals dared the return to their familiar water hole, bending to drink in the very shadow of the forsaken edifice that, after all, offered no more threat than a featureless cliffside. Although they skirted the looming walls at a respectful distance, perhaps scenting mysterious odors that made them nervous and flighty, the herds of tree-horns, giant bison, and even huge, shaggy serpent-noses with long, curving tusks made their way to the pool—and to the waiting spears of Strongest Man and his hunters.

The Humans had stayed. Fear had not driven them away from their territory. Had they not conquered the demons who had come to take their Land? Did not the finely formed skulls and bones of the slain creatures litter the ground before the entrance to the Mountain Thing? Strongest Man saw to it that these pathetic remains were raised on the points of long wooden stakes—a grisly triumphal display and a warning.

Strongest Man and his tribe knew that the tall, beast-eared ones had not all been destroyed. Sometimes a lithe, elfin figure could be glimpsed flitting furtively among the dense branches of the forest. And once in a great while, one of the wolf-eyed creatures would creep from the folds of night's dark cloak, would leave the sanctuary of the woods in an effort to regain entry into the Mountain Thing. But Strongest Man, even though he had taken many seasons on him since then, remembered in his hands the killing of demons. There was always a tribesman awake to give the signal. Then the hunters would descend on the terrified alien, who might escape but usually did not.

For the first time, the Humans' existence held a purpose

other than bare survival. The Mountain Thing stood as a reminder to the tribe's children and then to their children that evil spirits dwelt nearby, awaiting only an unguarded moment to return to the source of their power. Although the elfin beings who clung to a shadowy existence in the woods were seen less and less frequently by Strongest Man's descendants, the human tribe had by now grown roots as trees do. By its unavoidable presence, the Mountain Thing had become the common focus of their lives, had even inspired the beginnings of religious ceremony and the telling of stories.

The pitted skeletal remains, once regarded proudly as battle trophies, became sacred objects, seldom seen or touched and spoken of in apprehensive whispers. But eventually even these poor bits of evidence crumbled with age into dust, and the threat of the beast-eared strangers' unseen presence passed slowly into tribal legend.

The land began to grow cold. The change was gradual but inexorable. Grasses turned brown, succulent plants withered, and the drinking pond froze solid as stone. Many animals began to wander farther south in search of warmer grazing and feeding grounds. Even the hardy birds flew far beyond the forest, winging over neighboring mountains whose sparse growths of trees were soon buried under a thick blanket of snow. It was more than an ordinary winter. It was the beginning of an ice age.

Stoically the Humans accepted the change, adapting as well as they could to what was becoming a permanent season of White Cold. They wore snug furs and skins and built fires to warm themselves. But the land grew more inhospitable, it seemed, with each passing day, so much so that against all the ancient taboos, many of the Humans took shelter inside the Mountain Thing itself.

The massive alien structure withstood the icy wind, withstood the pressure of the ever-falling snow; indeed, the walls and spires seemed miraculously to repel it. The Humans made their rude camp in the colonnaded hallway just inside the Mountain Thing's portals. Their curiosity dulled by constant hunger and discomfort, and with legends of evil spirits still echoing in their minds from seasons long past, the Humans never sought to explore deep into the interior of the strange place. Instead they huddled by their fires and entertained themselves with fanciful explanations of all the strange objects they saw. To the Humans, the Mountain Thing was just that—a hollow mountain, an awesome and wonderful cave. They were unable to conceive that such an immense structure could be built with tools and hands or that the knowledge to fit such unwieldy masses of material into a whole even existed. In truth, the alien structure had not been shaped by hand or tool, for its creators had used far different means to bring it into being. But that knowledge, along with the reason for their cataclysmic arrival, had disappeared with those hunted strangers long ago.

So it was that the small tribe of primitive men and women found refuge for a time inside the mysterious dwelling of their ancient enemies. Soon, however, an advancing mile-high sheet of ice, grinding the land beneath it, drove even the hardiest of the game animals to seek warmer lands to the south. The Humans knew that they must follow or starve, and they chose not to starve.

Abandoned, the wondrous castle of the otherworldly beings continued to resist the snow and ice. Even as the mighty glacier flowed ponderously around and over it, hiding it completely from the eyes of all, the Mountain Thing remained whole and untouched, an immortal heart buried deep within the glacier's frozen breast. And locked within that heart, beyond reach, were the secrets of the long-vanished elfin beings.

They survived, some of them, although they did not belong to this harsh young world and were ill equipped to cope with its extremes. The aliens' few elemental powers—Humans would call it foul magic—worked badly or not at all in the strange atmosphere of this hostile place. The kindling of even a small fire for warmth took the combined energy of several of them, leaving them weak and trembling from the effort.

When the few survivors of the slaughter had recovered from their shock sufficiently to explore their forest surroundings, they fell into despair. Everything hurt them; brambles clawed through their flimsy garments, drawing blood. Low-hanging branches slashed their delicate faces and tangled in their flowing hair, holding them fast. The ground underfoot was painfully uneven to tread, and from it rose such an acrid stench of mold and decay that to inhale deeply was to choke and strangle.

It seemed that while the elf beings' powers to manipulate the flow of certain energies in this place were severely limited, their senses and sensitivities grew uncomfortably heightened. A laborious process of adaptation had begun, for they would need much more than their enfeebled magic merely to keep life within their bodies.

They adapted. Forced to fend for themselves in a nearly incomprehensible environment, barred by the watchful Humans from returning to their only dwelling place, they learned. They learned to eat what they could find, to find whatever shelter might be available, to fight for their lives when forced to, and even to kill living things for food and protective clothing. This last came hard, for the elves knew little of death save that it seemed irreversible and was therefore undesirable. The awful finality of killing repelled the gentle aliens even as they discovered that it was among the most necessary of their new skills. So they learned, and in time they even had teachers.

The creatures of the woodland, they discovered, possessed many instincts worthy of emulation—this was particularly true of the predators. As days and moons passed, these fanged and clawed ones grew accustomed to being observed as they prowled on their nightly hunts. The elfin beings never interfered with a kill but merely took note of the method and its timing. Eventually, catches were shared, for as the elves' hunting abilities became strengthened, they sometimes killed more than they needed.

Thus a loose alliance was formed between beast-eared aliens and native savage predators. But in all that time, not once did it occur to the elves to turn their newfound prowess against the Humans who had mercilessly slain so many of their kin. The concept of revenge had not yet entered the minds of the strangers, who were inoffensive and innocent of evil intent.

As death, with its often brutal finality, was a mystery to the elves, so the renewal of life was almost as mysterious. They did not feel death's inevitability, and so they were spared the need and urge to create progeny. In the sparing, however, also came a kind of forgetfulness. Although the elves were quite capable of siring and bearing children, there was no desire, in the wish or the act.

Again the woodland beasts, and more than once an oblivious human couple, provided unwitting guidance. With the new harshness of survival, it seemed, came a nearly forgotten promise of life; and this time the learning was sweet, opposed in its very essence to the cold immutability of death. This new skill, with its attendant perceptions, awakened life and reaffirmed it. A wondrous secret was shared in the curve of a knowing elfin smile, in the slant of a translucent, half-closed eyelid. The order of this world, previously hidden beneath dim hopelessness, suddenly revealed itself to the small band of aliens. Opposing dark, there was light. From the depths of despair one could ascend to the heights of joy. A body capable of feeling agonizing pain could also experience exquisite pleasure. Above all, counterbalancing death's bleak finality was an irrepressible, continuous renewal of life.

By the time the great cold began to grip the land, the elves were no longer the tall, frail beings they had been. Through many generations of swift adaptation they had changed so that most of them stood smaller and had greater endurance than their ethereal forebears. Even so, many died in those first icy days, and the survivors found food and shelter increasingly difficult to obtain. The elves had learned long ago not to resist the whim of nature but to flow with it; when they observed the animals scattering in search of a warmer, more hospitable clime, the elves imitated the beasts as they had often done. Small as their number was, the descendants of those who first emerged from the Mountain Thing went in different directions, hoping that at least a few of their kind would survive to feel warmth and see the land once again clothed with green, growing things.

One group of elves followed a pack of wolves.

Perhaps it was because the slender, four-fingered beings with pointed ears were so unlike Humans that the wolf pack accepted them. Perhaps the shaggy canines sensed that these were kindred spirits, as misunderstood by men as were the wolves themselves. Certainly both groups bore the scars of fear's insensate violence.

Whatever the reason, the travelers joined forces: great, fanged carnivores standing tall at the shoulder as a man's hip, and graceful, fur-clad outcasts from another time and place. When the wolf pack ran, their adopted charges ran with them, covering the deep snow drifts with strides so swift and even that their feet barely sank into the sparkling powder. And when a kill was made, wolf and elf alike shared in the warm, red meat, lending each other the heat of their bodies as they ate and afterward as they rested.

It was a pure and practical bond, a bond of kin and kind, destined to endure long after the thick sheets of ice covering the land had receded, baring the imperishable heart of the glacier once more to the sun.

Two

Cutter crawled lizardlike onto a broad, moss-covered boulder, pulling himself forward until his nose brushed the shrubbery that hid his view of the clearing. Cautiously, he parted the leafy screen with the tip of his short curved sword. The scene that greeted his gaze was not unexpected, but thorns of horror still pricked his insides.

Within a wide circle of stones, a ceremonial bonfire burned high and hungrily. Around the fire many tall men danced wildly, mimicking the leaping flames with the movements of their dark, nearly naked bodies. The ground itself seemed alive with the writhing shadows of the dancers; nearby, several drummers battered out a fiercely jubilant rhythm on their taut-skinned instruments. Beside them, his arms folded across his chest, his knee-length mantle of oily gray hair swaying slightly in the heated breeze, stood the Spirit Man. He was lean and muscular despite his advanced age, and he observed the proceedings with an air of smug approval and obvious self-satisfaction.

The focus of this sinister rite was an incongruously small and helpless figure whose arms were bound in mock embrace around a hand-hewn pillar of rock. The captive stood little more than half the height of those who were celebrating his bondage so triumphantly. His skin was very pale and showed with cruel clarity the deep cuts and bruises his tormentors had inflicted. As he sagged against the rough stone, his face hidden against one outstretched arm, a sudden surge of pain caused him to fling back his head. Revealed were two large and sharply pointed ears, beast ears that flanked a childlike face that was broad and sweet of feature and wholly unhuman.

The captive's eyes fluttered open to meet the comfortless,

22

unnerving stare of a polished skull. Hanging by a thong near the peak of the tall rock pillar, the skull had many companions, some more yellowed with age than others. But all showed the telling ridges of bone where ears had been and the large oval eye sockets that bespoke their kinship with the elfin prisoner below.

The beating of the drums increased in ferocity. One of the dancers whirled away from the ring of men circling the fire. In his outflung hand he clutched a sharp stone dagger, and as he turned round and round, the point of the blade swept closer and closer to the small captive's bare back. A shriek of delight burst suddenly from the dancer's lips, and new blood oozed from a long, deep slash across the prisoner's shoulders.

From his hiding place behind the bushes, Cutter watched and winced, his lips parting in a snarl to reveal sharp white teeth. Stretched out beside him on the boulder, Cutter's gray-clad companion Skywise trembled with anger and fear.

"Cutter. . . . Those skulls," he whispered.

"Don't worry," came the low response. "Redlance's won't hang among them. I swear it!"

Skywise nodded and gulped once, holding his breath for a moment to center himself. Cutter's intentions were very clear. Redlance must be rescued, and quickly, but that would mean fighting the humans.

Skywise could think of many other things he'd rather do.

"Cutter, what if they—"

Send, you fool! Do you want them to hear us?

Instantly chastened, his mind tingling from the vehemence of Cutter's mental retort, Skywise decided that it would be useless to express his apprehension. He glanced over his shoulder and saw that the others were ready, awaiting only Cutter's order to attack.

The drumming ceased abruptly, and the ring of panting dancers parted in deference to the Spirit Man, whose upraised arm commanded silence. He entered the ring, an impressive figure cloaked in his own long hair; tilting his head back in a kind of ecstasy, he pointed a bony finger at his helpless inhuman victim.

"O Gotara, Master of all Spirits," chanted the shaman. "Behold! We have captured another demon-spawn of the Evil Ones. Accept this offering, mighty Gotara. We avenge the corruption of our land!"

Where it was not matted with blood, Redlance's hair shone in the firelight, rivaling the angry tints of the evening sky. His large, moss-green eyes were bright with tears, for he understood the speech of the humans and had ceased begging their mercy some time ago. At the setting of the sun, which would happen in mere moments, he knew that they would kill him, and he knew how they would kill him. First they would cut off his pointed ears as trophies of the grim ceremony, and then they would slit his throat with the same obsidian blade that had steeped in the blood of other unlucky members of his tribe. Once more, Redlance looked up at the silent skulls of his kindred. In vain he tugged at the tough animal-gut thongs that bound him to the pillar of sacrifice.

Accompanied by the muttered assent of his followers, the Spirit Man's litany droned relentlessly on.

"Untold seasons ago the Evil Ones invaded our land, the land which Gotara gave to us in all its abundance that we might thrive. The Evil Ones came and twisted the shape of things with their foul magic, seeking to mold the land to their own likes and to their own ends. But ever we fought back, and ever shall we fight to do Gotara's will. Hear, Master of Spirits, the cries of this child of demons. Let his death agony appease your just wrath!"

"Get it over with, old man," murmured Redlance.

The Spirit Man's thin lips curled in an ugly, one-sided grin.

"Tabak," he said, turning to a handsome, broad-nosed man whose legs seemed too long for his thick torso. "Tabak, you and your hunters captured the demon. It is fitting that the greatest of honors should be yours."

From his low-slung belt of braided hide the shaman drew a short, shiny black knife, which he presented to Tabak. The muscular hunter accepted the blade with swelling pride, and the drummers struck up a slow, steady rhythm; it was almost like the pounding of a heartbeat, as if to accentuate the significance of the moment. At sunset the drumbeat would stop, and in the instant of that silence the demon would die.

Redlance closed his eyes as Tabak approached.

"Ayooooooah!"

The worshipers started and turned as one at the howling cry. The eyes of the humans went wide as the shrubbery at the edge of the sacred clearing seemed to burst apart, sending forth a pack of barking, slavering wolves—and riding each wolf, an elf-demon. The elves, moving with fluid and unnatural speed, brandished weapons of shining metal, a fearsome material foreign to the humans. Chaos broke; wolves and riders together became a disordered blur of fang and blade, leather and fur, sinew and claw. Caught completely off guard, the humans scrabbled for whatever weapons lay at hand; but stone knives and wooden spears were no match for the potent magic of the elves' metal blades, and naked human limbs proved especially vulnerable to the wolves' crushing jaws.

While his companions engaged the resisting humans, the pale-haired leader of the attack urged his huge canine mount straight for the pillar of sacrifice.

"Tabak! Now," screamed the Spirit Man.

The captive Redlance called out, "Cutter!" but that cry of joy turned into a gasp of pain as Tabak jerked the elf's head back, exposing the throat.

Cutter clung low to his wolf Nightrunner's hunched back as the great animal crossed the clearing in three powerful bounds.

"Too late, human," the elf growled as his wickedly keen sword plunged deep between Tabak's ribs just as the obsidian knife began its fall toward Redlance's throat.

Tabak collapsed with a rasping cry. The sacrificial blade clattered against the stones surrounding the fire as Cutter hacked impatiently at Redlance's bonds, freeing him at last from the cruel thongs. Too weak to stand, the injured elf was swept up by Cutter in one swift motion to ride across Nightrunner's shoulders.

The Spirit Man shook with rage. His followers were fleeing for cover at every turn.

"No! Stay and fight! You must stop the Wolf Demons! Destroy them! Gotara wills it! Gotara wills—"

Disgusted with such obstinacy, Skywise reared his wolf up behind the Spirit Man and rapped the human's head smartly with the rounded pommel of his sword. The Spirit Man's bony knees folded under him, and he caved in like a pile of dry twigs, long arms and legs jutting awkwardly from the tangle of his grizzled hair.

"I have Redlance," called Cutter. "Enough blood for now. Wolfriders, to the Holt!"

Instantly the elves and their mounts regrouped, leaving battered but still-living humans where they had fallen. As the Wolfriders loped away from the clearing and back into the darkened woods, Cutter, their chieftain, halted his animal beside the recovering Spirit Man.

The aged human brushed his hair away from his eyes, only to turn and stare up the length of his nose at the point of Cutter's gleaming sword. Outlined by the light of the rising moons, both elf and wolf made a single, menacing silhouette that started the Spirit Man trembling with earnest fear. He felt Nightrunner's hot breath blowing in fetid clouds against his face.

"Remember this, old man," said Cutter, his quiet tone underscored by the low and steady growling of the wolf. "Next time I'll skin you like a stag and let the wolves pick your bones!"

The Spirit Man blinked as Cutter's hard, gem-blue eyes, set at a feral slant, seemed to bore into his very brain. The shaman could not long meet the elf chieftain's unsettling gaze; when he saw that he had forced the human to look away, Cutter arched his neck and voiced a long, high-pitched howl that held a note of triumph. From deep in the wood came the answering howl of his tribefolk—or was it the pack song of the gathering wolves themselves?—and without a backward glance the chief of the Wolfriders went to join them. With disquieting swiftness, elf and beast were gone from the clearing; only a brief rustle of foliage in the deepening gloom marked his return to the shelter of the forest.

The Wolfriders were waiting for him beneath the drooping branches of a great willow tree that grew by the banks of a narrow stream. When Cutter arrived, he saw that many of his tribefolk bore the marks of battle. They were bruised and gashed, and one of the wolves had taken a spear point in the thigh. But none had suffered nearly so much as Redlance. Skywise rode his wolf forward and gazed with concern at the wounded elf.

"How bad is he?"

"I don't know," Cutter answered. "Ride on ahead and tell Nightfall we bring her lifemate back—somewhat less than whole."

Skywise nodded once and quickly trotted away. As he emerged from the double shadow of the willow tree, his silvery puff of hair glowed like a white fur-flower in the moonlight. Skywise was all the colors of the night, wearing leathers of gray and deep berry blue. His skin was as creamy pale as an egg's shell, and even his wolf, Starjumper, showed a sheen of blue-gray coloring in his fur. Like one of the fleeting, bright-tailed stars he loved to spend the entire night watching, Skywise whisked noiselessly through a clump of trees and was gone from sight.

Trusting Nightrunner to bear them both as smoothly and as gently as he could, Cutter carried Redlance home. Within that tortured body, Cutter sensed many things wrong; there were little disjointures, small inexplicable sounds that told of damage beyond reach, perhaps beyond repair. Redlance moaned, and Cutter could do nothing but cradle him close, wishing that he were a healer now instead of a chief.

The last vestige of twilight had faded when Skywise reached the Holt. This was the home of the Wolfriders, a dense grove of grotesquely shaped trees dominated by one immense grandfather of a tree whose age was no less great than its size. Weeds and night-blooming wild flowers grew in natural disorder around the trees' roots, and twinkling fireflies—Skywise liked to call them "little star cousins"—broke the tranquil scene with flashes of surprising brilliance. A shallow brook flowed through the center of the Holt, while crickets chirred their accompaniment to its splashing song. Like old friends the gnarled trees embraced one another, their many branches entwining to form a dense canopy high above the ground. Moonlight filtered through the thick network of leaves, spattering patterns of misty light, blue against the indigo curtain of night.

At any other time, Skywise might have paused to admire the Holt's special beauty. But as his wolf skidded to a halt near the base of the great central tree, Skywise could think only of the news he bore and of the one whose heart it would pierce more deeply than any arrow. He called her name.

"Nightfall!"

From one of the rounded holes in the tree's massive trunk a delicate, wide-eyed face peered down anxiously and then vanished. In moments Nightfall stepped from an opening between the twisted roots of the tree. She watched as Skywise dismounted but did not speak to him even when he stood before her, nervously running his fingers through Starjumper's rough collar of fur.

"Redlance was captured," he said finally. "By humans."

Nightfall shut her eyes. She had been braced for misfortune, sensing long before Skywise's arrival that ill had befallen someone she loved.

"He got separated from the hunting party," Skywise went

on. "I don't know why or how. The drums started up almost the instant we noticed he was gone."

"They . . . they killed him?" Her voice was hollow, her diminutive body uncharacteristically stiff. Skywise could not bear to witness her agony, suppressed though it was.

"Cutter's bringing him now. We saved him. The humans fought back, but—"

Nightfall put her hand to Skywise's lips. She gazed intently over his shoulder at a gathering of shadowy shapes in the distance, limned by slanting moonbeams. Before she could see them clearly, she caught the scent of the returning Wolfriders. Redlance was among them, alive. She ran to meet them, her soft catskin boots barely stirring the grasses beneath her flying feet.

Cutter slid off Nightrunner's back, gently carrying Redlance in his arms. The injured elf's face was hidden in the thick nap of his chief's bearhide vest. Nightfall took Redlance's hand and saw with only partial relief that his chest still rose and fell, though shakily. She looked up at Cutter, her golden eyes brimming with tears that could no longer be contained.

"He lives, Nightfall," Cutter said softly. "Luck was with us this time. Tonight the tall ones mourn their dead, not we."

Nightfall caught her breath, imagining what it must have been like for her tribefolk to engage in actual combat with the savage humans. Tenderly, she stroked her lifemate's long, robin-red braids, trying not to look at his many wounds or to think too deeply about their origins.

"He knows I don't like him to hunt," was all she said to Cutter as she helped him carry Redlance to the center of the grove where the Father Tree stood.

Just inside the opening at the tree's base a progression of thick, shelflike fungoid growths jutted from the bark, forming a kind of ladder. Climbing upward through the hollows in the heart of the ancient timber, Cutter noted that the living stairs were still firm despite countless seasons of use. The great tree's past inhabitants had each left their mark upon its body in some way, shaping a bole here, a limb there—all save Redlance, who as yet had shown no sign that he had even received the ancestral gift of the ability to mold the forms of living plants. This lack was a mystery to the Wolfriders, for the blood of "shapers" ran strong in Redlance's veins. In times past, the elves of the Holt had found much use for the talents of these artists; the strange and wonderful convolutions of the Father Tree's interior were just one example.

During the seemingly endless wait for his dormant powers to awaken, Redlance had tried to be of use to his tribe in ways that were often poorly suited to his mild nature. This time, the well-intentioned effort had cost him dearly.

Cutter and Nightfall carried Redlance up to a small, rough-walled chamber high within the tree's trunk. A single candle, no more than a wick pushed into a lump of animal fat, flickered in a shallow metal bowl beside a mound of sleeping-furs. Although the illumination was feeble, it was more than sufficient for the two night-sighted elves to tend their companion's injuries.

Redlance's cuts were cleaned and his ribs bandaged with strips of fine, petal-soft leather; when it was done, Cutter stood stiff and unspeaking, glowering at the red-haired elf. Meekly, Redlance looked up at his chief and smiled a weak, apologetic smile.

"You should have seen him, Cutter," Redlance ventured. "The finest, fattest buck in all the woods. I almost got him."

The explosion came.

"I don't care how sweet the game is near the humans' camp! You know that hunting alone is forbidden! And especially there! Why did you disobey me?"

Redlance looked away. "I'm sorry. Forgive me. I thought you would be proud of me if I brought the buck down by myself. That's why I slipped away after I spotted him. I didn't want the others to know."

Cutter tried to hold on to his flagging rage. Redlance had acted against the spirit of the pack. He had endangered himself and thereby the entire hunting party. The decision to save the captured elf had not been made without hesitation. It had been necessary to weigh the value of the single tribe member against the risk of other Wolfrider lives lost, perhaps many. Cutter bore the knowledge that he might have decided to abandon Redlance had the others not been so solidly in favor of attempting the rescue.

"You're lucky you're so well liked," growled the elf chieftain. "It was the rest of the pack wanted to peel you off that rock, not me. If you weren't my best tracker—and the High Ones know why you are since you can't find your own ears without help—I'd have left you to the humans."

Cutter's diatribe trailed off. Redlance was smiling at him. So was Nightfall. They knew him too well. Nevertheless, Redlance did truly regret his carelessness. He would be a long time healing, and the horror of his experience with the humans would stay with him long after his body recovered. That was punishment enough. He reached out a swollen hand and felt it immediately caught up in Cutter's solid, reassuring grip.

Nightfall sat beside the sleeping-furs on a low mushroom-shaped stool that she herself had carved. Earlier, when she heard Skywise call her name, she had been whittling designs in the handle of a wooden skewer; bits of the shavings still clung to her leather breeches. She brushed them away now and glanced affectionately at Cutter.

He looked tired and a little shaken. His wide, square-cut features and sensitive lips were drawn tight with tension. He started at the wail of a night-hunting bird, becoming no less edgy even though he could identify the sound easily.

Nightfall understood. The Wolfriders were a hardy, pragmatic pack, long accustomed to self-reliance. But Cutter had somehow fixed on the notion that the life of each and every tribe member was his responsibility, the death of one or many, solely his blame. No one, as yet, had been able to convince the zealous young leader otherwise. This concern was an endearing trait that had won him much-needed support, but his skill as a fighter and his decisiveness in taking the right action had earned Cutter an even greater prize: the Wolfriders' respect. To one so new to adulthood, on whom the self-imposed disciplines of a chief weighed heavily, that esteem was a source of comfort and a welcome font of strength.

The flickering candle glow highlighted the soft sheen of Cutter's buff-colored hair, part of which was caught up at the crown in the traditional chief's lock. Since the time of Timmorn Yellow-Eyes, the first Wolfrider and founder of the tribe, that crest had been the symbol of authority for each successor in the line of leadership.

Now Cutter was chief. For six turns of the seasons it had been so. Looking back on all she knew of him, Nightfall marveled at Cutter's swift adaptation to the role, at his devoted and unsparing efforts to remain worthy of the tribe's continued trust. From the moment when his fine, unruly mane had been gathered back into a leader's proud topknot, she had watched him mature. But the special friendship they shared, had shared since they were cubs, remained unchanged.

Often, during their sendings, Nightfall had come very close to touching Cutter's soul name. That pleased her, for she loved him in an effortless, soothing way. There had once been whisperings among the tribe, hopeful speculations that the young pair might become lifemates. But the passage of time evidenced that their loving friendship would be an end unto itself.

Then, too, there was Redlance. Nearly three times older than Nightfall, guileless and patient to a fault, he had drawn the spirited she-cub to his side almost unawares. What had begun as an arousal of her protective instincts had quickly changed to adoration, for the red-haired descendant of tree-shapers had proved neither meek nor reserved in matters of love. As lifemates, Nightfall and Redlance were known interchangeably as bee and flower, for that which one lacked the other provided, sustaining the perfect harmony of the bond.

"He's asleep," Cutter whispered, carefully replacing Redlance's hand on the furs.

Nightfall followed him as he went down through the hollow tree and stepped into the open night air.

"Why do the humans hate us so?" she asked. "We offer them no harm."

Cutter turned to answer her; his tone was matter-of-fact. "Humans have always hated our kind, ever since our foreparents, the High Ones, first set foot upon this world. That's just the way it is."

Nightfall folded her arms about herself, looking very small and very sad as she leaned against the knobbly bark of her tree home.

"I wish we could live in a place where there are no humans."

Cutter spread his hands. "I know. But this is home. Beyond the woods, what is there?"

The question required no answer. Indeed, there was none; the Holt and surrounding patch of territory that the Wolfriders claimed as their hunting ground was, to them, the world, the be-all and end-all of existence. By nature the elves were territorial. It was as if some distant, racial memory of having once been driven from a dwelling place spurred them to cling fiercely to whatever homeland they now had.

The Holt was situated in a particularly lush part of the forest in which water and game animals were to be had for the taking. The Wolfriders shared hunting rights with their bond-pack but also enjoyed the bounty of certain nut-bearing trees and berry bushes that, having been toyed with by shapers in the past, bore unnatural quantities of fruit in defiance of the seasons.

That the Wolfriders had altered the land somewhat for their own use was true; that they always lived in harmony and close communion with their surroundings was their unspoken law of life. The Wolfriders had killed only one human in their rescue of Redlance, for in accordance with the elves' regard for all living things, even human blood was not to be spilled wastefully or without regret.

Cutter walked alone to the top of a grassy hill that over-looked a shallow glen. As he sat there brooding with his knees drawn up to his chin, he slipped his sword from its scabbard and examined it carefully, making sure that he had cleaned it properly after the evening's ugly business. The blade was very beautiful, plain and gracefully curved like a crescent moon. It had been his father's weapon, passed on to Cutter when Bearclaw died six seasons ago. Because of its shape, the old chief had named the sword New Moon. Cutter treasured it above anything else he owned.

There was a rustle of leaves and a faint thump beside him; someone had jumped from a nearby tree. Without looking, Cutter knew that it was Skywise. The elves sat in silence together, two small shapes against the big night sky glittering above the hill.

"See, Cutter," said Skywise, pointing to a group of bright stars overhead. "The Great Wolf chases the Human Hunter across the sky. He's clumsy, that hunter. One day he'll trip, and the wolf will get him."

Cutter gave his friend a halfhearted smile. "You see all that up there, Skywise? Strange, I just see stars."

Once more the young elf fell to brooding, his downcast eyes all but hidden by long wisps of his shaggy, pale hair. He gnawed at one end of a broken twig and made no further effort to be pleasant. Skywise's face—which seemed to have been designed to accommodate grins and sly, know-ing glances—became grave.

"What's the matter?"

Cutter answered slowly. "I never killed a human before. Didn't think it could be done. Something bad will happen soon. I feel it."

Mustering a shadow of his usual flippancy, Skywise laughed. "You're full of dreamberries! What can the humans do to us? They're afraid to come near our Holt."

Cutter's only reply was the meaningful raising of one dark eyebrow, implying clearly to Skywise that where the humans were concerned, anything was possible.

Tabak's body lay stretched on a low bier that was covered with animal skins painted with magical charms and symbols. At either side of his head a torch sputtered. At his feet lay his weapons and the ceremonial jewelry he would wish to don before presenting himself to Gotara. Rudely woven baskets full of fruit, eggs, and dried meat rested by his side. He was well prepared for his Last Walk, for his death on the point of the Demon Chief's moon knife had earned him the highest honors his tribe could bestow. This was small consolation to Tabak's loudly mourning family, however; they had been utterly dependent on him as a provider and were now at the mercy of the Spirit Man's decree.

The old shaman was in a foul mood; his scowling face was as wrinkled and dark as the knee joint of a brown salamander.

"This is a sign from the spirits—a punishment," he cried, as much to himself as to his assembled followers. "We were weak. The Wolf Demons desecrated our ritual. They killed Tabak. And all because we were afraid to fight back!" He clenched one bony fist as his breath came in fierce, emotion-wracked gasps. "The spirits despise our cowardice and turn away from us. They no longer hear our prayers! We have delayed too long in carrying out Gotara's will!"

Suddenly the shaman's gaze fixed on one of the torches. The flames flickered in the depths of his hard, chestnut-brown eyes. He reached down and plucked the torch from the ground, holding it above his head so that its sparks fell treacherously close to his extravagant mane.

"Now we will do what must be done so that Tabak may rest!"

From a pool of darkness at the bottom of the hill near the Holt came an urgent cry, a howl made up of many voices raised in alarm. Cutter sat bolt upright, his skin tingling, his pointed ears pricked. Down in the glen, members of the wolf pack were gathering, moving about nervously, their eyes shining like fallen stars as they reflected the moons' light.

"Ayoooah, Nightrunner," Cutter called, running to meet the great wolf who scrambled toward him. In his excitement, Nightrunner nearly knocked Cutter over. The wolf was large, even for one of his kind; though comparatively brawny by elfin standards, Cutter was hard pressed to keep his balance as Nightrunner leaped up to place both huge forepaws on his shoulders.

"Speak, my friend," Cutter demanded. "What have you seen?"

Nightrunner licked the elf chieftain's face, whining and shivering. His thick fur stood on end, and his magnificent brush was bent in the sign of warning. Cutter tried to calm the wolf's agitated movements, tried to force the eye contact necessary for him to extract a clear image of the threat from the animal's mind. He grasped a handful of fur on either side of Nightrunner's massive head and held on tight until their eyes met.

It was like sending but much more difficult; it required more concentration and shaping of thought patterns to merge with the blunt, instinct-driven mind of the wolf. One image dominated all others, a memory of scent as much as of substance:

Humans-fire-humans-fire-humans-fire.

Instantly Cutter broke contact and turned to look at Skywise, who was waiting at the top of the hill.

"I was right," said Cutter. "The humans are coming against us—with fire!"

Skywise said nothing, but his left hand crept to the hilt of the straight, wide-based blade at his hip.

Treestump sat back on his haunches and surveyed his handiwork with satisfaction. His she-wolf, Lionskin, shifted her weight impatiently as the yellow-bearded elf made a

final, unnecessary adjustment on her bandage. During
Redlance's rescue, Lionskin's thigh had been punctured by
a wooden spear; the wound was not a serious one, but
Treestump made certain that it was clean and properly
dressed. He knew that he would have to watch her closely
over the next few days, or, left alone, the she-wolf would
gnaw and worry the thin leather bandage to shreds. She
seemed unusually nervous, not from pain but in response to
a sense of imminent danger that Treestump could not help
but share.

Strongbow stood at his favorite post, on the long-healed
stub of a fallen limb that protruded from the bole of the
Father Tree. The thrill of battle with the humans still coursed
through his veins, and it was as much with eager anticipation as with concern that he, too, scented trouble on the
rising wind.

Below him, Scouter and One-Eye emerged from the opening at the base of the tree, their faces solemn from their
visit with Redlance. Scouter glanced at his father, whose
rough-cut black eyepatch did little to conceal the blend of
sympathy and vengeful anger in his expression. One-Eye
was one of the oldest of the tribe. Several of the skulls the
humans displayed on their pillar of sacrifice were those of
friends and kinfolk he had known and loved. That gentle
Redlance, of all the Wolfriders, had nearly been the humans'
next victim was a difficult thought for One-Eye to bear. He
wordlessly embraced Scouter, grateful that his youthful son
had not suffered so much as a scratch in the daring attack.

Strongbow was the first to hear the distant warning howl
of the wolves and the first to receive Cutter's urgent sending that followed soon after.

Humans-fire-humans-fire.

The elfin archer responded to his chieftain's mental summons with practiced ease; he had long ago forsaken the use
of speech and communicated solely by sending.

Humans-fire-humans-fire-humans.

Treestump stood up, accepting Cutter's call with an air of

grim vindication. The message came as no surprise, for he had suspected all along that the humans would not permit the disruption of their sacrificial rite to go unavenged.

"So it's finally come to this, has it?" Treestump grumbled, stooping to pick up his gleaming double-headed throwing ax. "After all this time, the Tall Ones finally found the belly to come and meet us on our own ground!"

He heard the light steps of his daughter, Dewshine, and turned to see her standing behind him, tense and eager, with bow in hand and a dagger laced to her hip-belt.

"I heard the wolves, Father. There's more trouble, isn't there?"

Treestump nodded. "Cutter has sent the call."

"It didn't come to me."

"No," Treestump answered, fingering the white-gold curls at her temple. "Not this time, pretty cub."

Dewshine's narrow shoulders almost sagged with disappointment, but she quickly caught herself. "I understand," she murmured. She had killed the doe from which her tunic was made, and she knew that she could pin a running squirrel to a tree with one throw of her slender hunting knife. But even so, her body was slim and delicate. Most humans she had seen were nearly twice her height, with huge five-fingered hands capable of breaking her in half like a dried twig. She looked at her father, at his stocky frame and broad chest well sheathed in layers of muscle, and conceded that he was far better suited to face humans in combat than she.

The female Wolfriders were well trained in the use of bow, spear, and knife. They were no more strangers to the hunt than the males were unaccustomed to tanning hides or digging for tender roots. But there were close to twice as many males as females in the small elfin tribe; since becoming chief, Cutter had with good reason been more protective of his life-bearing tribeswomen than his predecessors had been. Even though she had taken part earlier in Redlance's rescue, firing arrows from the cover of the trees near the humans' sacred clearing, Dewshine realized that in the conflict to come she would be of no help once her barbs were spent. Now, as the wolves began to appear in the Holt, whining for their riders to mount and make the bond complete, Dewshine took comfort in knowing that her sister Wolfriders—Nightfall, Moonshade, and even One-Eye's sturdy mate, Clearbrook—must also remain behind to defend the Holt itself if need be. Of the males, only Woodlock, who had recently fathered a tiny son and who was needed to aid in its care, and the injured Redlance were not summoned with the others.

Lean and pale astride Nightrunner's supple back, Cutter circled through the Holt with sword raised high and saw that his armed hunters were ready to follow him. Deep within his breast a hard knot of fear seemed to press against his heart. Never within memory had the superstitious humans dared to broach the Wolfriders' stronghold. Never had the furtive elves been forced twice in one night to confront their ancient enemies hand to hand. Cutter had hoped with little reason that further bloodshed might be avoided, but the humans were bringing fire into the deep woods. That was a threat that had to be met and dealt with in one way or another.

"Weapons ready," ordered Cutter. "Follow Nightrunner!"

The wolf pack lit off at a run, close on the heels of their powerful leader. The elf warriors rode as one with their shaggy mounts, bursting through clumps of tall fern and forest shrubbery, weaving effortlessly around thick tree trunks and fallen branches. A stiff breeze had sprung up; it sang in the Wolfriders' large ears; and the treetops, yielding to the wind's mounting force, seemed to point like long-fingered hands back to the Holt. If it was a sign or warning for them to return, the Wolfriders paid no heed.

Cutter felt Nightrunner's pace begin to slacken. He dug his fingers deep into the wolf's gray-brown fur, sensing that the moment of confrontation was at hand. Skywise, riding abreast with his chief and friend, suddenly pointed to the closely grouped trees ahead.

"Look!"

The trees were edged with brightness, but it was not the silvery glow of the moons. The trunks were lit from behind by a sinister, ruddy light that could mean only one thing.

The running wolves pulled up short, barking and whining in panic as their instinctive fear of fire took hold. It was with the greatest difficulty that Cutter urged a resisting Nightrunner toward that yellow radiance, toward the sharp stink of humans waiting beyond the trees.

The Spirit Man smiled his evil half smile as Cutter emerged from the shadows, perched on a terrified wolf that snarled and crouched and held its ears flat against its bristling skull. For a moment the elf chieftain and the human shaman regarded each other in silence. Cutter felt uneasy, for this time the Wolfriders could not rely on surprising the humans as they had earlier. Clearly, this meeting had been anticipated, even arranged. The Spirit Man and his several torch-bearing companions had come; they had waited patiently, knowing that the wolves would carry the message of their arrival.

"I warned you, old man," Cutter growled. He knew the humans' language well, for Bearclaw had deemed it necessary that his son have that advantage over the enemy. "Go away or we must kill you!"

"No, demon-chief," the Spirit Man answered in even, almost conversational tones. "We shall live, but you and your kind will be ashes before sunrise."

At once the human's meaning was clear to Cutter. His eyes widened with alarm and disbelief.

"Are you mad, human? If you burn the woods, everyone will starve, your tribe as well as mine!"

The Spirit Man was unmoved. It seemed that he had already given thought to the possible consequences of his action and had dismissed them as unimportant. The men behind him, however, shifted uncomfortably.

"No matter!" the shaman's voice rang out as he swept his guttering torch before him in a wide arc. His body was drawn to its fullest height, and his bony chest swelled with self-righteous conviction. "Gotara wills a cleansing! Only Men must rule this land. All demons must burn!"

"No," cried Cutter.

At the same time, Strongbow fired an arrow with deadly accuracy; it pierced the raving shaman's throat. But it was too late; the Spirit Man had already thrust his torch into a nearby shrub. Fanned by the heavy breeze, the flames caught instantly. Cutter watched in horror as the other humans imitated their shaman's actions. In seconds, greedy tongues of flame began to lick the weathered trunks and limbs of trees that were part of a forest that was far older than men or elves could ever tell.

Three

The plump, pallid worm oozed slowly over the troll's left ankle, covered the distance between the troll's spraddled legs, and began with senseless determination to ascend the right ankle. Having nothing better to do at the moment, the troll observed the slithery process with mild amusement; then he lazily plucked the worm from his leg and inhaled it through pursed lips in a single slurp.

Munching contentedly, reluctant to swallow too quickly his juicy snack, the troll settled himself more comfortably within the depression his buttocks had worn in the dusty cave floor. As he had done every night, all night, for many turns of the seasons, he sat guard beside the round, stone door slab blocking the entrance to the Tunnel of the Green Wood.

The troll's name was Scurff the Doorkeeper, and this night's watch seemed destined to be as dull as any other night's.

The last of the worm pulp slid down his throat as Scurff nodded off, his shapeless chin disappearing into folds of warty flesh on his upper chest. He began to dream an agreeable dream in which a pretty troll wench drifted seductively toward him, her pendulant breasts swinging like mud-filled sacks suspended from her shoulders. Scurff was just about to bury his face in her quivering amplitude, when a loud, clashing noise jolted him awake and made his heart pound.

In the center of the round stone door a metal plate had been set so that it was visible on either side of the door. Someone outside now hammered at the metal disk with desperate urgency.

"Open up, tunnel-makers," a voice cried above the din. "We've no time to waste!"

Resentfully, Scurff the Doorkeeper roused himself, deliberately taking his time as he shuffled to the opposite wall of the cave, where the door-lock mechanism glimmered faintly in the dim light of a phosphorescent lantern.

"What do they want now?" the troll grumbled. "It's too soon since the last time they were here!"

He winced as the hammering without grew even more frantic. Reverberations spiraled down the pitch-black corridor that declined away from the guard chamber to connect with a maze of underground tunnels far below.

Scurff doubted that his shouting could be heard by those who were causing the disturbance, but he shouted, anyway. It did him good.

"All right! All right! Miserable, noisy elves! Give a body half a chance, will you!"

The mechanism that swung and locked the door was actually an intricate system of pulleys and gears concealed within the tunnel wall. The only exposed part of the works was an ornate metal wheel set upon an axle that projected stalklike from the cave floor. Like a disgruntled miller, Scurff leaned to the task of turning the wheel, which squealed and protested, revolving fitfully about its sturdy axle. The unpleasant grinding sounds coupled with the clatter at the door set the troll's teeth—few though they were—on painful edge.

Responding at last to the Doorkeeper's efforts, the ponderous stone began slowly to swing inward on its single monstrous hinge. In need of maintenance, the massive hinge creaked treacherously. Scurff ceased turning the wheel and shouted again.

"Stop your racket! I'm coming out now!"

The stone door stood barely half an arm's length ajar, the opening a crescent-shaped gash of yellow light in the otherwise inky mouth of the tunnel. Suddenly another crescent, much smaller and glinting with bright metallic reflections, was thrust through the crack. It was a short, curved blade, and it was brandished by a shadowy figure who quickly squeezed through the narrow opening to glare with icy blue eyes at the troll.

"You're wrong, Doorkeeper," said the shape. "We're coming in!"

Instantly recognizing the short sword and its wielder, Scurff gave a squeak of alarm and groped for the wheel. Confronted with an emergency he had never expected to face, the doorkeep tried frantically to reverse the unlocking process and to reseal the tunnel, but the gesture was futile.

With an animal howl, Cutter hurled himself at the squealing troll, who flung his arms before his face and doubled over like a startled sow bug. The elf's frightening tactic was immediately successful; before New Moon needed so much as to split a single hair on his tuberous scalp, Scurff lay groveling on the tunnel floor. Cutter twisted his lithe body in midleap and landed with a leather-shod foot planted squarely between the troll's shoulder blades.

Scurff did his best to eye Cutter reproachfully. Although he had spared himself further violence by his wisely submissive actions, he writhed with pangs of humiliation.

"Y-you can't do this," the troll stammered. "It's just not done! No one has ever violated our caverns before."

"No one's ever burned down the forest before," Cutter answered, jerking a thumb back at the partially open door. For the first time Scurff noticed wisps of acrid smoke seeping into the tunnel from outside.

Now several more elfin silhouettes squirmed through the opening and headed straight for the burnished glint of the metal wheel. Like a bone-diseased sloth, the mechanism groaned as Skywise, Treestump, and One-Eye set it slowly turning once more. At last the door scraped fully open.

Backlit by lurid orange light, huddled together, coughing, the entire Wolfrider tribe and their lupine mounts stood revealed. From his place at the wheel, yellow-bearded Treestump shouted at them.

"Don't stand there gawking! Come inside! Quickly!"

Sheltering her tiny newborn son, Wing, in her arms, Rainsong was the first to dash into the tunnel. Her lifemate, Woodlock, followed immediately, carrying their daughter, Newstar, on his back. As the elfin family sidled nervously around their chief and his prone troll captive, Cutter gave them a reassuring nod and waved them on deeper into the passageway.

Now a group of Wolfriders jammed the entrance, hindering one another in their frightened rush for refuge. Pike wriggled through, clutching his bone-tipped throwing spear as protectively as Rainsong cradled her infant. When he beheld the quietly outraged troll pinned beneath Cutter's foot, Pike's flushed, round-cheeked face split in a torrent of uncontrollable laughter.

Grim Strongbow cut the outburst short, shoving Pike forward into the gloomy cave. The gaunt-featured archer bore his plain, curved longbow in one hand and dragged his spindly son, Dart, along in the other. It seemed that weapon and child were interchangeable in terms of the handling they received, but Dart voiced no more complaint that did the inanimate bow.

Now nearly all seventeen Wolfriders and their bond-pack of fourteen wolves were inside the cave. Scurff the Doorkeeper began to wheeze as more elves and their shaggy mounts crowded around him. The air inside the tunnel was thick with swirling smoke, and a steadily growing shower of sparks warned that flames from the wind-swept inferno would reach them at any moment.

Still outside were Nightfall and Redlance. The injured elf could barely hold his seat atop his panicky wolf. Scouter and Dewshine hung back to assist the struggling pair, but it was petite Nightfall who all but carried her mate to safety within the passageway.

"What's going on here?"

The rude utterance startled the elves. At once Cutter abandoned Scurff and moved swiftly toward the source of the unpleasant voice. Three bulky shapes stood close together, blocking access to the lower tunnels. The central figure of the three flourished a thick-shafted stabbing spear and spoke again.

"Cutter! You're getting too bold for your own good, little elf chieftain."

"I have very good reason, Picknose," Cutter responded. "Or didn't you know there's a fire outside?"

Picknose's protuberant features made his scowl easily discernible, even in the gloom. He scoffed. "Outside? What do trolls care about outside? That's your business. Out! All of you! Get out!"

Cutter folded his arms, almost absentmindedly displaying New Moon in the casual gesture. Skywise moved, frowning, to stand beside his chief, while other Wolfriders let their hands drift to their weapons. At the same time, Picknose and the two stocky guards flanking him advanced with threatening intent toward the elves.

"You heard me," Picknose bellowed. "Get out!"

"Hospitable as ever, eh?" Cutter murmured.

A slight shift of stance and the merest incline of his head were the only signals the Wolfrider chieftain needed to give. Instantly the wolves glided into a growling ring around the three trolls. Whichever way they turned, the tunnel's guardians confronted a fanged grin and glaring yellow eyes.

Picknose was certain that the wolves were hungry. He was not at all certain that the elves could control their mounts, even if they wished to. Taking care to make no sudden movement, Picknose cast an accusing frown at Scurff the Doorkeeper.

"This is all your fault!"

"I did my best to stop them," whined Scurff, who was still rubbing the back of his negligible neck. "Will somebody please close that door!"

Cutter took a quick head count, saw that all his folk were inside, and then nodded to the three elves at the wheel to comply with the troll's request. Silent, stricken, the Wolfriders stood and watched as the great slab of rock slowly swung into place, shutting off forever their last glimpse of the burning Holt.

In the flight from their doomed tree-homes, the Wolfriders had managed, barely, to snatch up a precious few belongings. Among these were long, rawhide thongs, which the elves now used to bind the trolls' thick wrists behind their backs.

"You'll pay for this, mark me," Picknose swore through the curls of his long black beard.

One corner of Cutter's mouth turned up wryly at the threat. He knew with smug assurance that the troll folk were a basically cowardly lot, but he was also aware that that streak of cowardice was accompanied by malicious, unpredictable cunning. He gave the knot on Picknose's bonds an extra tug and then shouldered the impressive stabber the troll had earlier brandished with such menace. Skywise, too, hefted one of the other guard's weapons, pleased with the ease and tidiness of the capture.

"Perhaps with some similar 'persuasion' your old king, Greymung, will be only too glad to help us," Cutter commented, hopping onto Nightrunner's back.

Picknose responded with a string of sulfurous remarks pertaining to the elves' ancestry and a scowl that would, had green plants grown in the cave, have withered the leaves like a sudden frost.

Thus, a subdued procession of trolls, elves, and wolves began to file down the gloomful passageway. The corridor was narrow, the angle of its descent inconstant. Yet the elves knew that every padding step of their wolf-mounts carried them deeper underground, farther and father from a home that by now no longer existed. Until the fire had sated its raging appetite, there was nowhere to go but down into the forbidden caverns, which, in all the history of their tribe, only one Wolfrider had ever seen.

Scurff sulked openly as he stumped along at the head of the line, shrinking away from the baleful glances of his fellow trolls. Unjust, he thought. Their reproach was totally unfair, considering that he had always performed his inglorious duties faithfully and without complaint. Scurff held the post of Doorkeeper simply because no one else wanted it, but that had never bothered him. He preferred an uneventful existence.

Now he resented the Wolfriders more than ever, for not only had they shattered the understanding that had long existed between himself and them, they also had almost certainly cost him his comfortable post, as well as a pincertorn toenail or two if King Greymung was feeling particularly vindictive this day.

The tunnel took a sudden turn to the left and then inclined more steeply. Uneasily, Cutter realized that the trolls' night vision must be superior even to that of the Wolfriders. He rode along not speaking, concentrating all his attention on the four lumbering shapes ahead of him, certain that they'd soon attempt an escape. Soon enough, he heard rather than saw one of the captives suddenly leap to one side of the path, trying to escape through some kind of air shaft cut into the tunnel. Guided by the sounds and cool air, Cutter quickly thrust Picknose's spear between the escaping guard and the hole in the wall. With satisfaction, the elf chieftain heard a yelp of surprise and pain, and then the slap of two broad, flat feet reluctantly resumed their stride before him.

Have a troll and a hole, have a hole and no troll!

The sending came from Skywise, and it made Cutter grin. Snatches of mental communications among others of his tribe flittered through Cutter's brain like butterflies visiting a single flower. From each individual he gleaned a different impression: fear, apprehension, loss, hatred of the humans, despair, stoic acceptance, optimism—all of these washed over him, washed through the blood of the eight and two preceding chiefs that mingled in his veins.

Cutter thought of his dead father. If not for Bearclaw, the Wolfriders would not have had even this half-safe maze of underground passageways in which to take refuge. Evidently the captured trolls were also aware of this, and bitterly so, for among their mutterings Bearclaw's name surfaced—more than once—in tones that were none too fond.

It was long ago, when he had known but a few more turns of the seasons than his son's present twice eight and seven, that Bearclaw had discovered the trolls. Until that time, the arboreal Wolfriders, dwelling as they did above the forest floor, had been unaware of the thriving, tunnel-digging community deep beneath the ground. Obsessed with finding a way into their subterranean domain, Bearclaw had searched through many full changes of the greater moon. At last, he had discovered a forgotten above-ground vent that the normally conscientious trolls had neglected to conceal properly. The brash elf chieftain had been at first an unwelcome guest, but slowly the trolls became accustomed to his discreet visits; he had even kept the trolls' existence a secret from his own tribe for a long time. Eventually, though, the Wolfriders came to know of the underground dwellers, and the trolls began to offer bits of their fine metalwork in exchange for Bearclaw's—for he was still the only elf allowed to enter the tunnels—tempting gifts of furs and leathers. From these tentative beginnings a system of barter had evolved, one that delighted the Wolfriders yet gradually and inexplicably had incurred the mounting resentment of the trolls.

Cutter was summoned forcibly from his musings on the past as young Dart's voice suddenly piped, "Where are the hammer sounds? Aren't the trolls always supposed to be digging and hammering?"

The innocent query sent a ripple of disquiet through the elves. Indeed, the silence was profound. Although the meandering Tunnel of the Green Wood had now widened into a circular chamber faintly illuminated by a kind of phosphorescent lichen, there were no signs of troll activity or even habitation. The entrances to several other corridors hewn from solid rock gaped in the otherwise featureless walls of the cavern.

Cutter sensed a possible trap. He jostled Picknose with the butt of his spear.

"Your people know we're here, don't they?"

The sullen troll did not respond.

"Don't think you can trick us into the wrong tunnel, Picky," Cutter warned, deliberately choosing a calm and familiar manner. "Our ears are as sharp as they look, and you trolls do have a distinctive smell about you. If you have friends waiting for us in one of these dark passageways, tell them they're wasting their time. They can't surprise us." He paused to scratch Nightrunner behind the ears and then added evenly, "And they certainly can't outfight us."

Still silent, Picknose shifted his warty bulk and seemed to be considering this information carefully.

"By the way," Skywise offered, "Bearclaw told us about the concealed pit."

At this bit of news, Picknose became the picture of disconcertion, taking on the look of a toad caught between a fallen log and the beak of a hungry fisher-bird. Cutter blinked quizzically at his silver-haired friend.

Concealed pit? Skywise, when did Bearclaw ever mention a trap like that?

Delighted with himself, Skywise smirked.

He never did. I guessed!

Since the sending was open to all save the trolls, the Wolfriders' soft laughter quickly dispelled any aura of threat that remained in the gloomy chamber. The captive guards shuffled and looked at each other, obviously at a loss.

"You see, Picky," Cutter said amiably, "you're outnumbered and outfoxed! You have no choice but to take us straight to King Greymung's throne room."

Scurff the Doorkeeper shrugged, impatient with Picknose's refusal to submit with even slight grace to a hopeless situation.

"This way, Wolfriders," Scurff announced, indicating with his shoulder a part of the cavern where a large rectangular slab of rock was set flush with the wall. If the stone served any purpose, the elves could not guess what it was, but Picknose seemed truly incensed by Scurff's behavior.

"Idiot!" he shouted, the insult reverberating around the chamber for several moments afterward.

Scurff was unaffected. He made a rude noise at his fellow troll. Then he sidled as close to Cutter as he dared and cooed, "If you will untie me, good elf, I shall open this access for you. I swear it leads to the very foot of our king's throne."

Cutter studied the unmovable slab for a few moments, sighed, and nodded doubtfully.

Always an opportunist, Scurff reasoned that these uninvited elfin guests would so upset Greymung that the lesser matter of an ineffectual doorkeeper's punishment would be completely forgotten. Cutter, having correctly guessed the fawning troll's motive, eyed Scurff with amused contempt and then bent to sever his bonds. His sword, New Moon, flashed in the dimness.

As his hands were freed, the Doorkeeper trembled, secretly counting his fingers. The deadly blade had missed slicing them off by only a hair's breadth. Implicit in that deliberate, narrow miss was a warning that Scurff readily took with abject humility.

The Wolfriders watched curiously as the Doorkeeper fumbled and felt his way along one edge of the big, rectangular stone. Three times his stubby fingers seemed to disappear into random spots in the solid rock of the adjacent wall. Immediately, there was a scraping, squealing sound so loud that it startled the wolves and caused many of the elves to clap their hands in pain over their own sensitive ears.

A weighty flag began to totter away from the wall, its upper edge beginning to fall forward. Instinctively the wolves backed away. Skywise, however, noticed thick chains, previously hidden, bolted to the stone's upper corners, checking its fall.

"It's a door!" he exclaimed, grinning, as the ingenious

contraption slowly lowered itself to the dank-smelling floor. Behind it was an arched doorway, fashioned with some attempt at artistry. Beyond the arch stretched a long, torch-lit hall. The unexpected firelight made the elves squint.

Now it was the trolls' turn to be contemptuous, for the Wolfriders' wonderment at the relatively simple mechanics of the secret door was plain and unabashed. As the party passed over the fallen slab and entered the hallway, Skywise's questioning fingers brushed along the mighty links of the rust-spotted chain. He looked upward at the holes from which the chains emerged and tried to fathom how the door was raised and lowered and how many trolls it took to accomplish the task. Where were all these tunnel-diggers, these door-openers? he wondered. Why didn't they show themselves?

The floor of the passageway was cobbled with small stones, polished to a high gloss so that the patterns and intrusions within them, fashioned so intricately by nature, were shown to best advantage. Embedded in the mortar between the cobbles, sparkling gemstones winked like so many rainbow-hued eyes in the dancing torchlight.

Newstar wriggled off Woodlock's lap and dropped to the floor, laughing excitedly. She kept hold of her father's wolf's tail and trotted along, half crouching so that her delighted eyes would not miss a glint or a glimmer of color. Woodlock turned to watch his daughter, and for a moment his gaze met Rainsong's. No sending was needed to clarify the heartfelt message exchanged in that single glance. They envied their little she-cub, who could laugh and so soon forget all that had been lost.

"I wonder what Bearclaw thought of this," Cutter said aloud, sparing himself a moment to look around appreciatively before settling back to keep a suspicious eye on the captive troll guards.

"No Wolfrider has ever soiled these stones with his cursed footsteps," snarled Picknose. Highlighted by the torches, every wart and crag of the troll's furrowed features stood out in bold relief. He was not altogether ugly as his kind went. Evidently, he took great pride in his luxuriant black beard, for its tip was adorned with a pert red ribbon.

"What do you mean?" Cutter snapped. "Bearclaw came down here all the time. He said so."

"That braggart! Just because we tolerated his presence once in a while doesn't mean he ever had free run of our tunnels. Curse him for the snooping ferret he was. I hope you all end up the way he did! I—"

Picknose froze in midsentence, teeth clacking shut on a gasp. He knew that he had gone too far. The point of his own stabbing spear now pressed insistently against his spine. Cutter's wolf growl caused the procession to come to an ominous halt.

Moments passed.

"Forgive me," Picknose said, forcing out the words. "I meant no disrespect." He did not turn around, but his shoulders sagged with relief as he felt, finally, the spear's point withdrawn from his back. The orderly group continued on, but now Picknose walked in fuming silence, refusing to speak again.

At the end of the long, expanding passageway stood a magnificent arched portal. The curved sides of the arch stretched upward, meeting high overhead, and the structure bristled with many-faceted jewels set randomly in what seemed to be great patches of pure gold or silver. The appearance was almost that of hot wax, as if the semimolten metals had been poured in layers over the vaulting stone. Skywise assumed that the trolls possessed methods to cool the seething fluids quickly, for the melts had been built up in different spots to produce pleasing organic configurations of solid precious metal. He was therefore astonished when he inquisitively poked at one of the shining masses and easily scratched a fleck of gold away from the surface with the point of his blade. Dark, bare rock lay beneath, betraying the illusion.

Skywise frowned. He disliked being fooled, even uninten-
tionally. That the thinnest coating of leaf upon cleverly
shaped stone had deceived him so annoyed him that he
began to scrutinize his own troll-forged ornaments.

Skywise's wristbands were made of a lightweight, resilient
alloy that was permanently imbued with a rich smoky-blue
color. Of similar construction was the graceful face guard
he wore, more to keep his unruly burst of hair from his
eyes than for reasons of protection. When he brought his
wrists together sharply, there was no mistaking the bracelets' true metallic ring. Nevertheless, every golden nodule
and silvery stalagmite that Skywise observed beyond the
gem-encrusted archway was now suspect.

"In this place, what a thing looks like may not be what it
is," he muttered.

Preoccupied with their own concerns, none of his tribefolk
responded. But that mattered little, for Skywise was already
gnawing in his mind at the enigmatic bone of how the trolls
had managed to shape their rocky domain so artfully in the
first place. It was well known that the tunnel-diggers possessed no magic at all. Everything they accomplished was by
the skill of their brawny hands alone.

The long line of wolves and riders had passed beneath
the ostentatious portal. Now they were confronted by a
wide flight of stairs sweeping upward from the center of an
enormous high-domed vault. Here and there metal sconces
in the form of weird, open-mouthed reptiles craned their
long necks upward, emitting tongues of fire for light. The
feeble radiance was inadequate to penetrate the pitch darkness far above.

Looking up, Skywise had to remind himself that a ceiling
of solid rock enclosed the cavern high overhead. He tried to
imagine the black void to be a starless night sky. But a
feeling of overwhelming loneliness stole into his heart. He
wondered when, if ever, he would see the heavens in all
their richly populated glory again.

The spacious cavern was riddled with dark entrances and

exits of various sizes and shapes; many of these were inter-
connected by ramps or ladders cut from the living rock.
Clearly, this place was the central core of the trolls' underground habitat. From here, innumerable tunnels snaked
away in all directions, much like veins radiating from the
heart's beating place inside a living body.

Most alert and sharp-eyed of the Wolfriders, Scouter
jumped as he caught sight of several grotesque faces. They
were watching his tribefolk intently from dark, sheltered
crannies in the rock walls surrounding them. Like nervous
frogs startled from their hiding places in the shallows of a
murky pond, the peering spies darted furtively out of sight.
A quick shiver traveled up Scouter's spine as he thought he
glimpsed sudden, shadowy movements all around the chamber as well as above him on many of the overhanging
ledges. He gasped and whirled as something touched his
arm.

You're shivering like a little mouse on a wolf's tongue,
sent Dewshine. She let her fingers slide down his arm to
clasp his hand.

That's exactly how I feel, the elfin youth responded,
squeezing her hand briefly in turn.

Dewshine nodded, her wide-open eyes as blue and unflinch-
ing as those of her cousin, Cutter. She patted her wolf's pale
gray shoulder, urging the beast toward the foot of the
upward-soaring stairs.

The irregularly shaped steps shone with a warm, burnished glow, for they, too, had been covered with a layer of
gold. Time and much use had worn the plating away in
places, revealing a base of smooth gray stone. On either side
of the stairs stood a row of tall columns, formed by the
merging of gigantic stalactites and stalagmites. Swirling
throughout the lengths of these impressive formations were
delicate tints of pink, green, and yellow, as lovely in their
way as the varied hues of a sunset or a rainbow.

The trolls' world was a world of rock, cold and hard but
far from colorless. An appreciation of nature's incompara-

ble invention and artistry was one quality the tunnel-dwellers shared with their uninvited visitors. But in their compulsion to own, to dominate, to bend their surroundings in subservience to every selfish need, real or imagined, the trolls differed greatly from the Wolfriders. This difference had, in part, been at the root of much of the mutual contempt between the two races.

The captive guards hesitated, mounting the stairs only after much prodding by the elves. When they all reached the landing, it became easy to see why Picknose and his comrades had been so reluctant to make the ascent.

At the far end of the landing, just beyond a narrow entranceway that had been carved to resemble the open jaws of a bloodthirsty bat, lay the throne room of King Greymung. That regal troll was visible, sprawled on his massive chair, amid the splendors and comforts of his rank. He was alone, save for two rotund female attendants, beautiful by troll aesthetics, who fussed and fawned over the aged monarch with dutiful zeal.

Greymung himself was the epitome of dedicated self-indulgence—a gross, indolent creature, unsightly even to members of his own race. His appearance hardly harmonized with the subterranean elegance of his audience chamber, for though the room was somewhat small, it contained many objects to please the eye.

In keeping with his preferred bat motif, the backrest of Greymung's throne rose in the stylized shape of outspread wings; these were dappled with luminescent colors, a natural attribute of the stone from which the chair was carved. The room was lambent with a gentle spectrum of glowing tints, shown most spectacularly in gardens of crystalline, branchlike growths curving out of the walls.

The troll king insisted on being surrounded by the finest of his riches. There were heaped displays of brilliant fist-sized jewels, oddly designed weapons more beautiful than functional, and clever toys, heavy with intricate decorations of gold and silver. Whether or not constant exposure had

deadened Greymung's ability to appreciate his many trea-
sures, he sat among them like a bloated spider hoarding a
swarm of priceless and inedible flies in his sagging web.

He looked up as Scurff the Doorkeeper scuttled uncere-
moniously into his presence. "My king," Scurff began; then
he blurted, "The Wolfriders!"

Instantly, Greymung's expression changed from shock to
blackest fury. His subjects had been either unable or unwilling to warn him that elves were abroad in his tunnels.

"What's this?" screamed the troll king as Cutter led his
tribe, beasts and all, into the luminescent sanctum. "Wolfriders
invading my domain? Unthinkable!"

Scurff giggled nervously, made a perfunctory obeisance
to Greymung, and scurried as quickly as bulk and discretion
would allow through an exit to one side of the throne. The
Doorkeeper's cowardly flight hardly escaped his king's notice,
but Greymung's blood-freezing scowl was now fixed solely
on Picknose.

"You miserable worm! Is this how you defend your king?"

Still bound at the wrists and deeply embarrassed, Picknose
did his best to look contrite. However, to Cutter's observant
eye there appeared to be little love lost between the surly
troll guards and their irascible ruler. The elf chieftain dismounted and sauntered toward the throne, while his tribefolk
quickly made themselves at home. Greymung writhed on
his fur-draped seat as though the invading band of elves
were a swarm of bees.

"Relax, great troll," Cutter said, placing one foot on the
raised dais that supported the king's chair. "Our visit won't
be overlong. The Humans have burned us from our Holt.
We only came here to escape the flames."

"Batdung," spat the aged troll, his colorless whiskers
trembling in the epithet's wake. "We know your thieving
ways, elf. You and your wolf pack mean to rob us blind and
whet your blades on our gizzards in the process!"

Cutter turned to look around the chamber. The wolves
were prowling about hungrily, wagging their tails and utter-

ing plaintive whines. Several of them had already devoured the remnants of a stag's roasted haunch that lay among less appetizing leftovers atop a chiseled stone table. Dewshine, Pike, and Scouter were lustily digging into a huge bowl of plump mushrooms, and since there were plenty of these to go around, each Wolfrider soon gratefully received a handful. The weary elves sat or stood upon the gem-bestrewn floor, oblivious to Greymung's capacious coffers heaped high with gold nuggets, ignoring open chests full of magnificent jewelry in favor of a drink of water from the bubbling wellspring that served as the king's personal fountain.

Swinging around to confront Greymung once again, Cutter gave him a tolerant but significant glance.

"You judge us by your own greedy example, Greymung," said the Wolfriders' young chief. "We have nothing now. But you have more food and wealth than you know what to do with."

Fidgeting uncomfortably, Greymung shifted his small, rheumy eyes so that he would not have to meet the elf's penetrating gaze. "That doesn't give you the right to break in here and take what you want," he countered lamely.

"Maybe not," Cutter answered, accepting the choice mushroom that Skywise offered him. "But think a moment—" he paused to take a huge bite—"you owe us, troll. Your people are afraid to venture from their tunnels. What would you have done for meat all this time if we never shared our catches with you?"

"And when did we ever cheat you in a trade?" demanded Skywise. He grabbed a fold of the luxurious white fox fur robe that lined Greymung's throne and lifted it up for emphasis. "We barter only our finest pelts and leathers for the metals you forge!"

"And when one of you has fallen sick, haven't we, for kindness's sake, fetched you herbs and medicines, asking nothing in return?"

The voice came from a shadowy corner of the opulent chamber. It was Nightfall's, and the poignance of her question was a reminder of hardship to come. Who would shelter the Wolfriders now that the forest was destroyed? Where could they seek healing aid for Redlance, who looked so pale and strained as Nightfall hovered near him?

Picknose's scornful response left no doubt as to the trolls' position on the matter.

"Bah! You do us those favors because you know that only we trolls can forge the fine weapons and pretty trinkets you fools fancy. Anyone can learn to hunt. You need us far more than we need you!"

"Is that so?" Cutter swallowed the last of his mushroom and slowly drew New Moon from its scabbard. He examined the blade abstractedly, ran his thumb along its curved cutting edge, and then suddenly pointed the sword directly at Picknose. The troll jumped half his own height straight up; an instant later there was a smack as his big bare feet hit the polished floor.

"All right, then," growled the elf chieftain, "we'll see how you mighty hunters fare when the season of the White Cold comes and your store-holes remain empty!"

With his hands tied behind his back, his king decidedly disinterested in his fate, and a sword point threatening his sizable nose, there was little Picknose could do to retain even a shred of dignity. But the one expression of defiance he could make, he did; he stuck out his great slab of a tongue.

"Did you see that?" cried Dart. "I didn't know trolls' tongues were so long!"

"Or so green. Hey, Picky," japed Pike, "is that moss you have growing in your mouth?"

"Can't be," Cutter answered with a wicked gleam. "Moss only grows where it's quiet and still."

A few of the Wolfriders snickered, conceding even as they did that Picknose's emphatic gesture had demonstrated some respectable grit. This was more than could be said of Greymung, who huddled pettishly on his throne and did absolutely nothing.

Overcome by his own strong curiosity, Skywise had disappeared some moments before through the passageway that had faciliatated Scurff's escape. Now the elf hurriedly returned to the throne room, grinning his familiar grin of new discovery. He hopped onto the dais and clapped a hand on Cutter's shoulder.

"I've been down to see the forges! Bearclaw's old tales about what he found down here were true, except everything's bigger than he said. It's wonderful, Cutter! Come see for yourself."

Nestled amid folds of white fur at the base of Greymung's throne was a small boulder, round and pitted. At the moment it supported the king's regal right foot. It seemed a plain, inelegant footstool for such a regal personage, hardly worth anyone's notice. But as Skywise spoke, his left hand carelessly brushed against the boulder's dark, mottled surface—*clack*!—and held fast!

"My arm! It's stuck!" exclaimed the silver-eyed elf. Both he and Cutter gaped in surprise as other Wolfriders rushed up to see what had happened.

It took the elves a few moments to realize that the stone held Skywise not by the flesh of his arm but by the blue metal band about his wrist. The tugging force was powerful and frightening. Cutter grabbed his friend's hand, adding his strength to Skywise's frantic efforts to yank his wrist free. At last the mysterious rock released its grip, only to take sudden interest in Cutter's bright metal sword.

Ting! The blade struck the stone edge on. This time, however, the gripping power seemed much less strong. With a grunt and a two-fisted hold on the hilt, Cutter jerked his weapon free. He backed away from the boulder and eyed it warily, almost as if he expected it to pounce. Skywise whistled softly and began to inspect the dark object from all angles, taking care to touch it only with his fingertips; even in that position, he could sense the insistent pull at his wristbands.

"This stone has great power," he said in an awed murmur. He was smiling again.

"Get away from that!" ordered Greymung, fuming at Skywise's explorations. "It is sacred. There is not another like it in my realm."

Cutter's patience with the troll king was nearing an end. He uttered an oath of disgust and jammed New Moon into its sheath.

"Come on, Skywise. It's plain we're not welcome here. The tribe must assemble for a council."

"Hmmm?" Skywise mumbled as he knelt before the magical rock, enviously caressing its surface. He was so lost in fascination that he barely realized that his chief had addressed him.

Cutter shrugged and began to walk toward the far side of the chamber.

"A magic rock won't find us a new place to live," he said as he joined One-Eye, Clearbrook, Moonshade, and Strongbow. These were the elders of the tribe, whom Cutter, in their eyes still only a cub, often consulted. They regarded him expectantly, for as chief he would ultimately initiate the Wolfriders' next course of action.

A wave of uncertainty washed over Cutter then. He felt a great need for the calm and reliable counsel of his mother's brother, who was the oldest and most experienced Wolfrider of all. The young leader looked around until he saw the familiar crown of short, yellow curls belonging to the one he sought.

Treestump knelt in the cold, eerie glow of a phosphorescent lantern suspended from the ceiling. His wooden-handled ax was tucked inside his belt, the double-headed blade encased in a protective leather hood. With his weapon so concealed, Treestump was gruff and harmless as a golden honey bear. Yet the rock-hard muscles bulging beneath his tawny vest were tacit proof of his formidable store of strength.

He was with Nightfall and Redlance, trying with quiet determination to coax the injured one to eat. As Cutter came to squat beside him, Treestump heaved a discouraged sigh and shook his head. Redlance was trembling with weakness; his breathing had grown ragged and short.

Alarmed, Cutter impulsively laid his hand against his suffering tribeman's cheek. The red-haired elf responded, but the wan smile he was able to muster did little to ease anyone's concern.

"Later . . . I'll eat later . . . I promise," Redlance began, and then he was seized by a fit of coughing that left him doubled over in agony, unable to say more.

Cutter looked helplessly at Treestump, but the bearded elf had shut his eyes—a habitual response to sorrows for which he could provide no cure. He spoke to Cutter in tones that were soft and resigned.

"It's six turns of the seasons since Rain the Healer died, along with your father and mother and all the others. The loss never hit us harder than right now."

Treestump paused to lock minds with Cutter before continuing, sending in such a way that no one else could participate.

Redlance is broken inside. He needed long days of lying still, a rest he'll never get now. If Rain were alive and with us, he could lay hands on the damage—pull it all back together the way a tree-shaper mends a broken limb.

As though she guessed the nature of their sending, Nightfall put her arms around her lifemate, pressing his head against her breast. More beautiful than the trolls' precious gold, which they resembled, her eyes held a faraway look. She seemed to see where Redlance was going.

"Tree-shaper," whispered Cutter. "We waited so long for his powers to appear, and now the Holt is. . . ." He did not need to finish the thought. Their forest home was dead, and soon Redlance would follow. There was no help for it.

"Thieving, point-eared outsider! I said get away from that!"

Greymung's sudden shout was immediately followed by the sound of a blow and a sharp cry. Cutter spun around, automatically drawing New Moon. He saw Skywise lying in a little heap beneath the troll king's feet, and a wolf's snarl sprang to his lips.

"Grrreymung! You muck-eating son of a human!"

Cutter hurtled across the chamber, infused with all the strength of generations of fierce struggle for survival. Greymung's eyes bulged as the pale-haired Wolfrider landed before him on the dais, a compact, muscular bundle of murderous intent. The king turned in desperate appeal to his three guards, but they were still bound and were surrounded by guards of their own—furred ones, fanged and very hungry. Greymung felt ill. The look of anticipation, especially on Picknose's face as he and his fellows craned their bulbous necks to witness their ruler's fate, was poorly concealed.

"Stay back, elf! I am king!" The old troll's voice had dwindled to a quavering ghost of its former volume. "I command you!"

Crouched, ready to spring, his slanted, feral eyes wholly predatory beneath his frowning brows, the elf chieftain seemed quite disinclined to obey. Recovering groggily from the stunning impact of Greymung's fist, Skywise sat up just in time to hear Cutter's roar and to see New Moon slice a shining arc through the air toward the old king's head.

"No! No!" screamed the cowering troll.

Unexpectedly, the blade whizzed past his vulture's beak of a nose and cracked down hard, pommel first, against the cause of the whole incident—the mysterious, metal-loving sacred stone. A dark, finger-sized chip flew off, which Skywise gleefully caught.

"Here, friend," Cutter said wryly. "The king presents you with a gift."

"You're not going to kill me?" Greymung whimpered, peeking from behind jeweled fingers.

Cutter regarded him disdainfully. "A wolf doesn't kill an offender who knows all the proper signs of submission. You seem to have a knack for it, mighty king. The only difference is, you don't have a wolf's dignity, and you never will!"

Cutter leapt onto Greymung's broad belly and grabbed a fistful of his ragged beard.

"Troll, you are a big, fat fool, and your subjects know it. Where are they now? Hiding in their holes? Call them!"

Greymung stayed silent, wincing as the elf chieftain yanked at his whiskers.

"You can't call them, can you," Cutter jeered, "because you know they won't come. They're tired of you, you flabby old toad! I don't think they'd care if I chopped you to bits." Cutter paused for a moment and then continued. "It's lucky for you that all I care about is finding a new Holt for my tribe."

At this, a glimmer of hope creeped into Greymung's slitted eye. He delicately adjusted his slender, four-pronged crown, which had been jarred askew. Then he smiled. Of all the contorted, misshapen expressions the old troll had displayed so far, this was the least appealing.

"Well, why didn't you say so?" Greymung burbled.

He turned to Picknose and summoned him onto the dais with an unctuous gesture. The black-bearded guard stared at his king, no less mistrustful than the wary Wolfriders who began to group around the throne. Cutter jumped down and stood with his tribefolk, waiting to hear what Greymung would say next.

"Picknose, escort this noble chieftain and his tribe through the Tunnel of Golden Light."

Glancing quickly from the elves to the king and back again Picknose repeated, "Golden Light? But that one leads to . . ."

Boof!

The remark was suddenly interrupted by a harsh expulsion of air as Greymung, in a beatific, all-embracing gesture, flung his arms wide, coincidentally slamming his elbow into Picknose's middle.

"Leads to a beautiful land of bright promise, doesn't it, Picknose?" finished Greymung.

The Wolfriders' large, pointed ears visibly pricked up with interest.

"You need fear nothing, good elves," said the troll king. "Picknose will guide you all the way. When you reach the tunnel exit, I am certain you will not wish to return."

Cutter rested his elbow on one gilded arm of the throne. "This tunnel—it opens on green woods somewhere far from here?" He searched the aged troll's face, but if any subtle sign of deception rested there, it was lost amid too many warts and corrugations to be readily perceived.

"Green and peaceful," Greymung said, sighing. "If I could stand daylight, I'd live there myself. And just think—" he leaned forward conspiratorially "—no humans!"

The elves turned to one another with eyes alight. No humans. It was difficult to imagine a life without the constant eruptions of hatred and violence brought on by contact between Wolfriders and men.

No formal record of the elf tribe's history existed. What they knew of the distant past had been handed down through generations in the form of stories and legends, much embroidered. But at the truthful core of these tales one hard and bitter fact had not softened with the passing of time. Humans, the five-fingered Tall Ones, the hunters who wasted meat in the taking of a kill and who even killed one another with no greater provocation than anger or envy—these were the enemy.

Since the coming of the High Ones, the delicate elfin ancestors of Cutter's stocky wolf-riding tribe, human hostility had remained as cruel as it was blindly unreasoning. In all of nature, the elves had been able to find no example by which to understand such instinctive enmity. Among the animals, predator and prey bore each other no malice. Competition for territory or mating privileges was often bloody but was always solved without rancorous emotion. Only humans bore grudges, sought revenge, or hated for hate's sake. The torching of the forest had proved that nothing, not even a destructive act that would certainly threaten their own survival, was beyond the humans' need to annihilate that which they hated and feared.

A new Holt, a faraway green wood free of Man's treading foot. It was a painfully tempting dream, a chance for a new beginning. The trolls' tunnels obviously covered great distances underground. It was possible, just possible.

"Well, what do you think?" Cutter asked his tribe. "Shall we trust the trolls?"

"Seems they don't stand to gain much by lying to us," offered Treestump. "They don't like us down here any more than the humans liked us up there."

"If they really want to be rid of us, the truth is all to their advantage," added Skywise.

Dewshine, beaming with all the optimism of youth, grabbed her cousin's arm. "Oh, Cutter, it sounds so wonderful! Let's try it!"

Careful! This was Strongbow, whose sendings were always laden with truth as he perceived it. **It could be a trick. What if they intend to lose us in some maze of tunnels where we'll wander around till we starve?**

The warning sobered the elves considerably. Cutter pondered for several moments and then poured forth his thoughts in a strong, assured sending that enveloped the entire tribe.

The fire burns above us and will go on burning so long as trees still stand and a hot, dry wind fans the flames. We can't go back. And we can't live here. If we tried to find our way out without a guide, we'd surely become lost. The trolls know us well. The whole pack of us, elves *and* wolves, starving and angry, haunting their tunnels in search of prey would make life miserable for them. They want us out, I'm sure. As things stand right now, there isn't much to hope for. But gambling on this Tunnel of Golden Light is better than rotting here in these caverns where we're so unwelcome.

Cutter waited for a response, and it was not long in coming. With varying degrees of enthusiasm, the Wolfriders nodded their unanimous assent. Hands on hips, Cutter turned to confront the troll king. His youthful face was grim.

"All right, Greymung. If this new Holt is everything you say it is, we'll go there gladly and trouble you no more."

Once again the ugly grimace that passed for a smile twisted Greymung's doughy features.

"But if you're lying," Cutter warned, quickly slitting the knot on Picknose's bonds, "I'll send Picknose back to you in six separate pouches."

Troll king and newly freed guard exchanged malevolent glances.

"That won't be necessary," murmured Greymung, just loud enough for Picknose to hear. "I'll take care of that little matter myself, should he fail me."

Deliberately dampening their hopes with cautious reserve, the Wolfriders prepared for the long trek to their uncertain destination. Aided by the imposing presences of Treestump, the other tribal elders, and their wolves, Cutter persuaded Greymung to supply food and weapons to those elves who needed them. When the Wolfriders had filled their water-skins at the king's fountain and the wolves had shaken themselves fully awake and alert, the Howl began.

Raising their polished noses toward the ceiling, the great beasts sang their gathering song in the heart of the trolls' underground stronghold. The wailing harmonies filled the throne chamber, echoing through the vast adjacent cavern, around its multihued columns, down the long, burnished stairway. The stones rang with a wild song never heard before. Greymung and the three guards clamped their hands over their round, beringed ears, their faces puckering and folding inward like rotten fruit. Long adaptation to the squeaking of cave bats, the hiss of steam, and the clanging hammer blows of metalworkers at their forges had not prepared the trolls for this strident music from the surface world. To them it was a raucous and nerve-jarring dissonance

"Go! Go now! Get out!" shrieked the troll king. With hands wildly flailing, he motioned Picknose to begin the journey through the Tunnel of Golden Light.

Grumbling, Picknose stumped to the exit at Greymung's right and yelled at the elves to follow him. The howling died down as one by one the mounted Wolfriders filed past the throne and disappeared through the dark archway. Only Cutter paused for a moment to frown in puzzlement at the huddled, misshapen troll king.

"My father, Bearclaw, said that you were a great fighter once, Greymung. He told me how you led a successful rebellion against the trolls' first ruler, how you won the crown and your people's respect."

For just an instant, the fires of a faded youth kindled beneath his brows as Greymung glared at the young elf chieftain.

"Now, it seems, the crown is all that matters to you," Cutter said quietly. "Take care, old king. All the treasure in your realm can't replace the loyalty you've lost. No one came to your aid while we had you in our power. If a more deadly enemy comes, you're all alone. These subjects of yours"—he waved an arm to indicate the glittering riches scattered about the room—"will not rise to your defense, no matter how you beg them."

"Get out," repeated Greymung. "I never want to see you or your mangy, beast-eared pack again."

"You won't," Cutter promised. He patted Nightrunner's shoulder, and the great beast carried him silently from the throne room. In moments Cutter rode at the head of his tribe, guided by Picknose, who traveled on foot.

They descended several flights of rough-hewn stairs and came to the area where Skywise had seen the forges. Great fire-pits filled with smoldering, red coals yawned in the floor. The embers' dim glow revealed the batlike outlines of giant bellows overhanging the pits; nearby stood strong metal anvils shaped like huge black moles with pointed snouts. Small, two-handled carts with one or two stone wheels lay tipped on their sides, momentarily abandoned by the metalworkers whose lurking presence the Wolfriders could easily sense in the gloom beyond the fire-pits' sanguine light.

The odd party traveled in wary silence along twisting, ill-lit corridors: seventeen elves, fourteen wolves, and a troll whose thoughts were his own. At last they came to a tunnel that seemed older and more crudely excavated than any of the others; certainly it was less frequented. Cutter brought the line to a halt at the mouth of this unpromising passageway.

"What's this?" he asked Picknose.

The troll responded sullenly, "This is your path to a new life. It is the tunnel we call Golden Light."

Four

How much time had passed was difficult to estimate. The Tunnel of Golden Light was long and narrow and much darker than its misleading name suggested. But there was cause for optimism among the Wolfriders, for the tunnel neither rose nor descended. Its comfortably level and uncurving path beneath the ground reassured the elves that they were making straightforward progress on their journey to the new Holt.

Skywise never tired of toying with the chip from Greymung's mysterious footstool. He carried it affixed to one of his metal wristbands or let it cling to his face guard. The small object became a source of amusement to the Wolfriders; it was through the games they invented to play with his metal-holding stone that Skywise learned the limits of its power. It would adhere neither to the plain ring of gold that encircled Cutter's neck nor to the beaten-gold armlet decorated with two red feathers that Cutter wore on his left upper arm. Clearbrook's silver earrings, too, failed to attract the little chip of rock. But swords and daggers won its love instantly; thus Skywise concluded that the stone's powers were attuned to useful items rather than to decorative ones. Of course, the fact that it did cling to his own blue ornaments only served to prove Skywise's rightful ownership and mastery of the magical fragment. While his tribefolk sang songs or passed the time telling stories, Skywise used a small chisel he had found in the chamber of the forges to worry a hole through the center of the stone. He had definite plans for the fascinating trinket.

At one point Rainsong handed her infant, Wing, to Scouter and dropped back in line to ride beside Nightfall. Rainsong was the daughter of Rain the Healer, and she had inherited the instincts, if not the actual powers, of her dead father. She noted that Redlance sat slightly hunched over on his wolf but appeared a little more at ease, a little stronger than before. The guarded optimism that had recently lifted the elves' spirits had, it seemed, affected Redlance's condition as well.

"He looks better," Rainsong whispered to Nightfall.

The golden-eyed Wolfrider glanced sidelong at her lifemate. Her expression was hopeful.

"If he could just catch his breath," she said quietly.

Rainsong groped for an appropriate, reassuring response, but Scouter unexpectedly distracted her attention. The chestnut-haired youth was playfully tossing Wing into the air a little too roughly. The tiny babe had begun to cry.

At Woodlock's gentle remonstrance, Scouter immediately settled down. He cradled Wing in his arms with great tenderness, trying unsuccessfully to quiet the infant's outraged wails. Rainsong trotted up beside them and, without scolding, gathered Wing to her; his cries ceased as she nestled him against her breast. From her father's lap Newstar leaned over, stretching out a twig-thin arm to stroke her tiny brother's hair while he nursed.

Suddenly a yelp of pain came from the head of the line. Everyone looked up in surprise, and then surprise turned to amusement. Rubbing his scalp, which evidently smarted, Cutter was frowning irritably at a blissful and oblivious Skywise.

"Why do you want bits of everyone's hair, anyway?"

Busily plaiting the long silken strands he had already collected, Skywise answered without looking up. "To braid into a string for the magic stone. That way we'll all be touching it all the time. It will become our good-luck talisman."

The elf chieftain quirked a smile at his friend, shaking his head in wonderment. "I've never seen you so wrapped up in a thing before."

Considering the length of their friendship and the number of pet obsessions with which Skywise had preoccupied himself during his lifetime, Cutter's statement was rather broad. But it was also true.

"Don't ask me why. I just know this piece of rock is very powerful, unlike any other in the world." Skywise placed the fragment on his wrist and shook his arm violently. "See how it clings like a living thing? I wish I knew where it came from."

To oblige his inquisitive companion, Cutter gave Picknose a nudge with his soft-booted foot.

"Hey, Picky. The big stone we chipped this from—where'd you get it? What's it called?"

"It's a lodestone," the taciturn troll said. "They say it fell from the sky long ago. It's very old."

From the sky! Skywise thought triumphantly. He gazed with renewed affection at his humble-looking treasure. Quickly his fingers worked to finish the braided string made from his tribefolks' hair. When it was done, he passed the cord through the hole he'd chiseled in the lodestone's center and knotted the ends together tightly. Then for good measure, he pricked his fingertip with his sword point and sealed the knot with several drops of blood.

Cutter watched the process with interest, wondering what subtle magic Skywise might have wrought without his or anyone else's knowing. The silver-haired elf hung the lodestone about his neck and smiled.

"It will bring us luck, Cutter," he said confidently.

"We could use some, that's certain," was the wry reply.

Picknose's beetle-black eyes shifted and narrowed. He said nothing.

Like the wolves who could, if necessary, go for days without eating, the elves dealt well enough with their dwindling stores of food. Water, however, proved more of a problem, for many of the skins were less than half full. To spare their mounts' strength, the Wolfriders took to traveling on foot. Unfortunately, this meant more frequent stops to rest than before, and progress through the tunnel slowed considerably. During one such interim, while his tribefolk sprawled in exhausted heaps beside their panting wolves, Cutter confronted Picknose.

"Our water supply is getting low. The wolves are tired and thirsty. So are we. How much farther?"

"Don't worry," the troll answered soothingly. "You've almost reached the end of your journey."

Picknose's smiling assurances did not sit well with Cutter. Something was askew, perhaps a malicious gleam more intense than that which normally shone in the troll's eye. And yet, certain as he was that they had been in the Tunnel of Golden Light for at least several days, the young chief could not point to any clear-cut duplicity on Picknose's part. The troll had indeed led them a long way without mishap. What possible destination could lie at the end of the tunnel other than the beautiful green wood promised by Greymung?

Cutter collapsed at Nightrunner's side, pillowing his head on the great wolf's shaggy haunch. He fell asleep at once and dreamed of the Holt as it was in his childhood, lush and verdant and sheltering. But as the dream unwound, it took on a more sinister aspect. The sweet green foliage became spattered with bloody reds and oranges as in the Death-Sleep season. The vivid colors metamorphosed into ravenous tongues of flame that consumed the Holt in moments. The conflagration roared skyward, igniting the clouds, the very air itself, until nothing was left but an all-absorbing mass of white heat.

Cutter opened his eyes, awakened by a sick pounding in his temples and upper chest. Rivulets of perspiration trickled down his ribs. He felt as if he had touched the sun itself. The air in the tunnel seemed warm even now that he was awake.

He took a few sparing swallows from his water-skin. He poured some of the precious liquid into the cup of his palm and let Nightrunner lap it up. After a moment's hesitation he shrugged and gave the thirsty wolf another drink. There was no reasoning behind the act, considering how determined Cutter had been, so far, that the Wolfriders would make their water last. It simply seemed the thing to do, a final gesture of hope near the journey's end. The new Holt would have flowing streams, perhaps a lake. There would be tall trees to live in and game to hunt. And no humans. Hauling his ill-rested body to its feet, he set about rousing his tribefolk.

One-Eye helped Redlance to his feet, picked him up, and settled him on his wolf. He took Redlance's hands and closed them firmly on the animal's thick, reddish ruff.

"You hold on," One-Eye told the injured elf. "The troll says we're almost home."

Anticipation lent new vigor to all the tribe as they mounted their beasts in preparation for the final ride. Picknose had not taken them far on their resumed path, however, when they came to a turn in the tunnel. Splashed on the curving walls like a banner of welcome was a warm, yellow radiance. Skywise threw his arms above his head, fists clenched with fierce elation.

"Light! I see light ahead!"

"Golden Light," Cutter said breathily. "We've come through at last."

A sending of image rather than thought swept through the minds of all the elves, a primordial vision, and more than a vision, of cool green woodlands summoned from the deepmost part of every Wolfrider's soul. The forest was the first refuge, opening its leafy arms to enfold the fleeing High Ones so very long ago, and so the legendary pattern would repeat itself now with the much-changed descendants of those first elfin fugitives.

Unable to wait, Strongbow and Moonshade plunged toward the inviting light that marked the tunnel's end. But Picknose hung back, shrinking from the golden glow as from a disease-infested bog.

"This is as far as I go," he said, shielding his face with clawlike hands. "The light of day is harmful to trolls."

Cutter's smile was condescending. "We elves are night creatures, too, but the sun doesn't frighten us."

"How extremely fortunate," muttered the troll.

"Cutter, come on," Skywise urged. "Come see the new land."

"In a moment, friend." Cutter turned to Treestump, indicating his wish with a nod and a significant glance at Picknose. The powerfully built older elf had already stripped his ax of its protective hood. He grabbed a handful of Picknose's long, black beard and waved the double-bladed weapon before the troll's flinching eyes.

"Guard this crafty one until we make certain that old Greymung didn't lie."

Treestump acknowledged his young chief's command, forcefully backing Picknose against the tunnel wall and warning the troll in a low voice, "Pity you if you've led us astray, mud-grubber."

Meanwhile, the elves crowded toward the tunnel exit. Eager to be among the first to see what lay beyond the underground passageway, Cutter shoved past his tribefolk, wincing at the light's growing intensity. He assumed that his own eyes were at fault, having accustomed themselves too long to the near-total darkness of the trolls' domain. Brilliant, blinding light poured into the mouth of the tunnel and with it a blast of heat such as the Wolfriders had never before experienced.

"So bright!" exclaimed Cutter, blinking away the tears that welled in response to both heat and brilliance. As he came to the entrance, he felt his feet sink into a strange, gritty material unlike any soil he knew.

"Hurts! Can't see!" That was Skywise's anguished voice, sounding small and lost in the glare. Cutter could just make out the blurry figure of his friend, doubled over, rubbing his eyes frantically. Others, like Strongbow, staggered back a few paces, unable to endure the burning rays.

Finally Cutter was able to see something. The sound he made moments later was a mindless, animal groan.

A new land did exist beyond the confines of the tunnel. It rolled toward the distant, wavering horizon without a single distinguishable feature to relieve its stark and terrible uniformity. There were no trees, no bushes, no rocks, and no colors. The myriad low and rounded hills, swelling across the endless waste almost like ripples on water, seemed to be made of the same strange, pebbly soil that had drifted into the mouth of the tunnel. Everywhere, as far as eyes could see, the land was a single, lifeless tawny hue. There were no bodies of water, no animals, and certainly no humans. In that, at least, Greymung had been truthful.

Dominating all with its blazing, relentless power was the sun, but it was not the friendly, ruddy disk that announced the approach of evening to all who lived by night. This sun had no shape and could not be looked upon for even an instant. It filled the cloudless sky, searing the barren land below with fuming force. The heat was unbelievable, inconceivable to those who had known all their lives only the eternal shade and sanctuary of the forest.

Someone whimpered, "Where are we?"

Only one could answer that question—the troll, who at his king's behest had guided them through the Tunnel of Golden Light.

Suddenly, behind the Wolfriders, there was a rumbling sound and a trembling of the cave floor. Cutter turned in time to see part of the ceiling give way. He cried out, "The tunnel! It's collapsing!"

In moments the passageway was completely sealed by a huge pile of jagged and broken boulders. Treestump lay unconscious among the fallen stones, but the troll was nowhere in sight. Either he had been completely buried, or, more likely, he had escaped.

Dewshine ran to her father's side, helping him sit up. The other Wolfriders gathered around, not yet aware of the hideous scope of their predicament.

"What happened?" Cutter demanded of his reviving uncle. "Where's Picknose?"

"Don't know," Treestump mumbled. "He just touched the wall, and the stones came down like rain!"

With a curse Cutter stood up and examined the wall of rock blocking the tunnel. It extended well into the area above the false ceiling. There was no way to climb over it, and it was useless to contemplate trying to remove the stones one by one; Cutter was certain in the pit of his stomach that the blockage went far back into the tunnel. The effort would take more strength and time than the elves had left to them.

"Those lying trolls had it planned from the start," growled the young chieftain. "Picknose knew that once he got us here, he could cause a cave-in any time he chose. We're trapped!"

Dewshine stared in bewilderment at her chief and cousin. "But why? There was no need for them to do this."

"No need but revenge for Greymung's injured pride," he answered her. Cutter stood stiffly, fists clenched, his expression a bitter blending of regret and self-contempt. "I should have known just getting rid of us in a strange forest would never be enough to satisfy Greymung. But I didn't think he would go so far!"

"What now, lad?" asked Treestump.

"What now?" Cutter's hackles rose briefly until he realized that there was no malice in the question. He turned toward the entrance to the tunnel, toward the blazing, unfamiliar sun and the "new land" which seemed to mock him with its utter emptiness and desolation.

Silence was the only answer he could give.

Five

Cutter's fingers opened and closed with fretful repetition, working through Nightrunner's fur. While most of his tribefolk sought the relative coolness farther back in the blocked tunnel, the elf chieftain and his wolf stood at its mouth, staring disconsolately across the limitless burning waste.

"Cutter, don't blame yourself." Skywise's gentle voice broke the silence. "We all underestimated the treachery of the trolls."

"It's my fault, lad, if the truth be told," admitted Treestump as he moved to stand behind his crestfallen young chief. "Picknose caught me off guard. Your father would have tied me in knots for letting that happen."

Cutter's answering smile was both pained and bemused. "My father had a rotten temper, may the High Ones keep his soul." He glanced over his shoulder at Treestump and then dejectedly lowered his eyes. "Still," he went on, "I can't help but feel he'd have handled this better than I did. Bearclaw would never have tried to reason with the trolls, and he'd never have had even a little faith in Greymung's word."

The eldest Wolfrider hesitated and then placed his rugged hands on Cutter's fur-clad shoulders. In tones loud enough for everyone to hear, Treestump spoke earnestly to his dead sister's son. "Listen, lad, we all wanted to believe there'd be a new Holt waiting for us here. The decision to try for it wasn't yours alone."

"Strongbow warned us that we might be riding into a trap," Moonshade said, her near-whiteless eyes two pools of accusation in the semidarkness. "We should have listened to him!"

Treestump turned on her, his fists angrily clenched. "No! Fear is a trap! Standing still is a trap! How long do you think we could have survived in the troll caverns, eating mushrooms and mold, licking slime water from the walls, hemmed in by solid rock? There was only one path to try, and we took it. Blame me that we're pinned here now if you have to find blame, but don't question Cutter's choice. It was ours as well."

Although many of the Wolfriders voiced their agreement, Cutter's barely audible "Thanks" was unconvinced and unconvincing. He turned once more toward the barren vista that stretched on and on into the measureless distance. Nothing had moved. Nothing had changed. The desolation was neither a dream nor an illusion.

Cutter shook his head hopelessly. "No matter who's to blame, one thing is certain. This new land of ours is a death trap."

"Well, we can't stay in here forever," Skywise announced, drawing himself up with game resolve. His dark blue tunic and boots seemed like patches of cave shadow clinging to him as he stepped into the sunlight. Staggering brilliance washed over the small elfin form, swept away bravado, left total vulnerability exposed. Overwhelmed, Skywise retreated, reeling, into the tunnel's shady depths. There he leaned against the wall and waited, summoning the will to try again. He noticed that his body shivered as with extreme cold. It seemed very odd to him.

On his second venture forth, Cutter and Treestump accompanied the stargazer. Shielding their eyes as well as they could, the brave threesome took a few faltering steps into the sun-blasted waste. The yielding, gritty sand was so unbearably hot that the elves were forced to hop repeatedly from one foot to the other; soft leather boots proved to be inadequate protection against the penetrating heat.

Unable to see far with their large, light-sensitive eyes, Cutter, Treestump, and Skywise squinted through tears of pain, trying to orient themselves. They turned to look back toward the cave entrance, and suddenly a shared expression of horror and dismay crossed their faces.

In the tunnel, the watching Wolfriders were alarmed; they could not imagine what had so distressed the small scouting party. Unable to wait any longer to learn what fate lay in store for her children, Rainsong left the shelter of the cave, pulling the rim of her hoodlike cap down to shade her eyes. Trudging a short distance through the broiling sand, she stopped and turned to follow the gaze of her three tribesmen. The cry she uttered next was hoarse and full of despair.

Towering straight into the sun, stark and unscalable, a steep cliffside rose from the ground, stretching from horizon to horizon of the heat-roiled landscape. Some titanic swordsman, it seemed, had once used his world-spanning blade to cleave a mountain range in two, leaving one of the neatly severed halves erect as a monument to the deed. The soaring cliffs were made of many layers of rock, some tawny, some ruddy in hue. At their base, as insignificant as a tiny mousehole, opened the Tunnel of Golden Light.

"We can't go back," breathed Skywise. "These cliffs are sheer, and there's no getting around them."

Rainsong covered her face with her hands and ran for the tunnel. She stumbled, her usually nimble feet sinking to the ankles in the unfamiliar, shifting ground. Woodlock was there to catch her; he tenderly carried her back to the barrier of fallen boulders that marked the limit of their cave prison and set her down beside Newstar and Wing. The distraught mother hugged her children tightly; hot tears seeped through her feathery lashes.

The three who had gone out returned, gasping from the heat. Cutter slumped to the floor of the cave, propping his weary back against the hard coolness of the wall. The trolls' trap was as inescapable as it was merciless. There was nowhere to go and nothing to do but wait for an end that was too miserable and too inevitable to contemplate.

"I guess the lodestone didn't bring us much luck, after

all," Skywise said. He stood over Cutter, toying with the small chip of rock as it swung on its braided string. Slipping the pendant off over his head, Skywise held the cord by its knot and watched the stone spin like a caterpillar dangling from a silken thread.

Cutter sighed, absently tapping the lodestone with his forefinger to make it whirl faster; the hypnotic motion was soothing to regard. "You know, Skywise," he said, "even if we could go back, there's nothing left of the Holt by now but ashes."

To that there could be no reply. The two close friends fell silent, watching the lodestone spin more and more slowly until it finally came to a stop. Cutter tapped it again, setting it turning in the opposite direction. Again the pendant wound and unwound until it slowed to a halt. Although Skywise was usually the more observant of the two, it was Cutter who noticed a curious tendency in the lodestone's movement.

"Hey, look at that," he said, giving the stone one more sharp tap.

Several of the Wolfriders looked up incredulously, wondering whether the pair's sojourn in the sun had driven Cutter and Skywise to idle madness. But Skywise's face was alight with genuine wonder; he held the spinning lodestone before his eyes and studied it carefully as it lost momentum.

"See what I mean?" asked Cutter. "No matter which way it turns—"

"It always ends up pointing in the same direction!" Skywise finished excitedly.

Their curiosity piqued despite grim misfortune, Scouter and Dewshine came to see for themselves what was causing the stir. Soon all the Wolfriders were gathered around Skywise as he proudly displayed the lodestone's newly discovered property. They took turns spinning it round and round, watching with keen interest as the pendant twirled ever more slowly, always righting itself in one particular direction when motion had ceased. The lodestone was stubborn; it could not be made to aim in any other direction, no matter how the string was gripped or by whom.

"It's magic!" whispered an awed Scouter.

Skywise nodded, more pleased than ever with his treasured charm, for at last the Wolfriders respected its extraordinary powers. The wolves, however, were not so easily impressed, particularly Starjumper, who poked his nose beneath Skywise's arm and sniffed curiously at the lodestone. Discovering at once that the thing was not food, Starjumper snorted his disgust and justly shamed his elffriend with a look of extreme disappointment.

Her highly slanted eyes wide open with sudden awareness, Dewshine gestured excitedly at the pile of rocks that barred her tribe's only path of escape.

"Look! One end of the magic stone points back the way we came, and the other end points—" She swallowed back a hard lump of fear and extended a trembling forefinger toward the impossible brightness beyond the tunnel exit. There was no need for her to speak further; Skywise followed the slender huntress's reasoning and came to the same conclusion.

"Cutter, I think it's a sign," he said softly, holding up the lodestone to emphasize his words. "The tunnel is sealed behind us, so whatever hope we have must lie—"

"Out there in that strange, empty land," the young chief said, interrupting. "But maybe it's not so empty. Surely the trolls never explored it—not in *that* sun."

Nightfall came to stand by Cutter's side and put her hand on his arm. His words had retrieved her from the brink of hopelessness.

"That's right," she said. "The trolls led us here, hoping we'd die of starvation and thirst. But there could be food and water beyond those strange, wavy hills." Golden eyes met brilliant blue ones. "Couldn't there, Cutter?"

"Maybe, Nightfall, maybe." Cutter scanned the faces of his tribefolk. "What supplies have we got?" he barked.

The unexpected question brought a variety of responses.

"A water-skin less than half full and two pieces of dried meat," said One-Eye.

"Some double-shell nuts and a mouthful of brownberries," Moonshade added, searching the folds of the leather cloak she carried, tightly rolled, across her shoulders.

"I have a hunk of deer meat left," offered Pike. "Stole it from Greymung's table. It's gotten a little high, though." The spear carrier wrinkled his nose. "Sorry there isn't enough water in my skin to wash it down."

Each Wolfrider in turn told the sum of his or her remaining store. It was not a promising account: water to barely moisten the lips of seventeen for a day, perhaps two, and only enough food to share in one last meager meal. No more.

"Skywise, will the sun set?" Cutter asked his friend.

The silver-haired elf looked down and noted that the shadows cast by roughnesses in the tunnel's opening had shifted their positions on the ground.

"Yes," he answered. "The sun moves through the sky here as it did above the Holt. That, at least, we can depend on."

Cutter nodded, pursing his lips in thought. He eyed the wolves as they sat or lay, panting miserably, in the darkness of the troll-made cave. The great predators with their thick, shaggy coats were less able to endure the heat than were the elves themselves. Moreover, like their riders, the wolves were beginning to show signs of weakness from hunger.

Cutter made his decision.

"Give all the food to the wolves," he said, braced for the expressions of stunned disbelief he received. "They will need their strength to carry us where we're going."

"Where are we going?" Newstar shyly asked. She stood no taller than Cutter's waist, but her worn appearance belied the mere five turns of the seasons she had seen.

Cutter answered her as frankly as he would any full-grown member of the tribe.

"Out there," he gestured with a nod of his head toward the blazing vista beyond the mouth of the tunnel. "We will cross this land in the cool of night. The magic stone will guide our steps." He smiled, touching the talisman that Skywise wore again about his neck. "It may yet bring us luck."

Twilight's stealthy approach roused the elves from a sodden sleep. With its last breath, the sun's dying light whispered a promise of coolness, an assurance that the terrible heat of day would not linger to torment the homeless wanderers during their long nocturnal journey.

The wolves had already stolen from the shelter of the cave and were prowling about the cliff base, scent marking and hunting for anything remotely edible. They walked on the loose sand much as they would pad through powdery snow, lifting their feet carefully, stopping now and then to roll, to stretch muscles that were cramped and stiff from long days of underground confinement. Each sprint sent up sprays of gritty dust, but that was hardly enough to dampen lupine spirits. There were fleas to be scratched and orders of rank to be reasserted within the pack. And finally, when all the preliminary greetings and groomings were done, there was the Howl. Even pangs of hunger could not distract the wolves from their inborn urge to sing.

Nightrunner began. Deep within his throat the tone was born, sonorous and steady, rising in pitch as he tilted his head toward the emerging stars. Other pack members joined in, contributing their individual harmonies to the resonant, ritual music. Its volume enhanced by echoes from the steep cliffside, the wolfsong challenged the utter lifelessness of the surrounding land.

It was to the strains of this wild hymn to freedom, this swelling assertion of life, that the haggard elf tribe emerged from the tunnel. The Wolfriders were saddened by the innocence of their four-legged allies, who lacked the ability to foresee probable suffering or possible death. The most difficult part of their journey lay ahead, and yet the wolves sensed nothing beyond the fullness of the moment. They would carry their elf-friends as far as limited strength permitted across the desolate wilderness. But if nourishment and shelter could not be found before sunrise . . .

Cutter walked toward Nightrunner and crouched down, extending his arms. The wolf came to him and butted his huge skull against the elf chieftain's breast. Nestling his cheek in the broad space between Nightrunner's ears, Cutter rubbed the animal's neck, stroked his powerful shoulders, felt the sharp protrusion of backbone and ribs beneath his shaggy fur.

"Tomorrows mean nothing to you, Nightrunner." He sighed. "It's just as well."

The "now" of wolf-thought was hardly a foreign concept to Cutter. Since the beginning of his tribe's existence, wolves had been regarded as teachers, as models to be emulated. The pleasant limbo of "now" wherein the great beasts lived their lives, guided by instinct, habit, or occasional impulse, was an untroubled state of mind much cherished by the Wolfriders.

Cutter yearned for it with all his being. He wished to lose awareness of time, to know nothing of limits to endurance, and, most of all, to have no apprehension of death, whether his own or that of his fugitive tribe. Worry, anticipation, and fear were ticks gorging on his lifeblood, sapping his strength. Cutter knew this, but the chief's crest he wore and the responsibility it symbolized held him away from his own center; the very act of longing made "now" impossible to achieve.

Big Moon and Little Moon were nearly in alignment as the Wolfriders began their trek. Skywise rode at the head of the pack, holding the lodestone before him. He believed in its magic, was convinced that the talisman pointed the way to good fortune. It did not matter to him that some members of the tribe did not share his faith. The waxing moons cast their hard, metallic light upon the featureless terrain.

There were no landmarks to head for; neither tree nor jutting rock relieved the monotony of the shallow dunes as they rolled toward the distant horizon. At the very least the lodestone afforded a steady course for the elves to follow.

The still night air was surprisingly cold, a sudden change, difficult to comprehend in view of the day's scorching heat. Silently the small band rode on, overwhelmed by the immense, open spaces around and above them. Secrecy, stealth, the skill of seeing without being seen: these were survival ways ingrained in the Wolfriders' natures. Never before had they been forced to cope with complete exposure; and although the danger of some unknown enemy's surprise attack was very small, the elves peered about nervously like frightened fledglings turned too soon out of their nests.

Only Skywise did not flinch from the piercing brilliance of the stars. Only he felt more wonder than fear, forgetting even the chill of the air on his skin as he gazed happily at the innumerable points of light thickly sprinkled across absolute blackness. There in the sky, familiar and reassuring, though somewhat higher overhead than usual, were the star pictures that had captivated him since his early youth.

The Great Wolf still pursued the fleeing Human Hunter. The twin Eyes of Timmorn, cold and yellow as ever, glared balefully from within a cluster of less impressive lights. The four stars of the Longspear had not moved from the nearly straight line they made, nor had the pattern that Skywise called Goodtree's Rest changed its shape. Many were the stellar images that the stargazing elf had perceived and named through the turning seasons of his life. Now he recognized those images as dependable companions that would never desert him, no matter what alien landscape he might wander.

From time to time Cutter turned to see whether all was reasonably well with the other riders. There was little he could do to lift their spirits, especially Nightfall's. She seemed resigned to the certainty that her lifemate's injuries would eventually defeat him. Since departing the Tunnel of Golden Light, Redlance had quietly retreated to a private place beyond pain, beyond anyone's touch—even hers.

Cutter found himself murmuring, "Just as well." He shifted his backward gaze and noted that the vast range of cliffs, once so imposing to his tribefolk, had dwindled almost to nothing far behind them. The elves had traveled a long way without sighting a single living thing, and now the night was half gone. Tiredly, Cutter started to swing his gaze forward again.

"No, don't turn around," Skywise exclaimed, dropping back to ride beside Cutter. "Keep looking behind you. Now up . . . up."

"What am I supposed to be seeing?" the elf chieftain asked impatiently.

Skywise grinned. "I think I've discovered the secret of the lodestone's magic." He gripped one end of the dangling talisman's string in his right hand and pointed with his left to a middling-bright star directly behind them, about halfway up the dome of the sky.

"There! See? The Hub of the Great Sky Wheel: the only star that remains fixed while all the others whirl around it. See how it pulls at the lodestone?"

Cutter frowned, looking from pendant to star to pendant. There did seem to be a correspondence. The small chip of stone was shaped roughly like an eye, and its two tapering ends did appear to be aligned along an invisible path leading directly to the fixed star.

Impressed but not wholly certain that he liked the implications of this discovery, Cutter scratched his ear, still frowning.

"I guess so," he muttered, facing forward. "That strange rock Greymung used as a footstool . . . Picknose said it fell from the sky." Cutter cast one more nervous glance over his shoulder at the Hub Star. "Could the lodestone be a piece of that star?"

"It could be," Skywise said, agreeing, secretly amused by his chief's mounting anxiety. He took out the small chisel he kept inside his belt and began to scratch the lodestone's surface.

"I'm going to mark the end that points to the fixed star so that we can always tell our direction, even when we can't see the sky."

Instantly Cutter went stiff, his neck hairs rising, his blue eyes opening as wide as they could possibly open. "Careful," he cried, startling the other Wolfriders. "You don't know what evil magic you may release!"

The stargazer's expression remained calm, almost introspective. Smiling thoughtfully, he went on with his task.

"There is nothing evil in the stars, Cutter, or in anything that comes from them."

In a short while, the lodestone became an eye indeed, with iris and pupil carefully etched onto the point that looked homeward—home to the faraway parent star that seemed to shine sadly above the place where the Holt had once been. The Wolfriders followed not the eye but the tail of the stone; it guided them farther and farther from the ashes of the only life they had known. The elves had no reason to look back as the lodestone did. But what, they wondered, was there in all this life-forsaken new land to look forward to?

Six

The little lizard shot from the sand like a seed squeezed from the heart of a berry. Not far into his adulthood, Briersting reacted with the impulse of a hungry cub, scrambling clumsily after the small reptile as it skittered between his paws.

Strongbow cursed aloud—a sign of his great agitation—and dived off Briersting's back, locking a hunter's eye on the fleeing lizard. It was the merest scrap of meat, but it was meat nonetheless, and the elfin archer intended to have it. Unfortunately, the uncooperative wolf had similar designs; he, too, launched himself at the prey, kicking a spray of stinging particles into Strongbow's eyes.

As quickly as it had appeared, the lizard burrowed back beneath the soil. Briersting pounced on the spot, forelegs stiffly extended, jaws snapping shut a hair's breadth short of a disappearing tail tip. The wolf began to dig furiously, his growls and whines of frustration sounding for all the world like actual speech. But the tiny, scale-covered morsel of life—the first to be seen during all that long night—had vanished.

Angry and disappointed as he was, Strongbow felt some pity for his famished wolf-friend. He approached Briersting, was about to attempt to calm him, when he saw the lizard miraculously reemerge from the ground right below the unwitting wolf's tail. Acting purely on reflex, Strongbow bent and scooped up the reptile with ease.

Strongbow licked his dry lips and smiled, but the grin faded with his sudden awareness that he was the focus of intense, anxious observation. As he turned to face them, his tribefolk averted their eyes. His heart sank. They were so many, and all were so hungry. What could be done?

The archer looked at his lifemate, Moonshade. Her square, fine-boned features were drawn; her fathomless owl's eyes—the most alluring aspect of her dark and mystical beauty—were hollow. She was thinner than he had ever seen her, and her cheeks held no color. Seated before her, little Dart shifted uncomfortably on the bony spinal ridge of his mother's wolf. His arms and legs were fragile as slender reeds, and his leaf-red tunic, which had been skin-tight, now hung loosely about his ribs. Blinking at his anguished father, Dart knew in a vague way that he must neither expect nor demand that which his empty belly cried for.

Strongbow joined his family, a cold and guarded expression clouding his gaunt face. With one of his knife-sharp arrowheads he slit the lizard from throat to tail and gave Dart a bloody portion. Then the taciturn archer walked farther down the line of Wolfriders until he reached Rainsong.

She supposed, feeling deep gratitude, that he meant to give the remaining precious scrap to Newstar. But Strongbow's intent was quite different; Rainsong herself must accept the nourishment.

How long can you make milk for both your cubs if you go hungry, Life-Bearer?

His pointed sending humbled her. Although a selfless impulse had at first caused her to refuse the meat, Rainsong now accepted the offering without hesitation. Knowing what would please Strongbow more than any thanks she could speak or send, she bit heartily into the lizard's moist remains.

Strongbow was satisfied. With one pathetically small catch he had managed to feed four. That was something, at least.

Unseen hands lifted the black blanket of night from the shoulders of the land. The stars retreated before morning's inevitable invasion of their cold, celestial hall.

As Cutter had feared, the night's ride had left his tribe stranded in the middle of nowhere. The gently swelling dunes were no less regular and no less horribly barren than those the elves had already traversed. Water would have to fall from the sky to be found at all. And there was also the matter of shelter.

It will be hot again, won't it? Nightfall's sending was open; the others might just as well know the worst while there remained time to prepare.

Yes, responded Cutter, **so we'll do as we planned.** The afterthought he kept to himself: It's all we can do.

Pike carried two deerskin robes, supple and light, rolled tightly together and slung around his neck. It had not occurred to him when he snatched them from his tree hollow the night the Holt burned that the skins might later prove so vital to his tribe's survival. Now he handed the robes to Moonshade and helped her lace them together along with the long leather cloak that she herself bore.

When that work was done, Pike jammed his spear deep into the soft sand, creating a tent pole of sorts. Reluctantly, for he did not like doing without his weapon, Strongbow plunged his bow into the ground a short distance from Pike's spear. Several of the Wolfriders dug a shallow pit between the two poles and then lapped the interlaced skins over the protruding shafts, tying the edges securely.

The rude sun shade was finished none too soon. Dawn hovered in the air only moments before the edge of the sun's blinding disk burst above the horizon and began its slow, menacing ascent. Ten elves were all that could reasonably crowd beneath the makeshift tent; seven had to wait their turn, while the wolves were forced to endure the day as best they could.

With amazing swiftness the morning's heat increased. Outside the tent, hunched in its shortening shadow, Cutter took a sip from his water-skin and passed it to Skywise.

"It's only a quarter full," said the stargazer.

Cutter shrugged. "That's the last of it. That and whatever One-Eye has left. Drink."

Skywise did so, sparingly, and at Cutter's insistence offered the skin to Dewshine and Scouter, who also sat outside the shelter. The elves spoke little. Even sending became an effort as the sun climbed ever higher in the heat-hazed sky. By the time the blazing orb was directly overhead, burning down in all its fury, the Wolfriders had fallen into a half-conscious stupor. Those sheltered under the tent sat propped against one another, motionless save for the rising and falling of their chests as they labored to breathe the torrid air.

Cutter crouched with forehead resting on knees, arms wrapped around legs, and bearhide vest draped over as much exposed skin as possible. Somehow, though he had failed to notice just when or why, the "now" of wolf-thought had stolen upon him, detaching his mind from the influence of time. He knew that his body suffered terribly in the sun's direct rays; yet, abstracted, he experienced the discomfort without submitting to it. Dispassionately, Cutter's self-without-form acknowledged the heat and thirst perceived by his senses; but because he had no awareness of time's passage, his body was spared the added strain of fearful anticipation.

Thus the young chieftain spent more than half the searing day in a deep trance, curled about himself like an unborn cub suspended in dreamless limbo. He might have remained as he was until the sun had utterly consumed him but for One-Eye and Clearbrook, who each grabbed an arm and hauled his exhausted form into the shade.

At last the punishing ball of dayfire descended into orange oblivion below the horizon at Sun-Goes-Down. It took the Wolfriders more than a little while to make their nerveless limbs function, to gather their benumbed wits as evening settled. Cutter swayed to his feet, shaking with weakness. The wait for sunset had been the longest of his life.

"Break camp," he called hoarsely. "It's time to move on."

"Move on to where?" croaked Scouter. "We can't live through another day like this!" The youth's deep brown eyes gleamed with a hint of tears; he was worn out and frightened. When Dewshine knelt to put her arms around him, he shoved her away.

Lovemate. Her sending was intimate, not to be shut out. **We can't lie down and die here. We must keep going.**

Scouter rubbed his face and ran a hand through his fine, damp curls. He took a deep breath, let it out in a long sigh, and turned to Dewshine. So frail in appearance and yet so defiant, she made him smile his admiration in spite of himself. Her determination to survive was infectious. Scouter put his arm around Dewshine's delicate neck and touched his forehead to hers.

"Strongbow caught a lizard," he whispered. "Maybe there'll be others." It was the most hopeful thing he could think of to say.

Bedraggled, tongues swollen and sagging from their mouths, the wolves crept toward the elves, desperately pleading their thirst. Together, One-Eye and Cutter doled out precious handfuls of sun-warmed liquid from what remained in their water-skins. When each of the fourteen animals had lapped up its share, One-Eye gripped his water-skin by its narrow neck and shook it. Faint, hollow-sounding splashes told him that the container now held a mouthful of water at most. In Cutter's skin there was but little more.

"Tonight's the true test, Skywise," the weary chieftain told his friend.

"Don't worry, the lodestone will guide us," Skywise answered. He removed the pendant from around his neck and held it suspended by the cord. Although the fixed star was not yet visible, the lodestone single-mindedly pointed in its direction. "We've come a long way, and we're all holding up pretty well, considering."

All except Redlance, Cutter thought, watching with pity as several Wolfriders helped place the red-braided elf on his mount. No longer able to sit up at all, Redlance clung to his wolf as a helpless, newborn treewee would cling to its mother's back. A purely rational corner of Cutter's mind wondered what in the name of the High Ones was keeping the injured one alive. It seemed impossible that Redlance could last another day, especially without food or drink.

One-Eye's thoughts were similar. Deciding quickly, he uncapped his water-skin and held the opening to Redlance's lips, forcing him to drink the last priceless drop. The half-dead elf raised his eyelids, seeing little more of his compassionate helper than a blurred figure dressed in dark green. Nightfall embraced One-Eye, knowing that the elder Wolfrider felt pained by the futility of his gesture.

"For all the good it did," he murmured sadly, patting her shoulder.

"For all the good it did," she whispered, "thank you."

Skywise had trouble focusing his eyes. Whether he cared to admit it or not, the heat had drained his strength as well as that of the others. From the position of the moons, he guessed that the darkness had run perhaps two-eighths of its course. But the sky no longer held his rapt attention as it had the previous night. He was too tired. The lodestone seemed very heavy to him as he held it, swaying gently, above Starjumper's head.

The Wolfriders rode in silence. No one wished to speak, for words only grated painfully through parched throats, causing more misery. In all the vast, arid land only the labored panting of the wolves could be heard as the elfin tribe pressed onward.

With a shock, Skywise regained consciousness and lifted his head, realizing that he must have nodded off to sleep for a moment. The lodestone was not in his hand!

Panicking, Skywise tugged at Starjumper's ruff—a signal for the wolf to stop—and started to dismount. He fully intended to dig through the loose sand until he either found the talisman or fell over dead; but just at that moment Cutter rode up with arm outstretched, a dark, familiar object dangling from his fist. The stargazer closed his eyes in relief, mildly ashamed that his trembling was so noticeable.

98 WENDY AND RICHARD PINI

This may be yours, but now we know it won't jump up and stick to you if you drop it! The elf chieftain smiled and placed the magic pendant in his friend's waiting hand.

Skywise held the lodestone by its string and watched as it slowly righted itself. Wanting to make certain that his brief doze had not caused the Wolfriders to stray from their path, he turned and sighted along the length of the stone, following its carved eye back to the Hub Star. Satisfied that the travelers were still on course, he turned back and let his gaze follow the tail of the stone to where it pointed into the distance.

"By the wandering stars," he cried, shaking his head as if to clear it. "Am I seeing things?" Skywise blinked hard several times and squinted toward the land's edge once more. What he saw there made his heart leap in his breast.

"Scouter! Get your hawk's eyes up here," he shouted, not willing to trust his own weary senses.

Riding with his parents far back in the column of Wolfriders, Scouter glanced quizzically at One-Eye and Clearbrook and then urged his wolf toward the head of the line. As the keen-eyed youth drew abreast of him, Skywise clutched Scouter's gaunt shoulder, anxiously thrusting a forefinger toward the horizon.

"There, in the distance. What do you see?"

Scouter looked as he was directed, and as he stared, the pupils of his eyes dilated until the brown irises had all but disappeared. He frowned for a moment in concentration and then nearly choked on a gasp.

"Mountains," he cried. "I see mountains!"

"Yes." Skywise's voice was thick with emotion. "I was afraid it wasn't true. But the lodestone saved us!"

Had the discovery been of a garden full of luscious fruit growing by a sky-clear stream, it could not have renewed the elves' spirits more quickly than Scouter's stunning news. The Wolfriders crowded around the youngster, chattering excitedly, trying to see what he had seen.

Far away, where the ground met the black sky, stretched

a pale ridge of land, barely discernible but unmistakably different in nature from the tedious, rolling terrain the elves had crossed. The distant ribbon was too irregular, the surface too subtly mottled with shades of light and dark to be merely a continuation of the dunes. It had to be a mountain range.

Moonshade breathed aloud. "Praise the High Ones. Soon we'll see trees again."

Cutter, who had remained curiously reserved through the joy of the discovery, said, "Don't be hasty, Moonshade."

She stared at him, bewildered and slightly offended that he would discourage her from voicing her hopes.

"I'm sure I did see plants," Scouter insisted. "They looked like small bushes scattered all around the lower hills."

Scouter had been known to sit in a treetop on one shore of a wide lake, spot a bird's nest in the branches of a tree on the opposite shore, and not only correctly identify the type of nest it was but also count the number of eggs it contained. No one doubted his claim about plants now.

Separating from his gathered tribefolk, Cutter walked Nightrunner up the slope of one of the dunes so that everyone might see him. Once there, he addressed the elves curtly, much regretting the sobering effect he knew his words must have. His intent was not to dishearten but to caution. He held up the water-skin that hung across his chest.

"Who will drink to celebrate our good fortune?" he called to them. "There are still a few drops left. And after all, it's only another night's ride to the mountains—another night following another day's rest in the sun. Come! Who will drink?" He paused to see whether his ploy had worked.

It had. The band of elfin outcasts shook their heads. They had a visible destination at last, one that would give the courage of purpose to their trek. But in their elation they had momentarily forgotten the danger of assuming that the last leg of the journey would be an easy one. If they achieved their goal, there would be time for joy. But until then they must go carefully, sustained by hope tempered with calm determination.

The young chief saw that his tribe understood. Gazing down on them, he was a compelling figure with long, pale hair, luminous in the moonlight. Taut skin on his torso and arms revealed hard knots of muscle beneath. His youth did not hinder his leadership, for he was the embodiment of the Wolfriders' spirit. To follow him was to follow the living blood of the tribe's primal seed.

That red wellspring sang in Cutter's veins now. No chief before him had ever faced such a test. The Wolfriders' number was small: seventeen—more a family than a tribe. They were alone in a world claimed by humans, enemies who were physically larger and far more numerous than they. The elfin tree-dwellers had held their place in the forest for uncounted moons, despite all that nature and men had hurled at them. Now, in mere days, the fate of these survivors would be decided for all time. Cutter, son of Bearclaw, would lead them to new life or to extinction.

No one heard him as he muttered a grim vow: "They will reach the mountains alive, even if it is my blood they must drink."

The band set off again to the sighing of a cold breeze, which rose suddenly, stirring up the loose grains around the wolves' travel-sore paws. As the night wore on, the terrain began to change ever so subtly. Pebbles appeared among the fine sand, and scattered clumps of dry, dead-seeming weeds poked through the rough soil, hinting that plant growth was possible here.

At one point, Scouter turned to Cutter to inform him, "These roundy hills stop well before the mountains. There's a stretch of flat land we'll have to cross. But I see rocks there—some very tall, like tree trunks. If we can get there by sunup, we'll have shade."

Before Cutter had even parted his lips to speak, Scouter knew what the question would be, and what he must answer. "No, there's no water. None that I can see, anyway."

The elf chieftain nodded, staring grimly ahead. The prospect of another day in motionless battle with heat and thirst was not a pleasant one. Putting Scouter in the lead, he let the youth decide which far-off pillar of rock they should make for. Scouter chose one that seemed likely to provide the longest shadow and the most cover. He was proud to be entrusted with such a position of responsibility, for he knew that no one else could clearly distinguish the jutting formations that were so evident to his remarkable eyes. He also saw that the mountains still lay some distance beyond the tall rocks, but not quite so far as an entire night's walk.

Eventually, as Scouter had promised, the dunes lowered and gave way to a wide, flat expanse of ground, covered with a thin layer of dust. Rocks and boulders of every size lay scattered among thick clumps of brownish weed. And there were night-sounds, wonderful to hear after almost two days of oppressive silence. Insects softly buzzed and chirped in the shrubbery, falling still for a moment as the beast-riding strangers passed close by them. Occasionally, when a white-winged moth fluttered too close to a wolf's mouth, there would be an audible snap as the morsel of nourishment was snatched from midair.

Their hunting instincts dulled by extreme fatigue, the Wolfriders failed to notice the small, long-tailed lizards that often lay in plain sight atop boulders or by leafless bushes. The scaly creatures held so still and blended so well with their surroundings that they were easily mistaken for groups of stones or fallen twigs.

Sharply defined by the moons' brightness, the mountains beckoned to the elves, taunting the travelers with their deceptive nearness. The Wolfriders were all but spent, and morning was on its way. Soon the moons would begin to set, and the side of the sky where Sun-Goes-Up would lighten slowly and ominously. Knowing this, the elves put aside all thoughts of their ultimate destination and concentrated only on reaching, before sunrise, the tall rock pillar Scouter had chosen for them.

Redlance, beloved. Touch me. I cannot find you!

Nightfall sent repeatedly to her lifemate, frightened that she received no response. Ordinarily, the private touching of thoughts she sought could be accomplished during sleep or even unconsciousness. But to escape his pain, Redlance had sunk so deeply into himself that Nightfall could find only darkness as she searched through the passageways of his inner being. Again and again she called to him. Finally, there was a stirring, a hint of familiar warmth that flickered into a glow, wanly illuminating her path.

Beloved, he called faintly. **Come to me. I must give you my soul name.**

No! Her response was torn from her, a silent scream. **I will find it myself if I am meant to!**

Lifemate. Friend of my body and my spirit. I do not want to die without giving you all that I am.

Then live! I will not take your gift! I will not let you go!

She broke the communication with a suddenness that left her dazed and more frightened than ever.

Lying prone atop his wolf, Redlance shuddered, digging his hands into the beast's rank fur. With a supreme effort, he pushed himself partially upright, clutching his ribs and gasping for breath. Nightfall rode close beside him, brushing back one of his thick braids to touch his livid cheek.

"I called you back to pain," she said. "But I'm not sorry. You are with me now."

He gripped her hand with a strength that surprised her. "Where are we?"

"Near the mountains, beloved. We'll rest when day comes and travel through one more night, and then—"

"No!"

Cutter heard Redlance's agonized cry. He whirled and leaped from Nightrunner's back just as the dying elf crumpled to the hard-baked ground. The other Wolfriders kept a respectful distance as Cutter slid to his knees beside the broken, dust-covered form. He gathered Redlance in his arms and held him through an endless moment of suffering.

"No more . . . no more," the son of tree-shapers moaned.

Cutter's hand crept to the hilt of New Moon. He was still cradling Redlance as his wide blue eyes locked with Nightfall's. Understanding at once, she shook her head and spoke quietly, firmly, touching her own hunting knife strapped to her thigh.

"I'll do it, when my heart truly believes there's no hope left."

Relieved, Cutter readily concurred. His thoughts raced as he lifted Redlance from the ground, looking toward the lofty rock formation that would shield his tribe from the coming sun. The striated pillar did not seem so far away; even at their slow pace, the tribe should be there in less than a single eighth of a day's march. Unquestionably, riding any farther across his wolf's sharp spine would kill Redlance. But Nightrunner would collapse under the added weight if Cutter tried to ride double with the injured one. Time was growing short. Daylight approached. The column of rock was not far away.

He began to walk.

"No, lad, no." Treestump put out a hand, gently restraining his young chief. "There's a better way."

Once again the leather cloaks carried by Moonshade and Pike proved their value. In a sling made from the pliant skins, Redlance was lifted and carried, with Cutter and Treestump bearing the head and foot and Nightfall and Pike gripping the hides' edges on either side.

At first the other Wolfriders continued to ride while the four litter bearers trudged doggedly across the cracked and pebble-strewn ground. But then, one by one, the elves dismounted to march with finely formed jaws set and lucent eyes determinedly fixed on the nearing stone pillar. A kindred sympathy infused them all; their minds intertwined in an open sending that became a continuous, silent song. It kept their wilted bodies moving forward even as the sun poked its malevolent, fiery brow above the rim of the land.

"Mountains are beautiful in this light," murmured Skywise. "So near . . . and so far."

"We'll make it. We have to." Cutter's voice was a toneless rasp.

From what source the two friends had stolen the strength to climb the natural tower, once they had arrived, was a mystery even to them. Now they rested briefly upon the flat crown of the monolith, which was perhaps six or seven times the height of a Wolfrider. From their perch, Cutter and Skywise surveyed as much of their intriguing new surroundings as they could while the sun was yet low in the morning sky.

The land was flat but far from vacant. Dominating the elves' view were gnarled, eroded upward-reaching fingers of rock that were similar to, but not as tall as, the Wolfriders' chosen shade-place. So fluid were the weird, stony shapes that if they were not alive now, it seemed they surely must have lived once, writhing with all the abandon of a troll's fungus garden. For a moment, Cutter's thoughts floated back to Redlance, descendant of tree-shapers, and to the dead Holt with its Father Tree, all twisted and burled like these spires.

A riot of large, brambly shrubs, clinging to life with admirable tenacity, grew in clusters among the many boulders that shared their hard, dry bed. Although the bushes were not green like the bushes the elves had once known, they announced with sun-browned authority that survival was possible in this wilderness.

Of even greater moment to the Wolfriders and their immediate needs were the many signs of animal life evident around them. The time of half light before dawn seemed to be when small-winged and furred things foraged. Now that the sun had risen, most of these had already returned to their burrows or places of shade, but a few tiny mouselike creatures ended up lining the shrunken stomachs of several of the wolves. Treestump, Pike, and Strongbow caught two excessively thin and long-legged rabbits, a scavenger bird, and six lizards. One of the rabbits was so infested with fleshworms that it could not be eaten, but the rest of the catch was portioned out as equitably as possible among the elves and was gratefully downed, even to the bones. Slight though it was, the nourishment made the prospect of mid-day heat a little more bearable.

Feeling the ascending sun's rays more burningly on their skin, Cutter and Skywise climbed down from their vantage atop the rock pillar, but not before they spared the mountains a final, longing glance.

The mountains were not, in fact, the high peaks of a range but more closely resembled hills in height. The slopes, though, did not rise gently, mound upon mound. Rather, they clawed upward, with deep, irregular gashes scoring the bare rock as if a monstrous long-tooth cat had savaged it. Tortured by the elements, gouged and furrowed, the mountains were all the more beautiful, blending hard contrasts of light and shadow with the subtle and pleasing colors of the rock itself.

"One more night and we'll be there," whispered Cutter.

"One more night," Skywise repeated. "And what then?"

The elf chieftain shrugged. "You can say as well as I."

They joined the others in the stone pillar's long shadow.

As the shadow moved, the elves shifted their positions to keep within its protection. Treestump had the presence of mind to cut branches from the brittle weeds so that his folk might hold them against the sun's steep rays during the middle part of the day. Otherwise, the travelers slept or stared lethargically at the roasting landscape.

Somehow the day passed.

What was "Sorrow's End"? Even as he shouted the phrase at the top of his parched lungs, Cutter felt that something much older and wiser than he had shaped the words.

"Ayoooah, Wolfriders! We face the final trial. When next we rest, it will be in the foothills at Sorrow's End."

No one questioned his meaning; indeed, no one had the strength to question anything. It was all the Wolfriders could do to haul themselves onto their mounts' sagging backs. From dawn until dusk, the elves had been no more active than bears sleeping through the season of White Cold; yet they were exhausted, as though they had covered a great distance on foot at a dead run.

It seemed to Skywise that the sun, too, knew thirst, that it continually needed to drain the mortal strength out of every living thing on which it mercilessly shone. Perhaps, he thought, the greedy orb would soon exhaust its reservoir of life, drying up the last of its creeping, scampering, fluttering sources of renewal. Skywise cherished the fantasy that should his tribe perish before reaching the haven of the hills, the sun would then weaken and wither to a spark more feeble than the dimmest star in the night sky.

The final ride began. Cutter took the lead, his strange cry fading in his own mind even as it was wafted away on the dry evening breeze. Nightrunner's slow gait was disturbingly uneven, with his hipbones creaking audibly beneath folds of fleshless skin. Like his brethren, Nightrunner walked with his head hanging down, his back achingly bowed under the weight of his rider. The wolf panted incessantly, licking his lips for traces of moisture that had long since evaporated. Cutter's throat, too, was agonizingly sore from dryness, but there was nothing he could do for it; his near-empty waterskin had remained behind at the tall rock with Nightfall and Redlance.

Sorrow's End. There was no such thing. Only death could end sorrow, and only that of the dying one, not the pain of those who lived on and mourned.

In his mind, Cutter relived the sad events that had occurred just before sunset. He saw himself bending over Redlance, who lay with his head resting in his lifemate's lap. Cutter had called aloud, rather than sent, Redlance's name, as if to

rouse within the red-braided elf the last living bit of energy
needed for a spoken reply.

"Redlance, it's time to go."

The eyes opened, a look of disquieting calm in their pale
green depths.

"No, Cutter. You know as well as I that I must stay here."

"He can't ride, my chief. And I won't leave him." Nightfall's toneless pronouncement still haunted Cutter. Gently,
she hushed her lifemate's entreating protests with a firm,
"It's decided."

At that moment a torrent of images—Redlance's rescue
from the savage humans, the Spirit Man's vengeful torching
of the forest, the arrow, fired with deadly accuracy by
Strongbow, piercing the raving shaman's throat too late to
avert flaming tragedy—poured with relentless force upon
the painful open wound of Cutter's guilt.

"Forgive me," he asked. "If I'd killed that old man when I
had the chance, none of this would have happened."

At once Redlance's trembling fingers closed about his
sorrowful chief's hands.

"We are hunters, Cutter, not murderers. It has always
been our way to respect life." The words of comfort had
been offered without a trace of bitterness, in a voice that
sounded, at last, free of pain. "Please—" a pause for breath
"—I don't want that to change no matter what happens."

Unable to do more, Cutter embraced the mated lovers,
promising that he would return soon to fetch them both.
He quietly placed his water-skin at Redlance's feet. He did
not trust himself to meet his dear friend's eyes as she spoke
a vow of her own.

"We'll be here waiting, Cutter. That is *my* promise."

The pillar of stone shrank behind him, becoming one of
many pale, skeletal fingers groping at the full moons
overhead.

"Sorrow's End," the "no-such-thing," still waited for the
Wolfriders somewhere among the nearing mountains. Cutter had experienced premonitions before, but never one so

strong and inexplicable as this. If Sorrow's End were, indeed, death, why was he certain beyond all misgiving that the elfin tribe he led would find life once they reached their goal? He wondered if his desperate wish for their survival might be blinding him to the bleak truth: Sorrow ceased only when life ceased, and the Wolfriders must prepare to surrender and suffer no more.

Abruptly Moonshade's wolf, Shyhider, lurched to a stop, his legs stiff and trembling, his breath a harsh wheeze in his constricted throat. Ribs heaving like a bellows, he took one more shaky step and collapsed, tumbling Moonshade and Dart to the ground. As they stood up, Shyhider dragged himself forward and then rolled on his side, kicking convulsively. A cloud of disturbed dust settled upon his death agonies like a veil. Impulsively, Dart reached out to pet the beloved animal's muzzle, but Moonshade prevented him, lest in a spasm those still-mighty jaws should clamp shut on his arm, crushing the frail bones like the leg of a grasshopper.

Moonshade's eyes were dry and unblinking as they watched the wolf breathe its last. Shyhider was not a young male. Through twice-eight-and-two snows he had been Moonshade's wolf-friend, one of the many who had shared bonds of loyalty and affection with her. As with all the others she had known and lost through the span of her many seasons, Moonshade mourned Shyhider's death. But the loss of this mount was especially poignant, for the wolf had broken his steadfast heart while bearing both elf-friend and child, like part of his own flesh and fur, across this unknown and unforgiving ground.

Strongbow dismounted and held out his hand to Moonshade. She came to him listlessly and did not protest as he lifted her onto Briersting's back. The lean archer turned next to his small son and received a decided, negative shake of the child's tawny head.

"No, father. I don't want to ride. I can walk, like you."

Strongbow smiled faintly as Dart's little fingers crept into his palm. Father and son trudged on together, hand in hand, leaving Shyhider's matted and skeleton-thin carcass to the scavengers who would surely follow. No one suggested that the elves try to glean the meager bits of flesh from the wolf's bones.

Distance. Space. A straight line from place to place.
No.
Distance was not measured in straight lines, but in time. Space was a convoluted necklace of obstacles to be gone around or used to conceal. Travel through space was a winding, back-tracking, in-and-out process; from its beginning the goal could almost never be seen. One did not need to see the goal, however, to know that it would be reached after so much walking or riding time. But that was in familiar territory, where every tree had its scent-mark, where every fallen log or stream or steep embankment was a well-known part of the pattern.

With each staggering step, the Wolfriders could see the low mountains more clearly. It was their destination, and yet they felt more lost than if they had had to pick their way from one end of a dense overgrown wood to the other. Traveling in a straight line beneath an open sky demanded such a shift in thought and perception that the Wolfriders' weary minds could no longer cope with the strangeness. They rode with their heads lowered and eyes shut, their sensibilities beaten down to unconscious reflex.

Toward dawn, Woodlock's wolf dropped dead in its tracks, causing Newstar to squeal with fright. Her father lifted her from the dead beast's shoulders and carried her for a while on his back. The half-conscious child's slight weight soon became such a burden, however, that Woodlock wondered dimly how the wolf had borne them both so far without complaint. With the death of this second wolf, Treestump felt a muzzy pang of concern for his own Lionskin; a hazy memory of a human spear wounding the animal's leg made the stocky elf look to the wound's leather dressing. The wolf was limping somewhat but seemed well; Treestump grunted his satisfaction softly.

For the first time in three days there were clouds in the sky as the sun rose, painting the craggy peaks with delicious tints of orange, lavender, and pink. Stopping for a brief rest, as they had done many times since midnight, the elves noticed the fleecy golden clouds drifting low over the mountaintops and the rosy blush of day's first light on the land. Soon, they knew, the intense heat of morning would dispel the enchanted aura of color and beauty. But the mountains were close by. One last great effort would bring them to the foot of the jumbled crags before midday. The Wolfriders roused themselves and made ready to march, most of them deciding to spare their wolves by traveling the rest of the way on foot.

Rainsong could not be wakened from a deep, exhausted slumber. While Clearbrook held tiny Wing in her arms, noting with concern the infant's rapid breathing and feeble movements, One-Eye assisted as Woodlock strapped his lifemate's inert form across her wolf's back. Newstar wept in distress at the sight of her mother's limp body and dangling limbs, and there was little that could be said or done to comfort the child.

With murmured thanks, Woodlock took his son from Clearbrook and started to walk, halting in midstride when he saw that Rainsong's mount would not budge. The animal, whose name was Silvergrace, nuzzled and butted her forehead against Newstar, her protective instincts obviously stirred by the frail girl-cub's sobs. Acting with the parental devotion of her kind, Silvergrace made it quite clear that she would not move unless Newstar, too, rode upon her back. There was no arguing with the determined wolf, and so the little girl pulled herself up to ride with one hand tenderly caressing her unconscious mother's shoulder. Woodlock walked beside them, cradling Wing in the crook of one arm while resting his free hand on the she-wolf's rawboned hip.

A spark of fierce triumph ignited and flickered in Cutter's eyes. His people lived, and soon they would rest among the foothills as he had sworn. His feet dragged wearily across white-baked ground that was crosshatched with myriad shallow cracks. Ahead, he could see more dry, tan-colored bushes, but there were also leafless, lean-stemmed plants dotted with small yellow blossoms that the elves had not encountered before. The sight of the minute blooms kindled one hopeful thought: water. The thirsting Wolfriders knew well that no flowering thing could live, much less thrive, without some source of moisture.

Cutter halted, peering uneasily at what looked for all the world like a gathering of tall, log-shaped creatures standing with arms threateningly upraised. The things seemed prepared to bar the path of any intruder seeking the cover of the tumbled rocks at the mountain's base. The silent guardians were completely inanimate, but Cutter warned his followers to approach cautiously nonetheless.

They were plants, for their scent, however strange, was that of green, growing things; and from their long, cylindrical trunks jutted upward-curving branches—the menacing arms seen from the distance. Over the entire pale-green body of each plant grew a bristling coat of needle-sharp spines, like those of a quill-pig. Several of the wolves discovered the stinging efficiency of these needles while nosing about the bases of the unfamiliar growths.

By now the sun was high overhead; the Wolfriders cared little to stop and examine the peculiar vegetation when shade was so close, beckoning so enticingly. As they reached the jumbled slope at the foot of the mountains, the elves stumbled and dropped, one by one, to their knees, crawling into shadow-blackened crevices created by falls of large rocks.

Dewshine huddled in the dark place beneath an overhanging slab, laying her hollow cheek against the coolness of the rough stones beside her. Her small breasts heaved as she alternately sobbed and laughed, although no tears fell from her eyes.

"I'm withered and curled at the edges like a dead leaf," she told Scouter as he caved in beside her, rolling over so that his head lay in deep shadow.

Groping feebly for her arm, the elfin youth said between gasps, "The only thing that could look more beautiful than you to me right now would be a cloud bursting with rain. Even a drizzle would do."

Meanwhile, Cutter removed his sweat-soaked vest, letting it drag in the dust as he shuffled toward a likely-looking niche in which to rest. Heedlessly he brushed too close to one of the tall spine-covered plants. The sharp needles etched two bloody gashes on the back of his left hand.

It was too much.

With a growl and a curse, the outraged elf drew his sword and slashed at the offending plant, neatly severing the top with one deft slice. The prickly, dome-shaped upper half flipped through the air and landed with a satisfying thud in the dust. Cutter nodded sharply, smiling as if he had just beheaded a human, and started to sheathe New Moon.

Something sparkled on the blade, something that caught the light in a manner quite different from the natural moon-coolness of the sword's bright metal sheen. Cutter held the tip of the blade before his unbelieving eyes. There were moist streaks, like smeared drops of dew, clinging to the sword's edge. The elf chieftain emitted an inarticulate grunt of surprise.

"Uh? It's *wet!*"

Skywise hurried to his friend's side, no mean feat since the stargazer's knees were about to buckle. Staring at New Moon's tip, Skywise grasped Cutter's wrist, his silver-gray eyes bulging with disbelief.

"Where? How?"

They both looked down at the severed trunk of the needle-plant. It was full of pale, succulent meat that oozed a thin film of moisture. Carefully avoiding the spines, Cutter wasted no time in using New Moon to dig out a sizable chunk of the plant's pithy heart. He bit into it and chewed, working at the blunt-tasting mouthful as if it were a piece of stringy meat. Then his eyes lit up, and he looked at Skywise, nodding excitedly.

Pocketing the pulp in one cheek, Cutter managed to talk around it. "I'm getting juice," he exclaimed. "If you can stand the taste, this stuff is full of water!"

Those elves who had crept into the shadows now emerged, watching with eager anticipation and not a little wonder as Cutter and Skywise used their swords to gouge, chop, and gut the strange liquid-storing plant. Pike was the first, after Cutter, to sample the juicy, spongelike flesh. It was amusing to watch the spear bearer chew his portion, the shaggy tufts of honey-colored hair he wore over each ear wagging in and out with the working of his jaw and the accompanying motion of his still-round cheeks.

"Don't swallow it!" cautioned Cutter, but it was too late. Pike gulped and instantly regretted the mistake. While he choked and sputtered and received well-meaning slaps between his shoulder blades, One-Eye used his short sword to slash the top from another of the stunted sticker-plants. Soon all the Wolfriders were gleaning life-sustaining moisture from this most unexpected source—even Rainsong, who recovered from her swoon when Woodlock squeezed drops of liquid from the pulp onto her feverish skin.

Most gratifying of all was the sight of Dart and Newstar busily chewing and sucking the juice from their slices, almost perceptibly gaining strength. Wing, too, responded as he suckled droplets from his mother's fingers. Disliking the flavor, he gave forth his first lusty howl in days.

Recovered from his unpleasant experience, Pike mashed some of the pithy pulp-stuff between his palms, watching with delight as his wolf went through eager contortions to lap up the wetness that dripped from his fingers.

"How about that, Hotburr?" Pike laughed. "Leave it to Cutter! He found us plants that store their own water!"

In the midst of his tribe's happiness—the first they had

known since the raging flames had sent them flying from the forest into unimaginable hardship—Cutter quietly turned away. He walked over to a smooth, rounded boulder, where he sat and buried his face in his hands. Relief and fear both flooded him. Except for Nightfall and Redlance, the Wolfriders were still together, still alive and struggling to remain so despite their terrible ordeal. The humans had not won, after all, and neither had the trolls. But what would become of the small band of outcasts now? What did they really know of this place, of its danger or its ability to support the tribe, not to mention the wolf pack itself?

The weary chieftain felt a gentle touch on his shoulder. When Cutter looked up, Skywise did not remove his hand, or smile, or speak, or even shift his stance. Moments passed as the two friends simply shared each other's presence. There had never been much need for lengthy talk between them. Although Skywise had seen half again as many turns of the seasons as had Cutter, it was tacitly acknowledged that they were brothers in all but blood. Shared loss and shared suffering had only made the bond stronger.

At length Skywise spoke a single word, "Thanks." The levels of meaning were many, and none needed the clarification of sending. Fingering the lodestone thoughtfully, he walked to a jumble of rocks and sank down among them, stretching out in the shadows. He was unspeakably tired, too tired even to remove his blue metal wristbands and face guard, which were overheated by the sun. In moments he was not merely asleep but unconscious. Neither dreams nor sensations from the waking world disturbed the timeless oblivion of his much-needed rest.

Cutter crawled into the dark niche he had intended to occupy before his fortunate altercation with the spiny waterplant. Sleep would not come, however, despite his desperate weariness. Something gnawed at his mind and would not let him take his ease.

Sorrow's End. Sorrow's End. The phrase had a meaning beyond the shallow immediacy of the words. Cutter shifted uncomfortably, eyes shut, frowning. He tried to dismiss the irritating enigma that seemed determined to impose its rhythm upon the very beating of his heart. Sorrow's End. Sorrow's End. What did it mean? The answer was not the cessation of life; Cutter knew now that his first interpretation of the premonition had been wrong. But life was sorrow and joy and love and the hunt and battle all intermingled. The Wolfrider had not yet been born who could live through many turns of the seasons without being touched by all these experiences. How, then, could it be possible to find Sorrow's End while life endured?

Giving up his attempt at rest, Cutter uncurled and emerged from the confines of his rocky shade-place. Although white puffs of cloud, like balls of snow-rabbit fur, moved ever so slowly across the vivid blue sky, there was no breeze. The long trail of tracks left in the dust by the Wolfriders was undisturbed. Cutter wondered as he followed the trail with his eyes until it vanished beneath a fuming haze in the distance whether these were the first footprints the dust of this land had ever known. He thought of Nightfall, probably alone by now, waiting for him somewhere back along that path. Concern for her plight lifted him from his reverie, prompted him to act while his second wind still held.

"Umph," groaned Skywise, starting awake as a falling pebble loosened by Cutter's foot bounced off his head. The young chieftain had climbed atop the tumbled stones of his friend's shelter to gain a foothold in the low mountain's deeply scarred flank. Skywise mumbled under his breath and finally almost whined, "Cutter, will you please collapse? You're entitled!"

"Not yet," answered the pale-haired Wolfrider. "The juice from those sticker-plants is not enough for us. We have to find real water, and soon!"

Collecting his aching bones together and somehow hauling them to an upright position, Skywise watched Cutter climb for a moment, sighed hugely, and began to follow his willful chief.

"All right," grumbled the stargazer. "I suppose you won't sit still until you've found us a blasted waterfall!"

The climbing was simplicity itself for the two agile elves, who found ledges and handholds aplenty in the weather-worn rock of the mountainside. Keeping their grip, how-ever, was the difficult part of the ascent, for any more than an instant's contact between bare flesh and sun-baked stone brought searing pain. Like fleas dancing on a troll metal-worker's hot anvil, Cutter and Skywise leaped from boulder to shelf to rocky spur in search of a crack or fissure leading through the mountain. Their hope of finding a hidden wellspring faded as they zigzagged their way up to the summit without discovering a single promising access.

While Cutter climbed the rest of the way up to a broad, flat area from which he could survey the other side of the low range, Skywise paused to examine his sorely reddened skin. Gingerly touching his forearm, he sucked in his breath with pain. The stargazer's face, chest, and bare arms, and even his pointed ears, were a bright pink color, extremely sensitive to the touch. It did not take him long to guess that the sun was somehow responsible. Lifting one edge of his vest, he saw that the part of his chest that had been covered by the slate-blue leather was its normal pale color. But there was an embarrassingly sharp line between the pale, covered skin and the burned, exposed skin. Skywise decided that one of the first things he would do to adapt his clothes to this sun-swept environment would be to add a hooded cape and sleeves to his tunic.

Skywise! Up here! Quickly!

Cutter's mental cry sent all other thoughts flying from the stargazer's brain. As he climbed to join his chief, Skywise called, "What is it?"

No answer.

Worried, Skywise hastened to Cutter's side. The Wolfrider chieftain sprawled belly down, unmoving, on the flat expanse of rock. The attitude of his body was that of a long-tooth cat crouched in the bushes, sizing up its prey.

"What—" Skywise began, but Cutter's right hand shot out and clamped over the stargazer's lips.

"Shh," hissed Cutter; then, **Look!**

Skywise pulled himself to the rim of the rock and peeked over. His jaw fell open, and his eyes showed white all around the silver irises. Nearly crying out, he caught himself and silently drew in his breath instead. His sending was ragged with emotion.

I can't believe it! Elves! Elves!

Seven

Leetah stepped from the bead-curtained doorway of her hut, glowing like a ceremonial torch as the steep-angled rays of the early-afternoon sun fell upon her sparkling raiment and luxuriant auburn hair. Her brief bodice was as red as the fruit of a squatneedle plant; delicate gold threads woven into the fabric winked and glimmered provocatively. Her calf-length skirt was the blue of the sky, shot through with filaments of silver, and edged about her rounded hips and lower hem with golden fringes that fluttered gracefully as she walked. All of pure beaten gold, her jewelry was beautifully simple in design. Two ringlike bracelets adorned each wrist, calling attention to her sensuously articulated hands. From her upward-curving, sharply pointed ears dangled burnished oval disks, earrings whose yellow metal glinted brightly at the merest nod of Leetah's head. Crowning that lovely head, a wide circlet of gold held an unruly heap of curls in some semblance of order away from her brow.

The only other ornament Leetah wore was a neck ring from which three solid nuggets of gold, shaped like beads, were suspended. Fixed to each of the beads was the polished fang of a mountain lion, and the whiteness of the savage teeth stood out in shocking contrast against the deep brown softness of her swelling breasts.

As she walked along the whimsically winding path that led away from the door of her hut, she was suddenly stopped by someone who blocked her way, someone who wore three lion's teeth exactly like hers. He glowered at her with an expression that was calculated to intimidate; the desired effect, however, was not achieved.

"Well?" he said with an edge of impatience to his voice.

Leetah smiled, her own white teeth no less startling in

119

contrast to her dark skin than the curved fangs that gleamed upon her breast.

"How clever you are, Rayek," she said, glancing slyly at the glazed clay water jug balanced gracefully on her hip. "That is precisely where I am going."

Rayek's thin lips tightened into a hard, unamused line. Ordinarily he appreciated the delicate thorns of wit with which she often stung him, but on this day he had very little patience and certainly no sense of humor.

"I will go with you," was his low-voiced response.

Leetah realized that this flat statement of future events depended not in the least upon her approval. She shrugged, and answered him indifferently. "As you like."

A handsome couple, and coolly aware of it, they walked along the narrow, meandering path that would eventually take them to the Sun Village's communal well. If Leetah's body was a melody of curves, Rayek's lithe form was a counterpoint of angles and planes. He stood more than half a head taller than she, his skin as deeply tanned as hers but with sallow undertones. Naked save for two panels of brightly patterned cloth protecting his loins, Rayek moved in leonine rhythms, smoothly, unconsciously controlled, reserves of speed and endurance manifest in the elongated muscles of his torso and limbs.

The wide ornamental collar he wore and his wrist and ankle bands were made of plates woven of red and yellow grasses, lacquered to a high gloss and intertwined with delicate gold wires. Set between the plates of the collar were flakes of red-tinted clearstone, rare because of their size and flawless surfaces. On his chest, hanging from the lower part of the neckband, rested three lion fangs set into large gold beads, identical to Leetah's. He had killed the beast himself and had fashioned the trophies into ornaments for Leetah and himself.

Although the proud symmetry of his body was a feast for the eye, the onlooker's gaze rested longest on Rayek's face, not so much to take in the extreme beauty of his features but because once met, his penetrating amber eyes were impossible to avoid. They had a serpentine quality that never softened, never ceased to cause unease in others, even when he smiled. Only Leetah, above all the common folk of the Sun Village, had ever been able to look him in the eye without quailing; for this reason, among many others, she held Rayek's unending, frustrated fascination.

The two walked together in silence, skirting the rounded walls of other huts, nodding disinterested greetings to those in the small gardens who looked up from their spades to smile politely from the shadowy depths of broad-brimmed grass hats. Leetah had seen and dealt with this mood of Rayek's before. It was a periodic problem, much like the occasional blustery sandstorm, and no great cause for concern; she would weather the inevitable confrontation as she always had, and then there would be peace for a time, on her terms, until the next storm arose. Thus smugly armed, she gave her opponent a seductive glance from beneath half-closed lids as they approached the field of battle.

The well stood at the edge of the Sun Village, only a short distance away from the looming rock walls that embraced the cluster of clay-walled huts in a protective semicircle. This crescent of heaped and rubbled stone, pocked by shallow caves and crevices, formed a kind of natural, steep-walled amphitheater where the line of mountains crooked like an elbow. Within the afternoon shade cast by the belly of the crescent, the Sun Village nestled in serene and self-sustaining isolation, untouched for time without reckoning by the world beyond the mountains.

Among the village's inhabitants, legend had it that the well had been "shaped" long ago by a member of the revered family that had founded the Sun Village. The water had never failed the dark-skinned elves, even through times of poorest harvest when the sun drove fiery winds before it, parching grain on the stalk and withering flesh on the bone.

So that the villagers, like Leetah, who even now prepared to draw her daily supply of water, would never take the precious source of life for granted, much attention had been paid to the well and its appearance. The well house was covered with an ornate, peaked roof that was raised on four intricately carved miniature stone columns. These in turn were supported by a low circular wall built around the deep well itself, decorated with colorful tiles and surrounded by a profusion of lavender wild flowers.

The throat of the well was very narrow, and so the bucket used for drawing water was, of necessity, comparably small. Leetah had to lower and raise the bucket half eight times in order to fill her earthen jar; all the while Rayek stood aside with arms folded, silently studying her every movement, searching for any chink in the armor of her poise. Deliberately unflustered by her companion's piercing stare, Leetah did not know that other eyes were watching from above, strange, feral eyes that gazed down from the mountaintop with a predatory gleam upon her and the peacefully oblivious village.

Look at them! Who could've known? Skywise was still awed and thrilled by the incredible, unhoped-for discovery. **Elves! Just like us!**

Cutter's brows drew together blackly. **No, not like us, Skywise. They seem more like humans to me. They have no wolves, no tree-homes, and they live in the sun as men do.** Taking care not to reveal himself, he inspected the villagers within his line of vision more closely. The flow of sending went on uninterrupted. **Look at their skin. They're as dark as humans! I don't trust them.**

Skywise turned to his chief, crestfallen. **You mean you don't think they'd help us if we asked?**

The tone of the response was as flinty and sharp as angrily spoken words. **We're not going to ask. I learned a hard lesson from the trolls. From now on the Wolfriders take what they need—and no reasons given!**

Cutter had seen one of the dark-skinned elves draw water from an elaborately covered hole in the ground. He had seen the sparkling liquid flow as she transferred it from one container to another. Now he noticed that other elves were digging among tidy rows of plants; occasionally one of the swarthy strangers would pop part of a plant into his mouth, indicating that the odd vegetation was edible. That was all the Wolfriders' young chieftain needed to know.

Quickly, because both he and Skywise lay completely exposed to the sun atop their flat, high perch, Cutter sized up the strangers' camp—he had no concept of "village"—and decided on the best way to attack.

There were eight smaller shelters surrounding a very large one, and there seemed to be a good deal of coming and going from this big central place. The dark elves did not have any weapons at hand, at least none that Cutter could recognize. The stranger's movements were slow, almost languorous, like those of a sloth. But even though it seemed highly unlikely that there would or could be much of a fight, Cutter deemed it best to approach with stealth and attack by surprise. The crescent-shaped high stony wall surrounding the strangers' camp was, admittedly, good protection. But the inner curve of the wall was very rough, scored with deep crevasses, knobbled with rocky outcroppings—sufficient cover for the wolves and their riders to descend unnoticed.

Cutter touched Skywise's shoulder, nodding brusquely. The two friends hastily left their spying place to bring news of the strange dark-skinned elves to the rest of the Wolfriders.

Below in the village, Rayek felt a sudden inexplicable chill. He was filled with foreboding, and his original purpose was made all the more intent by a nameless, nagging dread. He moved to stand close behind Leetah, gripping her slender upper arms with proprietary firmness.

"Rayek, please." She laughed softly. "You'll make me spill the water!" As if to demonstrate, she turned to him, and the heavy jug tipped slightly, splashing a few drops over its rim.

Rayek's mouth curled sardonically. He opened his left hand, palm facing toward the listing piece of crockery.

Instantly, Leetah felt the vessel tremble and set itself upright, even as she held it in her hands. Her expression remained one of indifference; Rayek's tricks did not always impress her, especially when he flaunted them with such overbearing ease.

"How long will you torment me, Leetah?" he asked. "I have asked you to be my lifemate. Any maiden here would say yes." His tone was matter of fact; nevertheless, Leetah was amused by his unabashedly glowing, though not unfounded, opinion of himself.

"Then why pursue me, my arrogant one?" she parried, sensing that the game might take an uncomfortable turn if she lost her balance even for a moment.

Rayek's hands slid down her arms and locked tightly about her narrow waist, pulling her against him. "Because you are the only one worth having," he murmured, his breath softly stirring the russet curls at her temple. "Life is long. I have no wish to join with some adoring, wide-eyed bit of thistledown who would cringe at my every glance. And I would not choose a lifemate who could offer only respect born of worshipful ignorance to my use of the old powers." He held her even closer, whispering into her elegantly tapered ear. "You, Leetah, with your knowledge of ancient arts all but forgotten by the rest of our people— only you appreciate the old powers as I do, only you understand what I am and what I need!"

She shivered, his touch and his words conspiring to set her senses afire. Feeling him nuzzle the thick mesh of ringlets at the nape of her neck, she responded, caressing his dark, angular cheek with her lips.

"Have we not always understood one another, my friend?" she whispered. "Have we not shared in every way the sweetness of this understanding? Can you not be content that above all others, I take greatest delight in you?"

"That is not enough," he hissed. "I want to hear you say that you are mine, that we are destined lifemates, now and forever!"

She eyed him, with one delicate, highly arched brow lifting in haughty appraisal. He had voiced these demands many times before, and as many times she had declined to meet them, disguising her refusals with humor, with compassion, and with enough wit to distract both herself and him from any actual pain. But now Rayek seemed driven by secret demons sworn to torment him endlessly if he failed this time to win her consent. The reason for such urgency was beyond Leetah's imagining. Rayek had said, truly enough, that life was long, but to that she could not help adding the thought: And unbreakable alliances tend to limit one's freedom.

"Well?" he repeated, squeezing her waist with such pressure that she gasped.

"Oh! You're holding me too tight! Let me catch my breath, and I'll give you an answer."

Rayek hesitated, suspicious, and then reluctantly disentwined his arms from her. "Very well then, on that condition I release you!"

Clutching the heavy, water-filled vessel, Leetah fled in a shimmer of fluttering fringes. Dismayed, Rayek cried her name, but the auburn-haired beauty continued to run, laughing with relief. The battle had not gone in her favor this time. She needed a moment to summon her wits and plan new defenses before reentering the fray.

Suddenly a sound like nothing she had ever heard before brought Leetah skidding to a stop. The sound was neither the loud quarreling of a clan of kit foxes nor the rasping roar of a mountain lion. This chilling new noise was a high-pitched, many-throated howl, bestial and yet somehow mingled with the clear call of elfin voices. Other villagers, hearing the eerie wails, halted in midtask to look up in alarm.

Charging down the precipitous, boulder-strewn slopes on the village's north side, clearing huge blocks of stone with prodigious leaps, the Wolfriders attacked in full cry, weapons flailing and teeth bared. Instantly the elves of the Sun

Village flew into a panic, running for cover as Cutter and the male members of his tribe galloped zigzag around the closely grouped huts. Anything that even remotely resembled food or drink was swept up by the small band of invaders, with only the slightest show of resistance from the stunned villagers.

As a dark-skinned female strove hurriedly to gather up the fruit she had arranged to dry in the sun, scooping great handfuls into a woven basket, Pike rode up with spear outthrust and neatly threaded the weapon's tip through the basket's braided handle. The elf-woman screamed and collapsed in a faint as Hotburr vaulted over her head. Pieces of dried fruit flew everywhere, pattering like swollen raindrops as the basket swung crazily from the shaft of Pike's spear.

Skywise careened around a hut and came face to face with a plump villager, who clutched a golden-brown object protectively to her breast and tried to run backward. The silver-haired Wolfrider jabbed his sword, and the terrified elf dropped her burden, only to see it deftly skewered in midair.

"My bread," she cried. "My fresh-baked bread!"

Skywise did not know what bread was, but he noted that it had a wonderfully sweet scent; he flourished the punctured loaf with a triumphant howl and whipped Starjumper around to dash away in another direction.

Meanwhile, Scouter rode through someone's garden underbelly-style, with legs hooked over his wolf's back, pulling up as many tender rootlike vegetables as two hands and a grinning mouth could carry. Then, almost before he realized it, Scouter was clinging upside down for dear life as his wolf raced toward an enormous, long-legged humped creature that looked like the impossible offspring of a deer and a tree sloth. Wolf and rider shot between the monster's spindly legs, and it was all the young elf could do to keep his ravenous mount from trying to bring the gigantic beast down by herself.

Woodlock rode up to a rounded window opening of one

hut, thrust a hand through the beaded curtain, and withdrew it, clutching a round-bellied bottle full of something liquid—he did not care what. Screams of outrage and fear came from within the hut, and a thick-soled sandal hurtled through the beadwork, narrowly missing Woodlock's head.

At the same time, Treestump and Strongbow were busy chasing an angry villager away from an appetizing display of smoke-dried strips of meat. The meat hung from a string stretched between two poles; the dark elf had been coating each strip with a syrupy glaze when the raid began. As Strongbow grasped the string at its middle, Treestump chopped one end free with his ax and then the other. The elfin archer made away with the skein, trailing it after him like a banner. But Treestump did not escape unscathed; the villager hurled his pot of syrup at the fleeing ax-wielder's back. Unhurt by the ill-aimed missile, nevertheless both Treestump and Lionskin emerged from the encounter looking as if they had rolled in a honeycomb.

Cutter headed straight for the well, knowing only that water could somehow be gotten from it, although he had no idea how.

The moment the Wolfriders had descended, howling, upon his village, Rayek had run to fetch his long-spear. Now, as Cutter loped toward the well—and toward Leetah, who stood paralyzed nearby—Rayek dashed to intercept wolf and rider, setting himself squarely in Cutter's path. Nightrunner reared back on his hind legs, snarling and snapping as Rayek jabbed repeatedly at the wolf's vulnerable head. Clinging with practiced ease to his mount's back, Cutter urged Nightrunner to lunge this way and that to keep the belligerent spear bearer off balance. The young elf chieftain studied his opponent, noting that this one was different in many ways from the other swarthy strangers. Unlike the rest of his people, slow-moving and easily cowed, this flamboyantly clad elf was a fighter and a valiant one, one to respect. His hair, black and iridescent as a crow's wing, was pulled back tightly into what looked like a long, smooth chief's lock. This puzzled Cutter, for some instinct told him that the one he faced was not the leader of the dark-skinned tribe. The spear bearer stood alone without the support of his pack, and it seemed that this was his choice.

Rayek glared at the pale-haired Wolfrider, his eyes never wavering. Cutter realized with sudden disquiet that there was more to the piercing eye contact than the instinctive challenge of a staredown. The black-haired elf's most potent weapon was not his spear; it was the spellbinding power of his reptilian yellow eyes. Cutter sensed that he dared not meet his opponent's gaze much longer, for already he felt a subtle weakening of his will, a slight slowing of his forest-trained responses.

With a wild, animal roar Cutter shook himself free of the spell, brandished his sword, and brought it slashing down on Rayek's wooden spear. New Moon struck with such splintering force that the lance's sharp metal point went flying through the air, instantly severed from the shaft.

"Never point a weapon, Black Hair," Cutter growled as a disbelieving Rayek stared at the remains of his most prized hunting spear. "Unless you know how to use it!" With that, the Wolfrider's heel connected solidly with Rayek's jaw, sending the dark elf sprawling among the lavender wild flowers growing around the well. Cutter decided that this was a fighter who was not much accustomed to forceful opposition, not from his own kind, at any rate.

Guiding Nightrunner in a quick trot around the well, Cutter was about to dismount and try to make sense of the mysterious mechanics of bucket and windlass, when he glanced up and spotted Leetah standing not far away. Still clenched in her rigid arms was the glazed clay vessel full of water. Cutter's parched lips drew back from his sharp, white teeth, and his heels dug into Nightrunner's protruding ribs. The wolf sprang forward, bearing down on Leetah with slavering jaws agape, but she remained rooted where she stood, either holding her ground or too terrified to run.

At the last possible moment Cutter flung his arms around

Nightrunner's neck and pulled sharply back, nearly flipping the wolf on his side. A cloud of dust raised by the skidding quick stop billowed about elves and beast alike, finally settling so that Cutter got his first good look at the auburn-haired villager.

Her exquisite beauty was incidental, hardly worth noticing. Green as fresh young leaves, her glittering eyes were not nearly so enthralling as that which lay behind them. Had Cutter's thirsting mouth been at all moist, it would have gone dry instantly, for something was happening to him—something sudden and powerful, something too ancient in origin to be named.

He felt himself opening like the first flowering bud of the season of New Green; and hovering near, just waiting for the petals to part, was a russet-winged butterfly ready to draw the sweet, never-tasted nectar from the blossom's untouched heart. All that he was poured forth from Cutter's soul in a swift, uncontrollable stream. He felt frightened, uncomprehending; and yet the strange sensation was not altogether one of loss. For something new was introducing itself into his being, something that flowed in the opposite direction to his stream, washing through the inner passageways of his spirit like the deepest of sendings. Every muscle in his young body tied itself into a defensive knot, yet nothing could prevent the two currents from flowing together, their opposing tides creating a whirlpool in which the essence of each mingled with the other until there was only one pool, one source, one essence.

For Leetah the sensation was that of strong drafts of wind. The hut that housed her soul was battered unmercifully by the mindless, howling blast of a most unwelcome storm. Little by little the wind stole through cracks in the coverings of her windows and doorway; as the strange but oddly familiar gusts penetrated her house, the breath of Leetah's soul escaped, wafting away to be caught in the irresistible force of a whirlwind. Somewhere in that swirling maelstrom her soul's breath thinned to a sigh of grief. That part of herself was no longer safe, no longer insulated, and no longer hers alone.

The Wolfrider and the Sun Villager both reeled dizzily for a moment, trying to fathom all that had just passed between them. As chaos, in the form of snarling wolves and shrieking, stumbling villagers, reigned about them, Cutter and Leetah stood in the eye of the storm and simply stared at each other. Whatever it was, the sensation that had overwhelmed them at first sight certainly had nothing to do with love.

In the part of her mind that could still be objective, Leetah found Cutter not altogether repulsive. He was very young and very dirty, and his skin, even sunburned, was uncommonly pale. But his square features, sharp with hunger, were handsomely defined; his eyes, what could be seen of them beneath his ragged forelocks, were large and set well apart and seemed as luminous in color as two circles of rich blue sky—even to the pupils, which appeared to be deep indigo instead of black. His fine hair was more badly tangled than the branches of a rolling skeleton-weed but was a breathtaking blazing white. Certain rare, smooth strands caught the light in a pleasing way, suggesting that the unkempt mop might have seen tidier days. His fur vest was caked with dirt and active with sand fleas, and he smelled exactly like the beast he rode. In fact, Leetah was hard-pressed to decide whether this youthful pale-skinned stranger was an elf with animal blood or a wild animal that strongly resembled an elf. The distinction became even less clear to her as Cutter approached, staring down at her from his seat atop a huge gray creature the likes of which Leetah had never seen.

"What do you want?" she stammered in a very small voice.

Rayek was on his knees, rubbing his jaw and forcing his eyes to focus when he heard the scream. Without warning, Cutter had flung his arm about Leetah's waist and lifted her off her feet. The water-jug smashed to the ground, its wasted contents soaking a widening pool beneath Nightrunner's muddy paws. If Cutter noticed the loss of the water he'd come for, he did not care in the least, for he was gripped now by a wholly different kind of thirst. With Leetah caught securely under one arm, Cutter lifted New Moon high over his head and voiced the howling cry of the Wolfriders.

"*Ayooah!*"

As swiftly as they had descended moments ago, the Wolfriders swept to Cutter's side, laden with all the food and drink they could carry. Even a few of the wolves bore booty from the raid in their powerful jaws. The thieves' gaunt sunburned faces were merry and flushed with excitement. They galloped away in a shower of stones hurled by the villagers, who were just now recovering from their shock at the unexpected attack.

Skywise drew up beside Cutter, observing Leetah as she pelted his chief's chest with her fists. Even in the throes of writhing, leg-flailing outrage, she was the most beautiful creature the stargazer had ever seen.

"Uh, excuse me, but it doesn't look like you're carrying much water," Skywise remarked dryly.

"Huh?" was Cutter's eloquent reply. He seemed lost in a mist or sodden with overripe dreamberries. At last he connected his friend's comment with the struggling captive caught under his left arm.

"Oh," he elaborated, and then went on, "I'll explain later." They both ducked as a stone whizzed between them. "On higher ground!"

The Wolfriders made their clamourous escape, urging their tired mounts to climb among the ragged boulders and rocky outcroppings until they reached a good hiding place just below the peaks of the crescent-shaped mountain spur. Below, the village swarmed with activity, resembling an ant mound disturbed by the tread of some unwitting passerby.

Rayek had gotten another spear and was busily trying to mold a rescue party from the unlikely clay of the flustered gardeners, slow-moving weavers, and gentle-mannered artisans of all kinds who clustered about him, seeking guidance. Plainly, the dark-skinned inhabitants of the Sun Village had no experience in responding to such an emergency.

From the arched portal of the village's very large central hut came a figure clad in a long blue-green robe. His helmetlike headdress was made of shimmering, multicolored scales, and as he hurried toward the sound of Rayek's voice, he used a long smooth staff to guide his steps across the ground. His face was seamed and crosshatched with myriad fine lines, especially around the deep-set eyes, which were wide open and sightless. Although his clouded, milky irises were fixed in a blank, unseeing stare, the blind one's leathery features clearly expressed his perplexity and concern.

"Someone tell me what has happened," he called. "I heard strange voices—shouting!"

"Barbarians, Sun-Toucher," Rayek's furious voice answered, "riding huge, fanged beasts! They've taken Leetah!"

The Sun-Toucher's face tightened into a mask of dismay. He leaned on his staff for support.

"My daughter," he cried. "Save her, Rayek! You must!"

"I will," vowed the slim, dark-haired hunter. He turned to the gathered villagers and with a sweep of his arm ordered them to follow him.

Heading for the tumbled stones at the base of the sloping wall, Rayek began to climb, intending to comb the mountainside until he uncovered the Wolfriders' hiding place. To the best of their ability, Rayek's people imitated his agile ascent, bearing hoes and hand spades and blunt-bladed daggers and giving no indication that they had any idea how to use their weapons against the barbarians, even if their search brought them to a violent encounter.

"Follow me, you laggards," cried Rayek. "Follow for Leetah's sake!"

High above, from an overhanging ledge, Treestump and Strongbow observed the laborious progress of the rescue party. The afternoon sun beat down on their uncovered heads, but from chest to toe their bodies remained in shadow. Eager to get altogether into the shade, the archer and the ax-wielder quickly assessed the strength of the approaching enemy. The village held eight times five, perhaps eight times six full-grown inhabitants; of these, less than half had proved fit to join Rayek on his mission of rescue. Even now the strenuous climb was beginning to take its toll. One by one the followers dropped back to rest and catch a breath before gamely proceeding upward. Exasperated, Rayek turned and hurled curses at them, not once losing his footing as he continued to climb with all the ease of a squirrel maneuvering through the branches of a tree.

They're a pretty soft lot, Strongbow sent to his yellow-bearded companion, a contemptuous smile twisting his colorless lips. **I doubt most of them will make it up this far.**

Don't much like the look in that first one's eye, Treestump indicated Rayek with a nod and a cocked eyebrow. **Maybe you better pick him off, Strongbow.**

The elfin archer grinned maliciously, his russet eyes glinting as he reached back to his quiver for a sleek, deadly shaft fletched with the feathers of a black strutter-cock. The arrow was not half drawn when Strongbow received a swift and adamant sending from his chief.

No! No killing! Not if we can help it!

Not far away from the lookout ledge, Cutter sat upon a rock with a struggling Leetah firmly clutched in his arms. His hand was clamped over her mouth, but some muffled angry noises managed to escape through his fingers. Cutter glowered as Strongbow seemed about to protest the command against harming any of Leetah's people, but Treestump tapped the willfull archer's shoulder, and the two of them retreated from the ledge.

The Wolfrider's refuge was a relatively flat space notched in the mountainside; this shelf was littered with grotesquely shaped boulders, which afforded the elves ample cover as well as any number of vantage points from which they could secretly observe their pursuers. The first moments of their arrival in the lofty stronghold were spent in gasping, trembling exhaustion. Whatever meager strength the Wolfriders had gained from the sticker-plant juice was gone, depleted in the swift raid and the equally fleet escape. The elves devoured their stolen provisions with a ravenous will, sharing equally both food and drink with their half-starved wolf-friends.

Not quite understanding what Leetah was doing among them, Cutter's tribesmen indulgently helped him eat and quench his thirst. The captive villager was almost too much for the young chief's muscular arms to contain, but Cutter refused to let anyone else hold her, even though her struggles aggravated his fatigue.

No less curious about the strange new female elf than the Wolfriders themselves, the wolves prowled about Leetah's legs, discreetly analyzing her scent. Demonstrating the natural courtesy of wolfkind, they never raised their eyes to her or Cutter. Nightrunner, who had a greater personal interest in anything that affected his bond-rider, was a bit more straightforward in his inspections. Growling conversationally to himself, the huge, shaggy wolf sniffed Leetah from head to foot, examined her red, gold-trimmed boots thoroughly, and then poked his snout under her fringed skirt. Leetah's eyes darted frantically from the nosing beast to Cutter. She knew not to do anything that might irritate the still-hungry creature, much as she wanted to kick and flail and drive the hideous fanged monster away from her. Nightrunner's hot breath sent prickles of fright darting up the length of her spine and all through her slender limbs. But Cutter and his pale-skinned companions were oblivious to her predicament, as though being sniffed in the most intimate manner by a beast who would stand twice her height on his hind legs should not cause Leetah the slightest discomfort or alarm. As the wolf completed his investigation, turning and padding away with a disdainful snort, Leetah renewed her struggles, hoping that somehow her people would hear the muffled cries that Cutter's strong hand strove to suppress.

Pausing on a narrow spur of rock, Rayek looked back and saw that the two hardiest of his followers had at last given up the climb until they could gain their second wind.

"Come on, you weaklings! Climb!" shouted Rayek.

One of the two, a dark-haired elf with a round, gentle face, hauled himself up to the spur on which Rayek stood and clung there, panting. Sweat poured down the villager's glowing body in streams.

"You are the mountain lion among us, Rayek," he gasped. "We can't keep up."

Grunting with disgust, Rayek placed his sandaled foot on the villager's shoulder and gave him a forceful shove. The hapless elf cried out and tumbled down the rocky slope until he was caught by his companion. With injured expressions they both lifted their eyes to Rayek.

"Go back to your gardens, dirt diggers," he spat cruelly. "You're no use to me or to Leetah. I'll save her myself!"

So saying, Rayek hefted his spear, stretched his sinewy legs and in a matter of moments was lost from sight among the crags above. Left behind to do what they would, many of the rescue party sighed with relief and began to creep back down the mountainside. Treestump, peering carefully over the lookout ledge, glimpsed the fluttering of Rayek's boldly patterned garb. The hunter was threading his way toward the summit, unknowingly getting closer to the Wolfriders' hiding place with every long-legged step.

My, my! He's a persistent one, I'll give him that! Treestump's open sending was tinged with amused admiration.

Leetah seemed finally to have worn herself out. She lay rigidly in Cutter's arms with one delicate, four-fingered hand braced against his chest, pushing stiffly. Her ragged captor kept his hand over her mouth, all the while smiling dreamily into her flashing eyes. Skywise bent over to look at her, his silvery head cocked at a questioning angle.

Cutter, do you think she knows how to send? She might give away our position.

The youthful chieftain shook his head. **No. She'd have done it long before now if she could. But one thing's certain.** He brought his cheek close to hers, an incongruously friendly and affectionate gesture considering the circumstances. **She knows how to scream!**

For what her voice could not do, Leetah's brilliant green eyes compensated, blazing above Cutter's encumbering fingers with all the intensity of a shriek of rage. She was not afraid, but her brown cheeks were flushed with red humiliation; it was a new and most unpleasant experience to be carted about like a sack of grain and held against her will. The beastlike scent and shabby, begrimed appearance of the Wolfriders offended her. The barbarian's rough manner had quite successfully squelched the ember of curiosity that had glimmered briefly in her heart. She was not interested in who they were, where they came from, or how they had survived in the deadly heat of the desert. Her only concern was escape and how that might be done as swiftly as possible.

Among the few grudging compliments the Wolfriders had ever been paid by their long-time enemies, the humans, one was a particular favorite. It was said that the breathing of a baby inside its mother's belly was easier to hear than a Wolfrider in hiding. It was also said that one might hear a single snowflake fall to the ground with the noise of a thunderclap before one heard the footfall of a Wolfrider who wished to pass by unnoticed. If Cutter's forest-born tribefolk shared one supreme skill in common, it was that of remaining totally silent for as long as it took to avoid an enemy.

Knowing that Rayek was near, the small band crouched down quietly among the rocks, listening for his approach. They could hear the stealthy tread of his sandals as he searched every crevice and crag, the *clack* of his spear as the long shaft occasionally tapped against a stone. So keen was the hearing of the Wolfriders that even Rayek's breathing told them much. Although he did not realize it, Rayek's anger and frustration, betrayed by his rapid, forceful breaths, were a source of amusement to the objects of his pursuit.

Cutter did everything in his power to keep Leetah still; bracing himself with his back propped against a rock, he tried holding her between his knees. The problem was that she jangled, particularly her golden bracelets, which rang together like the antlers of two rutting stags whenever she moved her arms. Each time Cutter managed to pin down one of those shapely arms, the other escaped, hammering a tiny, defiant fist against whatever part of his anatomy was closest. His knees suffered the most, but the elf chieftain endured without making a sound of complaint, much as he was tempted.

Seated close behind his friend, calmly nibbling on a crust of stolen bread, Skywise watched the ongoing struggle and knew that eventually Cutter would lose. The young chieftain grimaced with pain, inadvertently slackening his bearpaw grip on the lower half of Leetah's face. Naturally, her smothered cries became more audible, and so he clapped both hands even more tightly over her mouth, thus leaving both her arms free to flail and pummel at will. Skywise wondered why it had not yet occurred to Cutter to simply remove her jingling jewelry, but the stargazer was enjoying himself far too much to offer any advice that might spoil the fun.

Skywise, she's *biting* me!

Feeling some sympathy, Skywise offered, **Well, hit her.**

Cutter's eyes filled with horror. Shocked out of his pain at the idea, he quickly replied, **I can't do that!**

Then just tell her you'll do something awful to her if she doesn't behave herself.

Any moment now, Cutter knew that those delicate but determined teeth would draw blood. He grasped at the straw of hope hidden in his friend's cryptic advice.

What's the awful thing I'll do?

Skywise winked. **Let her wonder!**

That seemed reasonable to Cutter, who could no more conceive of harming Leetah than he could devise a suitable threat with which to frighten her into submission. He brought his lips close to her ear, was momentarily dazed by the spicy-sweet scent of her skin, and then tried to sound gruff and implacable as he whispered to her.

"Uh, listen. I'm going to take my hand away from your mouth, but if you scream, well, you won't like what will happen to you."

Skywise rolled his eyes up beneath his lids. He shook his head hopelessly.

As her lips were freed from Cutter's tooth-marked hand, Leetah stared at her captor, weighing the implications of his veiled threat against the nearness of the rescue party from which, she assumed, the Wolfriders were hiding. If she screamed to reveal her whereabouts, her people might not find her in time to save her from the barbarian's promised retaliation. But as she studied Cutter's face, the thought stole upon her that somehow she knew much about this pale-skinned, flea-ridden stranger. Unpredictable though his behavior might be, Leetah sensed that he would do no more and no less than he had promised. She would not like what would happen to her if she screamed. Trusting her intuition while keeping Cutter's warning firmly in mind, Leetah made her decision.

It was a wonderful scream, long and loud and exuberantly defiant. Later, she would remember fondly the fullness of the reverberations, how the mountains seemed to tremble in awe as the echoes of her audacious cry rebounded from slope to craggy slope long after her breath had fled.

Poised on a treacherously slanting ridge of stone, Rayek started at the sound and quickly determined that it came from a jumble of huge rocks less than a spear throw away. Boldly he called out, "Leetah? Leetah, I'm coming!" and began to cover the distance with effortless leaps.

Glaring daggers at Skywise, Cutter growled, "What now, wise one?"

The keeper of the lodestone shrugged philosophically and answered with understandable foresight, "I think we're going to have a visitor."

Wishing vindictively for the whole of the lodestone's parent star to come crashing down on Skywise's head, Cutter hoisted Leetah over his shoulders.

"Let me go, you savage," she shouted, unable to believe that all her wrestling and wriggling had been in vain. She had never been physically overpowered before and could not understand how the pale-haired stranger could hold her in such a degrading position despite her continued protests and struggles. "Put me down!" The demand was punctuated by blows from her fist, which Cutter, to her absolute outrage, ignored. Finally she called out in a desperate appeal to the rescue party that she believed her valiant friend Rayek had led to her captors' stronghold.

"Leetah!" Rayek answered her cry for help. "Where are you?"

As he reached his quarry's hiding place, Rayek could smell the musky odor of the wolves. He knew beyond a doubt that the Wolfriders had followed the progress of his search since he first set foot on the mountainside. He was one against many, and he did not have the element of surprise in his favor. Rayek sensed the lurking presence of the pale ones and their ferocious mounts all around him, although they were quite thoroughly hidden from his eyes. Determined to demonstrate his fearlessness and utter contempt for the thieving strangers, he stood with feet firmly planted and chin haughtily high, daring the Wolfriders to attack him if they would.

"Where is Leetah?" he demanded aloud. "If you've harmed her, barbarians, I—"

"Calm down, Black Hair, she's fine!"

Remembering his sore jaw, Rayek whirled and pointed his spear at the sound of that hated voice. Cutter stood with one foot on a small rock and Leetah draped awkwardly over his shoulder like a rolled-up rug. She seemed uninjured, but her fallen countenance was proof that Rayek's lone arrival had disappointed her keenly. Now she regretted the cry that had guided him to her, for surely her brave but brashly arrogant friend would be taken even as she had been.

"In fact," Cutter said with a grin, assuring the solitary rescuer, "she's very strong!"

This prompted more kicking and scratching and pummeling with fists, all of which Cutter endured stoically. At her wit's end, the infuriated beauty shouted, "Rayek, do something!"

The black-haired hunter aimed his spear at Cutter's exposed middle.

"Release her, land-rat, or I'll—"

"No, I don't think so." The cheerful interruption came from behind and above him. Rayek felt something hard tap his shoulder; moving only his eyes, he saw that it was the sharp bone tip of a spear, crudely fashioned but nonetheless deadly. Rayek's gaze traveled up the length of the spear shaft and fixed upon the face of the weapon's owner.

"Boo," said Pike.

Rayek had not realized that the Wolfriders had managed to surround him so closely and so silently. Pike smirked down on him from atop a large oblong stone that lay lengthwise among other oddly shaped rocks bordering Rayek's intended path of escape. From the shadows of these rocks, six pairs of wickedly slanting eyes gleamed above six different but equally lethal tools for puncturing flesh and spilling blood. All were pointed at Rayek.

Still carrying Leetah across his shoulders, Cutter walked toward Rayek with a not-unfriendly smile. But Rayek spat in the dust at Cutter's feet, stopping the young chieftain cold in his tracks.

"Jackal! Leader of jackals!"

Cutter looked at the wad of spittle and then at Rayek. "I said, calm down. You're not impressing anyone." There was more menace in his tone now, although he continued to smile.

Forgetting her own humiliation, Leetah was aghast that anyone should speak so disrespectfully to Rayek. Even she, with her delicate gibes and tauntings, had never tempted fate by pushing him too far. Beneath the wide, colorfully striped headband he wore, Rayek's scowl was as black and brooding as any she had ever seen. It boded no good. Violence hovered in the air like a bird of prey; it was not long in making its swift descent.

Pike clambered over the oblong rock and hopped to the ground, casually strolling to Rayek's side. With his plain bone-tipped spear resting on his shoulder, Pike reached for the hunter's elegant metal-pointed lance.

"Let's have the pig poker, long face."

The instant he felt the cocky Wolfrider's fingers touch his weapon, Rayek spun around with a snarl that would have done the fiercest wolf credit.

"You dare?"

Rayek's amber eyes bored into Pike's blue-gray ones. Unable to look away, the round-faced Wolfrider stiffened until his posture was like that of a wooden doll. As Pike's jocular features sagged into a disturbing, empty-eyed blankness, his horrified tribesmen knew at once that Rayek's chilling stare was the direct cause.

Realizing that this was the sinister, will-sapping power whose paralyzing effect he had barely sampled during his first encounter with the black-haired one, Cutter yelled, "Whoa! This one can do more than send! Pin him down and cover his eyes. He may have other tricks!"

Even before the words were finished, Treestump, Strongbow, Woodlock, One-Eye, and Scouter had piled themselves on Rayek like a litter of new-weaned cubs fighting over a scrap of meat. They slammed him to the ground, rendering him helpless beneath their weight. Meanwhile, Skywise stayed with Pike, waving his hand before the stricken Wolfrider's eyes in an effort to bring him back to himself. Pike remained motionless and insensible as a petrified log.

"Pike? Wake up!" Skywise wasn't sure, but he thought he detected a flicker of awareness in his friend's unblinking eyes.

Since her capture, Leetah's emotions had ranged from livid incredulity to purple indignation to blackest outrage and all the tints between. But to her own surprise, fright had remained only a subtle, background color on the picture-wall of her passions. Why this was so she did not know, except that it had something to do with her young captor, who made her feel everything but fear—and one other emotion.

Untroubled by concern for her own safety, she felt Rayek's plight suddenly filling her heart with dread. From her uncomfortable vantage upon Cutter's fur-clad shoulders, she looked down at the writhing pile of barbarians and was able to glimpse only a dark clenched fist or a sandaled foot belonging to her overpowered champion. She was afraid for him, afraid of what the pale-skinned savages might do to him unless their chieftain willed otherwise.

"Don't let them kill Rayek. Please! I'll do anything you say." She spoke to Cutter softly, anxiously, in tones not unlike those of her first words to him.

Cutter was startled, partly because of the genuine fear in Leetah's voice and partly because she so mistakenly thought it necessary to bargain for her erstwhile rescuer's life with her own. He gently set her on her feet and looked at her, for once, as a being separate from himself. This was a very difficult thing to do, much like regarding his own hand or foot or tongue as an independent entity with needs and desires different from his. Her rebellious struggles had made no sense to him, and so he had dismissed them. Surely she knew, surely she understood the thing that had happened to them both so suddenly, the thing that could not be described in mere words.

He tried sending to her, hoping that she might at least be receptive to his thoughts if unable to give forth her own. He wanted her to know with the absolute soul-felt honesty of one mind touching another that he would not permit anyone she cared for to be harmed. But her inner mind-ways were constricted—deliberately, it seemed—protecting even the topmost layers of her self-without-form from unwanted contact. Never had sending been such an effort for the Wolfriders' young chief, and when his stream of thought had ceased its flow, he felt uncertain as never before that any communion had been achieved.

Gazing into the jewels—the color of leaves in New Green—that were Leetah's eyes, Cutter was silent for what seemed to her a very long time. With his altered perception of her as an individual rather than as an extension of himself came the full and stunning impact of her beauty, beauty that was alien and yet somehow familiar, like the recurrence of a forgotten dream. New responses awakened in Cutter in that moment, and he smiled; his first taste of desire was as sharp and sweet as honey from the comb.

"Take your filthy hands off me, you wild dogs!" Rayek lay spread-eagled on his back, with a Wolfrider holding down each straining limb. Scouter had slipped his fingers beneath the black-haired hunter's headband and was gleefully tugging the cloth down over those dangerous amber eyes. Rayek shouted again.

"By the lost dwelling of the High Ones, you'll pay for this!"

The effect of the words was instant and galvanic. Everyone froze in midmotion and stared at the blindfolded prisoner. A moment later, a buzz of startled "How's that?"s and "What?"s circulated among the Wolfriders like seedlings caught in a whirlwind. His large, pointed ears quivering as they took in the offensive oath, Cutter abruptly abandoned Leetah and stalked to Rayek's side.

"What do you know of the High Ones, Black Hair?" The sunburned chieftain stooped and roughly peeled back the band of cloth from the hunter's eyes. "Speak! You dare profane our ancient fathers?" Cutter was too incensed to fear Rayek's serpentlike, trance-inducing powers, and Rayek was not fool enough to use them in his vulnerable position. Glowering contemptuously at his enemy, the proud captive did not deign to respond.

"We are all descendants of the High Ones, stranger." Leetah came forward in a rustle of skirts and a chiming of golden jewelry. The Wolfriders watched her with puzzled frowns as she indicated her tapered ears and graceful, four-fingered hand. "Can you not see that we are all of one race?"

While Cutter and his tribesmen mulled this new idea over, Rayek, fuming, struggled to a sitting position and adjusted his skewed headband. "I claim no kinship with this vermin," he spat.

Leetah hastened to kneel beside her discomfited friend, reassuring herself that only his dignity had been harmed. She hushed him with a word and then addressed the Wolfriders, her attention directed particularly at Cutter. "Who are you, pale ones?"

The young chieftain rose, resting his arm on the head of the gray-furred beast to whom he seemed bonded in more than simple brotherhood. "We are Wolfriders from the faraway woodlands," he said. "And for three days we have journeyed through the burning waste." A sweep of his arm indicated the direction from which the group had come.

Rayek sprang to his feet, jabbing a finger at Cutter's face. "You lie! No one can cross the desert and live!"

"Desert, eh?" said Skywise, rolling the lodestone pensively between his fingers. He gazed beyond the village, past the wide gap in the curving flank of the mountain range that cradled the group of huts and gardens, and saw, beyond a great stone arch and a smoking mountain, more white flat ground stretching in near-unbroken smoothness toward Sun-Goes-Up. The elfin village was surrounded on all sides by the desert, the only spot of green in a wilderness of sand. Skywise gave Rayek a calculating look and said, "If this desert can't be crossed, how did *your* people get here, Black Hair?"

The sullen hunter's reply was not forthcoming, but Leetah impatiently spoke as if to interrupt him. "There are too many questions to be answered now. Come down to the village, all of you. My father, the Sun-Toucher, will know if you are telling the truth." There was an edge to her voice that hinted that she had not forgotten the indignities she had suffered at the Wolfriders' hands. "And if he finds no deceit in you, we will help you as we can."

Rayek believed this offer to be much too generous. Secretly, he hoped that the Sun-Toucher, with his infallible insight, would discover some evil motive behind the Wolfriders' unforeseen arrival. That the tribe of pale wanderers existed at all was a marvel that even Rayek could not dismiss. The Sun Village had nurtured its inhabitants in such perfect isolation for so long that the dark-skinned elves had never dreamed of encountering others of their kind or even imagined that "others" existed. Despite Leetah's assertion that the Wolfriders were of one race with the Sun Villagers, Rayek's mistrust of the strangers grew deeper by the moment;

antipathy toward Cutter inflamed his brain like the sting of a scorpion. Although he did not understand why, Leetah's handsome suitor sensed that the Wolfriders' mangy young chieftain would soon be his rival, in more ways than one.

A low, warning growl from the wolves alerted their elf-friends that something was amiss. The great beasts' ears were pricked, their nostrils twitching, as the wolves sniffed toward the lookout ledge. At a nod from Cutter, Scouter left his closely grouped tribesmen to find out what or who was approaching. The youth fell on his belly and crept to the rim of the overhanging shelf of rock. Meanwhile, Nightrunner uttered several deep, imperious woofs, his brush extended with hairs partially raised. Leetah and Rayek observed with rising curiosity the wordless but effective communication and wondered what it meant.

Almost immediately Scouter returned, barely suppressing a fit of chuckles. There was a momentary silence as he sent openly to share what he had just seen. Soft, sly smiles bloomed on the Wolfriders' lips. Leetah and Rayek sensed, uncomfortably, that they were the butt of some secret jest.

"What is it?" Rayek demanded.

"Your rescue party," laughed Cutter, "has finally arrived!"

A more bruised, bedraggled, woebegone group of would-be saviors never hauled one foot in front of the other. Of all the villagers who had started off in pursuit of Leetah's kidnappers, only six had persevered, lighting upon the Wolfriders' hiding place by merest chance. The puffing rescuers halted together in the space between two giant, crazily angled crags, looking up at their quarry, open-mouthed, panting, hoes and spades dangling uselessly from their limp hands.

"We'll save you, Leetah," said one between gasps.

She looked at them and shook her head, hiding a small smile behind her fingertips. To their credit, the Wolfriders did not exploit the opportunity to ridicule her people's lack of stamina. For that she was grateful. She turned and took Rayek's arm, preparing to descend the rocky slope to the village.

"Wait," called Cutter. "There are more of us hiding on the other side of the mountain."

Astonished, Leetah turned to him. "More of you?" she echoed.

Rayek scowled, his heart twisting within his breast. More than ever, he was one against many. The rivalry had begun.

"You will *not* send," hissed Clearbrook in a thirst-broken whisper. Her gray eyes flashed a stern rebuff at Dewshine.

The not-quite-adult huntress glared back at her elder; then, her defiance expressed, she crouched on lean, sun-reddened haunches and stared at the dust beneath her sandaled feet.

"It will be dark before long," Dewshine muttered sullenly. "The sun was much higher in the sky when they started over the mountain. What's happened to them?"

Clearbrook knew that Treestump's golden-haired daughter spoke for all her sister Wolfriders. Like she-wolves who must remain by the den to protect their cubs while the males hunt, Moonshade, Rainsong, Clearbrook, and Dewshine had been forbidden from adding their strength to the raiding party. Although they understood why Cutter had decided thus, the decision still rankled.

"It's hardest for me," Clearbrook quietly told her tribeswomen, aiming her words particularly at Dewshine. "I've borne my young. One is dead, and one lived to become your lovemate, pretty cub. Since Scouter's birth I have felt a stillness in me; there will come, I think, no more new life from my body. But what if I am mistaken? Only the High Ones know if Nightfall is gone, by now, with Redlance. We four, and Newstar when she is grown, are the last hope of renewal. That is why I am here with you instead of on the other side of the mountain with my son and lifemate."

"What has happened to them?" Moonshade said, echoing Dewshine's earlier query. "Are they in battle with these dark-skinned elves?" A thrill of wonder and dread at her own words caused Moonshade to shudder; even in her most

delirious moments during the past three days, she had
never dreamed that the journey's end would hold the discovery of others of her kind. "Are our mates captured?
Killed? Or do they wait for the cover of night to conceal
their attack?"

"We dare not send to find out," Clearbrook asserted.
"Who knows but these brown-skinned ones have powers
greater than ours. In our concern we could betray Cutter
and the others."

"Not if we lock-send," Dewshine interrupted. "How
could those strange elves possibly seize upon a lock-send? It
can't be done!" She stood up excitedly. "Let me try to reach
Scouter. The strangers won't detect my sending, I swear it!"

"No!" Clearbrook leaped instantly to her feet, ready to
strike the impetuous young one senseless if all else failed.
But just as her fingers rolled threateningly into a tightly
clenched fist, Clearbrook started and glanced quickly at the
peaks high above her.

At the same time, Rainsong went rigid, totally alert, while
Moonshade blinked her huge eyes and began to smile. Realizing what was happening, Dewshine cleared her mind of its
clutter of emotion and was rewarded by the sweet, reassuring touch of Scouter's projected thoughts glowing within
her being like a brilliant star. Almost at once, sendings from
both Treestump and Cutter jostled pleasantly for her attention against Scouter's insistent call.

"They live! They live, and we are to join them!" Rainsong
sighed, clinging to the last caress of Woodlock's sending
before his glow winked out of her mind.

Newstar, who was as yet unskilled at receiving the cast
thoughts of her tribefolk, understood her mother's relief
well enough to smile delightedly and fling her wasted arms
about Dart. The children's smudged and wan features had
never looked more beautiful to Rainsong than at that
moment.

Eight

Crowding and fluttering together like a flock of waterfowl encircling a hapless school of minnows, the dusky Sun Villagers vied with one another for the best view of the pale-skinned barbarians and their comely mates. Although less sudden and much less violent, the Wolfriders' second entry into the village caused almost as much commotion as their first. They had come, two eights less one strong, down the mountainside, led by Leetah and Rayek and flanked by straggling members of the rescue party, who gave the prowling wolves a respectfully wide berth.

Feelings, understandably sore over damage done during the raid, still hung in the hot afternoon air. The stares that greeted the wild forest folk were not altogether friendly, but the Wolfriders made no apology. They walked with chins high and eyes focused straight ahead, proud and strong despite their travails. The Wolfriders and their panting mounts followed Leetah and Rayek to a patch of grass growing by a cobbled walkway near the entrance to the village's tall central hut. There the forest elves gathered, wary and sullen now, shifting uncomfortably under the direct scrutiny of so many staring eyes. The wolves, pacing back and forth restlessly with lowered heads and drooping tails, stepped protectively between their elf-friends and the crowd of chattering strangers.

Although soft-mannered and physically frail, the dark-skinned desert folk evidently were not timid creatures. Inexperience with conflict, not cowardice, had caused their panic and flight during the Wolfriders' attack. Now, open curiosity all but supplanted the mistrust and resentment that had been visible moments before on their faces. It was difficult for the Wolfriders to gain a single clear impression of the desert elves' appearance, so confusingly bright and varied were the colors of their elaborate clothing. The villagers seemed taller than the forest-born intruders, but their eyes were similarly large and slanted, and their ears were as handsomely pointed at the tips as any elf could wish. They gabbled incessantly in tones much louder than those the Wolfriders habitually used for speaking; clearly, life in this desert hideaway was so tranquil and safe that these dark-skinned ones could raise their voices at any time without fear of altering a hidden enemy.

From among the confusion of unfamiliar scents that filled the air, a tangy-sweet odor of flowers wafted to Cutter's nostrils as the jeweled curtain covering the doorway to the central hut parted. The heady scent contained a presence that seemed both part and source of the aura that surrounded the entire tall structure. The heart and soul of the Sun Village lay behind the gossamer curtain—Cutter was positive of it, although he did not know why. Again, his body's inner rhythm merged with the insistent, repetitious riddle that pounded in his brain: Sorrow's End . . . Sorrow's End . . . Sorrow's End. What did it mean? Cutter feared he might go mad if the answer did not present itself soon.

Leetah flew into her father's arms as the Sun-Toucher stepped from the folds of the beaded curtain to greet her. Sightless eyes moist, lips parted in a tremulous smile, he softly spoke words of gratitude to Rayek. The black-haired hunter acknowledged the thanks with a sour expression, which, fortunately, the Sun-Toucher could not see. Draped in the flowing sleeves of her father's blue-green robe, Leetah rested against him a moment and then turned to embrace two of the female villagers to whom she bore a strong resemblance. The older of the two, dressed in a long hooded gown, was Leetah's mother, Toorah; the other, a maiden whose reddish-brown hair was twisted into two charming topknots on either side of her head, was Shenshen, Leetah's younger sister.

Sun-Toucher struck his staff against a carved stone pedestal. The sharp tapping caught the attention of the villagers immediately; their chatter subsided as they obediently backed away from the objects of their curiosity. With sure and steady steps, Leetah's leather-faced father came forward, stopping exactly two of his own body lengths away from the gathered Wolfriders.

Cutter had never seen an elf with so many seasons on him or one whose face was crisscrossed with fine lines like those that marred the skin of swiftly aging humans. His calm, commanding mien marked the Sun-Toucher as a figure of some authority. Yet as with Rayek, Cutter sensed that the blind one was not truly the leader of the village. Separating from his tribefolk, the young chieftain took several hesitant steps toward the regally garbed elf. Somehow, those sightless eyes put him at ease.

"Call me Sun-Toucher," said the elder, genially tilting his helmeted head. The iridescent scales covering his headdress winked and glimmered with the movement. "I do not see with my eyes, Wolfriders, for I gave them up to the almighty Daystar many years ago." He lifted his staff, indicating the afternoon sun. "But the heart can learn to see more deeply than the eye." Cutter shied back a step as the Sun-Toucher, still speaking in even, gentle tones, approached him with hand outstretched. "Let me 'look' at you now."

Nervously the Wolfriders' chief held his ground, not knowing what to expect. The robed elder's fingers never touched his pale skin, yet a weird, warm sensation spread through Cutter's mind and body, a feeling that could only imperfectly be described as contact-communion-exchange. The Sun-Toucher smiled an enigmatic half smile and laid down his staff, moving toward the other Wolfriders, some of whom could not conceal their misgivings. He held both hands before him now, brown palms facing outward. His fingers caressed the air, seeking, probing; but what they actually touched and tested, the tired "barbarians" could not guess. All of Cutter's tribefolk experienced in turn the strange feeling of unspoken communion—a feeling that was similar to sending but was not sending as they understood it. The Sun-Toucher's smile was soft with satisfaction, and when his many-seamed hands passed near Newstar, Dart, and Wing, a look of deepest empathy crinkled his brow.

"I sense great weariness and hidden sorrow for the loss of all that you have known," he murmured, his hands passing from Clearbrook and One-Eye to rest above Rainsong's leather-capped head. From the depths of a profound trance his voice rose in singsong fashion to embrace the entire tribe. "Your days have been perilous, yet you have endured them with courage and a ferocious will to survive. Life and all it means is precious to you, more so because your number is small."

Cutter gasped as though an arrow had thudded between his shoulder blades. He cried, "Redlance and Nightfall!" shattering the solemn hush that had settled on the village. The sudden interruption startled Leetah's father so that he tottered and nearly lost his balance.

Hastily picking up the discarded staff and placing it in its sightless owner's hand, Rayek shot a poisonous glance at Cutter; but the remonstrance was lost upon the Wolfriders' impulsive chief, for he had summoned Nightrunner to him and was about to clamber onto the wolf's lean back.

"Forgive me, Sun-Toucher," Cutter said, "but we had to leave two of us behind in the desert. One was injured, dying. I've got to go back for them before it's too late!"

The notion was so ridiculous that the Sun-Toucher could not believe his own instinctive urge to take it seriously. "But you are exhausted, young chieftain," he protested above the renewed jabber of the crowd, "and so is your beast!"

"No matter," Cutter insisted stubbornly. "I promised Redlance and Nightfall that I would return to fetch them after we reached the mountains. Redlance might still be alive." He paused and scanned the astonished faces of the villagers. "If there is a healer among you who dares follow me, let him do so now! I'm going!"

In his heart Cutter did not dare to hope that any of the dark strangers would answer the challenge. He could not blame them. It was too much to ask of anyone. Were he not too tired to reason clearly, even he would think twice about setting foot again on the burning, hard-baked flatland, vow or no vow. Then, too, he realized, he did not even know if among the village's chattering inhabitants there was a healer.

No healer came forward. Perhaps, thought Cutter, in the peace and safety of their total isolation, these strange, slow-moving elves had no sicknesses or injuries to mend. The young chieftain could no longer afford to waste time wondering; his madness had spread among the other Wolfriders with the speed of a brush fire in a dry wind. Spent as they all were, some even offered to go in his place, eager to render what aid they could to the two missing tribe members. But Cutter remained willfully determined to keep his word. Anyone might accompany him, but the first face Nightfall would see coming out of the darkness of this night would be his.

"Wait, Wolfrider. I am a healer."

Almost unnoticed, the day's second miracle occurred with the crisp utterance of those few words. Cutter turned Nightrunner around and rocked back on the wolf's bony spine. Like the waters of the Holt's small running stream, a calmness washed over his dirt-smeared features. Why not? he thought. She was the completion of his every half-dreamed dream. Why should he be at all surprised that Leetah was a healer? It was she who had spoken, and it was she who would help him keep his promise to Redlance and golden-eyed Nightfall. A crushing weight seemed suddenly to lift from him as Cutter realized that the wholeness of his people would never again rest solely on his shoulders.

Appalled, Rayek clutched Leetah's arm. "What are you saying?" He nearly choked on his own rage. "I forbid it!"

Her head swiveled with slow elegance until she looked directly at Rayek. Then only her eyes moved as she glanced coolly from the hand upon her arm to those amber orbs whose gaze, for once, lacked their usual piercing confidence.

"You forbid?" she asked evenly.

The clutching fingers relaxed their grip and reluctantly fell away.

"Forgive me," Rayek whispered. "But at least let me go with you."

Leetah's frown disappeared, and a smile of welcome blossomed in its place. Rayek had traveled boldly beyond the confines of the village many a time. He had even gone as far as the Sunken Peaks, a cruel desolation of crippling stones and barren dryness several days' walk, Rayek had told her, from the village. Leetah was careful not to reveal the full measure of her gladness at the hunter's offered company, for she was more frightened by the thought of venturing into the desert than she wished anyone to know.

"What will you ride?" Cutter asked her, anxious to be on his way. "You have no wolf."

In response, Leetah turned to a nearby villager and requested him to saddle two mounts, one for herself and one for Rayek. The Wolfriders were frankly curious to discover just what sort of beasts the dark elves would choose to ride. Scouter had his suspicions and saw them confirmed as the villager returned towing two of the hump-backed "deer-sloths" Scouter had glimpsed and so named during the raid.

Both of the peculiar creatures stood two elves tall at the shoulder, and much of their height was in their treacherously slender legs. Viewed from the front, the animals resembled nothing so much as fat bolls of twigs; their bodies bulged roundly above their reedy limbs and seemed likely, as Treestump put it, to snap clean off at the knees in a stiff breeze. At the point where neck met shoulder, each beast sported a large fleshy hump. Their backs sloped precipitously toward long, tufted tails, creating the illusion that their hind legs were shorter than their forelegs. The snouts were long and narrow with cleft upper lips and flaps of skin over the nostrils. The best that could be said of the dull eyes, partly hidden beneath stringy forelocks, was that they drooped.

Dewshine regarded the outlandish beasts doubtfully. "What are those queer things strapped to their backs?" she asked her father.

Treestump studied the quilted, wedge-shaped saddles. They made an odd kind of sense to him in view of the animals' hazardous design.

"I couldn't put a name to those things, pretty cub, but I'm guessing you sit on them. See how they're built up in back to make you ride level?"

Pursing her lips, the young huntress decided at once that she would not like to have such bulky trappings between her and her wolf's back. "I feel Trollhammer's muscles move beneath me when we run," she said, stroking her mount's coarse fur. "Our bodies talk to each other. We know things. That's the only way to ride."

Treestump chuckled. "Maybe so. Of course, I can't see one of these things actually running. But imagine straddling that tall beast's bare back." He pointed at one of the creatures as it shuffled around, giving the Wolfriders a full side view of its hilly contours. "Sit atop a slope like that, and you'll find yourself tumbling downhill faster than a mudbug rolling off a rotten log!"

During this conversation Leetah and Rayek had been collecting things for their ride, receiving a little too much well-meant assistance from their fellow villagers. His patience wearing thin, Cutter was glad that Rayek seemed to hold sway over his people. One sharp word from the black-haired hunter put an instant stop to the time-consuming suggestions and offers of supplies, most of which were more meddlesome than helpful. Finally, the saddles were fitted with water-bags, foodstuffs, blankets, and the materials for a litter, should one be needed. A ladder made of fine cord was hitched under the side flap of each saddle; when unrolled, the ladders brushed the ground, enabling Leetah and Rayek to climb up and seat themselves astride their huge mounts.

"We go north?" Rayek curtly asked Cutter. The pale chieftain answered him with a blank stare.

"We came from that way," Skywise offered, pointing. "From where the hub of the sky-wheel shines."

Rayek's mouth twisted disdainfully. "We go north," he said.

Sun-Toucher frowned, sensing the friction between Rayek and the newcomers. He heard plodding hoofbeats, the rustle of the crowd, and calls of "Farewell," "Good fortune," "Shade and sweet water."

It had been a day of new things, a day of changes, and the blind one saw that the shifting of patterns had only begun.

Nightfall awoke, dizzy and faint, to Woodshaver's nuzzlings. The wolf put his great paw on her shoulder and touched his nose to hers, whining softly. With a start she sat up and peered around. Mist clouded her vision, but whether the haze was born of the land and its tricks of light or rose behind her eyes from the marshes of her own overweary mind, she could not say. She looked down anxiously at Redlance. He lay very still beside her, barely breathing. His lips were cracked and dry, and his flesh was the color of sand.

Nightfall reached for Cutter's water-skin, knowing that it contained a few drops at most. She undid the cap and lay down beside her lifemate. Moistening her fingers, she gently brushed them across his lips and cheeks, watching him closely for the slightest response. He remained as motionless as death.

Beyond sorrow, she turned over and propped her back against the ragged column of stone that towered above her like some giant, silent guardian. Gripping the water-skin by its neck, she held it aloft, saluting her tribe's still-visible tracks, which pocked the smooth ground between skull-like boulders and scattered shrubs. Then she put the container to her parched lips and drained it in one swallow, casting the empty skin into the dust as though discarding the last of her futile hopes. Woodshaver got to his feet and trotted over to sniff the water-skin. He licked the rim of the opening, took the skin in his jaws, and worried it; then he moved off to lie down and methodically begin chewing the oiled but edible leather bag to bits. Nightfall shrugged.

When last she had measured the shadow of the pillar of rock, before dozing off, it had been shorter by half. Somehow, a leaf of time had fallen from the branch of day without her awareness. The sun was low, beginning to set. Had she slept? She could not remember. Nightfall wondered whether the Wolfriders had managed to reach the mountains; if they had, were they any better off than she?

Slowly, the sky's red hue deepened; tortured rock spires surrounding the solitary elfin pair bled lengthening pools of shadow across the cooling desert floor. The elongated purple shadows reminded Nightfall of tall trees mingling barren trunks against fire-colored snow. While she gazed absently at the slice of shadow in which she lay, her golden eyes tracing its jagged edge as it stabbed toward Sun-Goes-Up, Nightfall was startled by a sudden flutter of movement near the tip of the shadow. Something crouched upon the crown of the monolith—something alive. Nightfall turned and craned her slender neck to see what it was.

Hunched over, dumb and brutally calm in its singleness of purpose, a scavenger bird clung to the rock with its hooked talons, simply waiting. It cocked an eye downward, regarding the two elves almost disinterestedly, and then blinked and righted its ugly, blue, warty head and resumed its placid vigil. Nightfall felt hatred for the dark-plumed creature press within her—not for the bird's intentions, which were understandable, but for the infuriating lack of urgency with which those intentions were displayed. So certain was the blade-beaked carrion eater of its eventual feast that it did not show even the slightest impatience.

Nightfall clenched her teeth, snarling, alert now, her brown curls tossing about her shoulders as she whirled to snatch up a stone. Standing protectively over her nearly dead mate, she hurled the sharp-edged missile hard at the avian silhouette atop the stone pillar. Aimed well and true, the rock sped through the air and struck the startled bird squarely in the breast.

"Away, scavenger," Nightfall shouted. "Leave us alone!"

The ghoulish creature squawked indignantly, flapping its wings in an effort to regain its perch. A second stone, thrown unerringly, nearly split the bird's curved beak in two. Wisely, it vacated its watch and flew away a little unsteadily. Lost pinfeathers spun downward, unnoticed, to settle on the ground. Nightfall's eyes followed the scavenger as it glided toward a new perch atop a crooked finger of rock not far away; she knew that it would be back before long, peering coldly down at Redlance, simply waiting. Her breasts heaved as all strength drained at once from her diminutive body and her mighty spirit.

"Leave us alone," she whimpered, collapsing beside her lifemate.. Tears she had not thought were left to her coursed down her cheeks and fell upon the exposed skin above Redlance's travel-stained bandage. His arms lay limply at his sides, incapable of holding and comforting her. His lips, dry as dust, could not smile tenderly or speak. His eyelids were sealed shut.

"Alone," Nightfall sobbed, "forever!"

She laid her hollow, high-boned cheek against his chest, and once more the star of her sending blazed within the emptiness of his inner passages.

Beloved, she sent. **Give me your soul name. I will take it now and give you mine!**

The soul name of a Wolfrider; it was the sum and substance of his or her being. A word-sound-concept for all there is: flesh, bone, blood, thought, dream, instinct, spirit. A secret name. A cushion and barrier to protect the deepmost private self through a lifetime, however long or short. A name never spoken aloud, save by a chosen lifemate—the only one other than parent entitled to claim knowledge of the totality of a Wolfrider's being.

Redlance did not answer. No matter how desperate her call, Nightfall could not summon a response.

So the brief span of their seasons was over. There would be no more growing, no further intertwining, vinelike. No more bee and flower.

Beloved, I am Twen ... Twen, friend of your body and spirit. Twen. Nightfall gave freely now what she had always hoped her lifemate would find for himself. Her soul name swam in a bottomless black pool, small and insignificant in the fearsome void that heralded encroaching death. Her gift was not refused. It simply could not be received.

Unwilling to leave that place which had once been all that completed her, Nightfall took refuge in dreams of the past. Around her star she gathered fond memories of moments, of days, of seasons illuminated by the joy, quiet or fierce, of her bond with Redlance.

In gossamer remembrance she curled with him, asleep, her body not yet fully mature, in the secret breathing hollows of their tree-home. In those days they called him Redmark, marker of the faintest blood trail, marked by his long, flame-red hair, he who loved the hunt more than the kill.

Another fragment: She saw him, terrified, pale as a toadstool, set himself between the suddenly charging long-tooth cat and his chief, Bearclaw, who writhed madly to free himself from the constricting tendrils of a strangleweed. The powerful flesh eater launched itself at the two elves; Redmark braced the butt of his spear shaft against the ground, bright metal tip angled toward the descending monster's throat. The surprised long-tooth impaled itself fatally, the momentum of its convulsing body carrying it over Redmark's head to crash into Bearclaw. The bearded chieftain was flattened beneath the beast's weight; tusks the length of his forearm plunged deep into Bearclaw's shoulder. Nightfall saw her own bloodied hands next to Redmark's, working carefully to lift the gigantic feline's head while other Wolfriders rolled the twitching carcass off Bearclaw's mangled chest. It took Rain the Healer almost two cycles of the greater moon to mend his chief, and when he could talk, the first thing Bearclaw said to Redmark was, "Idiot." But he was smiling wickedly through his whiskers as he proclaimed that Redmark the Tracker would thereafter be known as Redlance the Long-Tooth Killer. Nightfall laughed within herself at the mixture of pride and embarrassment that had flushed her lovemate's skin nearly as red as his hair.

"I would rather it was Redlance the Tree-Shaper," he said shyly. How she hoped his wish would come true so that, at last, he would know himself and be happy.

More memories flowed, of hunts and Howls, of exquisite joinings, of tree-green cool-water scent-shining shadow-wood climbing-high home.

What was that? A call? Not from Redlance. He was beyond reach. A dream, then. Part of Nightfall's circle of images and sensations recalled.

The dreams began to smother her star of sending. She diminished bit by bit in the endless empty maze left behind by Redlance's retreating spirit. Somewhere his soul clung with the fragile talons of a dying butterfly to the broken matter of his body. It was a final ledge, a leaping-off place that not even she, with all her need, could find.

She withdrew her star, and it shimmered to her at great speed, growing larger and larger until it burst behind her eyes in a sheet of purest white light. Now that she was within herself again, her golden eyes opened, perceiving a reality that was the desert, a reality her other senses gradually confirmed.

It was night; nocturnal creatures filled the pallid moon-light with scuttling movements and tiny sounds. Hard-edged knots of cloud, gray trimmed with white, drifted beneath unnumbered burning knife pricks in the blue-black sky. The ground was cold and hard, and Nightfall's body ached from head to foot. But her own pains were unimportant, for after a brave struggle of many days, Redlance was surrendering at last. The cherished pulse beat that had lulled her, even at the worst of times, to peaceful sleep was fitful. Nightfall did not lift her head but kept her ear pressed hard against Redlance's breast. His heart thudded dully, unevenly, uselessly.

"Stop! Stop now," she ordered the cruelly stubborn organ. "Enough!" Redlance suffered, she was certain. As her head moved with his labored breaths, she reached to touch his cheek once with her left hand. Then that hand slid gently along his body and came to rest upon the wooden hilt of her hunting knife. It was time. Her heart held no hope, and she would not permit the suffering to continue another moment.

"*Ayooooah!*"

What? she thought. The dream call again?

"Nightfall!"

No! Not a dream! Incredibly, not a dream!

Cutter's arms were around her. She felt him, scented him, cried his name. Her legs would not support her, but his embrace held her upright, reassuring her. Somehow water passed her lips, cooled her throat. Her vision cleared. Before her were Cutter's large, blue eyes, reflecting doubled moons, examining her with deep concern. There was someone beside him—who? An elf, surely, but so dark!

"Who is she?" Nightfall stammered, her tearful eyes riveted upon Leetah.

"Shhh." Cutter soothed his friend. "This maiden can help Redlance."

Without hesitation Leetah sank to her knees beside the stricken Wolfrider. She took his hand in hers and touched him, and suddenly her look of detached interest altered to one of shock and disbelief.

"These wounds were deliberately inflicted!" She was horrified. "Who could have done such a thing?"

"Humans," Cutter growled. "The same ones who tried to destroy us with fire!"

Nightfall flinched and shrank against her chief as a second strange elf came to stand beside them. He was tall, with hair as black as night, and he was dark-skinned like the other. His manner was arrogance itself.

"Really?" said Rayek, his tone openly mocking. "Humans, you say? We have legends of such creatures, but I never believed them."

Cutter pointed angrily at Redlance. "You're looking at their handiwork right now."

"Silence," hissed the black-haired one. "The healing begins."

Leetah still knelt by Redlance, but now her back was arched, her head tilted toward the heavens. The curve of her throat revealed taut cords of strength beneath her supple flesh. Her arms stretched downward; her eight fingers spread wide and pressed hard upon Redlance's upper chest. Abruptly her hands snapped shut into tightly closed fists, as though she had just snatched an insect from the air. In the vulnerability of her exhaustion, Nightfall knew somehow that the thing that had been captured in midflight was nothing less than Redlance's life.

Not a word was spoken, not a sound uttered, yet great power surged and flowed as Leetah sank ever deeper into her dreamlike trance. Her hands, conduits for a radiant current of healing force, lay upon the center of the damage. Beneath her ministering fingers, splintered bones grated and began hesitantly to knit, torn tissues lapped and mended, and hidden bleeding subsided. At the same time, Leetah exerted her will upon the heart, coaxing, cajoling, ignoring its protests, making sure that its throbbing pace held steady until it could beat on its own.

A dazed, barely comprehending Nightfall observed the healing. She lacked the strength to be curious about the two strange elves, stunned though she was by their appearance. Cutter's arm about her hunger-pinched waist was supportive. She sagged against his fur vest and watched the subtle but purposeful movements of Leetah's hands. Rain the Healer's hands had been similarly sensitive, Nightfall remembered, but power so intensely focused that it was almost visible had never poured from his fingertips as it did now from Leetah's.

Redlance groaned. His head shifted uncomfortably from side to side. His body shuddered, at once fighting and yielding to the force that relentlessly and painfully summoned him back to life. Reawakened, his heart beat angrily now, staving off death with a fierce will. But Leetah was not satisfied. She continued with her work until the last piece of the puzzle was fitted in its proper place. Finished at last, she wilted like a flower with a broken stem, her long auburn hair falling in waves upon Redlance's steadily rising and falling chest.

Uttering a little cry, Nightfall broke away from Cutter and stumbled to her lifemate's side. She flung her arms about him and with indescribable joy felt him hug her weakly in turn. His eyes held an endearing, bewildered look.

Leetah brushed cold beads of perspiration from her brow, sighing. "I have given him the strength he needs to recover."

"And you have given me back a tribesman," added Cutter, his voice filled with relief and respect. He came to Leetah's side and, cupping his hand beneath her delicate chin, raised her weary head. "No words of thanks could say enough, beautiful Leetah," he murmured, frustrated that she was not capable of receiving his sending.

Leetah frowned and pulled away from him. "No! Don't," she said. "I don't want you to touch me again!" Her legs wobbled. She called out, "Rayek?"

Instantly her dark-haired suitor was there to lend her his strength. The healing had cost her much; she had never been obliged to expend so much energy in such a concentrated effort before. Death had never pitted itself against her arts with such greedy determination, but she had managed to wrest the prize from those black, grasping claws. The battle had left her trembling with weakness but triumphant. She leaned heavily against Rayek, glad of his presence, for the three barbarians disturbed her.

Rayek grinned maliciously at Cutter, thinking, *She has spurned you, barbarian. See how she turns to me? You are a fool and a filthy one at that!*

Cutter cocked his head, wolflike, puzzled. Why was Rayek so determined to stir up pointless rivalry between them? Surely the dark-skinned hunter was aware of what had passed between Cutter and Leetah? Yes. He was obviously aware. More so, apparently, than Leetah herself.

"Redlance lives, thanks to your daughter," Cutter told the Sun-Toucher. They stood to one side of the rowdy procession that wound through the Sun Village. Redlance was in danger of being spilled from his litter as the assembled Wolfriders jubilantly packed around him, howling their joy that he and Nightfall had been rescued from the desert. Amused at the chaotic welcome, Leetah supervised the progress of the parade, guiding the litter bearers, who alternated every few steps as the Wolfriders vied for the privilege of carrying their returned tribesman to her hut. The healer felt duty-bound to examine all the barbarians, for she was aware of the extremes they had endured. It was, besides, something of a miracle that this new tribe of elves had found its way to her village, when her people had always considered themselves unique and isolated in the world. Privately she admired the courageous, haggard strangers, despite the personal humiliation she had suffered at their hands.

"I hope that someday Leetah will forgive me for carrying her off like that," Cutter said softly.

Sun-Toucher listened with interest to the soft burr in the young chieftain's speech. Save for a sprinkling of unfamiliar words and phrases, the Wolfriders' language was almost identical to that of the Sun Villagers. The difference lay in inflection, emphasis, and pitch. Cutter's voice was youthful but deliberately low. He spoke each sentence as though divulging a secret, and always subtly underscoring his tone was a pleasant "thrumm," not unlike the sound a purring great cat might make if given the power of speech.

"I did it without thinking," Cutter continued, "almost as though I had no choice!"

Perhaps there was no choice, Leetah's blind parent thought wisely. More and more, the Sun-Toucher found himself liking this very young stranger, who, although impulsive, was earnest in his aim to do all that could be expected of a leader and more.

"We are the Sun Folk, and ours is the way of peace," said the robed elder, placing a darkly tanned hand on Cutter's shoulder. "We would have freely given you the provisions which you took by force. But though you came to us in violence, you are welcome now to stay and rest."

Cutter felt his throat thicken. Rest! Not all the rest in the world could make him forget the events that filled the last half cycle of Greater Moon. It had been at least an eight of days since the fire had taken the forest and the Wolfriders had fled for their lives underground. Cutter knew that however long he lived, he would remember the torturous journey to this haven in the desert for the rest of his life. He turned to the Sun-Toucher, knowing that the sightless one "saw" and understood him well enough; but there were words that needed saying.

"No one has ever been kind to us before. We thought we were all alone in a world where life was short and often bitter."

The pale-haired chieftain lifted his too-old eyes and searched through the milling villagers for a flutter of blue and gold, a shimmer of auburn curls. He found them, just disappearing through the beaded door curtain of the healer's hut. The Wolfriders had already taken Redlance inside.

Discovering the Sun Folk, here, is like a dream, Cutter thought. But Leetah . . . I know I've dreamed of you before.

The healer's hut, like the other clay-covered shelters of the village, was squat and potbellied with a tiered roof that rose to a rounded peak some four elves high from the ground. Set in odd places in the walls were window openings and smaller breathing holes, all covered by filmy curtains heavily weighted with intricate beadwork. The clay that covered the hut, applied with none too exacting an eye toward symmetry, was multicolored and had been worked into swirls of reddish-brown, yellow, and pink. Sprinkled upon the well-ventilated roof were specks of crushed clearstone, which caught the light pleasingly. Below, a garden of small needle-plants, flowering thistles, and clumps of tiny yellow seek-root blossoms made it impossible to tell where the ground stopped and the foundation of the hut began.

The hut's interior was divided into two chambers by a curved partition that also served to support the conical roof. On one side of the partition an oblong hole gaped in the floor; through this opening a short flight of stairs descended into the dimness of an underground chamber. Sunk into the floor on the other side of the wall was a round sleeping pit. It was padded with a large cushion, and fur blankets were tossed carelessly upon this soft surface. A stool-like, backless chair with elaborate armrests, a stand made of polished petrified wood, and a colorful scattering of pillows and fringed rugs gave the area an appearance both intimate and invitingly comfortable.

Leetah held her breath and stiffened as the litter bearers trooped into her home, tracking sand across the rugs and bumping into her free-hanging narrow tapestries. The rest of the Wolfriders passed through the beaded door curtain more carefully, although they were all still giddy with joy.

While Redlance, beaming and completely confused by his new surroundings, was gently settled in the sleeping pit, Dewshine and Scouter tiptoed to the head of the stairs, where they peered down curiously into the hut's mysterious lower chamber. Rainsong and Moonshade examined the pillows, puzzling over the texture of the fabric, for the Wolfriders had never seen woven cloth before. Pike sat down awkwardly on the stool-chair and promptly fell over backward. Recovering, he found himself nose to pugged nose with a small desert wildcat. Long, tufted ears flattened against its head; striped and spotted fur bristled along its spine. The little animal took a couple of tentative swipes at Pike's full cheeks and then hissed and streaked across the room to cower between Leetah's ankles. The healer bent to pick up her pet, stroking its fears away, but the barely calmed wildcat exploded into a screeching, clawing ball of terror as several of the wolves nosed their way through the door curtain, seeking their elf-friends. Hurtling itself from Leetah's arms, the cat shot between Dewshine and Scouter and vanished down the stairs. One of the wolves calmly trotted after the terrorized pet, licking his chops, but Leetah instantly grabbed the beast's tail, receiving for her bravery the lupine equivalent of a shrug.

"No! Absolutely no! I will not have these creatures in my house!" She was furious. The wolves were very large and very independent, and their tempers were unpredictable at best. In addition, their coats swarmed with sand fleas, and their pungent body stench was overpowering.

Some of the Wolfriders looked up with slightly hurt expressions. Strongbow was openly resentful, and Treestump cleared his throat uneasily. Realizing that to insult a wolf was to insult its rider, Leetah changed her tone at once.

"Please, if you will, send your mounts outside. Forgive me, but they frighten me terribly."

Nightfall rose from her seat upon the bed cushion beside Redlance. "They're hungry," she explained unnecessarily. "I'll take them to find meat."

As the petite, brown-haired Wolfrider strode past her to shoo the wolves out the door, Leetah breathed a small "thank you." Nightfall turned to smile at the healer, the sinuous curves of her body striped with shadow as daylight filtered through the vertical strands of beading.

"Remember this," said Nightfall. "Anything you ever want of me, I will do as soon as you ask it."

"There is no need," Leetah began, but something deep within Nightfall's eyes stopped her. In that moment the healer gained an inkling of Redlance's worth and of what she, Leetah, had saved. Had her mate died, much of Nightfall's spirit would have died with him. It was an unbearable image: the plucky, golden-eyed Wolfrider a walking husk, joyless, aimless.

What if my powers had not been equal to the task? the healer thought, shuddering. Why must lifemating cause lovers to lose themselves within each other? Why can two never form a bond without becoming one? Smugly, Leetah congratulated herself for her well-managed relationship with Rayek; but then, for no reason imaginable, she thought of Cutter. She frowned and shook her head as though trying to shiver a fly from her cheek.

Hastily Leetah examined each of the Wolfriders, asking questions, seeking hurts and hidden pains, anything to distract her from thoughts of the barbarians' conspicuously absent leader. The chief complaints were of blistered feet, riding sores, and sunburn, all new and unsettling ailments to the shy, forest-born elves.

When she came to One-Eye, Leetah asked that she be allowed to remove his eye patch. He hesitated, glancing uncertainly at Clearbrook.

"There's nothing you can do for it. Better let it be."

"I'll be the judge of that," Leetah answered tartly. She noticed that One-Eye was rather plain and blunt-featured for an elf. How unfortunate, she thought, that he must also be disfigured.

Carefully, she lifted the eye patch and was startled to behold a perfectly smooth, slightly indented area of pale skin where the Wolfrider's right eye should have been.

"A healer mended this for you, did she not?"

"He did, pretty one, aye! Rain the Healer. Some time ago. The eye's gone, but it's not a bad job, is it?" One-Eye seemed proud.

"Could not the eye itself be—?"

"No. There was nothing left to save." He had almost forgotten how it felt when the sharpened, smouldering point of the wooden stake was driven through his right eye socket. They had done it slowly, enjoying themselves, two of them holding down his arms and legs, the third with the stake straddling his slight body, crushing screams from him. They had told him that they were going to burn out his demon eyes first. Then they would lop off his beast ears before taking his skull. In a madness of pain and fear he had sent a "wolf-send" to his third wolf, Nestrobber, forgetting that the beast had recently died of bellyworms. Fortunately, the desperate call had reached the sympathetic channels of another lupine brain and had touched a chord of response. A big, black wolf with white muzzle and paws had come charging through the underbrush, frightening the three assailants away from their victim's writhing body. The tortured elf had managed to pull himself quickly onto the strange wolf's back. Then they had fled, vanishing into the thicket and leaving their pursuers far behind.

"How did it happen?" Leetah asked again, stirring One-Eye from his dark memories.

"Humans," he said simply, regarding her with the polished chestnut circle of his single eye.

The healer did not want to know more. She looked at Redlance lying on her bed, cured but still weak from the damage inflicted on him by humans. She looked at the other Wolfriders seated quietly along the round rim of the sleeping pit, homeless and half starved because humans had tried to destroy them with fire. The old legends came back to her, of the ten-fingered ones with their clubs and their knives and their hate. Now the legends were real—they were truth in the wounded flesh—and Leetah felt shame for any ill will she had harbored toward the courageous outcasts, who were nothing less than her people's distant kinsman.

"You are all wonderful," she said, her words inadequate to express the depth of her esteem. "You have done the impossible. You crossed the desert without food or water, and you survived!"

"Cutter brought us through," said Skywise. "He never gave up."

"Aye, he kept us going, all right," Treestump added.

"And he found us our first liquid in days: the juice from those sticker-plants. We'd all have died of thirst but for him," Skywise finished, speaking almost to himself.

Leetah studied the stargazer, remembering that during her captivity in the mountains she had noted the obvious closeness between the barbarian chief and his silver-haired adviser.

"You love him, don't you?"

Skywise's thin brows shot up toward the rim of his metal face guard. "Don't you?" he countered impishly.

Leetah flushed red as her bodice. "What a ridiculous thing to say!"

The Wolfriders exchanged knowing glances, chuckling softly, eying her as though she were a child caught at some prank for which she could invent no excuse. Leetah would have protested their insinuations vehemently but for the sharp tapping on the wall outside her door. A robed silhouette stood behind the beaded curtain, politely awaiting admittance.

"Yes, Father," called the healer, leaping to her feet and running with light, graceful steps to part the curtains.

"Are the Wolfriders well?" asked Sun-Toucher as his daughter ushered him into her hut.

"Surprisingly well," answered Leetah, peeking surreptitiously over her father's shoulder at the two figures who stood on the cobbled path outside. Cutter and Nightfall were talking together quietly, nodding, their stance relaxed and intimate. Cutter suddenly looked toward the curtains, and Leetah just as quickly sidled out of view. Feigning ease, she elaborated on her assessment of the Wolfriders' condition. "They need much rest, and their stomachs need gentle stretching with food—small amounts at first, then more until their strength is fully recovered."

"*She* has summoned them," the Sun-Toucher told her.

Leetah understood at once. "Yes. They are well enough for that."

Although the Sun Folk were calmer now, their fascination with their barbarian guests had not diminished. When the Sun-Toucher emerged from Leetah's hut, followed in single file by the entire Wolfrider tribe, the villagers pressed close, offering gifts of food and clothing, milk for Wing, and the open hospitality of their homes. Gently but firmly the Sun-Toucher waved them away.

"Where are we going now?" Scouter whispered to Cutter. "Haven't we seen everything there is to see here?"

Overhearing, the Sun-Toucher stopped and turned to address the Wolfriders. "Your hardships have caused you to forget what it means to be elves."

Nonplussed, the forest folk gaped at the elegantly robed elder. We? they thought. Forget what it means to be elves? We who have struggled and suffered so long precisely because we are what we are? We who have survived against all odds because we thought ourselves the last of our race? We, the children of the High Ones? Forget?

"Come now, all of you," the Sun-Toucher continued serenely. "It is time you were brought before the Mother of Memory."

Nine

"Those are trees?" Dart was skeptical.

"What else can they be, cub?" Treestump muttered. "Everything here is different from the way it was in the Holt."

The Wolfriders stood in a semicircle before the arched portal of the central hut. Not quite as tall as the building itself, the trees in question grew on either side and behind it, shading the first and second tiers of the hut's ornate, domed roof. Dark gray and narrow, the trunks rose in undulating curves, segmented like the bodies of worms. The bark was smooth and free of knots or other blemishes.

"They look like storm clouds," Dart exclaimed. The comparison was an accurate one, for smoky-pink puffs of foliage billowed from the forked branches, so feathery and cloud-like that it seemed like tree and all might rise into the sky on the wind.

The central hut was very grand, twice as large as any other structure in the village and much more colorful. Painted into the convex walls on either side of the entrance were graceful, elongated figures of elves who seemed to be floating toward each other, reaching out to clasp hands above the open doorway. Patterns of flowers and shining sun motifs spiraled and whorled on every available surface of the hut. There was nothing to equal it in charm, even among the most ostentatious gilded and bejeweled chambers to be found deep in the caverns of the trolls.

Sun-Toucher parted the curtains with the back of his hand and held one panel open, stepping aside to permit the Wolfriders access.

"Enter!" he said, wisely making the command sound like an invitation. "*She* is waiting."

Cutter hesitated, his senses awhirl as the tangy-sweet scent

173

permeating the hut's interior once again poured into his nostrils. He put a hand to his brow, blinking hard, dizzy. The rhythmic riddle pulsed within him, stronger than ever: Sorrow's End. Sorrow's End. Sorrow's End.

Concerned, Skywise put out a hand to steady his chief, but Cutter shrugged it away. His face a mask of wonder, Cutter stepped between the parted beads and came into the room.

The single chamber seemed far roomier than the exterior of the hut had led him to believe. Perhaps it was a trick of the room's curious light, perhaps not. He did not notice any other details of the place's construction, for his eyes were captured at once and held immovably by the source of that light. The rest of his tribefolk slowly entered, and they, too, were transfixed by what they saw.

In a shallow alcove on the far side of the chamber, a circular dais rose in two steps from the gleaming, tile-inlaid floor. Set at the center of the platform was a chair made of polished stone, its arms and backrest trimmed with rectangular panels of beaten gold. Behind the chair a perfectly round disk stood on edge, echoing the diameter of the dais. The disk was divided into a mosaic of large clearstone plates, all held in place by golden channels. As though lit from within, the great circle glowed, each section of clearstone a different, luminous pastel hue. The light was soft and soothing and achingly lovely.

The source of this ethereal radiance was the figure seated quietly upon the stone chair. Cautiously, the Wolfriders drew closer, stopping in midstep as the figure slowly raised one long-fingered, unnaturally narrow hand. The face was shadowed and could not easily be seen. Cutter's breath caught in his throat as a low, languid voice broke the silence.

"Welcome, my ragged young visitors," said the seated figure. "Welcome to Sorrow's End."

Rainsong gasped, glancing at Cutter. "Sorrow's End," she whispered to him. "That's what *you* named this place! How did you—"

Know? he finished her question in his mind. I don't know! I don't know anything!

"You are elves indeed, brave travelers." The shadowed figure was speaking again. "Our race is of one heart and one mind, no matter the circumstances which shape our behavior or—" the filmy draperies of her pale green gown rustled faintly as she stood up "—our bodies."

She was tall, fully two heads taller than Cutter, and she was beautiful beyond compare. Skywise decided at once that Leetah was the second loveliest creature he had ever seen.

Agog, the Wolfriders shrank back like wide-eyed cubs frightened by an intruder in their den. Tallness: it was a *human* trait, one that triggered the forest elves' instinctive urge to flee. Yet they stayed, because the luxuriantly gowned figure standing upon the dais could not possibly be—even remotely—human.

But if not human, what?

The leaf of an idea drifted down, breaking the surface of the pool that was the Wolfriders' collective memory. Outward spread the ripples, opening wider and wider until they touched the distant shore of legend, where tall and fragile beings walked in the mist of an age gone by.

Cutter came forward and sank to his knees before the radiant figure, feeling stupid, inept, and unworthy. He gulped back his uncertainty.

"High One? Are you one of the High Ones?" The tremulous query trailed off like the faraway cry of a marsh-piper. Wholly awed, Cutter looked at her with the round, upturned eyes of an owl, the pupils so enlarged as to make the entire iris seem deep purple.

She bent over him. She was smiling. "No, child, you flatter me." Her voice was thrillingly rich, and it contained a note of amusement. "Old I may be, but not that old. I am Savah of the Sun Folk, some of whom are pleased to call me Mother of Memory." Now the benign amusement was turned upon herself. She looked down at Cutter, her body tilted at a graceful angle, her long hands resting upon her knees. "Do not be afraid. Have you never seen an aged elf before?"

Still kneeling, the Wolfrider chieftain shook his head, unable to utter even a simple no. Savah lifted her heavy-lidded eyes and surveyed her other visitors. Then she stepped down from the dais and flowed past Cutter, the swirling, crenelated hem of her gown brushing his chest. He was glad that he was on his knees; he couldn't have stood up if he had wanted to.

"Ah, no," Savah said, approaching Treestump. "I see that even the oldest among you is but a stripling."

The yellow-bearded Wolfrider's reverence changed instantly to embarrassed indignation. He dug his fists into his hips and blustered. "Hrumph! Well, now." But he seemed aware that he looked quite small next to Savah.

Dewshine giggled hysterically behind her hand. Scouter's shoulders were shaking, and his lips were tightly compressed in an effort to hold back peals of laughter. Tiny crinkles appeared at the outer corners of Savah's rust-colored eyes. Her smile was so winning that Treestump could not maintain his pique. Like a toad puffed up to impress an indifferent female, he visibly deflated. The Wolfriders could not help but give in to the infectious humor of the situation. Their relief, found in laughter, was immense.

Finally Cutter managed to get to his feet. He was far from convinced that Savah was not a High One, despite her denial. She turned to him; the light that still glowed steadily behind her chair shimmered upon the folds of her clothing so that she appeared to be dressed in the foam and flow of a waterfall.

"And you," she said, beckoning him to her. "What is it they call you? Cutter?"

He drew himself up proudly, chin raised to emphasize his height and to better enable him to meet those marvelous eyes crinkling merrily above him.

"A fine name for a fighting cockerel," she said, running her long fingers affectionately through his soft spun-sunlight

hair. "Dear me," she went on, "there is even a crest here to complete the image." She patted his chief's lock and saw his cheeks flare even redder beneath his sunburn.

In several surprising ways Savah reminded Cutter of his mother, Joyleaf. The same ease and familiarity were there, the same unhurried motherly wisdom. But in addition to those qualities, Savah possessed the serene authority of vast age. Cutter knew that he stood before the heart and soul of the Sun Village. Here, at last, was the source, the memory, the eternal guiding spirit of the Sun Folk.

"My heart rejoices that you are here," said the Mother of Memory, gathering the Wolfriders about her like a brood of young quail. "Long have I believed that other children of the High Ones still dwelled in the lands beyond the desert." She led them to a section of curved wall to the right of her throne, where a picture-carving stood out in raised relief. It depicted five elves—three tall adults like Savah, a young female of Wolfrider height, and a male child—all walking across a stylized landscape of rolling dunes. Behind them rose a large round sun that dwarfed the five figures. Gazing at the carving, the Wolfriders remembered all too well how small the desert had made them feel, how helpless; but the figures in the picture walked proudly, undefeated by the merciless sun. That pride was reflected in Savah's stately posture as she gestured toward the scene.

"You Wolfriders come from that Green Growing Place which is legend to all but myself. You see, I am old enough to remember a time before the village, a time when my family crossed the burning waste, just as you have done, to settle here in the oasis we named Sorrow's End."

The pounding at Cutter's temples suddenly ceased; the riddle was solved. Somehow, in the sand, in the rooks, in the torrid breeze and the limitless sky there had lingered a trace of that first elf-family's determination to survive. It had waited through time unknown to strengthen the hearts and guide the steps of other elfin travelers. What had Savah said? "Our race is of one heart and one mind." And now, here were the Sun Folk, and they were not strangers but brothers and sisters to the Wolfriders, who had believed themselves the last of the elf race. And here too was Savah, a child of the forest, as were the Wolfriders. But that Green Growing Place which had birthed her was, no doubt, very far away in both distance and time.

Timidly, Dart crept to Savah's side and plucked at her long flowing skirts. She seemed as tall as a tree to the child as she turned and rested her ancient eyes on him.

"Did the humans chase you away from your Holt, too?" he asked.

"Humans," she repeated. The word seemed to strike her like a sharp blow. She walked thoughtfully to the other side of the dais. A second scene was etched in light and shadow on the wall opposite the depiction of Savah's family. The Mother of Memory's hand stroked the hollows and swellings of the half relief. Her noble features were masklike, hardened against a resurrection of deeply buried pain.

"This harsh world has wrought many changes in our kind," she murmured. "Countless years have passed since I was as young and resilient as you are, Wolfriders. But I remember. Oh, yes, I remember the humans."

The Wolfriders stared at the picture, their brows drawn together, their mouths hard and tight. It was all too familiar. A naked human with upraised club stood in triumph over the corpse of a tall elf. Austere representations of trees with spear-straight trunks and sharply angled branches surrounded the two figures, lending a morbid aura to the scene.

Savah shook her head, looking sadly at the chiseled image of the human. "And still they fear us? After all this time?" She sighed. "What a pity."

The Wolfriders could not comprehend the note of compassion in her voice.

"Humans don't change," Skywise said flatly. "They never change."

"All living things change," Savah said, gently correcting

him. "Your ancestors were my height, but as time passed, their children were born smaller and smaller. The small ones had a better chance against all their enemies, not just the two-legged ones. I cannot believe that humans have not changed at all since I was a child in the woods."

They were killers then; they're killers now. This was an open sending from Strongbow.

But why? Savah responded instantaneously, rocking the Wolfriders with the power and clarity of her thoughts; as far as they had known, no one in the Sun Village was capable of sending. **Humans are not altogether unlike us. They walk upright. They speak with words. They bear their young, and they sing, oh yes. I heard them singing once, a very long time ago. There must be a reason for their eternal enmity toward our kind. Perhaps we shall never know what it is.**

Without warning, the somber mood in the chamber lifted. Savah smiled and draped one slender arm across Cutter's shoulders, drawing Skywise to her with the other arm. She spoke aloud now, and her voice was more sensuously soothing then ever.

"Well, you are safe now, at any rate, my woodland cousins. There are no humans here."

Cutter began to chuckle, and soon he was holding his sides in an agony of uproarious laughter. "Greymung," he blurted between gasps. "He swore he'd send us to a land of bright promise! A land where there were no humans!" Cutter fell backward on the tiles, breathless, racked with spasms of mirth. Catching on, Skywise grinned slyly, smacked his hands together, and let out a howl.

"He told the truth, by Timmorn's blood," Treestump roared, grabbing his belly. "For the first time in his muck-eating life, I'll bet, that wart-covered sack of cave slugs told the truth! And he didn't even know it."

"Or did he?" Cutter sat bolt upright, his tear-blurred eyes leaping from the gold trim on Savah's throne to the beautiful peaked headdress she wore, its scalloped edges glittering like golden rays of the sun. "Mother of Memory," he asked warily, "are there trolls in these hills?"

"What are trolls, child?" she asked, genuinely perplexed.

"Where do your metal things come from? Who makes them for you?" he tried, thinking perhaps that the Sun Folk had another name for the tunnel-dwellers.

"Why, we take the metals of the sun and the moons from deep places in the mountains. It is an art of which we are most proud, for it takes skill and patience to mold and shape the raw metal by hand."

"There are no trolls here? No trolls and no humans?" Cutter looked around, seeing the faces of his tribefolk light up as the truth finally sank in. Ignoring all decorum, the young chieftain merrily pounded his fist on the floor. "No trolls and no humans! No trolls and no humans!"

All the Wolfriders began to laugh, to howl, to shout their happiness. They had never made so much noise in one day before. The very thought that they could live now in peace, that the young cubs could grow, fearless, in a land without enemies was enough to release the tensions of several lifetimes.

Frightened by the hubbub, Wing yowled in the cradle of Rainsong's arms, waving his tiny fists in the air. Savah reached out her hands, asking to hold the precious bundle. Rainsong hesitated only a moment and then gave Wing into the Mother of Memory's infinitely tender embrace. Holding the babe with practiced ease, her hand nearly as long as Wing's entire body, Savah lifted him up for all to see. Her eyes were shining, and the colors behind her chair glowed with redoubled intensity.

"New life has come to Sorrow's End," she cried. The Wolfriders sent up a cheer that made the domed ceiling resound like a great bell.

Rayek burst into the chamber, his spear outthrust. Caught by the threatening surprise, several of the Wolfriders hastily reached for their weapons. New Moon was drawn and brandished before Cutter had time to think about it.

"Mother of Memory, what is it?" Rayek demanded. "What is the reason for this vile outcry in your presence?"

"Lower your weapon, chief hunter," Savah said quietly. "We began the festivities a little early, that is all. Is your promised contribution to the feast already here?"

"Witness for yourself," Rayek answered darkly, standing his spear on the floor. "I fulfilled my promise and surpassed it." He held the curtains aside so that Savah could see the villagers filing past, each bearing one or more slain animals. There were hares, and wild bristle-boars, and tiny deer not much larger than rabbits, and plump quail, and even lizards that appeared to have a great deal of meat on their bones. In spite of themselves, the Wolfriders felt their mouths begin to water.

Noticing the avid attention being given by her guests to the passing display, Savah nodded her approval to Rayek. "Thank you, chief hunter. What you have done will bring great pleasure and contentment to our cousins from far away."

"What I have done I did because you requested it, Mother of Memory, and for no other reason." Rayek's voice was hard as ice. He bowed respectfully to Savah, turned on his heel, and left, his exit punctuated by a great clatter of beads.

Untroubled by Rayek's insolence, Savah replaced Wing in his mother's arms. Cutter sheathed his sword as the venerable elf-woman turned to him.

"Tonight we hold a grand celebration to welcome you and your tribe. You will learn of the Sun Folk through dance and song, and perhaps we shall begin to learn something of the Wolfriders."

Cutter lowered his eyes. "The first thing you should know, Mother of Memory, is that we are in the habit of keeping ourselves cleaner than this." The other shifted uncomfortably, suddenly very much aware of their soiled and stained leathers. Moonshade was especially embarrassed, for most of the Wolfriders' clothes were of her making. Her gift—

the skill to render any hide as supple and soft as a flower petal—was hardly being shown to best advantage. "We know water is scarce in the desert," Cutter continued, "but if there's a place where we can swim or even just wash . . ."

"Ah," Savah nodded, kindly giving no indication that she had even noticed the Wolfriders' aromatic state. "I will have the healer show you the way. You will surely be more comfortable when you have refreshed yourselves."

At the mere mention of Leetah, Cutter's stomach muscles tightened involuntarily. He wasn't at all sure he liked the way his body had begun to react, independent to his will, ever since he had so rashly swept Leetah away into the mountains. Stupid thing to do, anyway! he thought—so needless to have frightened and humiliated her that way! Yet every fiber of his being clung to the memory of her sleek, brown skin next to his. She was part of him. He felt strangely incomplete yet well able to make himself whole with a single simple cure.

The water steamed, its dark surface broken from time to time by streams of minute bubbles. The pool was large enough to hold all of them comfortably, yet not one of the Wolfriders made the first move to step into the vaporous bath.

Newstar held her nose. "It smells like trolls," she said with frank disgust.

"Smells like their forges at any rate," Skywise observed.

"I am told there is a vein of liquid fire underground which heats the spring so that the water issues into the pool comfortably warm." Leetah stood above them on a rock ledge that overlooked the steaming pool. Her manner was guarded. "All my people bathe here and afterward lie in the sun on blankets to dry themselves. It is very pleasant." She almost said "delicious" but, glancing at Cutter, thought better of it. His eyes would not leave her.

"Well, I'm game," Pike said jovially. He dipped his hand into the pool, yelped, and brought it back with a splash.

Cross-eyed, he blew on his fingers as though they had been boiled.

"Oh Pike, it can't be that hot, can it?" Dewshine nervously tested the water for herself. It was quite warm, a totally unfamiliar sensation to an elfin huntress who had known only the exhilarating, sometimes biting cold of the forest lakes and streams. But Leetah was right. It was not an unpleasant warmth. "Deceiver!" Dewshine laughed, splashing Pike's face. She slipped off her tunic, unlaced her sandals, and sat down at the pool's edge, dangling her bare legs in the water.

Moments later, Scouter was stripped to the waist, kneeling to wash his face and upper body. It felt glorious. Wriggling out of his breeches, he slipped carefully into the pool. His eyes nearly popped out of his head at the incredible feeling of being submerged in hot water for the first time.

"It's wonderful," he called to Leetah, and she answered him with a friendly smile.

Soon most of the Wolfriders had laid aside their worn and ragged clothing to cleanse many days' grime from their bodies. The older elves, unwilling immediately to try something so new and strange, did not care to immerse themselves. Scouter and Dewshine discovered that it tired them out very quickly to swim in the heated water. Together they hauled their lithe young bodies onto the rock rim of the spring and lay there, breathing hard.

"Look at me!" Dewshine twisted her neck to see down her moisture-beaded back. Her torso from shoulders to hips was milk white; her forearms and legs were an angry red. "I look like a white-stripe!" she groaned.

"We're all blotched from here to there, cub," Treestump growled. "It's just plain ridiculous!"

"Will we stay like this, Leetah?" Moonshade indicated her sunburned arms and legs. Palest and most nocturnal of all the Wolfriders, she was miserable at the thought.

"I will see what I can do for you, if you wish," Leetah said, reassuring her. "But if you lie bare in the sun a little each day, I think you will become a lovely dark color all over."

"Oh, no! How horrible," Moonshade cried, and then caught herself as she saw Leetah's green eyes cloud over and her smile falter ever so slightly.

Well, a touch for a touch, the healer thought wryly, remembering that she herself had been repelled at first by the Wolfriders' pale skins.

Cutter had long since discarded his fur vest and deerskin leggings and was dressed only in the triangular breechclout that also served as his sword belt. Although Leetah tried to look at him simply as one of the others, she knew that even the most dispassionate observer would concede that the Wolfrider chieftain possessed exceptional beauty. Unlike Rayek's, Cutter's lines were sinuously rounded; his shoulders and chest were broader, and his thighs more emphatically curved with muscle than those of the Sun Folk's chief hunter. This in itself did not set Cutter above Rayek in desirability, but his complete lack of self-consciousness—his innocence of the kind found only in animals—attracted Leetah to the young barbarian in a way that she had never been drawn to haughty Rayek.

Even so, the attraction had an element of compulsion to it that Leetah did not like. She had known many flavors of desire, both mild and sharp, in her lifetime, but this was not to her taste. A healer of the Sun Folk, she had given of herself in ways that few others would be willing to risk. It required immense strength of will to enter an injured body, to feel in part the guiding pain, to knit and sew and tie and reweave all that was frayed or torn or sundered by misfortune or disease. But Leetah had never turned away, and those life-giving hands had never failed to accomplish everything expected of them. Her pride and sense of duty gave her the strength to look death in the eye and to say no.

However, there was another side to her art that had nothing to do with duty. This was Leetah's self-given reward, her compensation for the risk and pain and dreadful vulnerability she experienced while healing another.

The body held many secrets, many hidden keys to both discomfort and pleasure, and Leetah knew them all. Moreover, everyone in the village knew that the healer could, when she chose, unlock those secrets and present them as gifts to whomever she favored. What she received, or took, in return was also of her own choosing, and it was whispered that the Sun-Toucher's daughter had more secrets than anyone else. It was also whispered that Rayek's vanity must be well founded in accomplishment, else why would he hold the greatest favor in Leetah's eyes?

Control over such power was a most satisfying thing to possess. Of all the villagers, only she had a hut to herself, the comings and goings from which could be regulated by her merest word. She deemed herself well entitled to that privacy as payment for the intensely intimate contact with those who needed her help. No wonder, then, that she kept her own needs to herself, never expressing them except from a position of strength and absolute control.

Leetah remembered the moment during the raid when winds blasted her defenseless soul and carried part away to merge with something else. She had been stripped of power then and had hated the feeling. Now, as she looked at Cutter, glistening wet in the sun and caressed by vapors from the heated pool, she knew that he had somehow gained possession of that missing part of her. And she, she owned something of his. It was a thing like a sound or a word—a word that would spell her absolute defeat if she ever dared to speak it aloud.

Tam ... Tam ... Tam. She wondered what this strange word, which sprang unbidden into her mind, could mean ...

Leetah had felt obligated to stay and watch over the Wolfriders on their first foray at bathing in a hot spring; but as Cutter rose and stretched, and it became very clear that he was about to shed the breechclout to dive into the water, she was beset by a sudden, frantic urge to flee. It was the height of idiocy, particularly unworthy of a healer, but the tension grew within her; she prayed that her unreasoning panic would not make itself evident by any outward sign to the Wolfriders.

Before she could move, Cutter stopped and turned. The breeze had shifted toward Sun-Goes-Down, and Cutter's nose tested the air, wolflike. There was an odor of smoke—he could see the plume rising from the edge of the village—and beneath that scent was something very much like the reek of human cooking fires.

"What's that smell?" Cutter asked apprehensively.

"The meat for your feast of welcome is being prepared," Leetah answered, surprised that he did not know it himself.

"They're burning it?" he yelled, horrified. Treestump, One-Eye, and Strongbow jumped up, their famished bellies braced for disappointment.

"I should hope not," Leetah replied archly. "Though we don't normally cook such large amounts of animal flesh, it will all be roasted with expert care."

Cutter growled an oath. "You mean you burn good red meat in fires the way humans do before you eat it?"

Dart and Newstar groaned, and Scouter and Dewshine added to the chorus of dashed hopes.

Treestump sighed. "Well, if that's the way it is, that's the way it is." He hunkered down despondently and flipped a pebble into the steaming water.

Leetah was nonplussed. "You do not eat cooked meat?"

As one, the Wolfriders shook their heads.

"Well, then, I'll see to it that everything gets done to your liking," Leetah promised, hurrying away, glad for an excuse to leave. Cutter watched her go until he could see no more of her than a flounce of auburn curls, vanishing behind the crest of a hill. Turning back, he met thirteen knowing pairs of eyes and thirteen maddening smiles—thirteen, not sixteen, because little Wing was asleep, and Dart and Newstar had no idea what was going on.

*   *   *

Luckily, little of the meat had been cooked when the order arrived to douse the fire-pit. The raw, red slabs and undressed carcasses were fastidiously laid aside for the Wolfriders to deal with however they chose. Three villagers, armed with large fronds from fan-bushes, kept the flies away.

Everyone agreed that the village looked almost as attractive as it had during the last festival of Flood and Flower. Of course, the luxurious blossoms brought by the heavy rains, signaling the turn of the year, had long since gone to sleep. The flowers were not missed, however, for gay cloth banners strung from poles and rooftops, along with candle lanterns made from plates of translucent clearstone, festooned the village almost as colorfully as nature's own perishable decorations.

Clean although still dressed in their old leathers, the Wolfriders were led to the Sun-Goes-Up edge of the village by a troupe of youthful, gauze-clad Sun Folk. These were the dancers, all very excited and eager for twilight to descend so that they could begin their performance. Savah had ordered that the oldest dance—the First Dance—of the Sun Folk be shown to the Wolfriders, for it told the story of the origin of Sorrow's End.

"You should see the wolves," Nightfall whispered to Cutter as they walked. "They're stretched out among the rocks, gorged and contented as you please! It was very kind of the Sun Folk to turn loose one of those big, humped—how did Leetah say it?"

Cutter helped her, molding his mouth around the strange word. "Zwoots, I think. Yes, she called them zwoots."

Nightfall chuckled. "I can barely say it. Well, anyway, all I had to do was ask, and they gave one of those beasts to the wolves. It was a fine, quick kill."

"I guess the Sun Folk don't bond with their mounts the way we do."

"How could they?" Nightfall made a face. "Zw . . . zwotes seem so stupid."

Thick-piled rugs had been arranged on the ground near
the stage where Savah was seated along with Leetah and her
parents. The Wolfriders, at Savah's gracious nod, sat down
cross-legged on the rugs and were immediately served heap-
ing platters of raw meat and bones. The entire populace of
the village had assembled in a circle around a specially
smoothed area of ground where the dancing would take
place. Cutter's tribe felt the curious eyes of the Sun Folk on
them, and they were glad when food and drink were passed
around in earnest, partially diverting the villagers' attention.

From beneath her long lashes Leetah watched the Wolfriders eat; she was not as revolted as she had expected to
be. Although ravenous, the forest elves did not wolf the
meat but wisely took time to chew, cutting larger chunks
into reasonable portions with their blades. Leetah had been
concerned that they might harm themselves by gorging, but
it was clear that they instinctively knew their limits. In this
they were unlike their wolf-friends, who had devoured a
full-grown zwoot down to the bones in a matter of moments
and were now so bloated that they could barely move.

Flies did not seem to bother the Wolfriders any more
than fleas did. The elves huddled together, hunching over
their food, and did not speak while they ate. Leetah saw
Rainsong take a well-chewed scrap from her own mouth
and place it on Newstar's tongue, caressing the child's cheek.
The Wolfriders touched each other often, unconsciously,
their interdependence an unspoken matter of fact.

The sun sank behind the peaks of the mountain spur that
encircled Sorrow's End, veiling all the village in purple
shadow. Resting between mouthfuls, Skywise leaned back
on his hands. He looked past the horn of the crescent-
shaped range, a middling run's distance from the village, to
where freestanding rock pillars rose into the air. One
formation in particular, larger than all the rest, engaged his
curiosity. He had noticed it earlier from the rocky heights
where the Wolfriders had hidden after the raid, and he had
wondered about it even then.

Two immense tapering columns of stone soared heavenward, their peaks curving toward each other like upraised cupped hands. One of the columns was larger than the other, as if it had at one time been part of a greater mass—a mountain spur, perhaps, that had since eroded. Linking the two peaks was a narrow, stone thread—a bridge. The whole thing conformed to no law of nature that Skywise knew.

A villager clad in a gaily striped loincloth came to offer Skywise and the others helpings of bright red, rough-skinned fruit. The stargazer selected two pieces for himself, asking, "Do those tall, joined peaks out there have a name?"

The villager smiled proudly. "That is the Bridge of Destiny," he answered. "You will learn all about it from the dancers."

Even as the villager spoke, Skywise saw Savah straighten in her chair, her narrow face set in an expression of deep concentration. The lanterns, strung from pole to pole around the dancers' circle, began to glow; although the candles within were not aflame, the clearstone plates gave off a brilliant yellow light. This was Savah's sign for the ceremony to commence.

Eight graceful maidens and youths drifted to the center of the circle, and as they did, a delicate chiming of bells accompanied their steps. An elf woman, gowned similarly to Savah but far younger, rose from her seat upon the edge of the stage and moved to stand beside the Mother of Memory. A moment's silence between them indicated a private sending. Then the young elf-woman inclined her head toward the Wolfriders.

"I am Ahdri, handmaiden to the Mother of Memory," she said in a musically sweet voice. "There are no words to speak our wonder and our joy that you, our brothers and sisters, have traveled from a place of dim legend to dwell with us here under the mighty Daystar. With one heart and one mind, we, the Sun Folk, bid you loving welcome."

Cutter looked at Skywise, hesitating, wondering whether

he should say some pleasantry in return; but Ahdri came to his rescue, continuing her impromptu greeting.

"The Green Growing Place was the first shelter, the first refuge of the High Ones. You Wolfriders know that place well, for you come from there, as does our revered Mother of Memory. But we, Savah's descendants, can only dream of the forest, for none of us has ever seen it. Our oldest dance—the First Dance—is the story of Savah's journey through the desert with her family and the founding of Sorrow's End."

Ahdri motioned with her hand to the waiting dancers who formed a ring within the larger circle of onlookers. Sun Villagers, standing in different places around the circle, began to play musical instruments. The Wolfriders were startled by the weird, unfamiliar sounds. There were high-pitched, whining pipes, tiny bells jingling on strings attached to rattles, and chimes and clap-rocks—all of which were played together, producing a sound more unsettling than interesting to the forest elves.

Of the dancers, two of the youths and three of the maidens had very long hair. These five, in slow, eloquent motions, mimed the shapes of trees with intertwining branches, their flowing locks symbolizing garlands of hanging moss. The three remaining dancers rested in languid poses against the "trunks" of the tree-players, while the pipes trilled softly, sounding much like birds.

"The Green Growing Place was home." Savah's voice now filled the circle with its richness; she spoke as if in a deep sleep, her unblinking eyes focused on the remote past. "My ancestors called themselves the Rootless Ones, for though they were part of the forest, they held no permanent place within it."

Responding to the Mother of Memory's words, the three dancers rose and wove with restless, whirling movements in and out of the clustered "trees." The tree-players swayed and undulated as though whipped by heavy winds, their dark hair rippling sensuously against their shoulders.

"My birth brought the number of the Rootless Ones to thrice eight and six. My people were great hunters, and they were fearless."

All the dancers energetically mimed the stalking and slaying of forest creatures, some of which fought back before dying. These actions, though stylized and far removed from the pulse-quickening truth they sought to embody, stirred still-vivid, aching memories of the Holt in the Wolfriders' breasts.

"The Rootless Ones made war, often and fiercely, on bands of humans who sought to drive them from the forest."

It was impossible for the lissome dancers to capture in their movements the bulk and menace of the five-fingered enemy. Although the Sun Villagers seemed impressed by the performers' feigned ferocity, the Wolfriders knew that the dance was only the faintest shadow of that which was real.

Savah's voice, which had been nearly expressionless before, took on a grim and solemn tone. "A time came when bands of humans united in war against the Rootless Ones. My people fought bravely, but the enemy's number overpowered us."

Three dancers fell to the ground, their transparent garments in disarray, suggesting other fallen bodies. Five remained standing.

"Of all the Rootless Ones, only five survived the long battle. They were my mother, Hassbet; her cousin, Maalvi; Yurek, the Rock Shaper; Dreen, a boy child adopted by my mother; and myself. My years then numbered eight and four."

Each of the five dancers assumed the role of one of the survivors. Their bodies reflected sorrow and deep mourning. Of all they had seen so far, this part of the story evoked the Wolfriders' deepest sympathies. Clearbrook looked at One-Eye, who sat beside her. A tear coursed down his left cheek, and she saw that his single eye brimmed with other tears to follow. She thought it best not to touch him, but to let the pent-up grief flow as it would.

"We decided to flee the forest, to seek a place where humans would not dare to go. To the north lay more woods; to the east, the flatlands where humans often hunted great bulls and fleet hoof-dogs. We chose to follow the setting sun until we came to tall mountains that sundered the passing clouds with their blue peaks."

Round and round the circle marched Savah's impersonated family. At the center two dancers knelt facing each other, their hands joined to make the shape of a mountain. Above them stood a maiden whose face, framed by her own encircling arms, became the face of the sun. She sank slowly to her knees, disappearing behind the peak. The other dancers crept stealthily into a ring around the central three.

"But even there we found fresh human spoor; and so, lest the enemy spy us among the green grasses of the valley, we fled away south. The land we came to was all bare rock; beyond it stretched an eternity of sand."

Those who portrayed Savah's family bowed their heads and trudged about the circle as though toiling their way across yielding dunes. At times together, at times separately, the three who served to represent elements of the environment whirled about like gusts of wind or tumbled and rolled like skeleton-weeds.

"Yurek the Rock Shaper became our leader and our salvation." Savah's voice was now melodious; her lips smiled as she continued the narrative. "He urged us into the desert, vowing that he would protect us with his powers."

The Yurek-dancer performed a series of ecstatic leaps, signifying the exultation of a Rock Shaper surrounded completely by his own element—an element, in all its many forms, now his to command.

"By day we slept, protected from the all-consuming sun, within shelters summoned from the sand by Yurek."

All eight dancers lay on the ground. Cleverly, the three "elementals" arched upward, pantomiming the growth of a bubble of sand, which became a smooth, solid dome covering the five "sleepers."

"When evening-light fell, Yurek would dissolve the shelter he had made—" Here the elementals burst apart. "—And he would summon water for us to drink from the rocks deep under the ground. Then we would walk all through the night, five tiny fragments of life in a barren wilderness. Only one thought cheered us. We knew humans could not exist in such a place."

Redlance was fascinated. **A Rock Shaper! Is it possible? I can't imagine shaping a thing that isn't alive!**

Nightfall received Redlance's sending as she had received water from Cutter the night before, hardly daring to believe that it was real. She smiled at her lifemate, reveling in his nearness and his living scent, knowing that she did not need to answer him, that there would always be time enough between them, even for silence.

The Mother of Memory continued. "For one full cycle of the Greater Moon, twice eight days, we wandered. The flesh melted from our bones, and we grew deathly weak from lack of food."

Inspired by their initial sight of the gaunt Wolfriders, the dancers infused their portrayal of Savah's sufferings with poignant realism.

"But Yurek guided us onward, his powers seeming to increase even as his body faded. The ground spoke to him, and it told him of a place where both water and food could be found in abundance."

The music swelled, and the dancers' movements became even more expressive, combining hope and desperation with near-total exhaustion. Cutter and several of the other Wolfriders could not watch this play of agonized yearning, so fresh was the actual experience in their minds.

"And so at last we came to the mountains and to this place of hot springs and teeming life, which we named Sorrow's End."

The dance suddenly became a celebration, wild and free-flying, with youths and maidens leaping, tumbling, tossing their long locks joyfully as the villagers clapped their hands and sang. The lanterns grew brighter, and all at once the candles within them flared into life. As often as they had seen it happen before, the Sun Folk jumped and then applauded and cheered. Having lit the candles, Savah emerged from her trance, her large, deep-set eyes fluttering as they focused once more on the present. She looked at the Wolfriders and saw that their mouths were open.

"Do you like the story so far, my woodland cousins?" she asked.

Still gaping, they nodded.

Savah chuckled. "There is more." She stood up and pointed to the cluster of huts, all lavender and orange with sunset's painting. "Not long after my family settled here, our number began to increase. My mother joined with her cousin, Maalvi, and though I was newly of an age to bear children, I had already recognized Yurek as my lifemate." Savah paused and sighed deeply "Yurek. I love him, though I have outlived him by so many years that the counting no longer matters. He used his powers to open the ground and create the well that never dries. He drew forth the foundation of the great central hut and raised its walls so that neither storm nor rockfall not trembling of the ground nor time itself can weaken or wear it down. He lived to see generations of his descendants, his and mine, grow in their numbers. He lived to see his powers passed on to his children's children. And even though his oneness with this place cost him the life within his body, his soul lives now in every rock and grain of sand that touches Sorrow's End."

The Mother of Memory turned slowly around, her hands uplifted and gesturing toward the Bridge of Destiny. The eight dancers glided without a whisper of sound to the base of the raised platform on which Savah stood; they knelt down in a row and stretched forth their arms even as she did. All eyes turned toward the magnificent rock formation that vaulted to a height even greater than that of the nearby mountains. Eager to have his curiosity satisfied, Skywise was specially attentive to the words now spoken by the Mother of Memory.

"The Bridge of Destiny is the high place closest to the sun. Each dawn the first light of the rising Daystar gleams through the space between the two horns. Long ago, however, when Sorrow's End was young, the tips of the horns were not joined, as they are now, by a narrow bridge of stone.

"It was Yurek's habit to meditate every day at sunrise atop one of the two peaks. As time passed, his willing senses absorbed every secret that the silent rock held. He learned that the pinnacles had once been united in a mighty arch, that harsh winds and rains and whirling sand had worn the span through, parting the rock masses in two forever. Yurek became obsessed with the desire to reconstruct the arch. He meant to test his power to the limit, and no one could dissuade him.

"One morning, Yurek did not come down from his place of meditation. Watching from far below, I saw a bud of stone suddenly erupt from the tip of either peak. The nodules began to grow toward each other; my lifemate was, by his will, forming a bridge of living rock from the substance of the two ancient pillars.

"Many days passed as Yurek drew the clay of his effort from the very ground itself, up through the two peaks. I brought food and water to him, which he would not touch. I brought love to him, which he would not take. To shape the stone he had become a thing of stone himself, immovable, unresponsive, at peace save for his desire to complete the bridge. The fingers of rock grew, closing the gap between them, until they touched and merged into one."

Savah paused and turned to face the Wolfriders. Skywise noted that her features were calm and composed, her hands clasped lightly upon her breast. He wondered why the Sun Folk had grown so solemn and quiet.

"My young woodland cousins," Savah said to them gently, "perhaps you cannot conceive that an elf would willingly part with life. For you, the living is all, an end unto itself. And a lifemate is just that—a mate for life—one who becomes part of you, completes you, loves you faithfully to the last." She paused again, with the faintest, most enigmatic of smiles touching her lips. "When Yurek's great task was done, I thought he would return to me, but the rock had taken him. That which he had shaped by his will had reshaped him. The essence of the primal stone suffused his being, and he no longer knew me. Neither did he know it when, as he stepped in his final exhaustion to the center of the slender arch, the strong wind carried his body away. He fell into the chasm which yawned below the bridge he had given his life to create."

Madness! Cutter's open sending to his tribe crackled with rage and distress. **Stupid, senseless way to die!**

The Wolfriders concurred, and Cutter, in his anger, half hoped that Savah was aware of their disapproval. She was.

"When you have dwelled among us a little while," she said to them, "you will begin to lose the urgency you feel toward bare survival that is such a part of your natures. You will learn that life here is neither short nor bitter and that death, if it comes, is change rather than ending or tragic loss. Your times of mourning are done, brave wanderers. You have come to Sorrow's End."

Once again the ageless beauty and powerful presence of the Mother of Memory assuaged the Wolfriders' concerns. The living source of her people's existence, proof in the flesh of her own spoken truth, tall and elegant, an all but weightless frailty of form belying the many powers at her command, she was the image of a High One come to life. The Wolfriders could not but place absolute faith in her.

"Gaily now, dancers!" Savah clapped her hands. "Your toes are too much in love with the ground!"

Obediently the eight maidens and youths sprang away, their effortless leaps carrying them like deer across the wide circle. The villagers played their instruments with redoubled vigor as the dancers danced, not for the telling of a

story now but for the sheer pleasure of movement. Other
Sun Folk left their blankets and their half-eaten meals to
enter the ring, skipping, kicking their legs high in the air,
deftly following the merry music's rhythm with intricate
steps and undulations of their darkly tanned bodies. Breathless laughter and cries of delight mingled with the clamor of
bells, pipes, and hand-held clap-rocks, tapping out an ener-
getic meter. The circle swirled, a kaleidoscope of multicolored garments, bouncing breasts, and wildly lashing hair.
However disinclined the Sun Folk might have been toward
battle, they seemed eager to expend all their strength in one
night's revelry.

Rayek kept himself away from the warm lantern light,
preferring to observe the celebration privately from the
shadows. He could barely contain his contempt for the
Wolfriders; that they displayed their bestial eating manners
and their lack of appreciation so boldly before the Mother
of Memory disgusted him. Why were the Sun Folk blind to
the crudity, the potential danger of these pale barbarians?
Why had Savah flatly refused his counsel when he urged
her to send these violent invaders back into the desert?

The music slowed to a more stately tempo as dancers
began to fall away to the sidelines, exhausted and disheveled. Now only male villagers moved within the circle, and
Rayek's nostrils flared with scorn at their prancing. He
could put them all to shame if he chose, for none could
match his grace or sureness of step. That would mean,
however, performing before the gog-eyed beast riders—who
obviously had no idea what they were seeing—and that
Rayek was not about to do. Unobtrusively, he half sat, half
leaned on a corner of the stage and glowered at the festively
garbed assemblage. What foolishness, he thought. What
oblivious fools you are to welcome seventeen deadly stingtails
into your midst!

Cutter felt that he had seen and heard too much. His
long ears ached from the piercing wails of the pipes, and his
eyes discerned only a blur as they tried to follow the male

villagers' rhythmic gyrations. Overfed with sensations, Cutter searched for some means to sort out his senses. It did not take him long to choose the ideal subject upon which to focus.

Leetah sat next to Savah on the raised platform, delicately sipping a cider made from the fermented juice of squatneedle fruit. The healer was aware that the Wolfriders' chieftain was studying her, but it bothered her very little. She enjoyed a celebration, whatever the occasion. Music cheered her spirits; dancing stirred her blood; and, unlike the effect it had on most others, the drink made Leetah feel unusually alert and interested in everything happening around her. She was more than willing to set aside her first impression of the Wolfriders and welcome them now with an open heart. Most of them were young and childlike, especially Cutter. Naturally, it would take them time to learn the ways of the village. Until then, she would be tolerant, helpful, and forgiving. She smiled and took another sip from her silver goblet, liking herself very much indeed.

Seated near Leetah's feet, her slightly plump legs dangling over the edge of the stage, Shenshen was busy trying to prop up her sagging companion. Having diligently downed six full goblets of squatneedle cider, he had decided that Shenshen's lap would provide the ideal pillow for the night. Leetah's younger sister, however, did not care to be bestowed with such an honor. She heaved the sodden elf into a sitting position and folded him over so that his head lay on his own knees. That feat accomplished, she glanced up and caught sight of Cutter, wildly handsome in the lanterns' golden light, staring in her direction as though entranced. Rounded cheeks reddening, Shenshen began to primp and fuss with her two topknots, until she realized that those fierce, gem-blue eyes were fixed not on her but on a higher objective. Envy lent a sharp edge to Shenshen's tongue as she turned and whispered up to her older sister.

"I think the Wolfrider intends to carry you off again if he can, Leetah. Best be on your guard."

"Nonsense," the healer replied.

"Oh, but it's true! Great Sun, look how he stares at you! Of course, a savage like that might well fix his desires on any one of us. Surely he is ruled by whim rather than discretion."

Receiving no response, Shenshen smirked, thinking that her barb had stung. The more she observed Cutter, however, and noted his attitude, his total concentration upon Leetah, so unshakable that it seemed he would draw her into himself by the power of his gaze, the more Shenshen began to suspect a force greater than simple desire at work. If her suspicions were borne out, oh, how dreadful, how delicious! She hopped down from her seat and quickly went to join a group of her cronies who were lolling contentedly near the edge of the circle. Soon they were all huddled together, chattering conspiratorially, casting furtive glances from Cutter to Leetah and nodding their general agreement to conclusions drawn. Shenshen's green-gold eyes twinkled wickedly. Oh, how delicious.

The pale-haired barbarian's fixation was not lost upon Rayek. The hunter wanted to shut those hungrily staring eyes permanently, to petrify the Wolfrider like a piece of bone and cast him into the sand. It was time to show the intruder what was what and whose was whose.

Rayek walked over to Leetah's chair and offered her his hand. She took it most willingly, allowing herself to be helped down from the platform. Her transparent, spangled veil slipped from her shoulders and floated behind her as she stepped to the center of the circle with her darkly intriguing companion.

Taking their cue from Rayek, the male dancers already within the circle selected partners from the crowd. The musicians struck up a lilting melody that sparkled with the subtle percussion of chimes. It was a circle dance of complicated maneuvers and steps contrived to display grace and virtuosity. Although all the dancers performed expertly, Rayek and Leetah, superior in every way, might as well have been alone in the circle. This was how Rayek had planned it. He intended the Wolfriders to know beyond doubt how perfectly, how inevitably he and the healer were matched.

Cutter snapped a bone in two and sucked out the marrow. Although he understood in a vague way what Rayek was attempting to do, he was more amazed than irritated that the black-haired one should trouble himself with such futile posturings. As if Rayek or any other elf could alter nature to suit personal desire!

Seeing that his ploy had had no effect—those maddening blue eyes still followed Leetah's every movement—Rayek rounded the circle twice more and then broke away from the other dancers, dragging Leetah along by the hand. Angrily, she planted her feet and jerked him to a halt. He fumed. She didn't care. The male villagers had glided from the ring, and now the females were dancing with one another. Leetah wanted to join them. She was disgusted with Rayek's open animosity toward Cutter, and she had no intention of being caught in the middle. Gathering her veil about her, Leetah abandoned the hunter in full view of the Wolfriders and quickly lost herself in the mindless pleasure of music and movement. Rayek walked back to the platform and sat down on one corner, his pain and feeling of betrayal carefully concealed.

Unable to sit still beside his parents any longer, Dart went off into the deep shadows beyond the pooling lantern light to relieve himself. Looking about warily as he had been taught to do while in such a vulnerable position, the young elf was delighted to see four spots of luminous gold approaching him. He sniffed the air, grinned, and called out, "Briersting! I know it's you! Who's with you?"

Two shadowy shapes became visible around the golden orbs. Dart heard a friendly growl and then felt the push of a cold, wet nose and the tickle of whiskers. He laughed and rubbed Brierstring's stomach.

"Oh, feel that," he exclaimed. "You're so full, your belly's dragging on the ground! Who's this? Is it Lionskin? Well, come on; Treestump's just over there by Mother and Father."

The Wolfriders were glad to make room on the rugs for the two wolves. Puzzled by all the lights and activity, the great beasts lay down beside their riders and observed the goings-on from beneath grizzled brows.

Within the circle, the dance had evolved into a threesome—Leetah and two other maidens—all of whom rivaled the moons and stars in beauty. Gorgeous clothing and glittering jewelry seemed too much for such exquisitely sculpted curves, yet their flowing garments and shimmering veils lent the dancers a dreamlike quality that held the Sun Folk as spellbound as the Wolfriders.

Wide-eyed, with a sigh of awe, Nightfall stood up to see the wonderful sight more clearly. In that moment her entire concept of dance was changed forever.

Like all of her folk, Nightfall had known the forbidden ecstasy of fleeing to some secret place and shedding her garments, there to dance to the lusty tune of purring crickets and the roars of love-maddened frogs, to leap in sublime awareness of her own milky flesh, her gleaming limbs all silvered with moonlight. It was dangerous, a very dangerous and private thing to do. Sometimes lovemates danced together and did more than dance in their chosen place of risk and fulfillment. Once in a great while, dancers did not return, dragged away in their fatal oblivion by prowling Tall Ones who had somehow managed to avoid or quietly kill guardian wolf-friends. The danger, though, was part of the pleasure, and the pleasure was incomparable. Every Wolfrider knew it and never spoke of it except with veiled eyes.

Yet here in Sorrow's End dancing was meant for the participation of all, in the open, in the light, and surrounded by great noise. In the forest, an enemy could with ease perceive such a display from a distance of a day's run or more. The brilliance, the boisterous, heedless joy, the safety of the Sun Folk's celebration was nearly incomprehensible

to the Wolfriders. They understood the dance, however, and it stirred them.

Entrusting Dart to the others' care, Strongbow took Moonshade's hand and disappeared with her into the night. If there were no sheltering trees in this place of sand and stone, the stone would do for a hollow tree, and the darkness would do for concealing leaves. The rest would be as sweet as always or perhaps even sweeter with the memory of near death burning brightly still.

For Cutter there was nothing to see, nothing to hear or scent, but Leetah's lovely form whirling before him, dazzling his senses, clouding his judgment. As the healer swept by him, the trailing end of her veil brushed his cheek. He grasped the filmy cloth and stood up. Twined in the veil, Leetah started in surprise as she felt herself being pulled away from the other dancers. Her head snapped around; she saw Cutter drawing her to him. She tried to tug the veil from his hand and was mortified that he ignored the open disapproval in her frown. He continued to pull her toward him until there was but a hand's breadth of cloth separating her body from his.

Rayek stiffened; with great difficulty, he held himself in check. Let the barbarian displace one hair upon her head, he thought, let him put his filthy hands on her matchless beauty, let him give me the slightest reason to defend her, and by the High Ones I shall, to the death—his death. Although Rayek could not kill a fellow elf, he decided that killing the pale-skinned barbarian would be a different matter altogether.

Cutter's heart pounded. Leetah could see the pulsing beat in his throat and in the veins of his wrist. Wild creature, barely rational, what did he expect of her? What could he give to her, half animal that he was. Yes, animal! She knew his secret, the secret that was shared by all the Wolfriders, learned by chance during her healing communion with Redlance. She doubted that Cutter himself knew exactly what it was that coursed through his veins. Beautiful young beast. Raw flesh eater. Yes, his lips were tinged with blood, and yes, she wanted to taste them.

Leetah ran from the circle, leaving the veil hanging limp in Cutter's hand. She ran from the light, from the multitude of prying eyes and gaping mouths that no doubt gleamed and muttered behind her. She stumbled through someone's tidy garden, passed several darkened huts, until she came to her own, her sanctuary. Beads broke and spattered on the floor as she burst through the curtained doorway of her dwelling.

The darkness was soothing; she did not trouble to light the night candle near the sleeping pit. Instead, she sat on her stool-chair for some moments, collecting herself. The little wildcat regarded her with slight interest from its favorite spot on the bed-cushion and then twitched its tufted ears and settled down to resume its nap.

Leetah rose and went to the round window in the wall above the sleeping pit. Unable to help it, she began to laugh softly. At herself? At Cutter? No. She laughed at nothing, because there was nothing else to do.

The door curtains rustled, but there was no wind. Leetah turned. A slim silhouette stood framed in the open entrance to the hut. Although she knew that form and figure as well as she knew her own, a moment's fleeting madness led her to believe that Cutter stood there, unmoving, watching her with hungry lupine eyes.

Leetah breathed deeply once and shuddered. The shadow-shape came to her side, wrapped her in its lean, strong arms, and held her with a need entirely uncharacteristic in its frank desperation. The unblinking eyes that searched hers were reptilian yellow, not wolfish blue; the amber gaze demanded a response to an unspoken question.

Gently, the healer laid her palms against Rayek's face. Her sensitive fingers brushed his high, smooth brow, caressed his upswept cheekbones and his parted lips. The physical reality of him had never failed to move her, for his was a tangible beauty, as easily experienced through touch as

through sight. On him, more than on any other, she had
lavished the full measure of her art, for only he possessed
the strength to appreciate it.

With unexpected desperation of her own, Leetah returned
Rayek's embrace. The uniqueness that had so often won
them pardon for their conceit, that had gained them indul-
gence for their pride and self-absorption was suddenly no
longer enough to tie the healer and the hunter together.
Sensing this, they tumbled wordlessly onto the soft cushion
of the sleeping pit and strove to mend that fraying bond
before it could part forever.

It was useless. Although Rayek fought to possess her as
never before, although she clung to him until their bodies
could press no closer, Leetah slipped inexorably away.
Inwardly she raged, struggling to oust the unsettling awareness that had invaded her mind—her soul—without warning.

Tam ... Tam ... Tam. The word was a sound, the
sound a concept, and the concept an identity. She wanted to
be afraid to know this; she craved the ability to be repelled
by this word-sound-concept so that the identity it repre-
sented could be more easily rejected. It was unsettling—but
not fearful. She had realized this unbidden, in a fleeting
moment, when her eyes met the Wolfrider's.

In a last effort to reclaim the self she had so carefully
constructed, the unchanging self that had contented her for
so long, Leetah willed her senses to take dominion over all
else. She could feel the fibers of the yielding fabric on
which she lay burning deep into her body's heightened
perceptions. A sudden breeze whistled through the open
window, rattling the beaded curtain; the sound washed over
her like cold water foam, and she welcomed the noise as
one more barrier between herself and the ancient voice
whose call she refused to acknowledge.

Beams of moonlight filtered through the pattern of the
window beads and fell upon the hut's curved inner wall,
lighting up the colorful dancers painted there. She thought
of the real dancers beyond, who yet celebrated the Wolfriders'

arrival in Sorrow's End. A pale image of the newcomers' callow chieftain hovered insistently before Leetah's inner eye. She closed the eye tightly and forced herself to see—to feel—only the black-haired lover whose arms ensnared her with such fierce possessiveness. How long had she taken for granted the angular grace of that slim form? How long had he been hers to hold at arm's length or to gather in close at her whim? And why had their many joinings failed to bring shared enrichment growing beyond impermanent pleasure? The irresolute alliance had run its course, heedless of time's influence or passing. Now an urgent need for resolution had arisen, and there was time enough only to realize that it was already too late.

The healer and the hunter lay quietly together in the darkened hut. His head rested on her shoulder; languidly, her hand stroke the smoothness of his fine, straight hair. There was no other movement between them.

Abruptly he rose, becoming once more a silent, black silhouette standing before the rounded window. Leetah did not watch him leave, for a quickening of the night breeze betrayed a coolness on her bare shoulder, a coolness whose source she understood even before her fingertips discovered the streaks of moisture dampening her soft, brown skin. His tears.

She folded her hands over the poignant evidence of Rayek's pain and turned to bury her face in the bed-cushion. For the first time in long memory, Leetah wept; her own tears were hot and uncomfortable and brought with them no relief, no solution.

Ten

Briersting flinched and snarled, brushing against Silvergrace as though seeking encouragement. The handsome she-wolf edged away with feigned indifference, watching Nightrunner from the corner of her black-rimmed eye. His thick ruff bristling, his massive head lowered to emphasize the threat, Nightrunner took several slow, deliberate steps toward his upstart challenger. Briersting moved away from Silvergrace but gave no indication that he was ready to submit to the growling packleader.

Silent observers, Strongbow and Cutter stood well away from the confrontation that was taking place on a plateau above the sandstone caves where the Wolfriders now made their homes. It was dawn. The lean archer and his young chief had just returned from a successful night's hunt on the other side of the mountains; each elf bore a catch of long-legged hares trussed together over his shoulder. Wishing to avoid any interference with their wolf-friends' business, the two hunters held quite still and waited respectfully for the conflict to be done.

Slightly larger and more powerful than his defiant opponent, Nightrunner opened his jaws amazingly wide and displayed rows of excellent white teeth, bright against black lips. His fangs, fully bared, were as long as a human's thumb and terrifying to behold, and his uninterrupted snarls echoed hideously from the surrounding rocks. Briersting lunged, pulled up short, backed away, and lunged again, snapping at Nightrunner's muzzle, deliberately avoiding actual bloodshed. Methodically, Nightrunner backed his challenger toward the rim of the plateau; when it became obvious to Briersting that his only choice was to submit or fall, Strongbow's wolf-friend crouched down and rolled his eyes so that the whites showed clearly. Whining as if to placate, Briersting offered his neck to his superior. Nightrunner's hugely yawning jaws closed upon the younger wolf's muzzle for only a moment. Then, having bravely acquitted himself, Briersting was released, honorably defeated.

Strongbow glanced at Cutter. **In another two turns of the seasons, Nightrunner will not win so easily.**

Cutter nodded. Both elves knew that the wolf pack's leader was almost past his prime. He was Cutter's first wolf-friend; the bond had been formed in the elf's seventh year. Then, Nightrunner had been only a gangly-legged pup. Now, as Nightrunner imperiously accepted Silvergrace's solicitous nuzzlings, Cutter saw how rawboned his well-loved mount had grown. He wondered whether the great gray wolf would ever fully recover from his ordeal in the desert.

With his bow slung across his chest, Strongbow climbed down the steep walls of the plateau and crawled into a small cave entrance halfway down the cliffside. This opening led to larger caves deep within the porous rock where the Wolfriders, still nocturnal in their habits, slept through most of the hot day. Half a moon had passed since the forest elves' arrival in Sorrow's End, and though the Sun Folk continually offered all the comforts of their open houses, the Wolfriders remained slow to give up their old ways of secrecy and solitude.

Listlessly, Cutter moved to follow Strongbow. Then, gazing down on the awakening Sun Village, the young chieftain paused. One by one, villagers emerged from their huts, exchanged greetings, and set about the day's heaviest tasks before the morning sun shone too fiercely. Some climbed atop their rounded roofs to mend worn spots in the outer layers of clay. Others turned the soil in their gardens or carried large baskets full of white grain called child's-teeth to be husked.

Cutter climbed to a higher vantage and watched the dark-skinned elves at work. This had become his habit of late, along with refusing food and sleep, and his behavior had not gone unnoticed by the Wolfriders. Their chief's loss of appetite and shortness of temper—shortness unusual even for him—had a cause, but it was a cause too sensitive for confrontation. Although most of the Wolfriders knew exactly what was troubling Cutter, courtesy demanded that they withhold their advice and opinions until he sought them.

Thus, a forlorn figure clad in deerskin breeches and fur vest sat atop a flat-crowned crag and observed the placid routine of village life, hoping for a glimpse of the source of his torment. This morning, to his relief and renewed yearning, he was rewarded.

Leetah came out of her hut, carrying a length of red cloth stretched onto a square frame. Seating herself on a small stone bench, she threaded several silver needles with colored threads, which she carefully unwound from a long silver spool. The thread was very fine, spun from the empty egg cases of sand-dwelling hood spiders. Expertly, Leetah guided the needles in and out of the cloth, mingling the different-colored filaments in an opalescent pattern.

"Shade and sweet water to you, sister." Shenshen came around the side of Leetah's hut, her green and orange skirt all but hidden by the furs she held in her arms.

"Shade and sweet water." Leetah glanced up from her embroidery, smiled as she returned Shenshen's greeting, and then focused her attention on pulling out a stitch that she did not like. Shenshen gave her older sister's work a casual appraisal, shrugged, and sighed like one who had more important things to do.

"Leetah, why don't you come with me? I'm taking these blankets to the Wolf Children. Those dark, cheerless caves must be so cold at night."

The auburn-haired healer wove the needles in and out with studied indifference. "They do not sleep at night. I'm surprised all their dreadful howling hasn't kept you awake."

"Oh, I think it's rather lovely, so mysterious! I just can't understand why the Wolfriders won't come into our huts. They're very fond of you, you know, because you saved that poor, simple redhead's life. Come with me. Perhaps you can persuade them not to be so shy."

Leetah hesitated. Would her sister think her a coward? Did it matter? "You go, Shenshen. I don't want to."

"Because of Cutter?" Shenshen's shining topknots bounced as she shook her head impatiently. "Really, sister, must you be so unforgiving? He may have frightened you at first, but he didn't do any harm. And he did apologize." Green-gold eyes sparkled with secret delight. "You ought to be more friendly."

Viper, Leetah thought. What do you imagine you know?

"Shenshen, you are a fool to encourage her!"

The two sisters turned, startled by the sudden shout. Rayek stood behind them, his fingers digging grooves into the clay-covered wall of the healer's hut. His eyes flashed lightning as he glared from one maiden to the other.

"Leetah would do well to avoid those barbarians altogether," he said, stalking angrily past the sisters. In calculated afterthought, he spat over his shoulder, "Especially Cutter!" He did not wait to witness the effect his words might have.

"Well! By the midday fumes!" Shenshen pouted. "Rayek grows more ill tempered every day."

Leetah bit a thread in two. Almost smiling, she murmured, "The strangers make him nervous, that's all." Neither sister believed it for a moment, and they exchanged glances that said so.

Shenshen scoffed, slyly closed one eye, and placed her forefinger against her dimpled cheek. "Chief hunter or no, Rayek's needed a good taking-down for some time. And Sun bless me, I think Cutter may be the one to do it."

None of the villagers took it much amiss when Rayek failed to acknowledge their polite greetings. The Sun Folk respected their chief hunter, but few liked him, and fewer still understood him. They felt his constant contempt, even though they knew that he reveled in their dependence upon him, especially during times of poor harvest. Those who had from time to time made an effort to unlock Rayek's heart had found him to be cold, evasive, and, above all, arrogant. Therefore, as he seemed to desire it, they left him alone.

Sluggish dirt diggers, Rayek thought as he passed by a family at work with their hand spades and hoes. Dull-brained as zwoots, all of you! his mind shouted. Which of you would spend a lifetime, as I have done, toiling with the clay of your own soul to summon forth the old powers, the magic of the High Ones? Which of you would, then, have the strength of will to retain those powers, refine them, make them do your bidding? None! None save Leetah. The Sun-Toucher became content with his own limits long ago. And Savah has grown weak in the body, overburdened with too many memories. My Leetah and I are the strength and hope of Sorrow's End. Curse the Wolfriders for coming here! Curse you in your gardens for admiring them! The barbarians will drag you down lower than you've sunk already.

Armed with only the golden dagger that hung at his hip, Rayek left the village to prowl around the mountain spur encircling Sorrow's End. It was a good time of day to hunt bristle-boar. The spine-covered desert pigs would be growing drowsy from the ascending Daystar's heat. Their burrows would invite them to lazy rest after a morning of rooting for grubs, lizard eggs, and any other edible thing that hid beneath the hard-baked soil.

Rayek spotted tracks in the dust, tracks made by small cloven hooves. Silent as the flame-striped snake that he resembled in his red, yellow, and black clothing, he glided among the boulders, listening for the telltale grunts of a bristle-boar tusking up some last tidbit before returning to its shade-place.

Soon the hunter's patience was rewarded. He peered over the top of a large rock and spied a hefty specimen—quite mature, judging from the curl of its large tusks—browsing through overturned clods of dirt. The boar stood fairly near to Rayek, its unconcerned snorts proving its ignorance of the elf's presence. Rayek was almost disappointed. This would be too easy.

The hunter made a sharp clicking sound in his throat. When the boar looked up, trying to identify the noise, Rayek trapped it. His method was simple; the effect, inescapable.

As he had tried to do to Cutter, as he had succeeded in doing to Pike, Rayek captured the mind of the boar with the paralyzing power of his stare. Fingers of force seemed to reach out from Rayek's amber eyes, to penetrate the beast's small brain and choke the center of movement. The bristle-boar stiffened, its squeal of surprise cut short. Suddenly, where a living creature had breathed and fed and turned the crust of the desert with strong tusks, there stood a thing as still and silent as stone. Its four stubby legs were as rigid as small pillars. Its jaw was frozen partially open; flies buzzed in and out of its mouth with impunity.

Rayek walked toward the motionless boar, his golden dagger unsheathed and gripped in his left hand. "Calmly now, my bristling friend," he said as he knelt before the spellbound animal. He placed the point of the blade on the soft spot just under the beast's right ear. "You will not feel this."

His left arm tensed for one quick, deadly thrust, but before the dark-skinned hunter could give the stroke, he was interrupted by a youthful, mocking voice—a hated voice.

"You do your prey no honor to take the fight out of it like that."

Rayek looked up. High above his head, atop a colorfully layered outcropping, perched the barbarians' pale-haired chieftain. Rayek scowled at him, squinting from the glare of sunlight on bare rock.

"What do you know of honor, Wolfrider? You are more beast than elf. Is it an honor for animals to die in terror and pain?" Rayek pointed to the stupefied boar. "My way spares them that suffering."

"Oh?" Cutter's smile was enigmatic. "Is that how you plan to get Leetah?"

Insulted beyond endurance, Rayek slowly rose to his feet. A murderous expression distorted his handsome features.

"Stay away from her, barbarian. I warn you." Rayek's voice was low; the dagger glinted menacingly as he transferred it to his right hand. Spreading the fingers of his left hand wide, he held them over the boar's rounded back. Cutter's eyes went wide, for the animal, still rigid and insensible as death, began to rise from the ground! Straight up it floated until it hovered on a level with Rayek's chest.

"Do not cross me," the hunter continued darkly, "or you will stand no more chance—than *this!*"

Blood spurted as Rayek drove his knife deep into the paralyzed boar's throat. It died instantly without a twitch or cry, thudding stiffly to the ground. Cutter's stomach turned over; any death, no matter how horribly painful, would be preferable to what he had just witnessed. He respected his rival's obvious magical prowess, but now, more than ever, he disliked and distrusted Rayek.

This is your enemy, Tam, the Wolfriders' chieftain thought to himself. You've never had an elf enemy before. He's much more dangerous than a human.

"You're sure of it? She's the one?" Skywise was tremendously relieved that his friend had finally decided to confide in him. The two elves sat together outside the largest of the sandstone caves. Cutter leaned upon Nightrunner's back, picking distractedly at the wolf's fur.

"Yes, I knew it the moment I saw her, and so did she. Leetah. She knows my soul name, Skywise. I'd stake my life on it."

The stargazer nodded sympathetically. "Then you should talk to her."

"I will," Cutter murmured, almost to himself. "Tomorrow."

Inside the cave, Dewshine sighed unhappily. It bothered her that her cousin-chief, who was not very much older than she, seemed on the verge of illness because of the thing that had happened between him and the Sun Village's healer. In the most vague way Dewshine empathized with his suffering. She and Scouter had recently begun to delve into the mysteries and pleasures of joining; drawing on her admittedly small store of experience, Dewshine was able to imagine something of the pain of thwarted desire. This "thing" was more than desire, however; it made her cousin gaunt and moody and joyless. She feared that someday she herself might suffer such an illness. What was it? And what was the cure?

"Cutter hasn't eaten a thing for two days," she commented to her father. "He thinks of nothing but Leetah."

Treestump understood his daughter's implicit question. He smiled and pretended to be interested in his belt buckle. "Uh huh. Sometimes it happens like that. There's no telling when or why."

Dewshine's round, wondering eyes egged him on. Farther back in the chamber, Scouter pricked up his ears. He, too, was seeking answers. Treestump looked out of the cave at his dead sister's son, who lay watching the quiet night-shrouded village as though the other half of his soul slept there.

"Sometimes an elf lad and maiden Recognize each other, and bang—" Treestump clapped his hands together under his daughter's nose "—it's fixed! There's nothing either one of them can do but accept it, poor cubs."

Dewshine gasped. "Fixed? Forever?"

"Forever," her father solemnly said. "Once you Recognize your lifemate, even death won't break the bond. You become one soul in two bodies." He paused. "Believe me, I know."

"And that's what's happened to Cutter? But Father, what about love? What about choice?" She lowered her voice to an anxious whisper. "Leetah hates Cutter! How can they become lifemates?"

Treestump petted his daughter's white-gold curls. "That's the problem, isn't it, pretty cub?"

Dewshine gulped. "Can this Recognizing happen to any-one? Any time?"

She was not at all happy to see her father's immediate nod.

It took Cutter most of the following day to summon the wherewithal to confront Leetah and yet maintain his self-control. The urge to carry her away was strong, although he tried to suppress it. He was strong, very strong. If he wanted to take her, he could, and she wouldn't be able to prevent him. Why shouldn't he take her? She was his, after all. But each time his thoughts reached that giddy height, the pathetic image of Rayek's bristle-boar—helpless, paralyzed, a poor puppet victim—shattered Cutter's dream of easy triumph. No. He would not violate Leetah's dignity. He would talk to her, show her that she had nothing to fear. Then, if she wanted to, she could carry him away. It didn't matter. Nothing mattered except the knot in his stomach and his need to be rid of it.

Cutter walked through the Sun Village, hunching up his shoulders as though to hide his face in the thick nap of his vest. Large dark eyes peered curiously at him from window holes or from behind tall fanlike growths of sticker-plants. Villagers tittered and scampered away as he approached Leetah's silent hut. He kept his head down, his long, pale bangs concealing his eyes. Pausing at her heavily curtained doorway, he thought a moment and went instead to a nearby window. Although the fabric of the beaded curtain was gauzy and translucent, he could not see inside the healer's dwelling. Even so, he was certain that she could see his shadow on the drapery. He leaned against the wall and spoke to the window.

"Leetah? Many days have passed without a word between us. Why do you deny the truth we both know?"

The chieftain scratched his knuckles, waiting. After what seemed a very long time, the curtain was parted by a shapely brown hand; two plain gold bracelets chimed together on the slender wrist. Leetah's exquisite features appeared in the opening. Her expression was part guarded puzzlement, part annoyance.

"Truth?" she repeated. "I don't know what you mean."

"Yes, you do," Cutter shot back instantly. He placed his hands on the broad lower rim of the window and looked hard at Leetah. It was all he could do to keep from climbing into the hut. "In my tribe we don't play games with our hearts. We *know*."

"Know what?"

The Wolfrider almost groaned aloud. When he had resolved to talk to Leetah, he had not realized that words appropriate to the situation did not exist. Either she understood or she did not. But of course she understood everything. Words were useless ornamentation, or ought to be, at a time like this.

"I won't hurt you," he said, blundering ahead.

"No, you won't," she said, agreeing, looking past his shoulder with an odd smile.

Suddenly the world spun around, and Cutter's back struck the ground hard, knocking the wind out of him. Sprawled face up, the young chieftain blinked and shook his head; his upper arm burned where his assailant's nails had raked the flesh. Cutter winced, able to make out a dark figure, heavily backlit by the sun, standing over him. It was Rayek. In the hunter's hand gleamed a long, pointed object.

Instinctively Cutter twisted his body as the missile knifed toward him. Its point struck and entered the ground just a hand's breadth away from his ribs. If he had not moved . . .

Rayek turned stiffly and walked away. Amazed, Cutter released his grip on New Moon's hilt and looked at the strange object beside him. Plucking it from the ground, he examined it from all angles and decided that it was not a weapon.

It was as long as his forearm, carved from cloud-tree wood. Three symbols, one on top of the other, made up the body of the pointed stick. The topmost symbol was the polished likeness of a noble elf's head. It reminded Cutter of Sun-Toucher. Supporting the sculpted head was an elf's four-fingered hand, and below that, the smoothly rounded representation of a heart. A short length of stick, tapering to a point, extended downward from the tip of the heart, presumably a handle.

Cutter held up the miniature totem and studied it, trying to fathom its meaning. He turned to Leetah for help but saw that she had vanished from the window. Her curtains were closed, and he knew that a barrier much stronger than those filmy, bejeweled drapes separated him from the healer.

Furious and frustrated, he clutched the symbol-stick as though it were Rayek's neck and dashed for the great central hut. Covering the distance with an arrow's speed, Cutter, in all his fury, burst into Savah's presence.

She was alone. This was very strange, for normally the comings and goings from her audience chamber were almost ceaseless. Villagers constantly visited her, seeking her wisdom, seeking memories. How it happened that he had caught Savah at this time of solitude—not even the ever-attentive Ahdri hovered near—Cutter could not guess. He was glad of it, though. Still wrought up and breathing hard, he sank to his knees before the Mother of Memory and waited for her to acknowledge his presence.

Her silver-lidded eyes were shut, yet she did not seem to be asleep. Her posture as she sat upon her tall-backed chair was erect and regal. The multihued disk behind her chair shimmered faintly, the only source of light in the chamber save for eight triangular vents cut high in the domed ceiling.

Cutter looked around. This was only the second time he had entered Savah's dwelling, and on his first visit he had been too overwhelmed by the sight of her to notice much else. He remembered the wall pictures on either side of the dais, but looking up, he noticed many more carvings ascending into the blue-shadowed dome above. So many memories. The bark of a tree has memories of its own, too, he thought, but the pictures there are always changing, always growing.

Suddenly Cutter felt tired and very lonely. The circular chamber was cool, but not with the breath of life like the living forest. The shadows were soothing but not many layers deep and mottled and in constant gentle motion like leaves. Nothing moved here. All was stillness under the blazing sun, and in that oppressive stillness a troubled heart seemed many times more heavy, lacking even the careless song of birds to lighten it.

"Come here, child." Savah's russet eyes were open. She held out one long birdlike hand to Cutter. He rose from his knees and came to stand before her on the dais. Seated as she was, their eyes were on a level. He tried to speak, but then without understanding how, he found himself at her feet, weeping silently, his face buried in her lap.

"Mother," he whispered. "Mother of Memory."

She stroked his hair and allowed him to rest against her long after his shoulders had ceased shaking. Straightening up, he hastily wiped his eyes with an impatient gesture and presented Savah with the symbol-stick. She took it and turned it thoughtfully in her hands.

"Rayek?"

Cutter answered her with a nod, although he suspected that he didn't have to. Somehow the Mother of Memory knew everything that went on in her village, even though she seldom stepped forth from her hut.

"What is it, Savah?" Cutter pointed to the stick.

"A challenge wand! I have not seen one in—" Ah, how to tell the Wolfrider how long it had been? Would he even believe, judging by the Sun Folk as they were now, that her people had once been warlike? That the first children of Sorrow's End had lived to train for battle, honing their bodies to perfect, sharp strength against the day that they must defend the village from humans? The challenge wand was a relic of ritual combat from long ago, forgotten as the years passed in their eights, and many eights of eights, forgotten, as were the humans who never came.

"This wand has an ancient voice, Wolfrider. I must teach you its language," Savah said. "When all involved are before me, I shall tell you what it means."

"Hear anything?" hissed Scouter.

"Not with you yelping like a wolf cub with a bee under its tail," Pike growled. "Keep quiet and let me listen."

Scouter clung to the limb of a cloud-tree, watching as Pike pressed his ear to a vent in the topmost tier of the central hut's roof. Climbing the tree to gain the roof and eavesdrop had been Scouter's idea, but Pike did not have a pair of scrupulous parents as Scouter did who would box his ears if they caught him. Hence, Pike was the eavesdropper and Scouter the envious hidden accomplice.

The elfin youth excused his misbehavior by reasoning that anything that affected Cutter mattered a great deal to the entire tribe. Respect and courtesy aside—far aside—the Wolfriders would surely want to know everything about the Sun Folk's strange attitude toward courtship and lifemating. The way Cutter had been acting lately, he'd probably keep it all to himself. So, Scouter concluded, someone had to find out.

Pike's expression revealed that he was indeed getting an earful. Within the large hut, an unusual ceremony was taking place.

Savah stood upon the dais, her arms outspread. In one hand she held the challenge wand. Before her on a curved stone bench sat Leetah, her mother at her left side and her father at her right. They had quickly obeyed Savah's summons, and Cutter had noted that even the venerable Sun-Toucher, interpreter of the voice of the mighty Daystar, was humble in the presence of the Mother of Memory.

Last to arrive had been Rayek. He had entered the chamber of audience with cool hauteur, wearing an elegant red robe partially caught up in graceful folds and tucked into his belt. Immediately he had gone to Savah's left hand, the hand that held the challenge wand. Ignorant of anything else to do, Cutter had positioned himself opposite Rayek, on Savah's right. Both rivals had looked at Leetah and then glared at each other, unspeaking.

Although she knew nothing of the ancient ritual about to begin, Leetah sensed that for good or ill, her long and tranquil life must soon change. Her wonder and anticipation were tinged with anger. Although she was the pivotal figure in this strange dance, she had not called the tune, nor was it to her liking. Apprehensively, she waited to learn what was expected of her, listening as Savah explained the origin of the challenge wand.

"Long ago, the way of the Sun Folk was not the way of peace. The earliest inhabitants of the village were hunters and fighters, pitting themselves against wild beasts, mastering the treasure-filled mountain peaks which surrounded Sorrow's End. As time passed, they devised difficult games to try their strength, wits, and courage to the limits. Life in the village centered on these mock battles, but one day a dispute arose which gave new purpose to the games.

"Two suitors loved the same maiden. Each desired her for his own. All were opposed to a three-mating, but the maiden cared for both suitors equally. When it became clear that the matter could lead to bloodshed, the maiden wisely proposed that her suitors compete in a game. To issue a formal challenge, one of the rivals carved a wooden wand which symbolized the three trials he would undergo, and he presented it to his opponent. The victor would win the right to court his love without interference from the defeated one. In that way, unhurried and without fear of violence, the maiden was able to examine both her suitors and make her choice.

"The event became known as the Trial of Hand, Head, and Heart, and in all the long history of Sorrow's End it has taken place only six times. This—" Savah held up the carved stick in her left hand "—is the seventh challenge wand."

Rayek folded his arms, noting with satisfaction the look of uncertainty in Cutter's eyes. Leetah was fascinated in spite of herself.

"Children of my children's children," the Mother of Memory intoned, "hear now a chant that is older than old and truer than truth itself."

> *"Heart to heart are lifemates bound.*
> *Soul meets soul when eyes meet eyes.*
> *Maiden, 'mongst those gathered round,*
> *Stands your true love Recognized?"*

Leetah blanched, but the chant continued.

> *"Speak his name and all is done.*
> *'Twixt these two, you must decide.*
> *Nay to both or aye to one?*
> *Which of them must step aside?"*

Silence.

Now, Leetah! You know the truth! Speak it now! We're Recognized! Cutter sent, knowing full well that Leetah would block him out as she had done before. He couldn't help it.

"Say what is in your heart, my daughter," Toorah said softly. "We will all abide by your decision."

Leetah turned first to Rayek. Underneath the arrogance, the self-assured pose, a lifelong friend who needed the vindication of her love begged—demanded—that she defy nature itself for her own sake and for his. She caressed him with her gaze. Then, slowly, almost against her will, Leetah's iridescent eyes were drawn to Cutter's.

The Wolfriders' young chieftain—so young, hardly more than a child—was Rayek's opposite in every respect: artless, frank-hearted, wild as a beast of prey. And yet . . .

"Soul meets soul when eyes meet eyes." Savah's chant echoed in the healer's mind. Leetah looked at Cutter and *knew* him, top to toe, within and without. He was that part of herself over which she had no control, the innocence that defied discipline or cynical scorn. He was courage; he was vulnerability. And he was passion, so raw and demanding and giving at once that Leetah was forced to look away from him, away from herself. She felt exposed down to the marrow of her delicate bones.

"Speak his name and all is done."

Tam . . . Tam . . . Tam.

Speak his name . . .

Leetah put her hands to her face. No! she cried inwardly. It can't be him! That savage? I'd rather be lifemate to his wolf! Curse the humans who sent him here! Shall I go about the village with a living mirror at my side, reflecting all that I would have no one know of me?

For long moments Leetah agonized in silence. Then she lifted her head and spoke very softly. "In truth, I—I can neither choose nor refuse either one."

Rayek's jaw dropped. Cutter drew in his breath. Unbelievable! He marveled. How could Leetah deny Recognition?

Savah nodded, her gold headdress glinting rainbows from the light of the many-colored disk. She did not seem surprised by Leetah's answer.

"If the maiden's heart is open to both who seek her love," the Mother of Memory said evenly, "then the trial may determine which suitor she'll approve."

Turning to Cutter, the aged elf extended the challenge wand. "Chief of Wolfriders, Rayek has challenged you to the Trial of Hand, Head, and Heart. The one of you who takes victory in each of three contests shall win the undisputed right to court Leetah."

"Strength, wits, and courage, Wolf," Rayek interrupted, raising a warning fist. "Three out of three! You cannot defeat me! Leetah will be mine once and for all!"

Instantly the healer was on her feet, stepping between the two rivals. She was indignant, her dark gleaming skin ruddy with inner fire, her eyes glittering more fiercely than the facets of her gold ornaments.

"Rayek! Do you know less of courtesy than this barbarian does?" she cried. "This is no child's game of toss-stone, and I am not some trinket to be handed out as a prize! The only thing the trial will resolve is your foolish rivalry, not my preference!"

"Peace," Savah commanded as Rayek flinched from the lash of Leetah's censure. "Let the Wolfrider speak. Does he accept the challenge?"

A single nod, more eloquent than any boast of prowess, was Cutter's only reply. He had no choice but to accept, just as Nightrunner could not have refused Briersting's challenge for Silvergrace on the plateau. It was the Way.

"Then let the rivals prepare," pronounced the Mother of Memory. "The trial begins at sunrise."

Suddenly, overhead there was a sound as of booted feet scuttling down the roof outside. Then came the rustle and creaking of dry, overburdened branches, a thump, a curse, another thump, and silence. Cutter smiled. He saluted Savah with a slight bow, as he had seen others do, and then turned and stared at Leetah, not angrily but without affection. She did her best to respond in kind. No one spoke as Cutter quietly walked from the chamber, parting the beaded curtain and closing it behind him without a sound.

"He is a stealthy one, this Wolfrider," Leetah's mother commented, easing the tension. "He did not speak once."

"It is better to judge him by his actions," said the Sun-Toucher. Although his words were discreet, something in the lines surrounding his sightless eyes suggested that he liked Cutter very much indeed.

"He is an animal," muttered Rayek, "and should be treated as one."

Savah regarded the chief hunter a little coldly. "Remember, the contest must be fair," she cautioned him. "Do not be tempted to use your magic against Cutter."

Rayek's slow grin was malevolent, chilling. "I will not need to, Mother of Memory."

He bowed his head respectfully to Savah, saluted Leetah and her parents in the same way, and turned to depart. Leetah caught him by the arm. Her grip was desperate.

"Win," she whispered. "Please win. Shield me from him. I cannot do it myself."

He touched her cheek but did not try to take her in his arms. "I don't understand you. You had the chance to choose me. You still do. Why let this nonsense go on?"

She lowered her eyes, ashamed. "Because there is something I must know. I cannot explain more."

Rayek smiled thinly. "I will win tomorrow, and you will be mine. I swear it."

She watched him leave the hut. The beads rattled noisily, and the curtains swayed for some time afterward.

Her hands—the life-giving hands that had never failed to accomplish everything expected of them—were trembling.

Eleven

Dawn.

It was a time of glorification, a time of golden mist through which the sun looked most kindly on the wakening face of the world, a time to set great events in motion, to see what changes the day would bring before it passed into darkness.

Sun-Toucher remembered the white brilliance of the Daystar, that blinding splendor that had claimed his sight little by little, enabling him to perceive the truth more and more clearly as his vision dimmed. He had learned that the sun was more than light and warmth; it was mother and father to all movement in the world. Wind, rain, day, night, plants that pushed roots deep underground in search of water, beasts that were stilled by its heat and active in its absence—all moved in answer to the Daystar's command. To hear the voice of the sun and to understand it perfectly, the young Sun-Toucher had meditated daily, staring into that face of indescribable brightness. Twice a cube-of-eights of years had passed since blackness had taken his sight.

The memories remained, however, and the Sun-Toucher remembered blue sky. He remembered the stirring beauty of morning's first rays, trickling over and down the mountainside like liquid flame, rousing each layer of color within the rock to full vitality. Never but at dawn were the hues of the desert so wonderfully alive. His memories growing more vivid with the time rather than fading, the Sun-Toucher sensed what his people saw as they gathered for the Trial of Hand, Head, and Heart.

The ring where the Sun Folk had danced to welcome and honor the Wolfriders had been transformed overnight into an arena. Weathered stones set tightly together bordered the flat, circular stretch of ground. The raised platform, which supported Savah's "chair in the sun" and two other seats, was shaded by a canopy of deep blue fabric held aloft on gaily painted poles. Golden fringes trimmed the canopy and glistened like amber raindrops. Nearby, smaller lean-tos waited for spectators who might wish shade during the contest.

Since the morning twilight, while stars yet shone in the purple sky, the folk of Sorrow's End had been awake, pre-paring for the day's events. The village buzzed with gossip and speculation about the forthcoming duel between Rayek and the Wolfrider.

Lifematings born of Recognition were extremely rare among the Sun Folk and were as much cause for great excitement as the equally rare elfin births. Ever since Leetah's healing skills had matured, no villager had died from injury or sickness. The Sun Folk treasured Leetah, held her nearly as high in their esteem as they held Savah herself. Unfortu-nately, the blessing of the healer's consummate skills carried with it an insidious curse. The laughter of very young children was heard less and less in Sorrow's End.

It was generally agreed that something remarkable had happened to Leetah since the barbarians' arrival, and what was more remarkable, she seemed to be fighting it with all her strength. Chief administrator of the rumors, which flew like flies around a pot of sweet-cider pulp, was Shenshen, self-appointed authority on her older sister's love troubles. She basked in the fluttering attentions of her fellows, all eager for some toothsome bit of insight into the mysterious triangle. Was it Recognition? they asked. Who had Recog-nized whom? Had Rayek or Cutter issued the challenge? Or was it all Leetah's idea? Coyly, Shenshen avoided direct answers. Thereby implying that she knew more than she told.

As the population of the village gathered around the rock-encircled arena, Shenshen and several other maidens clustered near the blue canopy, waiting breathlessly for all three points of the bellicose triangle to arrive.

Soon the gleaming, scalloped edges of Savah's peaked headdress could be seen above the milling crowd. The villagers parted to let her pass, and she spoke to them with affection and humor, her frail form never losing its stately bearing or its aura of mystic power. The Mother of Memory's arm rested upon Leetah's; with cool dignity the healer escorted the progenitress of Sorrow's End to her seat beneath the canopy. After lightly touching her father's hand in greeting, Leetah took her place beside Savah. The Sun-Toucher remained standing by the circle of rocks, for he was to preside over the Trial of Hand.

An outbreak of excited chatter heralded the coming of the Wolfriders from the caves. Through the spaces between the huts, they could be seen approaching the arena, all seventeen of them, even baby Wing riding in a doeskin cradle on Woodlock's back. The forest elves were grimly escorted by several fierce-looking, shaggy wolves; and Cutter, walking at the head of his tribe, seemed no less grim or fierce than the huge beasts skulking beside him.

He was bare to the waist, dressed only in leather breeches and soft boots. New Moon hung at his left hip, its silvery sheen accenting his natural swagger. Shenshen and her covey found themselves entranced by the simple green-feather ornament that decorated his breechclout.

"Cutter will win the trial," a dark-haired maiden announced, sighing. "He has to."

"Leetah Recognized him," added another. "Everyone knows it!"

"Everyone but Leetah." Shenshen tittered foolishly, unable to take her eyes from that fascinating feather.

The Wolfriders did not mingle with the crowd when they came to the circle of stones. Instead, they grouped together to one side of the platform, shielding their chief almost protectively from prying eyes.

"Where's the old pig poker?" Pike asked, craning his neck to look around for Rayek.

"Maybe he won't show. Maybe he's scared," Scouter offered.

"Not likely." Cutter half smiled. "His head may be on crooked, but he's no coward."

"You're right. Look." Treestump pointed to where a circular arch of rock jutted up from the mountainside. Within the arch a lone figure stood, casting a long shadow as the newly risen sun beamed through the aperture.

"It's Rayek," whispered Nightfall, glancing quickly at Leetah and wondering what turmoil the healer's icy composure concealed.

"He's still not impressing anyone," Treestump muttered, eliciting a giggle from Pike.

With a leisurely stride the chief hunter stepped down from his perch and approached the place of trial. He carried no spear but bore himself as though he were amply armed. Rayek did not deign to acknowledge his opponent's presence, but stepped directly into the arena. Taking that as a sign, Cutter entered the ring of stones as well. He was slightly shorter but no less formidable in appearance than the hunter. The outcome of the trial was anyone's guess.

Savah gestured for silence from the murmuring villagers. Everyone could clearly see the short, carved staff that she held in her hand.

"Yesterday the seventh challenge wand of Sorrow's End was hurled and accepted. Rayek, chief hunter of the Sun Folk, has challenged Cutter, chieftain of the Wolfriders, for the undisputed right to court Leetah the Healer."

Why not "Healer of the Sun Folk"? Leetah wondered. Perhaps Savah means that my powers are for the good of my kind, not just for my tribe. It is still difficult to believe that the Sun Folk are not the only elves in the world.

"Three trials shall test the strength, wits, and courage of the two opponents. Only he who wins all three shall be named victor. Let Rayek and Cutter each fail one trial, and the games shall be declared done."

If that happens, nobody will be any better off than they were before. What a waste of time! Strongbow sent to his tribefolk.

Cutter will win, Pike flashed back, too angrily. **Don't ever doubt that!** More vehement than it needed to be, his sending did not quite ring true. The memory of Rayek's paralyzing stare had shaken Pike's confidence. How could Cutter defeat one who had such power?

Savah's resonant voice assumed a commanding tone. "He who loses all three trials must abide by the rule. He shall in no way and by no means interfere with the victor's attentions to Leetah. Do the opponents understand and agree?"

They nodded.

"Then let the first contest begin."

"Bring forth the tools for the Trial of Hand," called the Sun-Toucher.

Quickly Skywise jumped into the ring. He stood in front of his chief, grinned a brotherly grin, and in one motion transferred the lodestone from his neck to Cutter's.

"Here. Wear the lodestone for luck," he said. "It led us away from the fixed star, away from our old life to here. Maybe it will guide you now!"

Surprised and honored beyond words, Cutter placed his hands on his friend's shoulders.

"Thanks, Skywise."

The stargazer grinned again and stepped aside as three male villagers, all dressed alike in red capelets and tunics, entered the arena. Two of the elves carried a pair of long poles between them. The third carefully rolled along the ground a large cylinder that was deeply grooved near either end. The drum appeared to be fashioned from a log of petrified wood. The Wolfriders could not begin to guess what such objects had to do with a test of strength.

One of the red-garbed elves gave Cutter a strip of yellow cloth to use as a blindfold; Skywise helped his friend adjust it over his large ears. Rayek pulled his wide, striped headband down to cover his own eyes. Seeing this, Pike breathed a sigh of relief; the black-haired one would not be allowed to use his deadly magic. It was going to be a fair fight.

Sun-Toucher spoke quietly to Rayek. "You have played

this game many times. The Wolfrider has not. I must instruct him."

"As you wish," Rayek said lightly. "He will gain no advantage if you do."

Cutter heard the swish of the elder's robes and caught the metallic scent of his helmet as the Sun-Toucher came to his side.

"Is it strange not to see, Wolfrider?" Leetah's father asked with gentle amusement.

"I've never had my eyes covered before," Cutter admitted. "So my ears and my nose must make up for it. I hear them doing something with the poles. How does this game work?"

"The attendants have placed the rolling drum in the center of the ring of challenge. Now they settle the poles into the grooves of the drum. You must straddle the poles on your own side of the roller while Rayek balances on the other side. Attendants will hold both ends of both poles off the ground. You must take care not to lose your balance and fall."

"So far, not bad," Skywise whispered.

"Shhh! What then, Sun-Toucher?"

"It is very simple. The Trial of Hand is a test of strength and agility. To win, you must cause your opponent to fall from the poles. It will be named a fall the moment your foot or his touches the ground, no matter how slightly. But remember one thing. All the while you and Rayek are wrestling hand to hand, the attendants will be tilting the poles and rolling the drum back and forth."

Skywise gulped and looked at the two elves who were already kneeling in position at opposite ends of the long shafts. Their wide faces were unreadable. Would they favor Rayek because he was one of them?

"Remember the lodestone," the stargazer said, gripping his chief's arm reassuringly. "It will bring you luck."

I'll need it, Cutter mused. He heard his friend's light steps as Skywise darted away to join the other Wolfriders.

Behind him, from the platform, Leetah's voice called out softly, "Mother, come sit by me."

Was the healer as worried as he was? This contest is senseless, Cutter thought. I don't see the need of it, but I'll do as Leetah wants.

He felt his way forward until his shin bumped into one of the poles. The third attendant helped him find his footing atop the two slender beams. His tree-dweller's toes were accustomed to gripping the narrowest, smoothest limbs, and Cutter felt pleasantly at home for the first time in days.

A slight shuddering of each pole told the Wolfrider that Rayek had taken his position. The cylinder rolled suddenly, catching Cutter off guard. His arms spun in the air as he strove to maintain his balance. Rayek snickered nastily, able to imagine what he could not see.

Fed up with his rival's sly mockery, Cutter jumped straight into the air and came down hard on his side of the poles, quickly hopping from one foot to the other. The two attendants were so startled, they nearly lost their grip, and Rayek found himself tipped up on one leg, groping in space with his free foot for the other, crazily bobbing pole.

The Wolfriders howled with glee, and even some of the Sun Folk chortled behind their hands.

Sun-Toucher banged his staff against the base of the stage. Everyone settled down, or tried to.

"One fall loses all," the blind elder called out imperiously. "Ready yourselves."

Cutter and Rayek crouched down, fully aware that this trial would set the pace for the rest of the duel. One of them had to lose, and the most the defeated one could hope for was to best his opponent in one of the two remaining trials. In that way, no one would win; but neither Cutter nor Rayek had any intention of losing the Trial of Hand.

"Good luck, Black Hair!" Treestump called from the sideline.

Pike's eyes bulged like strutter-hen eggs. "Huh? You're on Rayek's side?" he gasped at the eldest wolfrider.

WENDY
©82.PINI

234 WENDY AND RICHARD PINI

"Nope," Treestump drawled, stroking his beard complacently, "just sympathetic. Cutter'll beat the living bear fat out of him."

Pike sniggered. "Oh!"

"Begin!"

Cutter felt the rolling of the drum and the alternating tilting of the poles beneath his feet. With his left arm extended for balance, he groped about until his right hand found Rayek's. Their fingers locked in a crushing grip, and Rayek quickly made the first move, jerking the Wolfrider's arm far to one side. Cutter, however, had correctly anticipated that his rival would use such a tactic, and he was braced to counterbalance the move.

"No," Cutter growled. "You won't end this fight so quickly!"

The poles suddenly tipped down on Cutter's side; he took advantage of it and pulled Rayek toward him. The hunter bent his knees deeply, shifting his weight to keep himself from falling forward. As the beams once again came level, Rayek sprang up and jerked Cutter's arm from side to side to confuse him. Amazingly, the Wolfrider kept his foothold even when Rayek risked toppling himself by throwing his full weight into a mighty pull to his right.

"Give up, flea scratcher," warned the hunter. "No one can best me at this game."

Cutter laughed. "This is easier than walking a tree branch in a light breeze!"

"Think so?"

Rayek suddenly cranked Cutter's extended arm in a complete circle and pulled him hard to Cutter's right. Gleefully, he felt his young opponent keel onto one foot and heard the Wolfrider's whoop of surprise. "You were saying, cur?" Rayek jeered.

Trained through a lifetime of tree walking to avoid a fall in any way possible, Cutter jumped completely off the pole on which he tottered. Twisting his lithe body in midair, he dived for the pole, grabbed it with his left hand, and then let both feet drop solidly onto the other pole. He was in a dangerously awkward position, but his feet had not touched the ground.

"Mother, why are you chewing on your hat?" Newstar asked, looking with innocent wonder at Rainsong.

"Hush! Or I'll chew on your ears," Rainsong muttered nervously through the leather. With tremendous relief she saw Cutter, still clinging with his left hand, straddle the teetering poles in a crouch. Then, abruptly, he stood up and yanked Rayek forward. To keep himself upright, the hunter had to brace one sandaled foot against the drum. It rolled toward him, and his heel, moving with it, almost brushed the ground. Rayek spat out an oath as he regained his foothold.

"Bead rattler," taunted Cutter.

"Bone polisher," Rayek shot back, squatting down and forcing his rival to lean far over the rolling drum. Powerful leg muscles launching him like an arrow from the strongest bowstring, Rayek sprang up and rammed his shoulder against Cutter's. The Wolfrider's feet skidded back along the poles with the impact.

"Snake," he shouted.

"Dog," came the hunter's reply.

Cutter leaned into Rayek, his stockier build and slightly greater weight serving him well against his lanky opponent. Both contestants were locked now in a two-handed death grip, pushing against each other, straining, each hoping for his own brute strength to prevail. The tilting of the beams meant little now, for Cutter and Rayek were perched directly over the drum, where motion was slight. Their bodies glistened with sweat, and their interlocked fingers were white from loss of blood flow.

Leetah had seen Rayek dance the twin-pole dance many times. She had seen his challengers fall many times, so easily that Rayek's victories had seldom impressed her. Now she held her breath, watching her black-haired friend strive as never before to cast down his opponent.

Suddenly it was over. There was a slight shifting of Cutter's weight—a coiling, almost—a burst of strength from some yet-untapped reserve. And then Rayek was flying, head over heels, his colorful loincloths fluttering, his lips shaping a silent "No!" He struck the ground shoulders first, raising plumes of dust.

The Wolfriders went wild, giving forth their howling cry over and over again. "Ayoooah! Ayooooah!"

Stunned, unsure whether they should be pleased for Cutter, the Sun Folk stared dumbly at their chief hunter as he picked himself up and pushed his headband back from his eyes. He would not look at his people or at Cutter, who still perched on the poles, fussing with the knot of his blindfold. Rayek stood silently before the platform, before Leetah's seated figure all stiff with shock and amazement.

Disgusted with the knot, Cutter ripped the cloth from his eyes and whirled it over his head. He howled, and his tribefolk howled back at him, waving and smiling their pride.

"Ha! What did I tell you?" Treestump crowed. "He's old Bearclaw's son sure as birds fly!"

"And Rayek's chewing nettles now, sure as snakes crawl." Skywise laughed. He didn't care who heard him.

Cutter bounced to the foot of Savah's chair. He looked up at her, seeking some sign of approval, and was disappointed by her complete neutrality. Sun-Toucher nodded at the Mother of Memory; she held the challenge wand above Cutter's topknot as a sign of victory.

"The Trial of Hand goes to the Wolfrider," the Sun-Toucher announced.

More cheers and shouts of congratulation came from the forest elves. With chest puffed proudly, Cutter turned to Leetah, again seeking favor, but again he was met with cold indifference. Somehow the healer had built a wall around herself, one that would not permit even anger to show through. As though the moment of Eyes-Meeting-Eyes had never occurred, she gave no sign that he had moved her in any way. Hurt and bewildered by her impossible behavior,

Cutter slunk away from the canopy, all triumph drained out of him.

"Well, my kitling," Toorah said, casually adjusting the loose folds of her cowl about her throat, "Rayek has lost his solitary claim on you. Perhaps the Wolfrider—"

"Mother! Physical strength is but a trifle," Leetah answered, interrupting too hastily.

Although much time had passed since Toorah had held any maternal sway over her headstrong daughter, the richly gowned elf-woman thought that she glimpsed just then something of the child she had known long ago—the emerald-eyed child of silences and secrets who could be coaxed to reveal her heart's burdens only indirectly.

"Surely the barbarian will fail the test of wits," Leetah said as though to reassure herself.

And if he succeeds in all three trials, daughter, what then? Toorah wondered. Onto what strange turning in your life's path will this pale young stranger lead you?

A scuffle had broken out at the edge of the arena. Five embattled villagers lunged, pounced, and were flung back, shouting, amid clouds of dust; and in the center of it all—predictably—stood Cutter, his shining sword held high above his head as he fended off those who tried to wrest it from him. It was an impressive sight: the muscular Wolfrider holding his own against five astonished dark-skinned elves who simply could not get near him long enough to reach the silvery blade.

"No," he yelled, outraged. "You can't have it! Get away!"

The only thing his battered assailants could do was back him toward the stage and corner him like an animal. Cutter whirled and looked at the Mother of Memory with betrayed, pleading eyes.

"Savah, you can have anything I own but this!" He clutched the hilt of his weapon fiercely. "Not New Moon! Not my father's sword!"

At a sign from Savah, the panting villagers left Cutter alone. He stood there, disheveled and dirt-streaked, the lodestone tangled in his long hair. He had all but made up his mind to forfeit the second trial—even the whole contest— rather than put up with this impossible loss. Part with New Moon? Give it away? They might as well ask for his heart wrapped in a leaf.

"Tradition demands that both opponents give over their weapons," Savah said quietly. Rayek's golden dagger already lay across her palm, proof that the hunter was willing to obey without question the code of the trial of wits.

"The blades will be hidden deep and well in secret caverns within the mountains," continued the Mother of Memory. "He who regains his weapon and returns here first by use of his wits shall be declared the victor."

"Sounds fair enough," Treestump said to Skywise. "I know how the lad feels about Bearclaw's sword, but it would be a shame if he let his heart rule his head just now."

Skywise nodded. Strength and courage Cutter had in abundance, but there was not a guileful bone in his body. Skywise knew that his young chieftain could not meet defeat at Rayek's hands this day. Unfortunately, in a trial of wits, Cutter's impulsive, flammable emotions were his own worst enemies. Not the fiery, reckless blood of Bearclaw but the calm, reasoning blood of Joyleaf must rise in Cutter's veins now, or he would be lost. Skywise wished he could somehow summon the spirit of that dead mother-chief to guide her son to victory.

"Go on, Cutter," the stargazer said, walking to his friend's side. "Luck is with you today, I know it." Carefully, Skywise disentwined the lodestone from the snarls of his chief's fine hair and arranged the talisman properly around Cutter's neck.

Savah held out her hand, gazing steadily at the grim, tight-lipped leader of the Wolfriders. He hesitated one moment longer and then very reluctantly laid his precious sword in the ancient elf-woman's palm. His back was turned to the chair next to Savah's; without turning, he spoke over his shoulder to the red, blue, and gold-garbed figure who sat behind him.

"Only you could make me do this, Leetah. But I still don't understand why you must."

It was past midmorning when the elves who had been sent to hide the two weapons returned from the mountains, riding a pair of the bizarre zwoots. The Sun Villagers had gradually dispersed after the Trial of Hand, knowing that there would be little to see for much of the day until either Cutter or Rayek emerged triumphant from the Trial of Head. With the return of the weapon hiders, however, many of the dark elves poked their heads out of doors and windows and came into the hot sun to watch the combatants depart in search of their concealed blades.

Rayek and Cutter had remained in the Sun-Toucher's care, each buried in his own thoughts, since the first contest. Now, as Savah instructed them, the rivals were once again required to wear blindfolds. This time, however, the red-caped attendants tied their hands behind their backs as well.

Nightrunner became frantic as his bound and blindfolded elf-friend was helped into the saddle of a tawny-colored zwoot. The humped animal bawled irritably, not wishing to be ridden again so soon after its trek to and from the mountains. Whining with jealousy, Nightrunner fought to follow Cutter, nearly dragging Skywise and Treestump along with him.

"Easy," Skywise said, trying to soothe the lunging wolf, holding onto the beast's ruff while Treestump grabbed the tail. "Cutter will be all right. It's all part of the test."

Hardly convinced, Nightrunner continued his writhings, calming down only when a firm but compassionate sending from Cutter touched him. Nightrunner sat down on his haunches, panting, while Skywise and Treestump wiped their brows and sighed with relief.

Rayek's zwoot was a darker color than Cutter's, with dusky

markings on its lower legs. The hunter straddled his mount comfortably, little troubled by the tightly knotted rope binding his wrists. Cutter and Rayek each had two attendants who led them away from the village. It was a quiet departure. No one called out farewells, but the Wolfriders joined in a mass sending of "good luck" to their chief.

Completely disoriented, Cutter could only hope for the best as he was led along an unknown path to an unknown place. The air was torrid and still. No breeze carried faraway scents to his seeking nostrils; the sun's rays, almost vertical, gave him no clue to the direction in which he traveled. The two attendants would not speak to him, and so he rode in silence, listening to the steady plod of his mount's great, soft hooves.

He thought of Leetah. How unlike Nightfall the healer was! Leetah had no sense of the pack, no love of group bonding. In many ways she was just like Rayek. Cutter did not question Recognition; no right-headed Wolfrider would. It saddened him, though, to think that even if he won all three trials, Leetah probably would not accept him with open arms. Her beauty haunted him. How could one so lovely behave in such an unelflike manner? By rights, he shouldn't have to prove himself; Recognition was enough. The ways of the Sun Folk, however, were not the ways of the Wolfriders, and he consoled himself with the hope that Leetah's feelings might change if he did indeed prove himself worthy of her.

Cutter felt a shadow pass over him. Faint echoes of the zwoot's hooves told him that he was surrounded by stone; perhaps it was some kind of arch or natural tunnel. Soon enough the sun again beat down on his head. The attendants led him along for a short distance and then stopped his mount. They helped him climb out of the saddle but would not let him place his feet on the ground. Not liking it at all, Cutter had to allow them to carry him by the arms and legs like a dead deer. They covered a stretch of very uneven ground and nearly dropped him twice. Finally, he felt himself being borne into shadow again, blessedly cool shadow. His surroundings smelled like a very dry cave, not at all like the dank and dripping troll caverns that were a lifetime away. His sightlessness made him increasingly edgy.

"I'm getting sick of blindfolds," he grumbled.

The attendants deposited him on cool, hard rock. "Then take the blindfold off," one of them said with a trace of amusement in his voice. "If you can free your hands."

"We'll come back and find you if you don't show up in the village by sunset," added the other.

Cutter heard the patter of their sandals growing fainter behind him. They had left him utterly alone, cloaked in darkness, his hands bound behind his back.

"Thanks," he muttered.

Rayek ignored the cramping pain in the muscles of his upper arms and continued determinedly to saw at his bonds. The jagged point of a rock, which he had cursed earlier for gouging his spine, had become the means by which he would gain his freedom. Rapidly his arms worked up and down, scraping the ropes that bound his wrists against the sharp cutting edge of the stone.

At last he felt a loosening. Ferociously he twisted his hands, straining them apart until the rope gave and fell away. Rayek breathed deeply and spared himself a moment to flex his blood-starved fingers. He was in pain from nails to shoulders, but he was free.

He pushed his headband back from his eyes and looked around. He was in a dark cave, seated on a mound of rocks that sloped gently down to what looked like a smooth area of floor. Slender threads of light beamed into the cave from a number of tiny natural vents in the low ceiling; at least he would not have to locate his dagger in total darkness.

Carefully, for the piled rocks had a tendency to give unexpectedly beneath his feet, Rayek worked his way down to the dust-coated level below. He knelt down and scrutinized the floor of the cave, seeking some clue that would provide a starting point in his search.

No one, not even the most sharp-eyed Wolfrider, could have detected the faint, deliberately but not altogether carefully obliterated sandal prints as quickly as Rayek. A subtle heel mark here, an all-but-invisible toe print there—both seemed to be facing in the same direction. If his attendants had backed out of the cave, wiping their tracks as they went, it was likely that his dagger lay somewhere in the direction the toe prints pointed. He followed them with his eyes and saw that they led to a tunnel formed by a fallen slab. Crawling on hands and knees, he squirmed through the narrow opening; as he did so, his hunter's eye spotted a tiny red thread caught in a crack in the rock.

The barbarian will lose *this* trial, Rayek thought, but even so, I've no time to waste!

Crouched slightly to avoid bumping his head on the low ceiling of the cave, Cutter stood up and looked around, his keen night vision piercing the gloom. In his hand dangled the blindfold. His wrists were raw and red. He looked at the short piece of knotted rope that lay at his feet and decided that it would probably be of no use to him in his task to come.

Releasing himself from his bonds had not been particularly difficult; it had simply required patience and forest-born dexterity. Cutter had squirmed free of strangle-weed before. Working his hands loose from the binding rope was not so different; it may have been easier, in fact, since the rope was not alive and did not constrict like the hungry weeds.

The cave was low and long and full of scents: bat droppings, the musty remains of small, dead animals, dirt and sand, and good plain rock. Cutter sought one scent in particular: the trail of those who had gone before to hide New Moon. He wondered if the Sun Folk had any idea how sensitive his nose was. Given reasonable closeness, he could distinguish his sword's unique scent even if it were buried under a pile of weapons made of a different metal. Something about the composition of the troll-created alloy called brightmetal gave it a sharp and hard odor.

Down on all fours, Cutter sniffed along the floor of the cave and soon was rewarded by a fairly strong scent-trail, laid down earlier in the day around midmorning. It smelled something like one of the attendants who had led him to the cave, perhaps the one with squatneedle cider on his breath. Cutter smiled to himself and followed the trail up an incline until he came to a jumble of large boulders. It seemed that the roof in this part of the cave had collapsed long moons ago, leaving a great open space above the tall pile of debris. Some instinct told Cutter to climb to the top of that pile, which he did. From there, he saw that although a nearby wall was almost black with layer upon layer of shadow, he could just make out a hole yawning between two deep furrows in the rock. The little cave within a cave was on a level with the summit of the boulder mound. Cutter could make it easily in one short leap. But should he try? He wondered. Was that the way to New Moon?

He closed his eyes and tested the musty air with his nose. Something was there, more subtle than a fleeting dream image, thinner than the cry of an owl on the other side of a high hill. With only his hunch to go on, Cutter leaped through space and landed within the niche, which was large enough for him to stand upright.

Peering deep into the hole, he could see nothing but blackness; his sense of smell, however, proved more rewarding. The scent of the weapon hiders permeated the little cave, and he knew that somewhere in the gloom ahead lay something hard and sharp and familiar. He walked forward a few steps and banged his forehead against rock. Cursing, he hunched down and felt his way along; after a while he was forced to crawl like a worm on his belly. He fairly wallowed in the two villagers' wake.

Unexpectedly, Cutter spied luminous highlights on the

rough stone ahead. The tunnel widened, and soon the Wolfrider was not only able to crawl comfortably on hands and knees but could also see exactly where he was going. Apparently his crawl-space exited into a place where there was light. Cutter's nostrils quivered with excitement. The scent of brightmetal was not strong, but its tinge in the air was unmistakable.

Still on all fours, he came to the end of the tunnel. There he discovered as he climbed out onto a little shelf of rock that the source of the light was located in the ceiling of a breathtakingly large and beautiful chamber. A shaft of sunlight streamed through a gaping hole in the roof of the cavern, an opening that clearly led to the outside world, perhaps a way for Cutter to escape once his task was done. But there was no way he could get to it from the ledge. Cutter decided to worry about one thing at a time.

Far below the jutting shelf, more than ten elves deep, it seemed, lay a garden of wonderful cave growths all dried and hardened by the penetrating sun; Cutter guessed that the gap in the ceiling was recently made. Mottled stalactites and stalagmites reflected pallid, sandy hues, their surfaces crumbling in spots, showing the effects of exposure. Even so, the lumpy, conical shapes and clustered bars hanging like icicles from the walls were marvelous to behold.

New Moon was somewhere down there!

Cutter studied the floor of the chamber. It was encrusted with sharp-edged rocks; especially long and jagged ones seemed to be concentrated directly below his high perch. He could jump safely from such a height if there was soft ground or sand below; obviously, that was not the case.

Well, he thought, either I jump and risk a broken neck, or I use my wits! If I had a vine . . . or a rope!

The young elf chieftain sat down on the narrow ledge and began to unlace the outer legs of his leather breeches. Soon he had two long, tough strips of hide, which he tied together, fashioning a makeshift rope. He supposed that the weapon hiders had come earlier to the caves with all sorts of climbing aids to make their jobs easy, but he and Rayek were supposed to be clever and resourceful.

Rayek!

The Wolfrider's heart began to pound in earnest. Surely his rival was at that very moment searching as actively for his golden weapon as Cutter was hunting for New Moon. Perhaps the black-haired elf, knowing every pebble in his desert domain as he did, had already located his hidden dagger! Time was slipping away.

There were several deep cracks in the rim of the ledge, and Cutter hastily looked around for some way to wedge his leather rope into one of them. He picked up a loose stone; tying one end of the long leather strip securely around the rock, he did his best to wedge the crude anchor as tightly as possible into one of the cracks. Lying on his stomach, he leaned his upper body precariously over the rim to reach down and pull at the rope, testing its strength. The rock held firm in the crack, but Cutter knew that he would have to slide down with extreme care to avoid jarring it loose.

When all was ready, the Wolfrider grasped Skywise's talisman on his breast and held it for a moment for luck. Then he carefully slid, belly down and feet first, over the edge of the jutting shelf and hung there by one hand. He gave the thong one more tug and then eased himself onto it. The anchor rock made a slight grating noise as it took Cutter's full weight, but it did not shift. Letting out his breath, he slid, hand over hand, down the line, spinning slowly in space like the lodestone on the end of its string.

The rope was not long enough. Even dangling by both hands from its end, Cutter saw that his feet were still almost three times his own height off the floor of the cavern. What lay below him was not soft ground or sand.

He would survive the fall, but it would hurt. Cutter opened the fingers of his left hand and let himself hang by one arm. The trick now was to persuade his right hand to let go. He looked down. The stony teeth grinned at him.

"Oh well." He sighed.

Cutter was lucky. His feet struck reasonably smooth spaces to either side of the spiky, fist-shaped rock. His knees bent to absorb the shock, and he rolled over and over; then the pain began. Ragged fangs of stone bit into his flesh; he heard his head crack sickeningly against something hard an instant before he felt it. Time seemed to stretch. He lay on his back, gasping, unable to move. His head swam. The shaft of sunlight seemed a solid thing as he looked up at it. New Moon's scent was gone.

A gleam of gold.

Rayek had thought it an illusion at first, a trick played on him by his eyes. He was tired and bruised from head to foot, but he had only himself to blame. He should have taken the time to stack those three boulders more carefully; he had needed the extra height they would give him to jump up and grasp the lower lip of the second tunnel he had found after squirming through the first. In his haste, however, he had not balanced the large stones quite perfectly. They had toppled under him, and he had ended up on his face with a palm-sized bruise throbbing beneath his right eye. Eventually he succeeded in gaining the edge of the opening, hauling himself through and sliding down its slanting length. The climb would have been much simpler with a length of rope and a hook such as those the weapon hiders had surely used. Better yet, if he could have used his magic . . .

Still, his discomforts had not been in vain. Beyond the tunnel he had discovered a small chamber lit by slivers of light that poked between adjoining rocks overhead. The floor of the cave was dusty, but not a sandal print showed; all tracks had been obliterated carefully. All the same, Rayek knew that someone had ventured there, and recently, by the way the dust was disturbed. He had prowled about the chamber, looking high and low; and finally, in a small crevasse near the far wall, he had spotted a gleam of gold.

He dropped on all fours, straddling the deep, narrow

crack, and peered down into its shadows. The cool yellow glint revealed itself as a highlight on the faceted pommel of his dagger. Uttering a sound that was both a laugh and a shout of triumph, Rayek lay prone over the fissure and reached down into it. His hand groped about in emptiness and scraped against the walls of the deep crack but did not touch the blade. Impatiently Rayek twisted and turned, straining his arm until he nearly wrenched it from its socket, but to no avail. The dagger was beyond his reach.

Willing himself to be calm, the hunter studied the problem. He could just make out his weapon; it seemed that the hilt was upright. He removed his headband and used the loop of fabric to extend his reach. Very gently, it brushed the tip of the pommel. Rayek withdrew his arm and saw that the hilt rocked back and forth ever so slightly. At last he understood.

The weapon hiders had delicately balanced the crosspiece of the dagger between the close-set walls of the fissure. The blade was so precariously supported that one hasty touch would send it plunging into unknown depths.

"Cleverly done, my people." Rayek had to give them due credit. This was a test of wits indeed!

The loop of his headband was of no use to him, for the hilt, upright, could not be snared. A hook would be the ideal tool to catch under the crosspiece and lift the dagger out. He thought of the gold wires woven through his collar, but they were too thin, too flimsy. Rayek pondered deeply, all the while aware that his rival was probably striving at that very moment to solve a similar problem.

How simple it would be to levitate the dagger, Rayek thought—but Savah would know. She could never be fooled, and the barbarian would be declared winner by default. There must be another way! If only my grasp were longer.

As Rayek thought, his hand toyed absently with the mountain lion fangs that decorated his elaborate collar.

*   *   *

The small groan of pain was magnified by hollow echoes singing among the stalagmites.

Cutter supposed that he could move, but he did not care to try. Sharp stones jabbed him from all angles, and he knew that if he stayed still, he wouldn't feel them so insistently. He stared up at the rope he had fashioned from his leather lacings. It dangled high overhead, useless. He'd never be able to reach it again unless he learned how to fly. Shifting his half-closed eyes, he fixed them on the radiant beam of light that stabbed into the chamber from above. Its angle told him that it was well past midday outside.

Suddenly Cutter remembered with stomach-wrenching worry that the Trial of Head was as much a race as a test of wits. He did not think he had lost consciousness after his fall, but he had unquestionably lost precious time just getting his breath back. He would have to get up and continue his search for New Moon. Now that his senses were swimming back to him, the tantalizing tang of brightmetal returned to his nostrils, stronger than ever.

Gingerly, he sat up, feeling a dozen different small agonies as he pulled away from his bed of jagged rock. With relief he determined that his hurts were all on the outside. What must Redlance have gone through? he wondered. The thought made him shudder.

Rising shakily to his feet, Cutter flexed his knees and began to pick his way through the garden of stone teeth. The soles of his soft boots were worn thin, and he felt every cruel jab of the hard-edged rocks. Finally he came to a smoother area and stood there for a moment, sniffing the air all around him. His nose guided him toward one of the many-layered, iciclelike growths on the wall opposite the entrance side of the chamber. As he walked, his unlaced breeches flapped loosely about his legs, but Cutter was so intent on sniffing out his sword that he hardly noticed them.

The scent—so strong! He felt elated. I must be right on top of it.

Cutter, son of Bearclaw, eleventh chieftain of the Wolf-riders, slayer of enemies and savior of his tribe, tripped over his flapping breeches and fell nose first across a narrow crack in the cave floor.

New Moon!

There in the shadowy cleft, like a firefly winking within a hollow log, hung Cutter's sword, its blade pointing down into darkness, its hilt shining a cheerful greeting to its master. Cutter could see it plainly; but the joy of discovery quickly faded, for all his efforts to reach his weapon ended in frustration.

Limber as he was, Cutter could just barely tap a fingernail against the pommel. His arm would stretch no farther than that. The makings of a hook did not exist within the cavern; the ends of the gold ring he wore around his neck were hammered together and would not come apart. The Wolf-rider went through every conceivable contortion; he even tried using his toes to grasp the crescent-shaped crosspiece and almost kicked the sword into the depths of the crevasse. At last he lay over the fissure, resting his head on his forearm, which spanned the narrow crack. He pounded the ground with his fist.

Can't grab it, can't fish it out. Come on, Tam, you fool! *Think!*

The lodestone, seemingly unwilling to part with any more of its luck, dangled from his throat like any common rock on a string. It felt heavy.

Rayek smiled and held the makeshift hook before his amber eyes, watching it turn gently on its length of cord. He was certain that it would work as well as magic. It was really a simple device, even a toy, but Rayek felt the warmth of pride as he recalled its inception and construction.

He had been lost in thought, fingers working the golden beads and mountain-lion fangs that hung from his collar, when suddenly two of the great teeth accidentally pinched his finger. Muttering a curse, he had released the fangs in disgust; but then the thought had come to him: Even though the lion is long dead, his teeth still find a way to seize. If they can clasp my finger, why not my dagger? The beginnings of an ingenious idea took root and grew in his mind.

Using the thumb and first two fingers of his left hand, he mimicked the clawlike action he wanted from the device in his thoughts. Yes, he reflected, I will need all three of the fangs to be certain that once gripped, the dagger does not fall; this contest shall not be given to the Wolfrider!

Rayek began to undo the golden wires that held the bead-and-fang pendants to his collar; then he hesitated. A subtle realization stole into his mind; he had fashioned the twin sets of trophies himself: one to adorn Leetah's gold neck-ring, the other for his own clearstone collar. Now, to win the Trial of Head, he was destroying—however symbolically—that identity which had existed between hunter and healer. It was a passing thought, however; time was of the essence, and Rayek had delicate work to do. Besides, he wondered as his sensitive fingers worked at the gold wiring, when he emerged triumphant from this test, would Leetah even care that she was no longer his twin in adornment?

Laying the lion's teeth and large gold beads on the dusty floor of the cave, Rayek began to work. Fastening a short length of wire to the small eye in the setting of each tooth, he then tied the other ends of the wires together so that he had all three fangs hanging from a single point. By twisting the flexible gold filaments, he managed to make all three teeth hang just so, curved inward to make a grasping claw. Unraveling a long, heavy thread from the edge of his loincloth, the hunter fastened it to the joining of the three wires; now he had the reach he needed.

"Closer," he murmured to himself. "This work is almost at an end."

The grabbing device he had made was now certainly long enough to reach his dagger, but Rayek knew that it had no power; it would not clutch even if he were able to place the three curved fangs around the pommel of his weapon.

Somehow he must make his makeshift hand accomplish two opposite things at the same time; he must find a way to hold the gleaming white teeth apart until they were over the dagger's faceted pommel, and then he must arrange for those same teeth to close tightly to grasp the knife securely so that he could lift it out by the thread.

Again, Rayek found his solutions in his now-ragged collar. If the fangs had more weight on them, he reasoned, they would fall together more tightly. Using bits of thread, he tied one of the heavy gold beads to each lion's tooth so that the nugget hung below the tooth's point. Then, slivering a large flake of clearstone from one of the plates of his collar, Rayek separated the weighted fangs of the claw device and gingerly positioned the clearstone chip between them. He took his hand away from the pendant teeth and—success! The three fangs were propped open like the talon of a desert hawk about to pounce on its prey. Rayek breathed deeply, satisfaction crossing his features. Yes, he thought, it will work as well as magic.

Now he knew, he must be as delicate as he had been clever. The glittering mechanism must be lowered ever so gently over the dagger so that the three inward-curving teeth would surround the weapon's pommel. The pommel itself must push the clearstone chip out of the way so that the weighted fangs, no longer set open, could clasp the faceted ball. The most exacting touch and the greatest patience would be needed; a wrong tap with one of the teeth or golden beads would send the dagger forever out of his reach.

Carefully, the hunter lowered the slowly twirling device into the fissure. Working the thread in his fingers to keep the pendants from striking the hilt or crosspiece, Rayek gingerly dropped the claw over the knife, stopping just as the flake of clearstone touched the pommel. The true test was now. Would the red chip fall away as planned, or would it be wedged too tightly by the down-pulling weight of the fangs and beads to be dislodged? Beads of sweat stood on

Rayek's face; his body, lying over the crevasse, was stone still; only the tips of his fingers moved gently as he lowered his contrivance the last bit.

There was the faintest of scraping noises as the clearstone moved against one of the lion's teeth; then, suddenly, the flake fell away, and the three fangs closed with a *clack* around the sword's hilt. The movement was so abrupt that Rayek, in surprise, almost let go the thread he gripped; but when he looked into the fissure, his elation soared. The makeshift device had worked! The dagger was held!

Bit by bit, for he still was not absolutely certain that the device would take the full weight of his weapon, Rayek began to lift the thread. The three fangs slid upward along the hilt until they reached the bulging pommel; then they stopped. Painfully slowly, a hair's breadth at a time, the dagger rose, until first hilt, then crosspiece, and then blade cleared the crack in the cave floor.

Rayek did not take the dagger in his hand right away; instead, with a feeling of great well-being washing over him, he held the knife up by the cord and looked at it, saw how it was clutched at the pommel by those three sharp fangs, caught under the crosspiece by the gold beads. He savored it, watched it turn, regarded the light playing on the blade.

"I'd like to see the Wolfrider figure this out." He chuckled.

Suddenly everything seemed uncomplicated. True, he had lost the Trial of Hand, but the trial of Head was his. Now he and the Wolfrider were even in terms of the contest, less than even in Leetah's eyes. Rayek knew his lovely friend well. She would choose a mate with wit over a mate with brute strength on any day the sun rose and set. He had only to go back to the village to wait with Leetah for the barbarian's sad, shameful return from his failed trial. Then she would see the Wolfrider for what he was, and she would look at the chief hunter with new eyes. I will help my Leetah recover from the illness inflicted on her by the barbarian, he vowed silently. I will heal the healer!

It did not take him long to find a way out to the open air.

He emerged from a small cave hole into welcome afternoon sunlight, certain of his triumph. Rayek saw that he had been taken into a part of the mountains quite close to the Bridge of Destiny. The massive wind-sculpted formation loomed high into the blue sky. It was like an old friend bending over him, reminding him to hasten back to the village so that the Wolfrider's later arrival would be that much more humiliating.

Rayek saluted the towering double horns and dashed down the mountainside. He startled a tawny lioness as she nursed her cubs in her den and roared back at her when she threatened him. All the way to the village he ran with long, unbroken strides. When Savah's blue canopy came into view, he was surprised to see a crowd waiting there in the hot afternoon sun.

Perhaps Savah sensed my victory, he thought happily. She knows so many things.

The chief hunter slowed to a dignified walk and held up his recovered knife as he approached the arena. Everyone watched him. No one spoke. He looked at Leetah, seated beside the Mother of Memory under the canopy; her expression was difficult to interpret. The Wolfriders were gathered in a group separate from the villagers. For barbarians, they seemed to be taking their leader's defeat rather well.

"What kept you, O mighty slayer of toads?" Skywise grinned as Rayek passed by him.

Offended, the hunter turned to give the stargazer what he had given Pike on the day of the raid. Unperturbed, Skywise casually stepped to one side. Rayek froze, his yellow eyes wide with disbelief.

There on the ground behind Skywise sat the chief of the Wolfriders, lacing up his breeches. At his feet lay New Moon, cradled in its sheath, safe and sound.

"Cutter's been back a good while." Skywise jerked a thumb at his friend.

Rayek's darkly tanned face drained of blood. He shook his head slowly from side to side.

"No . . . no! How?"

Slanted blue eyes smiling beneath his thick brows, Cutter unsheathed his sword and stood up from his cross-legged position in one smooth motion. The strange, homely chip of rock still hung about his neck. Cutter held it by its string and touched the top of New Moon's pommel to the lodestone.

He had done this at least an eight of times since his return to the village, but the reaction of the Sun Folk was still one of amazement and delight. Carefully, tenderly, he let go the hilt of his sword, and there it hung for a few moments, suspended by nothing but the force of the metal-attracting lodestone. Finally, the weapon's weight caused it to fall away, just as it had done in the cavern; and just as he had done in the cavern, Cutter grabbed for the hilt and caught it with the speed of a striking snake.

Rayek exploded with outrage. "Cheat! Deceiver! What proof of wit is it to use a magic stone? I could have used my powers, but I did not!"

Sun-Toucher came forward to address the chief hunter's entirely warranted outrage.

"Cutter used no magic," the robed elder said gently. "He thought of the stone only as a talisman of luck. That its natural power to adhere to metal would work for him was Cutter's accidental discovery."

It was true. Cutter had thought the lodestone would work only for Skywise. When he had first felt the stone's tugging at his neck as he lay over the fissure, Cutter had not been able to believe it. He had experimented, however, dipping the stone into the crack and feeling its pull increase the closer it got to New Moon; and he had decided to chance pulling his sword out of the crevasse by means of the lodestone's power.

"I still say it's magic," Skywise whispered behind his hand to Treestump.

Beyond anger, Rayek turned to the only one who might yet see the injustice of the second trial's outcome.

"Leetah? It is not fair! I—"

She laid her hand on his cheek, speaking from the depths of her heart. "Oh, Rayek, my dear friend. I know you are wiser than the Wolfrider. But he returned here first, and Savah has ruled him the winner."

It was too much to bear. Rayek embraced the healer, needing her comfort, burying his face in her auburn hair.

"It is not over yet," he murmured. "I still have one chance left to defeat him."

Leetah's great green eyes were limpid with tears. She held him away from her and searched his face, lightly touching the ugly bruise beneath his right eye. Her fingers remained upon his cheek, and through them flowed the healing force that made her all that she was. The angry purple blemish faded and then vanished. Rayek's face, in all its lonely, clean-lined beauty, pierced her to the heart.

Cutter watched the exchange and felt the stirrings of a most unwolflike jealousy. Among the wolves, challenges for mating rights were highly ritualized, with elaborate displays of threat and little actual combat. Once a dispute was settled, it usually stayed settled; and for the sake of the pack's harmony, grudges were very rarely held. There was a black, gnawing feeling in the pit of Cutter's stomach, however, that he sensed would not go away so long as Leetah looked at Rayek the way she was looking at him now. There was no question that she had a right to love anyone she pleased. Everyone had that right, but no one had the right to defy nature, not even a healer as powerful as Leetah. Recognition was Recognition. When was she going to make up her mind to accept it?

Savah noted the puzzled frowns on the faces of the Wolfriders, the head scratchings and bewildered mutterings that demonstrated that Leetah's behavior was beyond their comprehension.

"Things are not as simple here as they were in the forest, are they, little cousin?" The Mother of Memory smiled as Cutter came to stand, almost sulking, before her.

Rayek left Leetah and went to stand beside Cutter, roughly

edging the Wolfrider over so that they both faced Savah squarely. Cutter's teeth showed in a snarl, but he said nothing to his rival. The third test would tell the tale; after that, Cutter hoped, he would see Rayek's arrogant face rarely, if at all.

"We come now to the Trial of Heart." Savah raised her voice so that the villagers and Wolfriders could hear her clearly. "It is the last and most difficult test of all. For either of you to win—" she pointed from one rival to the other with the challange wand "—you must overcome your greatest fear."

Cutter made a noise in his throat like a wolf's bark. "Then the contest is ended," he announced. "My greatest fear is for the safety of my tribe. I would not change that if I could!"

"Fool," muttered Rayek, scowling sideways at his opponent.

With an indulgent look, the Mother of Memory laid the challenge wand across her lap and touched her fingertips together. "How little you know yourself, Wolfrider. Buried deep within your mind are fears that you never imagined were yours. It is from these that I shall select the appropriate test for each of you."

Leetah observed with deep admiration Savah's consummate command of the lost art of sending. Only Sun-Toucher and Ahdri, Savah's handmaiden, approached the level of skill that the aged elf-woman demonstrated with ease. Although the Wolfriders obviously sent as often as they spoke, Leetah guessed that their technique must be unrefined, crude compared to Savah's supreme artistry.

Fascinated, the healer watched as Savah motioned Cutter to her and pressed her warm, dry fingertips to the Wolfrider's sweating brow. Cutter closed his eyes, unable to do more than receive, completely, the radiant presence of the Mother of Memory within the shadowed tunnels of his mind. Almost at once she moved toward his soul name; his sudden panic flared a red warning to her, a warning she respected. Calmly, she searched around that forbidden, private core. That which she wished to find, she knew, lay quite close by.

Cutter began to tremble visibly. Even from a distance the Wolfriders noticed it and were concerned. His eyes flew open, filled to their depths with a sudden, nameless dread. They met Savah's hooded gaze and pleaded with her, but she remained immovable. In that terrible instant Cutter knew that there could be no escape.

She knows!

Without pause Savah turned to Rayek, probing the hunter's deepest fears. He too was left shaken and dazed when the Mother of Memory completed her search. Savah lifted her finely featured, veiled head, the chiseled lines of her jaw accentuated by the length and curve of her throat. She looked first toward the lowering sun and then to the east, to that monument which had glorified and doomed her lifemate in the long-past days of their unconcluded union.

"For Cutter's trial we must go where the carrion birds nest and where the wind moans sadly like a beast in pain— to the Bridge of Destiny, where others in the past have tried to prove their courage—tried and failed."

The crowd of elves buzzed excitedly. All of them knew the story of Yurek's obsession and fatal plunge from the bridge. What was Cutter's greatest fear? Would he be asked to follow in Yurek's path? Would Leetah permit him to?

"Savah, I—" Cutter began.

"Do you forfeit the Trial of Heart, Wolfrider?"

He glanced at Rayek. "No. I'll go through with it. I just wish . . ."

There was nothing left to say.

How the wind sighed at great heights, even though its breath barely whispered to the ground far below. The climb itself had not been an unpleasant one, Cutter had to admit. He stood atop the lesser horn of the Bridge of Destiny, surrounded by many of his tribefolk, along with Savah, Leetah, Rayek, and Sun-Toucher. Even the blind one had made the ascent without difficulty, for the upward slope of the curved peak was gradual, steepening only near the summit.

From the height, the Wolfriders could look out over all there was to see of their new homeland. In the direction of the Hub Star stretched the brittle, cracked surface of the flatland. Toward Sun-Goes-Down, the bony ridge of mountains the Sun Folk called World's Spine wandered as far as the eye could see. From these mountains curved the crescent-shaped spur that encircled the village. Away from the Hub Star, more hills littered the horizon, isolated from Sorrow's End by sheets of flat rock and wave upon wave of drifting sand.

The view of greatest interest lay in the direction of Sun-Goes-Up. The greater horn of the Bridge of Destiny grew from the base of World's Spine, and the mountains continued on toward the sunrise edge of the land, shallowing to hills and thence to scattered mounds of rock. There was another stretch of hard-baked flatland, vented by great cracks and fissures; and then, rearing its great smooth-sided cone above the otherwise featureless vista, there was a smoking mountain.

The Wolfriders knew about these fuming peaks; they had seen one before, in the distance, from the highest treetops of the Holt. That cone, however, had been much farther away from the forest than this one was from Sorrow's End. Pure white clouds billowed from the top of the volcano, creeping ponderously up the vast blue dome of the sky. Soon all would be touched by the yellows and fiery oranges of sunset. It would be a sight worth remembering.

At the moment, Cutter was not inclined toward medita-tion. His eyes were trained along the narrow sliver of rock that connected the two horns of the Bridge of Destiny. The span of stone created by "mad Yurek"—Cutter hoped that Savah would not suspect his appraisal of her long-dead lifemate—was perhaps thrice eight paces long. It arched gently across a void whose depth Cutter had not yet dared to judge by sight. Deliberately looking anywhere but down, he let his eyes wander instead across the narrow bridge. He noted that there was some kind of symbol or totem erected on the other side. On closer inspection, he saw that the upright shaft of rock was actually part and issue of the curved peak, just as the bridge was. The pillar was crowned by a stone disk that was shaped like a sun with eight blunt points radiating from its rim.

"Did your lifemate make that symbol too, before he . . ." Cutter asked Savah.

"Alekah, my first great-granddaughter, made the stone sun-symbol, my little cousin. She had to cross the bridge to do it."

Cutter swallowed hard. "Did she come back?"

The Mother of Memory's eyes crinkled. "Yes, she did; but only three have duplicated her feat since then. The winds are strong here. Hear them howling? They make balancing very difficult. The span is not wide, as you can see. Few have even attempted a crossing. Fewer still have gone farther than several steps out."

"Why would anyone want to?" blurted Pike.

Nightfall shushed the spear bearer. The shifting currents of wind made her skin prickle. She did not like the turn the game had taken. When Savah held up the challenge wand once more for all to see, Nightfall knew with dread certainty what would come next. She took Redlance's hand and squeezed it tightly.

"Cutter, chief of Wolfriders, your final trial awaits you," Savah said above the wind. She placed her hand on his shoulder as though to steady him. "You must walk to the sun-symbol on the far side of the bridge, touch it, and return, all without aid."

His worst suspicions confirmed, Cutter shrank away from Savah, leaning heavily on one of the two protrusions of rock that flanked his end of the bridge like a gate. He glanced over the edge of the peak on which he stood, shuddered, and clamped his eyes shut. He had glimpsed tiny flecks of color at the base of the rocky horn; his stomach knotted up like a rope twisted too many times, for he knew what the flecks were. They were villagers, gaily garbed, staring up at him and wondering whether he would come down the slow way or the fast and final way.

Skywise was troubled by his friend's shivering. Beneath its sun-reddened surface, Cutter's skin was bloodless, and beads of fear-sweat stood out on his cheeks.

"I told you luck was with you today," the stargazer ventured, touching the lodestone still hanging about Cutter's neck. "You can do it. It should be easy for you. Why, I've seen you walk a tree branch no wider than this—" Skywise held the thumb and forefinger of his right hand a small span apart "—without stirring a leaf!"

"But it wasn't so far to fall, Skywise, never so far to fall!"

Although Cutter's fear was surely justified, it seemed to his friend that it was all out of proportion. A little fear was healthy in a dangerous situation, but this thing inside Cutter was a danger in itself. Trembling as he was, unsteady and weak, how could he be a match for the winds that would assail him if he made it to the bridge's center?

"He's the best climber of us all. Why is he so afraid?" Scouter whispered in Dewshine's ear. She shook her head, as bewildered as her lovemate. Never had she seen her chief-cousin paralyzed by his own lack of control.

"I ask you again, Wolfrider. Do you forfeit the Trial of Heart?" Savah's voice had grown stern.

Cutter stood between the two upthrust rocks, one hand resting on each. Wind whipped his fine, pale mane about his face. His eyes were wide and fixed on the foot of the bridge. The drop below him was beyond his mind's acceptance.

Now Treestump took Skywise's place beside his young chief. "Give it a try, lad." The yellow-bearded elder's voice was calm and sensible. "She's worth it, isn't she?"

That jarred Cutter from his trance. He looked over his trembling shoulder at Leetah. She stood a short distance away from him, wrapped in a filmy, brilliant red shawl. Her heavy russet curls danced enticingly, framing her piquant features in ever-shifting shimmering waves. He could not read her thoughts. Did she want him to succeed? To fail? To fall? One smile, one small nod of encouragement from her, and he might get through this. She seemed further than ever from him, so unlike the Leetah of Eyes-Meeting-Eyes, whose every slap and kick was more an affirmation of caring than a rebuff. Water-bearer. Healer of Redlance. Could she not spare him one kind glance?

Behind and a little to one side of Leetah, Rayek stood with arms folded across his chest. If the healer's eyes were unreadable, Rayek's fairly shouted his thoughts. Fall, Wolfrider! Fall and let me be rid of you once and for all!

From Rayek's hate rather than Leetah's coolness, Cutter drew strength. Gingerly, he placed one foot on the slender stone bridge, his hands still braced against the rocks for support. He took a step. His hands came off the rocks with a sudden lurch and went out stiffly from his sides. Another step. The bridge was as wide as two wolves side by side, wider than a fallen log spanning a stream. He didn't have to see his feet to know where to put them. Skywise was right; it was easy. He would do it. He would cross the bridge and come back, and it would be no different from walking a tree branch.

Cutter's lips pulled back from his teeth in a grimace of determination. The wind flowed around him like a swift-rushing river, keening in his ears like an endless bird cry. Balancing himself with his outstretched arms, he took another step; then, contrary to all good sense or reason, he looked down.

The stone bridge seemed to shrink to a mere thread beneath his feet, compressed inward by the empty air on either side of it. All around him was an immensity of nothing—nothing to lean upon, nothing to grasp, nothing to leap onto. Far below, the ground, all jagged with sharp shadows, seemed to pull him to it like the lodestone pulled at metal.

"No," screamed Skywise. "He's going to fall!"

Instantly Treestump, Pike, and Skywise formed a chain, each grasping the other's hand. Skywise edged his way onto the bridge as quickly as minimal caution allowed, reaching out for any part of Cutter that he could catch. The swaying chieftain's arms sawed the air; Skywise grabbed for a flailing hand, missed, saw a second chance, grabbed again, and miraculously caught a wrist. Slowly, Pike and Treestump began to step backward, little by little hauling Skywise and a fainting Cutter in from the bridge.

"C—can't do it," the young chief mumbled. "My heart's beating like a rabbit's!"

"Here," Skywise said softly, helping his friend sit down and lean back against one of the jutting rocks. "You're safe now."

Cutter's shivering had returned, many times worse. His breath came in shaky gasps, and he could not speak for the thudding of his heart in his throat. He curled into a miserable ball, knees drawn up, face buried in his folded arms. A ghost of his voice escaped. "Too high . . . too high."

Treestump wiped his brow and let out his breath. Pike sank down upon the other rock, leaning on his spear. The other Wolfriders showed various signs of relief and distress, but Pike summed up their general feeling.

"Hmph! It's a stupid test! I wouldn't do it—" he glared deliberately at Leetah "—for anything!"

She cocked an eyebrow at the cheeky elf and then turned her back to him and looked down at Cutter. Skywise knelt at his chief's side, not quite knowing what to do. Slowly, running a hand over his face and rubbing the back of his neck, Cutter emerged from his retreat. He looked up at the healer with a sad but thoughtful expression.

"Leetah," he said softly, "if I die for you, what would be the sense?"

Maintaining his mask of indifference, Rayek smiled inwardly. There's an end to you, Wolfrider, and you've brought it about by your own words. Leetah is worth dying for, or she is worth nothing—and she knows what she is worth to me!

Leetah's reaction, however, was not at all what Rayek had

expected. She seemed to melt for a moment from ice to cool, gentle water. There was tenderness in her manner as she bent over the Wolfrider chieftain.

"Leetah, I . . ."

"Don't apologize," Skywise said, interrupting Cutter. "You tried. What more should she expect?" The stargazer's eyes were hard and full of contempt, so much so that Leetah could not meet them.

She turned to the Sun-Toucher. "Father, this is . . ." She groped for words to express her shame and yet leave her a vestige of dignity. "This is not right."

"You seem troubled, daughter," the blind elder replied. "Were you hoping that Cutter's humiliation would soothe the indignity of your first meeting? The Wolfriders will not turn on one of their own."

She blinked at her father. Of course he was correct in part. She had wanted revenge. The Wolfriders had had no right to upset her life so. She had hoped that Rayek would win the trials so that she would not have to change that life. But she had also hoped to see Rayek's arrogance and possessiveness punctured somehow by the upstart barbarian. She had wanted them both under her control—Rayek and Cutter, Sun and Moon, Day and Night. In the end, the trials had settled nothing. The opposing forces, which had never truly been in her hands, were now out of her hands altogether.

"So! The fierce wolf cowers like a frightened squirrel." Rayek gloated, looking down at Cutter's hunched and huddled form. "Look, Leetah! What do you think now of your wild barbarian suitor?"

Savah studied the chief hunter's every word and action. The Trial of Heart was not yet done.

Before anyone realized what was happening, Rayek stepped onto the stone bridge, almost dancing to its center. He called to Leetah, "Your choice of a lifemate has become easier!"

"Rayek! What are you doing?" cried the Sun-Toucher.

Showing off his clear superiority to his rival, Rayek walked backward, turned about in a circle, and swept his hands gracefully through the air, ignoring the light and untroublesome breeze.

"As if a stroll across the Bridge of Destiny were something to be feared." He laughed. "See, Leetah? It is nothing. He is a coward to the very heart!"

"The wind," cried Leetah. "Rayek, be careful!"

What was the matter with her? the hunter wondered. Couldn't she understand that even the wind was on his side now? He had been twice defeated, once by brute strength and once by trickery, but the Trial of Heart was his for all to see.

"The wind? What of it? I know the rocks. They are my second home." Rayek grinned maliciously at Cutter. "Go live in a tree, Wolfrider! You were not made for life here in Sorrow's End!"

Cutter got to his feet, supporting himself against the rock, which had until now hidden him in its shadow. He stood close to Leetah, and his expression mirrored hers: helplessness and open concern.

Yurek ... Rayek ... they're both mad, thought the Wolfrider, and this one is going to end up the way the other one did!

"Rayek," Leetah screamed, "come back!"

Suddenly the wind howled like an angry wolf, blowing in heavy gusts against the proud figure on the center of the stone bridge. Rayek's lean body arched to one side like a bow. Overbalanced, he flung his arms to the other side in a desperate attempt to right himself, but the wind drove relentlessly into him. He toppled, and only a tiny spur of rock, caught by the fingertips of one wildly flailing hand, saved Rayek from swift and certain death. His body dangled in space, teased by the shifting air currents.

Horrified, Cutter slammed his fist into the rock. He shouted at Leetah, "His magic! Can't he use it to float himself up?"

What a time, the healer marveled, to think of the High Ones' legendary capabilities! "That power is lost to all of us," she shouted back. "Rayek! Oh, Rayek!"

In moments it would be over, unless . . .

Cutter closed his eyes, the sweat and trembling returning

in full force. No! he thought. No elf must die, even if he is my enemy.

Dropping to all fours, the Wolfrider crawled out onto the bridge. Several of his tribefolk rushed to stop him, but Savah barred their way. Little by little Cutter crept like a worm toward Rayek, clinging desperately with hands and legs to the slender bridge. The young chieftain's mind was bare of thought; blind instinct—to guard the survival of his kind, the instinct that had driven him to lead his tribe across open desert—drove him now to overcome insurmountable fear. Nearing the center of the bridge, Cutter strained a hand toward Rayek's bloody, rigid fingers.

A name that was not Rayek's sprang to Leetah's lips, a name she dared not yet voice, much as she wished to. In her mind she repeated the word-sound-concept, wondering whether it would remain part of her forever, even if Cutter should fall.

Tam . . . Tam . . . Tam.

The Wolfrider worked himself around, facing back the way he had come so that he could get a right-handed grip on Rayek. The hunter was almost exhausted, his face drawn with agony. Straddling the bridge as though it were a broad-backed wolf, Cutter reached for his rival.

"Here, grab my hand!"

Rayek's eyes slitted open. With his free hand he clawed for Cutter's, locking his fingers about his rival's wrist, not in a death-grip but a grip of life. Completely numb, the hand that had clutched the minute spur of salvation slipped its hold, and Rayek's full weight suddenly pulled Cutter's right arm down, slamming the Wolfrider's chest against stone.

Terrified, Rayek looked down once and then tired to curl his body upward, groping with his sandaled feet for any purchase on the bridge's rough underside. At the same time Cutter exerted all his strength to lift Rayek up by the arm. His left hand still useless, the hunter tried to double his grip on Cutter's wrist, but that was little help. By main force the muscular forest elf raised his upper body, lifting up nearly his own weight with one hand. When he could reach

it, Rayek seized the top of the bridge with his left hand.
Helped by Cutter, he got one leg up and then suddenly
slipped, with both feet dangling free in space.

"One wrong move and they'll both fall." Treestump's
beard quivered. Skywise felt his own heart against the back
of his tongue.

Once again Rayek hauled his right leg onto the bridge
while Cutter held him by the arm. Struggling, the hunter
managed to hook his leg over the top of the span.

"Come on! You've almost got it," Cutter encouraged him.

In another moment the two rivals lay prone, facing each
other in the center of the Bridge of Destiny.

"He did it! Cutter saved him," Skywise yelled. The
Wolfriders cheered, releasing breaths they had held through
the eternity of the rescue.

"Praise the High Ones," whispered Leetah, holding part
of her shawl to her face.

Gasping, Cutter and Rayek rested while the wind played
over their sweating backs. Then, at the same time, they
lifted their heads and looked at each other. Cutter's small
smile faded instantly. In the black-haired hunter's amber
eyes was a look of hatred as raw and red as an open wound.

You!

The unexpected sending blasted its way into Cutter's brain,
rocking him back as though he had been struck with a club.
He cried out in pain.

Rayek had never sent before. He had had no reason to;
but there were no words for his humiliation, his frustration,
his defeat.

Reeling from the searing impact of his rival's envy and
hate, Cutter collapsed, arms and legs wrapped loosely about
the rounded span of stone. Incredibly, Rayek began to back
away from him, leaving Cutter helpless and alone, equally
far from the safety to be found at either end of the bridge.

With a curse Skywise drew his short-sword, taking a step
onto the narrow walkway. Rayek stopped abruptly, surprised
as he backed into the thorn-sharp point of the stargazer's

weapon. It pricked his spine and threatened to go deeper.

"He saved your worthless hide, and you're just leaving him there?" Skywise growled in deadly tones. "Go back and help him or I'll—"

"No, little Silver-hair. You will do nothing."

Baffled, Skywise looked up at Savah, sputtering. "But—but Cutter can't—"

"Wait and see," said the Mother of Memory.

Since the beginning of the Trial of Heart, the fires of evening had gradually tinged the sky, turning the clouds creamy yellow from white, suffusing infinite blue with a whisper of pink. As long moments passed in tense silence, as the elves waited for the Wolfrider chieftain to move, those delicate hues deepened to angry gold and orange, and far below shadows lengthened on the ground.

Without warning, Cutter's eyes snapped open. He lifted his head, and all his trembling was stilled. Slowly, deliberately, he rose to his feet, standing erect against the capricious currents of the wind. He faced the peak of the lesser horn, where Leetah, Savah, his friends and his enemy all stood watching him expectantly. A few short steps would take him to them, and he would be safe.

In the middle of the Bridge of Destiny, Cutter, blood of ten chiefs, turned around. He looked at the sun-symbol on the far side. He knew what he had to do, and he did it without hesitation, without feeling. His steps were quick and sure, speed giving him added momentum to combat the forceful wind. In moments he had reached the sun-symbol and touched the weather-beaten stone disk with his hand. It was a meaningless act and proved nothing, at least to the watching Wolfriders, who never doubted their chief's courage or expected of him more than he could give. Had he returned to them at once, never crossing the bridge, they would have thought no less of him.

With the same swift, even placement of one foot in front of the other, Cutter almost ran back across the arch, his body barely wavering, his arms extended for trifling corrections of balance. This was the chieftain the Wolfriders knew, the agile one who could walk a tree branch no bigger than this without stirring a leaf. This was Bearclaw's son.

"You were right, Skywise," Cutter panted, draping an arm over his friend's shoulders. "The lodestone did bring me luck." He removed the talisman from his neck and handed it with gratitude to its rightful owner. Skywise beamed.

"Is that it? Is this contest business finally over and done?" Pike asked peevishly. He was impatient to get back down to the ground. More important, he was hungry.

Everyone slowly turned to the motionless figure standing apart from them, alone and friendless, no longer by choice. The Mother of Memory eyed him coolly but with the barest hint of compassion.

"Rayek?"

All trace of haughty self-satisfaction had vanished from the hunter's bearing. He was beaten, and for the first time his eyes allowed others to know it. Shoulders shaking, he turned and fled down the slope of the lesser peak.

"So be it. The Trial of Hand, Head, and Heart is ended," proclaimed Savah.

"Rayek," called Leetah. She started to follow him, but Savah enfolded her in the swirling mist-green sleeve of her gown.

"Let him go, healer. Fears born of outside sources, such as Cutter's fear of great heights, are far easier to overcome than fears born within the soul. Rayek defeated himself the moment he set foot on the bridge."

"But what was he afraid of, Savah?" Cutter asked.

She inclined her regally crowned head toward the Wolf-rider and answered him with a pensive sigh. "He is afraid of loss. He must be first in all things, or he is nothing. And now you are here."

Cutter mulled it over. "Strange! The contest would have ended in a draw if he hadn't gone onto the bridge. Didn't he know that?"

Savah did not answer. She did not need to.

"I don't care," Leetah cried, turning her back on them all. "Rayek is still my friend. I love him!"

"That would not comfort him now," the Sun-Toucher advised. "Give him time, my daughter, to see himself with new eyes."

"Well, at least he won't be meddling with you and Leetah any more, eh, lad?" Treestump jovially clapped Cutter on the back. "Your way to her is clear."

With a determined frown, the young chieftain went to stand close behind Leetah, so close that she felt his breath upon her ear.

"Treestump is right," he told her. "Enough is enough! I defeated Rayek in fair combat for you, and I'm through playing foolish games!"

Leetah's reply was sardonic. "Typically, you misinterpret, Wolfrider. You have not won me. You have won the right to woo me. No more, no less. But the final decision is mine."

Exasperated, Cutter spun her around and shouted in her face. "Decision? What decision? You can't refuse Recognition! No one can!"

His outburst simplified things enormously for her. As long as he behaved like a savage, she would find it easy to treat him like one.

"That is the difference between us," she said calmly. "To me, Recognition is more than mere blind instinct. I am many times your elder, Wolfrider, and you have much to learn."

With that Leetah drew her shawl about her and started down to the village. Rayek had vanished from sight.

"I don't understand her," Cutter grumbled to Skywise.

"Neither do I," said the stargazer. The corners of his mouth quirked into a sly grin. "After all," he purred, "what does it matter that you have a foul disposition—" Cutter's head jerked up "—and the manners of a troll? She's just the fussy type, I suppose."

Skywise got ready to run; he didn't think Cutter would swat him, but he wasn't absolutely certain. The other Wolfriders chuckled as they began to make their way back down from the Bridge of Destiny.

At last, thought Pike with satisfaction, food!

Twelve

The blanket was warm, made of many skins taken from brown bush-rabbits; its softness had a soothing magic all its own. Leetah pulled the cover over her head, hiding within its furry folds. Her hut seemed huge and empty to her, and the night was unusually chilly.

She lay wrapped in darkness, burrowing into the cushion of her sleeping pit as she had seen small birds work their bodies into the warm, soft dust-beds of the desert. All was quiet save for the chirring of insects in the gardens outside.

The healer's thoughts were anything but peaceful. Fantastic images darted through her mind. Although she could control the memories, choose which ones to bring forward and which to leave in the shadows, the phantoms born of her imagination would not be ruled; they seemed as tangible to her as remembered reality. Soon she gave up trying to sort one from the other.

Her turmoil had begun earlier that night with the dream. Tossing restlessly in her sleep, Leetah had been visited by a ghostly image: Cutter's face hovering above her, his translucent eyes wild and staring with a kind of madness. The leering face had spoken to her, baring sharply pointed tearing teeth in a fearsome snarl.

"What is my name?" he had demanded.

"Cutter!"

"My soul name, Leetah, say it!" The shape of his face had begun to shift then, snout and jaw eerily elongating, eyes losing their whites, gracefully tapered ears growing blunt and blurred around the edges by sprouting hairs.

"Tam. . . . No! I do not love you! You are not even my friend!"

The ferocious visage had continued to transform, the

271

nose and mouth pushing forward in such a way that speech should have been impossible; yet grotesquely, words had poured forth unimpaired.

"You can't refuse Recognition!" The dream-image had further distorted: forehead sloping sharply back, jowls bristling with fur, fangs sprouting like stalactites within a huge cave of a mouth. "No one can! No one. *No one. Noooooooo!*" Cutter's face had become that of a howling white wolf, his blood-chilling wails drowning Leetah in a pool of sound.

Curled up at her feet, the little wildcat had been startled from its sleep by Leetah's bolt-upright, shivering escape from nightmare. Although the vision had burst with her sudden awakening, the howls had continued.

Now, half the night later, as Leetah lay once more in her sleeping pit, feeling the sandy grit still between her slender toes, she relieved her moment of comprehension that the howling was real, that it had in fact invaded her slumbering senses and molded her disturbing dream.

Leetah remembered . . .

She had risen from her bed, tiptoed to the entrance of her hut, and peeked out between the parted curtains. Mother Moon was nearly full, swimming in the center of the deep, star-sprinkled well that was the night sky. Just disappearing behind the ragged mountain range to the west, Child Moon's face was half in shadow, showing its fear of venturing alone from its great protectress's sight.

Riddling the inner curve of the mountain spur's belly, the sandstone caves peered out upon the Sun Village like so many blank, black eyes. Above the caves rose a scored and runneled brow of rock that culminated in a broad, flat crown. There, atop that moonlit plateau, the Wolfriders were gathered with their mounts, singing. The harmony of their mingled voices was so pure that the howls of the forest elves could not be told from those of the wolves.

In spite of herself, Leetah had stepped outside in her gossamer idle-gown. The cold desert night clutched at her bare shoulders and nibbled at her upswept ears. She ignored the discomfort, for the wild, lonely howling—both frightening and painfully beautiful—seemed to have a purpose. Overcome with curiosity, she padded on bare feet to the caves and climbed from there up the rugged slope to the plateau, concealing herself among tall rocks just below the ledge.

They had all been there, all seventeen Wolfriders, although her vantage was such that a few of them were visible only from the chest up. Moonshade and Strongbow were nearest the edge of the plateau. Dart stood beside his seated mother, his little hand resting on her shoulder. Vigilant Strongbow held his bow at the ready as though expecting an enemy—perhaps Rayek—in a surprise attack. Leetah made certain that she was well hidden; she did not trust the archer to hold his fire if he spotted her. Rainsong and Treestump sat cross-legged together, and near them Woodlock looked after Wing under Newstar's strict supervision. Nightfall cuddled against Redlance, his strength nearly recovered. Pike toyed with his stone spear point, checking its bindings, while Scouter and Dewshine seemed lost in their own worlds, together yet apart in the uncertainty of youthful pairing. Clearbrook and One-Eye had ceased howling for a moment to share some secret that made them smile. Characteristically, Skywise's mind and heart were in the heavens; even as he tilted his head back to howl with his tribefolk, his silvery eyes picked out favorite star-pictures or discovered new relationships between the brilliant points of light.

In constant motion, the wolves wove among their riders, sniffing, touching, wagging tails, taking great sensual pleasure in the singing and in the sense of unity it evoked. It was an eerie, haunting communion of kindred spirits. Leetah shivered, feeling very much the intruder; but the wolves continued their full-throated song, unaware of her presence.

Suddenly Cutter stood, lean and pale in the center of the roughly formed circle, and drew his sword. A hush fell over the gathering as he held out his left palm and pricked its center sharply with the point of New Moon. He did not wince.

Ten bright droplets of blood fell one by one from Cutter's overturned hand, and for every tiny, red jewel that fell, the Wolfriders intoned a name.

"Timmorn Yellow-Eyes . . . Rahnee the She-Wolf . . . Prey-Pacer . . . Two-Spear . . . Huntress Skyfire."

A strange feeling crept up Leetah's spine as she listened to those softly chanted names. Each one conjured an image of its owner in her mind, and they were, all of them, more wolf than elf. The red droplets continued to fall.

"Freefoot . . . Tanner." Relentlessly the spool of names unwound, and as it did, Cutter's clear young voice spoke above it.

"Ten chiefs before me have sung the wolfsong, have run with the pack, and have kept the laws of our forest brothers."

"Goodtree . . . Mantricker."

"When our foreparents, the High Ones, first came to this world, it was the wolves who taught them to eat good red meat and to shun the sunny places where humans prowl."

Swiftly Cutter brought the flat of his blade under his palm to catch the final drop of name-blood.

"Bearclaw," the Wolfriders called out.

Cutter looked at the crimson spot spreading on his sword tip. "This night's howl is for him, for Bearclaw, my father—and for all our brothers and sisters who died as he did." The young chieftain pressed his lips to the blade, taking his father's blood back into himself. Then he sheathed New Moon and turned to his uncle. "Treestump, brother of my mother and oldest among us, you speak first."

The yellow-bearded elf settled back against Lionskin, who sat panting softly behind him. "My pleasure, lad," he drawled, his dark blue eyes twinkling as he plucked the ripest berries of his memory to offer up for everyone's enjoyment. "Bearclaw, eh?" He chuckled. "Now there was one grand, wicked elf! He's been gone six turns of the seasons, aye, but he was half again as old as me when he died, and I guess he knew more about living than most of us ever will."

The Wolfriders looked at one another, nodding in agreement. Each one had his or her own favorite Bearclaw stories, and the moons could easily rise and set many times before they might all be told.

"No Wolfrider ever lived longer, got into more scrapes, or had more fun getting out of them than Bearclaw," Treestump went on. "Nothing scared him. Why, he'd steal a human whelp right off its mother's back just to stir things up. Can't say I ever blamed the Tall Ones for not taking kindly to Bearclaw, but they never caught him. He'd leave the round-eared brats hanging on branches, or sometimes he'd give one to a she-wolf to be raised with her cubs."

"I always said those wolf-reared humans turned out the better for having been stolen," One-Eye interrupted. "Best of all, they left us alone and preyed on their own kind!"

"Served them right," Scouter chimed in importantly.

"Aye, Bearclaw could deal with humans one moment and end up in a game of stones down in the troll caverns the next. I never could figure out why Greymung's guards put up with him for so long. He'd cheat them out of belts, buckles, britches, and all and come back next day for their beards!" Treestump paused to scratch his own whiskers. "Oh, he was a mean son of a she-wolf, all right. But he had a merry heart and a tolerance for dreamberries that I've yet to see equaled!"

Clearbrook stood up, her single silver-white braid gleaming as it swayed against her thigh. She was the second oldest of the Holt elves, and her voice was heeded by them with great respect.

"You speak truly, old friend," she said, "but if we howl this night for Bearclaw, we must also howl for your sister, Joyleaf, for she was as much a chieftess as Bearclaw was a chief."

Pleased, Treestump readily conceded. Bearclaw would certainly not have been half the leader he was without

Joyleaf's influence, and the yellow-bearded elder did not think that his sister's praises could be sung too often.

"Perhaps Joyleaf's arrows were not always as sure to the mark as Bearclaw's," said Clearbrook, "but her patience often brought better results than Bearclaw's recklessness, and not just in the hunt! She was never one to act without thought and never one to think without wisdom. When Bearclaw, in one of his rages, would have led us into battle with the humans—just as chief Two-Spear led our wolf-riding ancestors into war and nearly destroyed them all—Joyleaf's wise counsel always turned his anger aside. She believed that someday there would be no hatred between humans and elves, and she led her life as she believed, in harmony with all that moved and breathed and grew."

Clearbrook turned to Cutter, seeing in him all that remained of two friends whom she missed and still mourned. "Together, Bearclaw and Joyleaf raised a beautiful son who even now bears the best qualities of both his parents." Cutter lowered his eyes as Clearbrook continued. "They were lifemates. They completed each other, just as any two who have Recognized each other should."

This last, Leetah knew as she eavesdropped, was for Cutter's benefit and, indirectly, was also a stab at her. Ah, Clearbrook! the healer thought ruefully, you and your folk have lived too long with the wolves. They, too, never question their instincts.

What was Recognition? It was a need particular to the elf race, a need that demanded fulfillment regardless of loves or friendships already formed. Although she knew that this was so, Leetah could not believe that that mindless need and the inevitable merging of two into one was the best for which she could hope. Neither could she sympathize with the Wolfriders' calm, unquestioning submission to such enslavement.

At that point Leetah had almost left her hiding place to return to her hut, but Cutter's voice had caught her attention and held it. There was something very somber, very pensive in his tone, almost as if he, too, had just been pondering the worth of certain time-honored notions.

"Savah, the Mother of Memory, is very, very old," he said, "but I've learned that any of us can live as long as she has—even longer. Sun-Toucher said we'd forgotten what it means to be elves. We aren't meant to die as humans and animals do but to live on and on like great trees in a forest, trees that saw the High Ones come to the world and that will see everything, forever, unless someone comes and burns them down."

The Wolfriders exchanged thoughtful glances. What had this to do with Bearclaw's howl? Their young chieftain seemed far away, seeing everything from a different place and a different angle than they.

"Bearclaw used to tell me that a Wolfrider's life was short and sharp—a bolt of bright fire in the night, like his sword, New Moon. He'd lived a long time, but I guess he'd seen so many others die for one reason or another that he just never looked ahead or behind. 'Now' was all that mattered to him. That was the way he lived. But he didn't have to die. He chose to."

Even Strongbow relaxed and sat down quietly to hear his chief's words. Dart and Newstar sensed a tale in the air, and they huddled next to their parents, rapt with attention.

"Speak on, Cutter," said Rainsong. "My children were not yet born when it happened."

"And Dart was too little to know," Moonshade added.

The young chieftain took a breath. "All right. I'm no storyteller, but I'll do the best I can . . ."

What does a forest look like?

Curled within her fur blanket, the chill of her night-spying upon the Wolfriders still gripping her bones, Leetah tried to fix images to all that she had heard. Cutter's story had been told in simple, quiet words, and it had terrified and touched her deeply. Now her imagination played havoc with the simplicity of those remembered words, conjuring mind-pictures that were distorted recombinations of all that she had seen and experienced in her life.

What does a forest look like?

Cutter had spoken of the Holt. It appeared now in Leetah's fancies as a place of deep-hued green and gold, of moist, supple foliage and intoxicating scents. She imagined gigantic needle-plants, smoothed of spines, growing so closely together that the sun could barely peep through chinks in their tangled branches. She crowned those branches with cloud-tree plumes, dark green rather than smoky pink, and she populated the shadows beneath them with all manner of strange beasts and birds. The boles of her "trees" were shaped like huts, and inside them the Wolfriders slept by day. At night they ventured forth to hunt, riding their fearsome mounts through the damp, green gloom.

It was during such a hunt, six years ago as Cutter had told it, that the terror had descended upon them.

"The humans say there's magic left in the woods from the time of the High Ones' coming," Cutter began.

Leetah warmed at these words; it thrilled her to think that something of the elves' very first ancestors had survived to her day.

"Small magic that went bad, like pools of stagnant water," Cutter went on, "because the High Ones couldn't control their powers here at first. If that's true, then I guess we've paid for it in a way we'll never forget."

The Sun Folk's oldest legends hint at the early struggles of the High Ones, thought Leetah. How frail they must have been if Savah, born well after their time, is of sturdier mettle than they!

For some reason, Leetah could envision Cutter's parents most clearly. Bearclaw was taller than his young son, sharp-boned, sly-featured, bewhiskered, and ragged—one who stabbed through life ungently. Joyleaf's hair was spun from sunbeams. Her eyes were her son's eyes, and she bore a bow as capably as she had borne her son seventeen years before. As she listened, Leetah imagined these makers of Cutter riding at the head of their hunting party, riding through the dark wood in search of game, riding toward a fate as yet unsuspected.

Something was in the woods. Something unnatural waited there in the darkness. Cutter described it as a scent like nothing the Wolfriders had known before. They felt its eyes fixed upon them, gagged on its stench; but no matter how they searched, they could not uncover the terrible presence that had invaded their domain. It was there, watching them, shadowing their trail, but always just beyond arrow range, always just quiet enough to make them doubt their senses. It seemed to possess a malevolent kind of intelligence, yet it smelled of beast and something else all twisted together.

The hunt for the intruder went on all night, fruitlessly, until toward dawn they discovered a young wolf lying dead in a clearing. Its stomach was torn out and its ribs exposed, and it weltered in a puddle of its own gore. The stench of the killer hung so thickly in the air that it had no source, no direction. It was all around them.

Death came suddenly, without warning. From the bushes a great curved claw struck out, slitting the throat of its first elfin victim. He was called Rain the Healer, and he was the first to die, as if by design. His powers would not help the next ones to fall.

Cutter's words had begun to fail him here as he attempted to relate from memory what had happened. Skywise remembered, and One-Eye, and Treestump, for they had been among the ill-fated hunting party. Only open sending could have conveyed the jumble of nightmare images that defied description, and Cutter refused to do this, knowing that such agony relived would do no one any good.

In her mind's eye, Leetah found herself there, then, among the hunters.

To have senses was to be witness to chaos: a monstrous, black shape rearing up in the half light before dawn, the glint of sword-sharp fangs, the pain of cruel talons raking unprotected skin, wolves and riders flung back, broken, a serpentine body as big around as a tree, thrashing and coiling with unassailable power. And most horrible of all, the monster was sending! It was able to attack the mind as well as the body!

Leetah saw it all: the images of the monster, in greater detail than Cutter had described them. Her imagination squirmed. Lightning and fire, a long-tooth cat and a huge black serpent locked in mortal combat, a pocket of the High Ones' forgotten magic rekindled by the flames and charged with the blood madness of the struggling beasts.

The magic! An ancient spell, asleep for untold time. A fire-spell perhaps. Fire was the great changer, the transformer of all things: metal to molten liquid, water to steam, wood to ash. Perhaps a group of High Ones, cold and homeless, had sought to warm themselves with a fire-spell. The magic had failed, but the seed of the magic had remained, asleep, for countless years, until lightning struck the spot and brought the seed to life. Two mighty creatures—the long-tooth cat and its enemy, the black serpent—battling to slay each other, had rolled unwittingly into the pool of fire-magic. Like metal or water or wood they had been transformed.

Change . . . joining—a twisted, newborn brain ablaze with the joy of slaughter. The monster had a name! The Wolfriders named it even as they died in its jaws. It was Madcoil, and it was death!

Tightly closed eyes could not shut out the hideous phantom that writhed in Leetah's mind. A snake with the head and claws of a lion, all black and scaly, stippled with random tufts of fur. And the head! The glowing, red slits that were eyes; the poisonous fangs; the jaws that nearly folded back on themselves, so wide did they gape! So huge that head and those rending fangs! So swift and silent that rushing, gliding body slithering about the wood to kill—anything— because that was all it knew to do!

The battle between Cutter and his fellow hunters and the ravening monster became a rout. Nearly mindless from the pain of the creature's distorted sending, half blinded by their own blood, they gave up and scattered, somehow

ending up high in the trees as Madcoil's howls of fury died behind them. The survivors began to call for friends and kin; a sick fear washed over them as they realized that half the hunting party—including Joyleaf—was missing. Ignoring the danger, for the monster might still lurk in the shadows below, Bearclaw leaped down to the forest floor and stood still as a stone, sending. It was a special call, meant only for his lifemate, but he was silent too long . . . too long.

Tam-Cutter, I feel your sorrow, Leetah cried silently, though it is softer now than it was six years ago. I see you, bloody with claw stripes, learning of your mother's death from your father's half-murdered eyes.

"The hunting party had been ten. Madcoil made it five. Treestump, Skywise, and One-Eye went back to the Holt. I went with Bearclaw to find the monster and kill it."

So simple, those words; so much had lain beneath their surface.

Forcing the frightening image of Madcoil into a misty corner of her mind, Leetah saw Bearclaw, wild with grief and utterly careless of his own life, dashing through the Green Growing Place in search of vengeance, in search, too, of release from unendurable loneliness. Cutter had said of his father that with the realization of Joyleaf's death, he never spoke again. Bearclaw was a chieftain whose weaknesses were as mighty as his strengths.

Madcoil's noisome scent led Cutter and Bearclaw deep into an unknown part of the woods beyond the boundaries of the Holt. A sinister bond grew between hunters and prey, but it was the prey that led the chase, controlled it, toyed with its vengeful pursuers and lured them with growls and grisly spoor on an endless, vain search.

Then, as though the monster wished it, Bearclaw discovered Madcoil's empty den. There was no telling how long the creature had dwelled there in the foul-smelling hole or what senseless impulse had brought it slithering to the Holt days before to do its bloody work.

Within the den were bones, strewn everywhere. What the monster did not choose to swallow whole, it plainly took pleasure in rending to shreds. There were the bones of beasts, human bones, and a punctured skull newly stripped of flesh, with large, oval eye sockets and tiny ridges where the large ears . . .

Father and son hid by the den and waited for the monster's return; but the waiting was long, and Cutter was exhausted. He fell asleep while Bearclaw kept watch, alone, as he had desired from the first.

Did the monster call you while your son slept, bearded chieftain? Did it promise you that which you craved? Did you make your silent farewell to your chief-son so that he would not wake? In her seething mind, Leetah became Cutter, reliving his and her father's death, illuminating his account of the tragedy with images of her own conjuring.

Madcoil's piercing shriek startled Cutter awake. Instantly he guessed what had happened. He ran like a frightened child, following his father's trail. The reek of the monster was all around, but the smell of fresh-spilled blood led Cutter straight as an arrow to his father's side.

Bearclaw was dying.

He was bitten clean through by Madcoil's great poisonous fangs, but he had managed to wound the monster badly. Cutter saw its serpentine tail winding away into the shelter of the wood; it left a blood-trail thick and black as pitch. For that, at least, Cutter was glad.

Fading, Bearclaw lifted up his beautiful crescent-curved sword and, with the last of his strength, gave it to his son. As Cutter knelt numbly by his dead father's side, something stirred on an embankment above him, gazing down on his sorrow with gleaming yellow eyes.

Wolves. Strangers from a far-wandering pack, all except for one. Blackfell. He was Bearclaw's mount, and the wolf had come for his rider. The great beast's coat was the color of a starless night, and it seemed that one could walk right through him, as through a deep, dark hole, to some other place. Blackfell carried Bearclaw's body away, melting like a shadow into the dark eternity of the forest, and somehow Cutter was comforted. Always closer to the wolves than to

his own kind, Bearclaw would run with them forever, a part
of their spirit and their blood.

Now the frightened child became a chief, calling upon
Blackfell's rogue companions to help him summon the
Wolfriders. It would be safe for his folk to come to him
now, for the monster lay wounded in its den. The wolves
obeyed him; from hill to glen to flea-infested cub-hole the
howling call was taken up until all the woodland rang with
Cutter's summons. Before the sun had set on the following
day, the call was answered. All save the new mothers,
Moonshade and Rainsong—and Rainsong's lifemate Woodlock, who guarded them—came swiftly with their weapons
and their avenging rage to join their new chief.

Dart and Newstar had fidgeted excitedly when Cutter
paused in the telling of his tale to look right at them. The
other Wolfriders knew the ending of the story very well, for
they had helped to shape it. Thus, to the children—especially
Wing and Newstar, who had been the first to renew the
Wolfriders' number after Madcoil's attack—Cutter spoke
with great respect as he finished his narration.

"I knew that Madcoil could die, because Bearclaw had
wounded it. But my father was wrong to think he could
destroy the monster alone. I needed all the Wolfriders to
help me keep the promise I had made to finish what Bearclaw
began."

And there you showed your true colors, Tam-Cutter,
thought Leetah. The colors of one who holds the idea of
pack more dear than personal glory.

To kill the monster, the Wolfriders made a great net
from vines. They weighted it with rocks and coated it with
sticky sap and carried it high into the trees. They stretched
the net from branch to branch so that it hung spread out
and level with the ground like a huge spider's web. Then
they waited while Cutter crept to the entrance of Madcoil's
den, hurling taunts and shouts to draw the monster out.
The cave gaped like a black, toothless mouth, and from it
poured a near-suffocating stench. It was the smell of conta-

gion, of fear and madness mingled with terrible pain. Poisoned by its own filth, the monster was greatly weakened; but that it would die on its own was too much to hope.

Leetah closed her eyes and imagined that the darkness was a cave and that she stood before it, throwing rocks, taunting, challenging the horror that dwelt within to come out and face her.

What courage it takes, she mused. Or is courage just anger strong enough to overcome fear?

She whispered, repeating the words she had heard from her hiding place below the plateau. "You took my parents and the others. Now try to take me! Don't think! Just come on, bloodsucker, I'm waiting!"

Fast, so fast that she had no chance to control her thoughts, the monstrous face of Madcoil lunged at her, slavering blood and venom, its great eyes filmy and starting out from its dark head. She gasped and opened her eyes, but the vision remained.

The young chief had run—faster than ever in his life— for never had death in such hideous, unnatural form pursued him so closely. He ran for the trees where his tribefolk waited with the net. Madcoil glided after him, crushing bushes and snapping off branches in its path. Cutter felt the tip of its forked tongue flicker upon his heels, and with a burst of renewed speed he dashed under the net, crying, *"Now!"*

As one, the Wolfriders plunged down upon the creature, covering it with the net, trapping it within the sticky meshes. It screamed and hissed, thrashing about in an effort to free itself, but the Wolfriders held on to the net by its edges, and the rocks woven into the snare pulled the monster down.

Voicing the howling cry of his people, Cutter sprang at the creature's head. Madcoil attacked his mind with a storm of confusing, frightening images, but the young chieftain knew them for what they were and was not cowed. A huge eye glared before him, and straight for the red slit of a pupil Cutter aimed New Moon's point, calling out, "Bearclaw!

Joyleaf! Guide me!" The sword pierced the monster's eye to the hilt, and as Madcoil's deafening shriek split the air, Cutter ground the blade back and forth, slicing the corrupted brain to mushy shreds.

Silence hovered over the plateau as the story ended. Cutter sat for a while with one arm encircling his knee, staring at nothing. Reflecting on their own impressions of that sad, eventful time, the Wolfriders had all withdrawn into themselves. Then, suddenly, Cutter brightened up and winked at Dart and Newstar, whose eyes were as big around as their open mouths.

"So that's how we, in a way, brought a monster on ourselves and how we destroyed it together," Cutter said. Then he added, smiling, "And if Bearclaw were here, he'd howl for dreamberries after such a long tale!"

Nightfall stood up, her golden-brown hair rippling from beneath her green kerchief like water spilling from a bowl. "Well, I say you left something out, Cutter," she announced, walking over to place her hands affectionately on his shoulders. "Bearclaw gave us a good, hard life—harder, perhaps, than it had to be at times—but you've given us a whole new way to live, here in a wondrous new land with others of our kind. And that's something Bearclaw never dreamed of. We howl for *you*, Cutter, blood of ten chiefs, and come what may, we follow you."

They had all tilted their heads back, howling once more at the broad face of Mother Moon. Not one of them noticed Leetah as she slipped away, padding delicately down the rocky slopes to the village, her cheeks moist with tender tears.

And now she lay under the blanket of many rabbit skins, and there was grit between her toes and a chill in her bones. The night was still as morning approached, save for the chirring of insects in the gardens.

And the tears still welled in her eyes.

Tam . . . Tam. It seems that I, too, have much to learn.

Thirteen

There was not much wood in Sorrow's End, and what did exist was not very useful, especially for making weapons. The scattered cloud-trees that gave shade to the village had only two or three thick limbs forking upward from their crutches, and from those limbs sprouted short, stubby branches, useless for decent butts for hunting knives. The wood itself was of poor quality, brittle and weak.

The troll king, Greymung, had grudgingly supplied the needy Wolfriders with finely balanced metal knives, good for throwing and piercing game on the run. In addition, many of the elves had their own short swords, which they were seldom without. Strongbow, however, had the only bow. The Sun Folk seemed never to have heard of one. This was understandable, considering that their erstwhile chief hunter required no weapon at all to catch game; he needed only to trick his prey into making eye contact with him, and the hunt was over. It was simple, but it was nothing to rouse the killing lust and make the blood sing.

Much to the delight of the curious and hospitable Sun Folk, certain of the Wolfriders came into the village more and more frequently during the day. Boredom drew them there, for unlike the endlessly changing environment of the forest, the bare rock and sand of the desert seemed to possess an eternal sameness, a sterility for which the spectacular vistas and sunsets could not compensate.

Since the night of Bearclaw's howl, the Wolfrider's had spent a large part of their waking time hunting. Except for the zwoots, which could not be hunted because they belonged to the village, most of the game to be found in and around the mountains was small. It took many rabbits, bristle-boar, and quail to keep the seventeen-strong tribe fed. For the first time since the desert trek, the Wolfriders found themselves in the peculiar position of having to compete with their own wolf-friends for food.

This did not go unnoticed by Minyah, a village elder who was acknowledged to be the finest gardener in Sorrow's End. Unwilling to listen to what she considered nonsense, she lectured the Wolfriders whenever possible that their strict diet of meat was derived from habit, not necessity. Redlance argued back that meat was meat and that desert plants were strange and not to the Wolfriders' taste. Minyah then proposed a wager that she could make a gardener of Redlance in less than one cycle of Greater Moon and that he would like it. Intrigued, Redlance and Nightfall had become the first Wolfriders to leave the caves during the daylight expressly to learn the ways and customs of Sorrow's End.

Pike, too, slept less during the day now than before. He enjoyed helping the villagers mend the colorful outer layers of clay upon the walls of their huts; he had always liked playing with mud, and clay was just as much fun. Pike was also fascinated by the metal-tappers, elves who worked and reworked pure soft metal by rapping it with small hammers. The Sun Folk were very fond of jewelry and liked to change the shape of the pieces they wore quite often. Once Pike came back to the caves waving a trinket he'd been allowed to hammer, shouting, "I'm a troll! I'm a troll!" The faces he made sent Dart and Newstar tumbling in fits of laughter.

Even Skywise, normally alone in his curiosity about the workings of the heavens, found a mentor in the kindly Sun-Toucher. He had chanced one morning to observe the blind elder leaving Savah's hut while it was still dark. Alone and unaided, the Sun-Toucher walked through the sleeping village, walked past the boundary of Sorrow's End to ascend the Bridge of Destiny. By the time he had arrived at the summit, the sun was just peeking above the horizon. The stargazer had learned from later observations that this was an everyday ritual of the blind one. Eventually Skywise found himself accompanying the Sun-Toucher on his daily climb to greet the morning sun. The two shared quiet conversation or pleasant silences, and each was tacitly glad of the other's company.

So began the merging of two very different tribes. It was a slow process, for most of the Wolfriders were reserved and hesitant to change their ways. Their memory of the Holt was still green, and Sorrow's End seemed, especially to Strongbow and One-Eye, a place of frustration and deep puzzlement.

"I don't like it." One-Eye sat on a lump of sandstone, braiding Clearbrook's long, silvery hair. "Cutter's ribs are starting to stick out like bare branches. That Leetah's got him so turned around, he forgets to eat or sleep."

The light of early morning poured directly into the cave. Scouter sat near his parents with his chin propped on one hand. At the youth's feet, Dewshine lounged with her legs raised and resting against the wall of the cave.

"I know," Scouter said. "Cutter told me that Recognition feels like you're sitting in a thorn-bush, gulping overripe dreamberries, with a sand flea up your nose. And it's supposed to be *good* for you!" The young elf shook his head. "I hope I never have to go through it."

"Nor I," Dewshine added fervently. "Love is much more pleasant. Think of Nightfall and Redlance. They aren't Recognized."

Clearbrook laughed, leaning against One-Eye's knee. "They might as well be, cub," she said. "Lovemates join for pleasure; lifemates join for love; but Recognition . . . ah! I wouldn't be surprised if it sneaks up and catches those two some day. That's how it happened with Bearclaw and Joyleaf. They were lovemates before they were lifemates, and lifemates long before they Recognized each other."

Dewshine sat up. "Then what is the difference between love and Recognition?"

Clearbrook and One-Eye looked at each other. "The difference is you, cub," said the silver-braided Wolfrider. "You and Scouter, Dart, Newstar, Wing—you're all here because of Eyes-Meeting-Eyes. Elf cubs are rare enough, but they are almost never born outside of Recognition."

Suddenly Dewshine understood. Her eyes grew wide. "You mean Cutter and Leetah have to—"

"They had better, or they're both going to get pretty sick," growled One-Eye as he finished tying Clearbrook's braid.

Silhouetted just within the cave entrance, Strongbow looked out on the Sun Village. Beside him, Moonshade busily scraped a stretched hide free of its nap of hair. She sighed.

"Well, hopefully Leetah will come to her senses soon, for her sake and Cutter's."

Strongbow leaned sullenly against the sandstone wall, chewing on a piece of rawhide. **I say he should just take her, and to the humans' cook fires with what she wants! Leetah claims the right of choice, but there is none. Recognition is Recognition!**

Outside, unaware of their critical observers in the cave, Cutter and Leetah stood on opposite sides of a stone watering trough. She loosely held the reins of a zwoot, letting the long-legged beast drink its fill. Cutter leaned on the edge of the trough, trying to get Leetah to look at him. Stubbornly, her eyes examined the grass at her feet as she chatted about unimportant things.

"We call them zwoots," she said unnecessarily, patting the animal's shoulder, which she could barely reach. "There are five of them in the village now. Rayek brought them back one at a time from the canyon near the smoking mountain."

At the mention of his one-time rival's name, Cutter frowned.

"That may be where he has been these past few days." She sighed. "I hope he returns soon."

"Do you really miss him, or are you afraid you might forget him?"

She glanced up, and it was her turn to frown. Cutter knew that he had pricked a sore spot. He reached into the trough and filled his cupped hands, holding them up carefully, apart from each other.

"Look. Two handfuls of water." He brought them together, letting their contents mingle. "Join them, and the water becomes one with itself. That's how we are meant to be, Leetah. Joined forever."

He looked very handsome to her just then, and she knew that he was trying very hard to be reasonable. She put her hand under his, catching the drops that seeped through his fingers. An interesting image, that: Recognition as two handfuls of water joined.

"Forever. Without love?" she said softly. "What then?"

The moment was like no other he had experienced with her. She was not fighting him in any way; she seemed in fact to want him near. He needed to touch her somehow, if only to brush her soft brown cheek with his lips. He leaned over the trough, bringing his face close to hers. She turned her head slightly but did not draw away from him. He whispered her name.

"Leetah."

"Shade and sweet water to you both this glorious morning!"

Cutter's hands flew open, spilling his hopes back into the trough. He whirled, ready to kill or at the very least to lop off ears. Shenshen and her covey of maiden friends fluttered past the watering trough, carrying baskets and giggling behind their hands.

"Do not mind us," Leetah's younger sister chirped. "We are off to fetch lizard eggs—" she looked Cutter up and down "—before the day grows too hot."

Grimacing, the Wolfrider clutched his sword hilt, turned, and stalked away. Leetah's shoulders sagged as she watched him go. It would do no good to call him back; his barbarian temper would make him demand what she had just now almost given him.

"Sun bless me," exclaimed Shenshen. "Did I say something wrong?"

Leetah glared.

*   *   *

Nightfall knelt by the side of one of the huts, near Minyah's garden plot, a strange and pleasant anticipation welling warmly within her. Although she and Redlance were not Recognized, she felt certain that not even that—the Eyes-Meeting-Eyes—could bring her closer to him. The part of her that had nearly shriveled away as Redlance had lain dying in the desert now blossomed with the feeling that she was witness to a long-delayed birth. Her lifemate, the source of that feeling, sat nearby.

"Redlance, dear, you are not listening." Minyah leaned on her hoe handle, exasperated but much too fond of the gentle-mannered Wolfrider to be cross. "A seed takes time to grow after it is planted."

She could hardly believe his simplicity. There he sat, cross-legged on a clear patch of ground by her family hut, gazing fixedly at a little mound of dirt. Beside him, Nightfall knelt with a peculiar smile on her lips. She seemed to think that she knew more about seeds than Minyah, which piqued the gardener no end.

Unperturbed, Redlance continued to concentrate on the little mound in which he had planted a kernel of child's-teeth. Only one kernel! He seemed to be waiting for it to do something. Minyah could not tolerate such nonsensical single-mindedness.

"I tell you, you cannot make it sprout simply by staring . . . at . . . it . . ."

Her voice trailed off, and her eyes bugged beneath the rim of her woven-grass sun hat. The mound of dirt at Redlance's feet had moved, almost like the shell of a hatching egg. A few grains of soil rolled down the miniature slope, and then a tiny sliver of green ruptured the surface and poked its way toward the sun. Then another leaflet and yet another struggled out of the ground. Finally a perfect little seedling, no bigger than Redlance's forefinger, stood forth in its minuscule splendor for the world to see.

The red-braided Wolfrider looked up at Minyah and

grinned hugely. She gripped her hoe for support and started to stammer something about watering and weeding. But then, looking from Redlance's beaming face to the tiny green miracle at his feet, Minyah began to laugh with outright joy. She had won her wager. In less than a moon the Wolfrider had certainly come to like gardening!

At that same moment, atop the lesser horn of the Bridge of Destiny, Skywise and the Sun-Toucher were preparing to make their descent to the village. The sunrise had been a beautiful one, and Skywise thought wistfully how sad it was that his mentor could feel the coming of dawn but could never see it.

"Your daughter Leetah's healing powers are the strongest I've ever seen," he said. "Why don't you have her restore your sight?"

The blind elf smiled and answered at once. "Because the sun teaches me more through my other senses. Wind, rain, the times to plant and harvest—all are governed by the mighty, life-giving Daystar." Sun-Toucher lifted his staff to the brilliant yellow disk, his blue-green robe billowing in a sudden breeze. "I interpret the sun's voice for my people. Through me, the Daystar speaks its intentions so that we may live in harmony with the land."

The stargazer cocked his head, a wonderful fancy taking him. "You called the sun a star! Wouldn't it be something if it turned out that all the stars were suns?" Shielding his eyes with his hands, Skywise looked into that brilliance for a moment. He did not know that his mentor stood smiling, both amused and impressed, behind him.

Barely audible at first but rapidly gaining volume, a rumble of thunder sounded in the distance. Sun-Toucher turned an ear to the east. His seamed face tightened with concern.

"There's no storm coming, if that's what's worrying you," Skywise offered, puzzled.

Sun-Toucher shrugged off the well-meaning comment with slight irritation. He listened very hard to the faraway sound, comparing it to certain other rumblings that were kept within his memory. "As long as it grows no louder," he muttered.

"It's only the smoking mountain grumbling about something, Sun-Toucher." Skywise couldn't understand why the elder should give it a second thought. In his experience, sounds like that were sheer bluster, as harmless as the throaty roar of a fat swamp-toad.

"Yes, it is the mountain, and its grumblings could mean little or much. Skywise, is there not one more among your tribe with especially far-seeing eyes?"

"You mean Scouter? He can spot a white fox against a snowdrift in a blizzard from five tall tree lengths away," the stargazer answered.

Sun-Toucher had no idea what all that meant, but he presumed that Scouter's eyesight could be termed at least keen.

"You want me to get him here quick?" Skywise asked.

"There is need here of his gift, I assure you."

The Wolfrider grinned. "Just listen to this!"

Filling his lower belly with air like a bellows, Skywise set out a howl that rocked the Sun-Toucher back on his sandaled heels.

"*Ayoooah-yoh!*" The inflection at the end of the cry was a summons for a particular Wolfrider. "*Ayoooah-yoh!*" The call outdid the distant rumblings by far, carried itself down into the Sun Village, down to the sandstone caves where Scouter and Dewshine tried their hands at the Sun Folk's game of toss-stone.

"Skywise wants you," Dewshine said casually.

The chestnut-haired youth had already flung his game pieces aside. Jamming on his hat with its tapering, tasseled crown, he dashed out of the cave, delighted to answer a call that he had not heard in many long days. Bounding through the village as fast as he could go, he nearly collided with Cutter. When the troubled chieftain continued walking and did not return his greeting, Scouter did the same. It was still a goodly run to the Bridge of Destiny, and Skywise's call had sounded urgent.

Nightfall watched Scouter's exuberant exit from the village, grateful for the small distraction he provided. Moments earlier, the first deeply felt rumbles from the smoking mountain had proved an even more timely interruption to her awkward situation. After Redlance's demonstration of his newly awakened power, she had witnessed Shenshen blunder between Cutter and Leetah at the most delicate of moments, and she had then gone to offer the healer what little solace she could.

"Nightfall, of all your tribe, are you my friend?" Leetah had asked her.

The golden-eyed Wolfrider had taken Leetah's hand at once. "Of course! You saved Redlance's life. I'll never forget that. Never!"

Pulling Nightfall to her in close conspiracy, the healer had urgently whispered, "Then you must tell me. What is a soul name? I must know what it means!"

The question had shocked and bewildered Nightfall, who could not comprehend Leetah's need to ask it. Such a thing was never spoken of lightly, not even among the closest of friends. Nightfall had opened her mouth to say just that, when the low, throbbing thunder momentarily startled them both.

Now there were no more distractions. Leetah's anxious, vivid eyes begged for an answer. It occurred to Nightfall that the Sun Folk might perhaps acquire their soul names much later in life than the Wolfriders. That would explain much.

"For us it happens just as soon as we are no longer children. It is a coming of age," Nightfall said, hoping that the healer would understand. "We go into the woods alone when the time is right, and we survive, and we wait until the soul name comes. It is the only way, being alone. You'll find out some day." Feeling not at all successful in her explanation, Nightfall made her way slowly back to Redlance and Minyah.

Some day, Leetah thought ironically. She had nearly said it to Cutter, at the trough, over his two strong hands cupped full of water. She had wanted to say it then, carelessly, the word-sound-concept that she knew to be his soul name, his *Tam* . . . Perhaps Shenshen's interruption had been fortunate. What would it have cost her, how would it have enslaved her to have said that name aloud?

The mutterings of the smoking mountain rolled through the Sun Village, and now many of the villagers looked up from their neatly rowed gardens or their small hand looms and wondered how much longer the noise would go on.

Skywise knew that the small puff of dust sputtering toward the base of the horn was Scouter. The lad has strength, mused the stargazer, and it's been stored up for too many days. He watched One-Eye's son race up the slope and wondered what task the Sun-Toucher had in mind for the sharp-eyed youth.

"I still don't understand why the noise from the smoking mountain worries you so," Skywise told the robed elder. "It can't hurt us. Where I came from, you could see a peak just like that one from the treetops, and all it ever did was belch up a few clouds now and then. We called it the Sleeping Troll because it vented smelly wind in its sleep."

The Sun-Toucher did not smile. "The danger is not in the noise, Skywise," he said, "but in the effect it may have." He turned at the sound of Scouter's running steps and motioned the panting youth to his side. "Scouter, you must be eyes for the village since Rayek is not here. There is a shallow canyon near the base of the smoking mountain. I want you to tell me if you see any movement there."

Still collecting his breath, Scouter could not quite stand upright. He blinked the perspiration out of his eyes and squinted at the distant, fuming cone. "I'll try," he said.

It was so much easier to see a long way at night; the sun distorted faraway things and made them wavery. It hurt, too, to stare at all that brightness for more than a moment, but Scouter tried. Although it was at least half a day's leisurely walk away, he focused his gaze on the volcano, on its surroundings, and especially on the shadow at its foot, which surely was evidence of the chasm Sun-Toucher had mentioned.

Around the cone's base he saw white rocks and colorless bushes. He picked out a scavenger bird lighting atop a lone, twisted sticker-plant, and he could just see into the mouth of what looked like a great jagged crack in the ground. The canyon seemed to follow the curve of the foot of the volcano as it disappeared behind one side of the cone.

The volcano grew angrier, emitting thunderous bursts of sound like explosions that punctuated its ceaseless rumbling. Suddenly, at the mouth of the distant chasm, Scouter saw dust—curling clouds of it—obscuring the deep shadows there, rising high into the fume-roiled air. He rubbed his eyes and looked again. The dust cloud was even larger than it had been a moment before, and he could see now what was causing it.

"By the High Ones," he gasped.

Again the volcano sent forth its thunder, and throughout the village the Sun Folk instantly dropped whatever they were doing. As if by some unspoken signal they calmly began to gather up their tools and other belongings and tie them into bundles. Villagers went in and out of their huts repeatedly, bringing out clothing, favorite bits of furniture, and food. For Nightfall and Redlance it was a very bewildering sight.

Minyah shouldered her hoe, her practical side subduing that part of her which still held Redlance's accomplishment in deepest awe. "Well, that has done it for certain," she clucked, referring to the smoking mountain's latest blast of sound. "Come along, young ones. We must prepare to go to the caves." She started to herd the Wolfriders into her hut.

"But why, Minyah?" asked Redlance. "It's only noise!"

"We shall see, child. Now, hop!" She gave his bottom a maternal swat.

Like all his tribefolk, Cutter thought nothing of the volcano's roar. He brooded disconsolately in the cave he shared with Treestump, unaware that anything was amiss outside. The young chieftain half leaned, half lay on a cave rock, toying with a bone and finally snapping it in two.

"That bad, is it, lad?" Treestump sat quietly in the shadows, willing to offer what help he could, but only if asked.

"What am I going to do, Treestump? I can't court Leetah. That's crazy! Every time I get near her, I need her, the way green growing things need rain." Cutter's eyes were hollow and full of yearning. "She's mine, and I'm hers. Why won't she accept that?"

"Well, my guess is Leetah likes to be in charge of herself," Treestump said thoughtfully. "Recognition scares her. But don't worry. I've got reason to believe your troubles aren't as bad as you think." The yellow-bearded elf was about to tell his young chief that on the night of Bearclaw's howl he had caught a glimpse of Leetah darting lightly from her hiding place, that he knew what none of the other Wolfriders even suspected: She had overheard everything. But suddenly there was an unexpected commotion at the entrance to their cave. Villagers began to pour in, carrying baskets and parcels as though they were prepared to stay for some time.

Treestump, what's going on? Cutter sat up in surprise. **I'll be cursed if I know!**

Among the group of dark-skinned elves invading his shelter and his misery, Cutter noticed Leetah's sister. New grudges not quite forgotten, he grabbed her and demanded, "Shenshen! What's going on?"

She seemed surprised that he didn't know. "Oh, do not worry, Cutter," she said, flirting with him and coyly adjusting the shawl full of bread and dried fruit that she carried upon her shoulder. "We have plenty of time. It is lucky that Scouter was here to do Rayek's job."

"Time? Time for what?"

More elves poured past Cutter, jostling him from side to side. Shenshen was swept along by the tide, leaving him as much in the dark as before. He heard someone yelling his name. A small figure far at the back of the oncoming crowd jumped up and down, gesticulating wildly. It was Scouter. Cutter pushed against the flow of villagers to reach the shouting youth.

"Cutter, Cutter! I saw them! They're big! Bigger than *that* one!" Scouter pointed between bounds at the zwoot Leetah had watered earlier that morning. "And they're headed straight for the village!"

"Easy, now!" Cutter grabbed his arm. "What are you yipping about?"

"Zwoots! A whole big herd of them!"

Another rumble from the smoking mountain rattled beads on curtains. Other Wolfriders, some groggy with sleep, began to gather around their chief.

"Hear that?" One-Eye asked Cutter. "All that noise scared the things up from the chasm where they live."

"That doesn't mean we're in any danger," a just-returned Skywise said, noticing that two attractive, darkly tanned maidens were definitely noticing him. He drew himself up a little more importantly. "It's a long way for the beasts to run from the smoking mountain to here. Maybe they'll tire out or turn aside before they reach the village."

The two maidens had drifted closer to him during this speech. They were both seductively attentive, one with extremely long, straight hair and the other dressed in gauzy ruffles. The ruffled one giggled charmingly.

"What's so funny?" Skywise eyed her from under half-closed lids.

"You do not know how strong zwoots are." She smiled.

"Or how stupid," added the long-haired one. "They will get here."

A villager wearing a gaudy tunic stroked a tethered zwoot's nose and said in all good humor, "Nothing stops them unless they plow head on into something they can't knock over."

"Indeed," Minyah chimed in. Her eyes rolled heavenward as she prepared to relate her trials with the humped creatures. "You should have seen my garden after the last time they—"

Cutter interrupted. "What? You mean this has happened before?"

"Once in a great while," said the Sun-Toucher, who had arrived with Skywise from the Bridge of Destiny. "It was Rayek who journeyed to the canyon, alone and on foot, and only he with his exceptional powers was able to capture and tame the few beasts you see here in the village. They have proved very useful to us in many ways. But when the entire herd is driven to flight, there is nothing we can do but get out of the way. The canyon leads them in this direction, and when they run, they run straight."

Now Cutter had something real on which to vent the frustration of thwarted desire. He looked around contemptuously at the Sun Villagers who had not yet entered the caves. Among them, climbing gently ascending natural steps to a cave entrance high above Cutter's head, were Leetah, Toorah, and the Mother of Memory.

"So," he said a bit loudly, "you're going to let these zwoot things kick holes in your houses and tear up your food plants, and you won't try to stop them?"

Leetah paused. "What would you suggest, Wolfrider," she asked dryly, "a net?"

The tone of her gibe was almost affectionate. Cutter stared up at her, baffled, wondering why she had chosen those particular words. Her smile was enigmatic but not unfriendly.

Taking heart, Cutter shouted, "Sorrow's End is our home now, too! We Wolfriders fight to protect our territory." He looked at his gathered tribefolk and saw that they were with him. "We'll turn the herd before it reaches the village and have fresh meat tonight in the bargain!"

Drawing their swords and daggers, raising bow, spear, and ax to the sky, the Wolfriders howled for their wolf-friends to come down from the mountains. It had been many quiet days since they had enjoyed a full pack-hunt.

After a short wait, Pike shouted, "Look! Here they come."

One by one the wolves appeared from behind crags and boulders and slunk down the mountainside to join their elf-friends below. Straggling villagers hastened their retreat into the caves, not a little confounded by the dual nature of the Wolfriders. Honest and innocent as children, the forest elves were nonetheless brothers to vicious predators. For Leetah the paradox was irreconcilable.

How could anyone revel so in the thought of slaughter and bloodshed one moment and tenderly place a child on an affectionate animal's back the next, as Strongbow was now doing with his son? The Wolfriders greeted their mounts with great joy and much petting. Soon, though, they would be rending open the bellies of living creatures, rummaging through the gaping red wounds for the choicest parts. Leetah understood completely why the Wolfriders were the way they were—it was in their blood. But at the thought of that blood mingling with hers, something inside her closed up.

A slender figure dashed from one of the empty huts, bearing coils of hempen rope. It was Dewshine.

"Look what I found," she cried to the Wolfriders. "Now we can catch the beasts as well as turn them!"

Leetah hurried to a tier of rock nearer the ground. "Dewshine," she called. "You are not going with them, are you?"

"Of course," the young huntress sang.

The healer was distressed. Dewshine had always seemed to her the most fragile, the most truly elflike of the Wolfriders. Leetah spluttered, "But it is not a maiden's place to—"

"To what?" the golden-curled she-cub called over her shoulder. "Why not?"

"Well, because . . . because . . ."

Dewshine laughed heartily. "Shame on you, Leetah! Don't you know your own mind about anything?" She handed out lengths of rope until there were only two left, one for Scouter and one for herself. "I'm going to catch the biggest zwoot of the lot," she said, giggling as her tongue slid over the funny word.

The Wolfriders mounted up, but before they could leave, some of the Sun Villagers gave them colorful woven cloths to use as head wrappings. Treestump thought that he looked silly but guessed that it was better than frying his brains. The day had grown very hot, and there was no telling how long he'd be dashing around in the open sun with his tribefolk.

Leetah noticed that Woodlock and Rainsong were staying behind to look after their brood and Dart. She wished she could have convinced Dewshine to stay as well, and she said so to Toorah.

"And what would you suggest, kitling," her mother quipped as she followed Savah into the cave, "a net?"

Perhaps, thought Leetah. They're all as hotheaded as their chief.

Led by Cutter, the Wolfriders positioned themselves in the shadow of the Bridge of Destiny. Beneath the smoking mountain's insistent rumble, eight and four pairs of sharp elfin ears caught the ominous pounding of scores of broad heavy hooves. Through the gap between the horns of the Bridge the Wolfriders could see what appeared to be an approaching dust storm. The terrain between volcano and village was such that it guided the beasts like thread through a needle's eye toward the Bridge of Destiny. Although they had run far in blind, instinctive escape from the canyon, their pace was still rapid. In a short while the zwoots would be charging full force under the rock span, and then they would have to be dealt with.

Clutching her rope excitedly, Dewshine said, "Let's run at them now, cousin."

"No," snapped Cutter. "The wolves aren't made to run

far in this heat. Let the zwoots come to us." He adjusted the
cloth hood about his face. Skywise had presented it to him,
saying with a grin that it was from Leetah. Cutter wasn't
sure, but he liked to think that it was. The cloth did hold
her scent in its folds.

Nearer and nearer came the stampede. Lumbering,
humped shapes stood out in the haze of dust, and strange
bawling cries grew in volume.

The Wolfriders fanned out, ready to split into two groups
to harry the onrushing beasts on two sides. The elves meant
to redirect the course of the stampede to some place where
they could entrap the creatures and bypass the village
altogether.

Now the lead animals came clearly into view. It was hard
to tell how many zwoots made up the lot, but it seemed
there were at least three for every Wolfrider. The rampag-
ing herd thundered beneath the bridge, their weird bawling
echoing to the very peaks of the twin horns.

"Wolfriders ready," Cutter said slowly. *"Go!"*

As one they charged the onrushing herd, scattering at the
last moment to run along either side of the lead animals.
Elves and their mounts harried the ungainly beasts with
spear, blade, and tooth. Terrified of the wolves, the zwoots
shied away even in their running madness, veering in the
direction the Wolfriders wished them to go. Howling their
elation, the forest elves turned the headlong rush.

For Cutter all care was momentarily forgotten. He knew
only the thrill of riding Nightrunner again at full speed,
feeling the great wolf's powerful muscles rippling under his
spare flesh. Cutter saw a zwoot toward the rear of the herd
break away from the others. A slight shifting of his weight
told Nightrunner to turn back, and the elf chieftain headed
after the rogue animal. Nightrunner galloped round and
round the humpbacked creature, confusing it so that it did
not know which way to snap or lash its hooves at its tormentors. Nipping at the zwoot's hind legs, Nightrunner drove

304 WENDY AND RICHARD PINI

the beast under the Bridge of Destiny and back to the rear of the stampede.

Ahead, the Wolfriders knew, there was a gap in the mountain spur that led to a dead end. Toward that gap the elves herded the lead zwoots; the rest followed, thundering into the cul-de-sac, well away from the huts and well-tended gardens of the Sun Village.

We saved the village! Now the hunt can begin! sent Strongbow, knowing that even the gentlest Wolfriders, like his own Moonshade, would respond to that primal urge. Grinning viciously, the archer pulled his bow from around his upper body and felt to make sure that he had lost none of his arrows. The other Wolfriders readied their weapons. They would kill only what they could use, but they would enjoy it. It was the Way.

Watching from the caves and ledges, the astonished Sun Folk could not believe how easily the feat had been accomplished. Events they had always accepted with graceful submission seemed now to have alternate courses and alterable outcomes. They cheered the Wolfriders' ability to choose action over inaction; however, they did so from afar.

"How exciting," Shenshen exclaimed, running back into the largest of the sandstone caves, where her family was. "How exciting!" She caught sight of Rainsong, who was sitting on the floor of the cave with her two cubs. Woodlock hovered nearby, his children's soft-spoken, strong-armed protector.

"Rainsong, your people are so full of life's fire," Shenshen bubbled. "Especially Cutter!" She shot a glance at her older sister. "Why, next to him Rayek seems as sour as a green fig!"

Moving away to where her sister could not see her, Leetah stood still for a moment, scowling, a rush of emotions playing over her face. Then she softened, letting her tears fall. She felt a presence behind her and could not mistake who it was. She would not have permitted anyone but Savah to see her weep.

"Child, your tears reveal your heart's struggle," said the Mother of Memory. "Will you confide in me?"

The ancient elf-woman sat down upon a root-shaped ridge of sandstone. Leetah knelt before her, resting her head on Savah's knees. The Mother of Memory reflected that it was not so long ago that another had wept in her lap for much the same reason. He too had been lonely and in great need of comfort.

Leetah looked up, her eyes swimming with tears. "Oh, Savah! Recognition is a curse on our kind. It has far less to do with love and is far more involuntary than I dreamed. I suffer as the Wolfrider does from unbearable need. But he is like a wild, young animal to me." She lowered her voice to the faintest whisper. "Savah, if I join with him . . . there will be children!"

"I dare say there will." Savah smiled with gentle gravity. "You and Cutter were drawn together for a reason. You both possess remarkable qualities—some, as yet, unguessed. Beyond a spiritual bonding, Recognition ensures that your offspring will number among the strongest and most gifted of our race. So it has always been with elves, even in the distant time of the High Ones."

Leetah's worries were not yet soothed. "But he is so rough! What kind of father would he be?"

"And you—what kind of mother?"

Taken aback, Leetah thought for a moment. She looked around the chamber and saw Rainsong nursing Wing while Newstar played with her mother's hat.

"Not like Rainsong," the healer answered truthfully. "She has devoted her whole being to her family."

Savah nodded, standing up and urging Leetah to her feet as well. "You fear for your freedom, healer."

"That is true, Mother of Memory."

"But Cutter understands and values freedom, too."

Leetah could not deny that. Many had been the times when he could have slipped into her hut in the night and overpowered her. But he had not. His youth may have been part of the reason, but Leetah suspected a sense of fairness in him that transcended age.

Savah could see Leetah's thoughts churning; she gave them one final push to set them in motion. "Perhaps the desire which binds you to him is more benevolent than you think."

The healer put a finger to her chin, smiling, silently recalling two handfuls of water joined. Abruptly, she was jarred from her first moment of peace in days by the sound of commotion outside.

"Savah! Savah! Come here quick!"

Leetah gasped. "That's Cutter!"

"Well!" The Mother of Memory smiled, gathering up her swirling skirts. "It seems I must make haste or risk his wrath!" She walked with grand dignity to the mouth of the cave, knowing that Leetah's curiosity would draw her there, too.

Cutter, Pike, and Skywise had a zwoot—or more precisely, it had them—and they were trying to tie it to a cloud-tree by the three ropes they had managed to slip around its neck.

"Look! We caught one for you," Cutter yelled as Savah appeared at the mouth of the cave. "It's only a little one," he yelped as he flew through the air, hanging on to his rope when it might have been wiser to let go, "but it's hard to hold!"

"So I see." Savah cocked a feathery eyebrow. "Allow me to help."

The three Wolfriders did their best to hold the creature still as Savah approached it. She hadn't done this sort of thing since Rayek, her pupil, had surpassed his teacher. Staring into the zwoot's bulging eye, she calmed the small brain beneath it. Hers was not Rayek's paralyzing spell but rather one that subdued all sense of fear. She stroked the little zwoot's nose—its shoulder hump barely reached the height of her chin—and sent to it, soothingly, thoughts that meant far less to it than the pleasant sensation of no fear.

Perhaps you'd like to live here? Shall we discuss it, you and I?

The creature lowered its head, a blank, stupid look in its eyes.

"Hah! I told you she could do it," crowed Pike. "Who needs Rayek?"

"Let's go get another one," suggested Cutter.

The three elves were bloody from the hunt and filthy from getting the worst of the young zwoot's struggles, but their exuberance was infectious. As they leaped onto their wolves' backs and lolloped away, Leetah ran from the cave, calling, "Cutter! Cutter, wait! I—" She stopped, smiling at herself. She was, she discovered, not quite ready to test her newfound resolve.

At the same time, Scouter and Dewshine rode up to the caves, towing a truly enormous zwoot with their ropes. Standing under it, the two young Wolfriders would barely have brushed its belly with the tops of their heads.

"This one is huge," Dewshine said, "but he's being very cooperative."

"So far," Scouter added doubtfully. "I guess he's tired out from running. Bet he'll do a lot of hard work for the village once he's tamed."

Shaking off its lethargy, the zwoot snorted. Scouter and Dewshine struggled to lead the animal around the rocks to a place in the village where they could tie it safely. Suddenly, with a bunching of thick muscles, the creature reared its head; Dewshine felt the rough rope yanked from her hands.

"Scouter, I've lost him," she cried.

Skittishly, the huge beast sidled around. Scouter, still gripping his own rope, which was looped high on the zwoot's thick neck, found himself trying in vain to hold the brute by himself. With a powerful jerk the beast tossed its head, and Scouter's light body went sailing through the air like a stone on a string. Bucking wildly now, throwing its heavy head from side to side, the zwoot stumbled back as the young elf and both flailing ropes tangled and collided with the beast's hump. Strapped against the frenzied animal, Scouter cried out as the zwoot pitched and reared, trying to throw him off its back.

The two wolves harried the zwoot, confusing it so that it could not run away. Drawing her dagger, Dewshine stood up on Trollhammer's back and leaped for the enraged beast. Grabbing hold of a tangle of rope near the beast's shoulder, she struggled against the wildly bucking motion to slip her dagger under a taut line holding down Scouter's left arm. He begged her to be careful; the giant zwoot's every plunge and buck flung the delicate maiden about like a leaf. Finally she sliced through the rope, and Scouter felt his arm come free. The zwoot chose just that moment to rear up on its hind legs, and the force of its flailing movement shook loose Dewshine's grip. Thrown free of the beast, she plummeted to the ground; her head struck a rock with a sickening crack.

At last able to draw his short-sword, Scouter plunged the blade to the hilt in the creature's neck. Again and again the dagger rose and fell, but the creature's strength was incredible. It continued to buck and kick and stumble about, its massive hooves pounding dangerously close to Dewshine's deathly-still form.

Horrified, Leetah watched, standing by the wall of caves. Other villagers saw what was happening, but no one moved to help the young elves, and the elder Wolfriders were nowhere in sight. Leetah saw that Dewshine would be trampled in moments.

Had she stopped to think, Leetah would not have acted, but her mind was suddenly very clear. There were no options. No choice existed and no time. She dashed to Dewshine's side and scooped the injured Wolfrider up in her arms just as the zwoot's lashing hooves stamped down on the spot where Dewshine had lain.

Leetah ran, and the maddened zwoot pursued her, frothing blood at its mouth. Scouter kept stabbing at the creature, but the blade only enraged the brute.

"Run, Leetah," cried Scouter. "The beast refuses to die!"

She ran with Dewshine's frail, all but weightless body in her arms. She ran as she had never run before, for she had never been in danger of her life before, and she found that she very much wanted to live.

The zwoot bore down on her; she imagined its hot breath at her back. She was gasping; she would not be able to run much farther before she stumbled. Suddenly there was a quick singing sound and a meaty thud. As if it had instantly and miraculously grown there, a black-fletched shaft protruded from deep within the zwoot's temple. The beast died even as it ran, stumbling to its knees and keeling over on its side with frightening swiftness.

Leetah stood, looking at the twitching animal. Unhurt, Scouter crawled off its back. A short distance away, Strongbow lowered his weapon, pleased that he had hit the zwoot on the run and cleanly. The other Wolfriders began to appear on the scene.

When Scouter learned that Dewshine still lived, his relief was inexpressible; but she was so pale and so still that he could not feel happiness until he saw her open her eyes. Treestump jumped off Lionskin's back and came running toward Leetah. There was a cold fear in him; he said only one word—"no"—and reached out to caress his only child's curls.

"Little cousin," Cutter cried, his pale hair flying as he rushed to see if she lived.

Leetah's eyes were cold and accusing. She wanted to shout, "Why? You who boast your brotherhood and love to the sky, why did you fail to protect this child of yours?" But the answer rested in her arms, in Dewshine's deathly white face. She was not a child but a Wolfrider, free to run and hunt and face danger with the pack as she willed.

"She could die from a blow like that," Cutter groaned softly. "Leetah, please help her! I know I've disappointed you in many ways, but I'll do anything, even go far away forever if only you'll . . ."

"I don't care what you do," the healer cried, her eyes filled with venom. "Just let me do my work!" She turned and bore Dewshine to her hut. The Wolfriders followed her, fervently hoping that their defense of the village had not cost them yet another of their number.

Dewshine's eyes fluttered open. She blinked in the dim light and tried to focus on the ceiling, unable to think where she was. She remembered freeing Scouter, flying through the air, and then nothing.

". . . mmm . . . Where'd the sky go?" she mumbled, putting a hand to her face. She was lying on something very soft, and a fur blanket was draped over her.

"You're in Leetah's hut, pretty cub." Her father's bearded face appeared in her field of vision; it wore a look of mingled relief and concern.

"Leetah's hut?" repeated Dewshine.

"Aye, cub. She healed you."

Dewshine looked around carefully, for her head was still tender. She recognized the sleeping pit in which she lay as something she had seen before. There were many of her tribefolk in the room. Pike sat on the stool-chair, eying its arms suspiciously as though he expected them to bite. Scouter sat on a soft cushion beside her. He was talking to someone whom she could not see.

"How can we thank you?"

"No need," said Leetah's voice. "Her hurt was not as great as I feared, thank the High Ones."

Leetah sat upon the ledge that rose from the floor beneath her window. She was propped all around with many pillows, and the little wildcat purred in her lap. She stroked her pet absently, watching as Scouter lay down on his stomach beside Dewshine, smiling into her blue eyes, whispering intimate, innocent secrets.

Weary and vulnerable as always after a healing, Leetah gazed wistfully at the two young lovers. Although still young as elves reckoned age, she was fully half as old as her father,

the Sun-Toucher—some six hundred years. In her heart now welled that familiar loneliness for which she knew there was only one cure.

Staring into space, she asked, "Where is Cutter?"

"He's gone," Skywise growled at her from across the room. He stood silhouetted against the beaded curtain covering the doorway, his arms folded and his feet planted defiantly apart.

"What?" Leetah rose from her comfortable cushions and ran to the door, lifting up the curtain on one side. Cutter was already close to the northern boundary of the village, heading for the mountains. Beside him Nightrunner walked stolidly, a loyal friend. The two figures, already small, were growing smaller with every passing moment.

"Oh, that foolish, infuriating barbarian," she cried. "He misunderstands everything!"

"Does he?" Skywise snapped, a sparkle hidden in his hooded eyes. "You've made it pretty clear that you don't care if he stays or goes."

Leetah whirled, stood nose to nose with the keeper of the lodestone, and shouted at him. "You stargazing oaf! You're just as thick-witted as he is!" She pushed him aside roughly and stormed through the door curtain. "Out of my way!"

Waiting only a moment, Skywise held the curtain open and peeked out. Leetah had started to walk after Cutter.

Skywise smiled.

She broke into a trot.

He grinned.

Finally she ran to catch up with the Wolfrider chieftain.

Skywise beamed, and when Leetah came to Cutter's side at the edge of the village, the stargazer gently let the curtain fall. Turning the lodestone in his fingers, he whistled smugly to himself.

At first they did not speak or even look at each other. They walked together for some time, heading nowhere in particular, hugging the base of World's Spine and losing themselves among great tumbled boulders. Nightrunner walked between the two elves, acting as both cushion and wedge.

"I will not live in a cave by day and howl at the moons by night," Leetah said finally.

Cutter shrugged. "I won't eat cooked meat."

"I still do not like you very much," continued the healer.

Cutter was not surprised. "We're too different. Maybe you can refuse Recognition."

She liked the resignation in his tone even less than she liked him. It was uncharacteristic of the Wolfrider and not suited to the situation at all.

"Rayek would be a better lifemate for you," he said. "I know that now."

Leetah frowned. This talk was going in a most unsatisfactory direction. "You can barely think for yourself. Do not presume to think for me," she snapped.

Once again a wall of anger rose between them. It was more than Cutter could bear. He stopped short just ahead of her. She saw only his smooth, muscled back as he spoke.

"Leetah, if it makes you feel any better . . ." He turned around slowly. A tear had already coursed down his cheek, and another welled in the corner of his eye. His was a look of pain unlike any she, as a healer, had ever seen. "I'm not sure I can live without you."

Turning away from her suddenly, he ground the tears from his eyes with the back of his fist.

"This isn't Sorrow's End for me," he finished. "It's sorrow's beginning."

Time held its breath.

"Tam?"

Cutter froze.

She came up behind him. He felt with a shock her touch on his skin, her fingertips running along his back. Slowly, sensually, her arms embraced him from behind. He tilted his head back, every fiber of his being alive with the warmth of her, the miracle of her body pressing close to his.

"You are trembling," she whispered. "Oh, I have wanted to touch you." There, it was said; she felt a pressure disappear from within her. Her hands caressed his chest, his stomach, feeling the hard knots of muscle that were elements of his beauty. She knew without seeing that his eyes were shut and that his throat arched upward. Her fingers moved with the pounding of his heart.

"Strange," she said, her eyes half closed, unfocused. "Now that I have said it aloud, I know what a soul name is and what it means." Her cheek rested upon his shoulder. "Cutter, blood of ten chiefs, all that you are is *Tam*." She breathed the word over and over into his shoulder, into his long, soft hair as fine as hers. She loved the smell of his hair. She accepted him entirely, and in the doing she was not enslaved but set free.

For a long time Cutter could not speak, would not have dared to even if he could, for fear of shattering a moment that might be only the most fragile of dreams. Eventually the two sat down together in the shadow of an overhanging rock. He held her hand upon his knee, content with that because he had to speak and could not have done so were she closer to him.

"I . . . searched for your soul name."

She understood the intimacy of that confession. "And found only Leetah? I know. Except for Savah, my people have all but forgotten how to send. We have lost the need for the silence of sending to keep us hidden from enemies. Even I can do it only when I heal." She hoped that he understood the intimacy of that confession. "Unlike you Wolfriders, we Sun Folk have never needed secret names to guard our deepmost private selves." Cutter lowered his eyes shyly, and she leaned close to him, placing her hand on his shoulder. "But though your sending batters me with the force of a sandstorm," she said, "I can no longer deny that you are part of me. The bond is true."

They sat together a little longer, quietly savoring the peace that had decended upon them. Then Cutter rose and made a growling sound that brought Nightrunner to him from the wolf's bed of dry brush. Cutter lifted Leetah up and placed her on Nightrunner's back, letting his hands linger upon her slender waist. The wolf tolerated her weight—barely.

"I will confess that you are not at all what I expected in a lifemate, my fair young Tam."

He grinned. "You're right. I guess I am a bar—barbarian." He led Nightrunner away toward the Sun Village. Leetah found the sinuous rolling of the wolf's spine strange but knew that she would not become a Wolfrider overnight.

Cutter spoke softly. "I've lived by the night, hunted and killed in darkness."

"And here all is light," she answered him. "The Daystar never veers from its path, and it gives order to our lives." Leetah looked up at the blazing disk, comfortable saying words she could not have said earlier. "Recognition is part of that order, no more to be denied than the voice of the sun. It is part of what we are." She looked at Cutter, thinking, And that is what you knew and accepted all along, is it not, Tam? At least we have that much in common, my barbarian.

That night he came to the window of her hut as he had done the day of the challenge. This time, though, when her hand parted the curtains, it revealed a face radiant with promise. Together they walked hand in hand to the Bridge of Destiny. When they came near the shorter horn, they ran all the way up to its peak. Breathless, his blood soaring, Cutter took Leetah in his arms, and she wrapped him in the silken blanket she had thoughtfully brought with her. The two sank slowly to the bridge. The star of a single sending—**Yes**—glowed within both their minds; neither could say if the other had sent it.

Their first joining was, as Leetah knew it must be, urgent and brief; but the promise of ecstasy swirled through her veins as she held her child-mate close, stroking the harmonious whole of flesh, muscle, and bone that housed his Tam—now her Tam. Cutter allowed himself to be turned gently onto his back, sensing that she would teach him things—things that until now the whispering voice of his youthful blood had only hinted were possible—things that would prove in their sudden, inescapable reality almost too exquisite to bear. The healer's knowing touch, infinitely sensitive, divined with instinctive ease each and every hidden well of sensation and brought forth in him such surging responses that he was frightened by their intensity. It was she who entered now, she who pervaded while he became her helpless, living instrument played from within. She saw his face contort, heard him gasp, felt his young body, drawn tight as a hunter's bowstring, straining against her. Wisely, compassionately, she then revealed her knowledge to him at a slower pace so that he might more fully appreciate each gift she bestowed. For Cutter it was a night of revelation, akin in wonderment only to the night when his soul name had come to him. Tam was all that he was, and Tam no longer barred the pathway into his deepmost self. Now Leetah walked there, singing, and soon he would learn to return her every loving gift in its fullest measure.

Now the blood of wolves springs in me, Leetah thought, and I shall love the night as I do the day. It is old, my Tam's secret, the great secret of the Wolfriders, and no one shall ever learn it from my lips. The High Ones must have found this world utterly strange when they came to it. For whatever they did to survive, I thank them.

Fourteen

"Rayek?"

The black-haired elf's head turned a little to one side, although he had not exactly heard the questioning voice with his ears. World's Spine lay between him and the one who inquired. He sat with his knees drawn up on a pouting lip of rock on the mountains' north side. Behind him rose a smooth, weather-sanded wall; from the corner of his eye he saw the ghostly light-that-was-not-light that emanated from it.

"Savah," he said, acknowledging her at last. "I sensed you searching for me." Rayek knew that if he turned around, he would see a rare and awe-inspiring sight. The Mother of Memory did not often send her conscious image, for it drained her strength to do so. But when the need or purpose was great enough, she could cast her speaking self-without-form beyond the limits of the village. The recipient of the apparition saw a transparent reflection of Savah, unmoving save for the lips from which issued a hollow ghost of her voice.

"I cannot remain thus very long. It costs me much," said the image. Then, without hesitation: "Cutter and Leetah have joined. They are lifemates."

As still as the luminous shadow behind him, Rayek accepted the news calmly. His days of solitary hiding and wandering the hills after the Trial of Heart had tired him. Brooding and hating had tired him. The weariness, at last, allowed him to treat himself somewhat more kindly now.

"Hmmm, a swift reconciliation indeed," he mused. "How unlike Leetah!" His back still turned to Savah's image, Rayek stood up and began to put on the hooded red robe that had lain folded beside him. "I'd have thought she'd let the barbarian dangle for at least a year. But no matter. I wish them well."

"Will you return to us?"

Rayek drew the hood up over his head. "What for? I saw the wolfriders turn the stampede. Sorrow's end has seventeen new protectors." He crouched and swung his body over the ledge, easily finding footholds in the rock to help him climb down. Not far below a gray zwoot grazed in the shadow of the mountainside, its quilted saddle fitted with provisions for a long journey. "There is no need here for me," said the chief hunter.

"What of your love for Leetah and hers for you?" Savah's eerily close yet distant voice stopped him. Hanging onto the ledge, he pressed his forehead against the warm rock and closed his eyes. "There is an alternative to your stepping aside," she offered.

For the first time he lifted his eyes to the phantom image. It was a beautiful, pale, elongated version of the serene Mother of Memory. Its eyes were shut, and there were already signs of strain and fatigue on the fine-boned features.

"Although it is not common practice, others in the village have from time to time taken more than one mate. Is it unthinkable that you and Cutter and Leetah together might—"

Rayek interrupted her but not rudely. "Yes, Savah, it is—" he smiled with amused irony "—unthinkable!" He resumed his descent from the ledge, knowing that she could still hear him. "The Wolfriders found Sorrow's End as though some force drew them here. I have no lodestone, but perhaps I too will be guided by the High Ones' unseen hands."

With that, the black-haired elf jumped the remaining short distance into his zwoot's saddle and gathered up the reins. He had three water-bags and food to last him a moon if he were sparing in appetite. He looked up at the wall above the ledge and saw that the luminous image wavered on the verge of extinction. He called to it. "Farewell, Mother of Memory. I mean to find my place, wherever it may be. It is not here!"

Rayek slapped the zwoot's rump, and it whined pettishly, less than eager to move from the pleasant shade. As his mount reluctantly lumbered away from the rocks, Rayek heard, or thought he heard, a final faint call.

"Farewell then, my dear one. You are better loved than you know. And you will be missed." Her voice sighed, like a dying breeze, into silence.

Savah regarded all the Sun Folk as her children, but Rayek knew that he and Yurek, the long-dead rock-shaper, had qualities in common. Savah had tolerated the chief hunter's restless, brooding nature with more true understanding than anyone else in the village. Rayek left Sorrow's End feeling a warmth he had not expected to feel.

Skywise came out of the largest of the sandstone caves, the last of his tribefolk to make his way toward the noisy, brightly lit festivities going on at the far side of the village. He had chosen to straggle behind. Looking up, he saw that the stars were beautiful and very clear, and he knew that he would not be able to see them as well once he entered the circle of yellow lantern light. The celebration would last long into the night; he could afford the time.

The blue-and-gray-clad Wolfrider climbed up to the plateau known now as the howling place. It had been a while since he had taken a good look at the night sky, but everything was just as he had left it: the star-pictures, the wanderers, the pretty cloudlike clusters. The Sun-Toucher had taught him to hear the voice of the sun a little, but Skywise knew the language of the stars in the depths of his soul. He always would, because the stars would never change.

He looked at the star-picture he had named Goodtree's Rest. He remembered thinking, when he had given it its name, that the points of light seemed to him to resemble a great tree: two bright stars, one yellow and one ice-blue at the tree's base, and a spray of lesser lights making the branches. It made him think of the Holt.

Strange, he thought. The stars whirl around the hub of

the sky wheel, never straying from their paths, while the world below changes and changes without reason or rule. One day the Holt was there, the next it was ashes. The Wolfriders lived in the forest; now we live among our own kind in a place of rock and sand. All things considered, it's not a bad change. The village is interesting—especially the maidens—and Cutter and Leetah are lifemates now, thank the High Ones.

Skywise turned to look out over the village from his high vantage. The little huts were dark. Everyone had gathered around the dancers' ring to celebrate the union of the two tribes, a union sparkled by the joining of Cutter and Leetah. In that bright pool of light, surrounded by the desert night's dark-blue veil, Skywise could see tiny elfin figures frolicking in the dancer's ring. He heard the thin strains of a joyful song echoing from the mountainside.

No, it was not a bad change at all, he thought. We came here with so little, just our clothes and a few weapons. I wish I had something to give Cutter and Leetah in remembrance of this night.

He looked again at Goodtree's Rest spangling the dark sky. An idea came into his mind as he regarded the two bright stars near each other, one yellow as the bright sunlight, the other silvery blue as the radiance of a full moon. Sun and moon. Day and night. Desert and forest. Leetah and Cutter.

Well, why not, he asked himself. Maybe I can't change the stars, but I can give the pictures new names. I named them in the first place! I'll give those two stars to Cutter and Leetah. They'll always have them. They'll always be together.

Extremely pleased with himself, Skywise hopped down like an agile squirrel from ridge to ridge in the sloping wall of the plateau. The lantern light and music beckoned more strongly now, for there were good things to eat and drink, maidens to dance with, and, most specially, a gift to give.